The Scarecrow

in the Vineyard

By Robert W. Gregg

INFINITY
PUBLISHING.COM

Copyright © 2009 by Robert W. Gregg

ISBN 0-7414-5600-1

Cover photograph courtesy of Brett Steeves (www.somersart.com) and Steve Knapp (www.keukaview.com).

Published by:

PUBLISHING.COM

1094 New DeHaven Street, Suite 100
West Conshohocken, PA 19428-2713
Info@buybooksontheweb.com
www.buybooksontheweb.com
Toll-free (877) BUY BOOK
Local Phone (610) 941-9999
Fax (610) 941-9959

Printed in the United States of America

Published October 2009

Acknowledgments

For advice on critical plot points by
Dr. Melissa Brassell, forensic pathologist,
and Fred Bailey, C.P.A.

To the memory of my parents,
Hugh and Marjorie Gregg

PROLOGUE

No travel brochure could have painted a more beautiful picture of New York State's Finger Lakes. The October foliage was spectacular under a bright blue sky, a brilliant blend of reds and golds, broken up here and there by stands of evergreen trees. The Robinsons, Kate and Brad, were enjoying the day, pleased with themselves that they had decided to take a drive and visit several of the area's wineries.

Their last stop of the day had been for a wine tasting at the Random Harvest Vineyards on a hill high above Crooked Lake. While Kate was a devotee of Chardonnay, she had read somewhere that the region's best wines were Rieslings. So they had dutifully sampled what Random Harvest had to offer, both dry and semi-dry, and concluded that praise for the Rieslings was amply justified. When they climbed into their car and headed home, a case of dry Riesling accompanied them in the trunk.

The road they were taking wound through acres and acres of vineyards. It was the middle of grape harvest season, and many of these vineyards were filled with pickers. In some places, the pickers were human, small figures that stretched out into the distance as far as the eye could see. In other places, the pickers were mechanical harvesters, their paddles dislodging the grapes and collecting them in holding bins. Brad, who had never observed the process, found it fascinating and drove slowly along the upper lake road the better to watch it.

"It's a wonder the birds don't beat the pickers to the grapes," he said to his wife.

"Maybe they would if it weren't for those things," Kate said, pointing to small, balloonlike objects which were attached to poles from place to place in the vineyards and seemed to be dancing around in the afternoon breeze.

"They must be some sort of newfangled scarecrows." Brad slowed down to get a better look at the balloons.

"Hey," he said, bringing the car to a stop on the shoulder. "There's a real scarecrow. The old-fashioned kind. See it? Down the hill there to the right."

It soon became apparent that whoever owned the vineyard had erected a variety of objects to keep the birds from the grapes. Some were no more substantial than old tattered shirts. But the one to which Brad Robinson was pointing looked surprisingly human.

"Somebody sure went to a lot of trouble fixing that one up," he said. "I think I'd like to go down there and get a picture of it."

His wife didn't think this was a very good idea.

"Let's not do that," she said. "I don't imagine they want people tromping around in their vineyards."

"It's not a big deal, Kate. Can't be more than sixty, seventy yards down the hill. It'll only take a few minutes. Just hand me the camera."

Dismissing his wife's worry that he might be trespassing, Brad left the car and, finding a path where there were no posts and wires, worked his way down the hill toward the scarecrow.

A cool autumn wind brushed across his face, and the view across the lake to the bluff was even more impressive than it had been from the road. It is, he thought, a great day to be alive.

The scarecrow was now off to his left, perhaps twenty or thirty feet away, standing between two rows of vines loaded with grapes. It had obviously done the job for which it had been created. The birds had not gotten to these grapes.

Brad was about a dozen feet from it when he first realized that this was no ordinary scarecrow. It stood against a tall post, its arms stretched out at right angles to the body and lashed to a wooden crossbar. The effect was that of a crucifixion. Brad was momentarily reminded of the many depictions of Jesus on the cross he had witnessed over many years in the church. But the scarecrow did not resemble the Biblical Jesus. It looked much more like scarecrows he remembered from Halloweens past. It was dressed in a pair of blue jeans, a dark blue work shirt, and a straw hat. The face beneath the hat did not, however, look at all like the familiar straw-filled sack with crudely painted eyes. What it resembled was a human head, and it took Brad only a few more steps to confirm that what he was looking at was indeed a human head.

The scarecrow in the vineyard was not some hastily assembled dummy whose sole function was to keep the crows away. It was a dead man. A dead man who in all probability had never imagined that he would end his life as a scarecrow in a vineyard high above Crooked Lake.

CHAPTER 1

Thirteen Months Earlier

The late September sun was setting, and the light coming through the west window of the rectory study did little to brighten the room. The man sitting at the desk in the corner would soon need to turn on the lamp, but he showed no inclination to do so. He slumped in his chair, chin almost on his chest, eyes closed. Anyone entering the room would have assumed that he was asleep. He was breathing deeply. More accurately, he seemed to be gasping for air.

The truth of the matter was that Father Brendan Rafferty had just experienced one of the most shocking incidents in his largely uneventful life. Not five minutes earlier Gerald Flanagan had stood over him and administered the worst tongue-lashing he had ever endured. Much worse than those his parents had resorted to on occasion when he disappointed them in some way. Much worse than those of his high school basketball coach when he seemed not to be putting forth his best effort.

Heavyset, face florid, dark eyes hooded, there had always been something menacing about Flanagan. But today the man had actually threatened him. The torrent of words, of accusations, had come so fast, so unexpectedly, that he had been stunned. Too stunned to think about what he was hearing, to speak up in his own defense, to reason with his accuser.

Now Father Rafferty was trying to recreate the brief, verbally violent scene in his own mind. It wasn't easy, because he felt a terrible emptiness in his chest. An emptiness that said he was afraid. He had always felt safe in his vocation. His parishioners came to him for help. He ministered to their needs. But in the last few minutes of this autumn afternoon he had suddenly become a man in trouble. He knew that he wouldn't be helping people. He would himself need help.

What was it that Flanagan had said? That his collar wouldn't save him. That his days of spreading perversion in the church were over.

He took another deep breath and finally got up from the desk. He felt unsteady on his feet as he left the study and went into the kitchen. Thank God, he thought, that Mrs. Burley was not at the rectory that day, that she had not overheard what had been said in the study. His housekeeper would not understand. Who would understand? The charge hurled at him had been so loud, so forceful, so unequivocal, that anyone hearing it would, at the very least, have assumed that there must be some truth in it. Why would a good Catholic parent be saying such things if they were not true?

He was not in the habit of regularly taking a drink. But he did have a bottle of Irish whiskey in the cupboard, and tonight he would make an exception. It might do him more good than water. It would calm his nerves, help him to focus on what he would have to do before the charge that Flanagan had leveled at him became general knowledge. And it would become general knowledge, of that he was reasonably certain. He knew Gerald Flanagan well enough to know that in all likelihood he would not rest until he had rid the parish of the priest he believed to be responsible for his son's condition.

The accusation was, of course, absurd. His mind was now clear enough that he could begin to make sense of what had happened that afternoon. And what had happened before that that had led to the confrontation in the study.

The Flanagans had belonged to St. Anthony's for many years, long antedating Father Rafferty's arrival as the parish priest. He had initially been pleased to find this large family among his flock. They were regular attenders at mass, and two of the younger generation, Paul and Philip, served as altar boys. But Gerald had gradually revealed himself to be a hothead and a troublemaker. His opinion of him had begun to change one day a few months earlier when Flanagan had earned himself some notoriety in the area by leading a widely publicized demonstration at what was believed to be an abortion clinic in a nearby town. There had been an ugly confrontation with local police, and although no one had been hurt, it had been a close call. Flanagan had visited him at the rectory shortly thereafter and demanded that a strongly worded homily should be delivered to the congregation condemning not only abortion but other practices which were an abomination in the eyes of the church. Foremost among these, apparently, was the gay lifestyle.

He knew full well that the practices to which Gerald Flanagan had referred were viewed by the church as sinful. When it came to homosexuality, he was thoroughly familiar with both divine law and natural law arguments against it. He could readily quote relevant scripture, including Paul's New Testament rejection of homosexuality in his letters to the Romans and the Corinthians. But Father Rafferty was also a priest who believed that homosexuality was not a matter of conscious choice, and that gays deserved his love and respect. He had chosen not to take up Flanagan's call for what would have been a blistering anti-gay homily.

Unfortunately, the rash of charges that priests had been engaging in acts of pedophilia with boys in their parishes had recently acquired front-page prominence around the country. His reaction to this development had been one of dismay. Gerald Flanagan's reaction had been one of ill-concealed fury. If a growing number of priests lusted after boys and young men, then priests in general must be suspect. The church had become a haven for homosexuals who could hide behind their cloth and collar and prey on those who trusted them and sought their guidance. He had watched with growing alarm as Flanagan had taken public positions espousing this view.

It might have come to no more than that had it not been for the fact that Philip Flanagan had sought him out on a recent Sunday after mass. He could remember his conversation with the young man as if it had taken place only minutes earlier.

"Father, I need to talk with you," Philip had said after looking over his shoulder, apparently to make sure that the rest of his family had headed for home.

"Of course, Philip. Come with me. We'll go over to the rectory."

"I have a problem." That is the way their conversation had begun, and for an awkward moment it went no further than that. But he had gradually coaxed Philip to say what was on his mind, and once started, the words poured forth in a veritable torrent. And they were accompanied by tears.

"I think I'm gay. I've been worried about it for quite awhile, but now I'm sure. Well, almost sure. I haven't done anything. You know, anything with another guy. But—" Philip paused, swallowed. "I'd know, wouldn't I? I mean, doesn't somebody sort of feel that way?"

This was bad news. Bad, certainly, for a fifteen-year-old boy raised in the Catholic Church. But especially bad for the son of a father who wore his loathing of homosexuals on his sleeve. How could this revelation have a happy ending?

"Philip, I don't really know how you would know the answer to your question. But I think you have done a very brave thing by choosing to talk about it. There are probably people who could give you better advice than I can, but the most important thing is that you have decided to be honest with yourself, not pretend that these feelings will go away."

"But what should I do?"

There was no question but that the boy meant what he should say, or not say, to his father.

"I think you should wait, be patient. You're only—what, fifteen? It's too soon to be having a serious relationship. I mean with anybody. It's one thing to have feelings, desires. That is no sin, not for you or anybody else. Acting on those feelings is something else. So you should go slow. Give yourself some time."

This was what he would have told any other teenager, boy or girl, straight or gay. But he knew it wasn't what Philip had in mind.

"I know. But that's not what I meant. What should I tell my parents? Especially my father."

There was no way young Flanagan could not have been aware that his father detested gays. Everyone in town knew it.

"I won't pretend that it will be easy, but I think you should be frank with him. I wouldn't treat it as an argument. I'd say just what you told me, that you think you may be gay and that you want his support in what is likely to be a difficult time for you. He's your father, and I'm sure he loves you, whatever he may feel about the issue."

"I'll go to hell, won't I?"

It was a question, but it didn't sound like one.

"No, Philip, you will not go to hell."

He knew he was treading on dangerous ground, but he was dealing with a very troubled young man who found himself in a very difficult situation. This was not the moment to remind him that church teaching defines homosexual acts as acts of great depravity. That he would be violating God's law.

He had put his arm around Philip Flanagan's shoulder and walked him to the door. He remembered his last words to the boy.

"If you find that your father can't talk with you about this, tell him to come and talk with me."

And Gerald Flanagan *had* come to talk with him. No, that wasn't what had happened. Philip's father had come to talk *at* him, even to shout at him. The boy had done what he had urged him to do. He had told his father that he might be gay. That he had discussed the matter with his priest and that the priest had been understanding, had sought to comfort him, had assured him that he would not go to hell.

If upon hearing this Flanagan had experienced conflicting emotions, it was hatred of gays, not love for his son, that had won out.

Father Rafferty took his glass of whiskey back into the study, turned on the desk lamp, and settled back into his chair. He knew that there was no need to waste time reconstructing the one-sided conversation he had had with Flanagan. The man had bluntly accused him of encouraging his son to become homosexual—"turning him into a pervert like yourself" was the way he had put it—and changing his mind seemed to be out of the question. So what was he to do?

He was not by nature a fighter. He had always tried to avoid conflict, and over time had discovered that the easiest and least painful course of action was neither confrontation nor a search for compromise, but rather distancing himself from problems. How could he distance himself from this problem, now much larger than Philip Flanagan's worry that he might be gay?

What he wanted to do, he realized, was to be somewhere else. To be someone else. Anywhere but East Moncton, Massachusetts. Anybody but the parish priest at St. Anthony's. But how could he do this? He could, of course, seek the help of his superior in the diocese. But that would take time, and there wasn't time. Nor would it silence Flanagan. Even if exonerated, even if transferred to another parish, he would forever carry the taint of a priest who had been accused of pedophilia.

Perhaps he could be laicized. He disliked that word. In fact, he disliked many of the words with which the church sought to mystify relatively simple things. But in plain language it meant that the church would relieve him of his vows, making him once again a layman. In spite of his faith and his belief in his chosen vocation, he knew that he would fare better if he no longer had to live with the rumors he would have to deal with if he remained a priest.

But laicization would also take time. The church seemed never to be in a hurry. As he nursed his whiskey it occurred to him with sudden, startling clarity that he had to leave East Moncton and St. Anthony's. Not soon, but now. And that would happen only if he simply took off his cassock and walked away.

It shouldn't be that hard to do. His possessions were meager. Everything he valued could be stuffed into the car. He knew he should notify the diocese of what he was doing, but that would only complicate things. He could not imagine them simply wishing him well. He would be told to stay where he was while they put in motion whatever investigative machinery the church used in cases like this. No, he would have to pack the car, leave the key to the rectory on his desk, and lock the door behind him. Much as he would like to say good-bye to Mrs. Burley, he couldn't do that. She would be the first to discover that he was gone. She would be puzzled, of course, and she would eventually call the diocese. By that time he would be miles away.

Father Brendan Rafferty had no idea where he would be. Or what he would do. He'd think about that as he drove. First he would pack.

CHAPTER 2

Thirteen Weeks Earlier

"Do I make myself clear?" The voice on the other end of the line was neither loud nor angry, but there was no mistaking the threat.

Frightened by the threat, he wanted to say something, something which would reassure Carl Sadowsky of his good intentions, something which would buy more time. But he couldn't find the words.

"I have been very patient," Sadowsky went on. "But now I'm regretting it. I know I'm repeating myself, but let me say it again. We had an understanding. I'd prefer to call it a contract. You needed money. I've given you money. A lot of money. If it hadn't been for me, you would have been out on the street. That would have been extremely unpleasant, don't you think? But thanks to me, you've had a roof over your head. You've had food on your table. And you've enjoyed the fun and games at the casino, haven't you? But have you paid your debt? Oh, excuse me. I almost forgot. You did give me five hundred dollars, and I thanked you. But that was almost six weeks ago. My records show that you owe me exactly twenty-one thousand, seven hundred dollars. That's what you owe me today. By the weekend, you will owe me twenty-two thousand. You do realize that, don't you?"

There was silence on the line. What could he say? He didn't have twenty-one thousand, seven hundred dollars. He didn't have seven hundred dollars.

"I'm trying," he said, a plea for understanding. "I'm doing everything I can. Maybe by Thursday."

"I'm afraid my patience is exhausted." The voice had taken on a sharper edge. "I would prefer not to have to make an example of you. I really would. It would be very unpleasant. But I am a businessman, not a philanthropist. Tell you what. I will give you until Saturday. You see, I'm being generous. You say Thursday, I say Saturday. I expect the twenty-two thousand by Saturday. Let's make it noon. And I want it in cash. I never accept checks. Do you understand? Saturday. You know where to find me."

He couldn't say "yes." It would be a lie. But he couldn't say "no." Something told him that he had finally run out of excuses, that he had run out of time. He had pretended to himself that Sadowsky was reasonable. He now knew that he had seriously, perhaps fatally, misjudged him. The man was not reasonable, had never been reasonable. He was dangerous. Very dangerous.

If more needed to be said to make clear just how dangerous, Sadowsky said it.

"If I do not see you at noon on Saturday, my man will pay you a visit." He paused. "Perhaps I will come myself. Yes, I think that's what I will do. I don't think you will like that. And don't even think of skipping town. I'll find you, and you will pay."

———

It had been many months since Father Brendan Rafferty had come to realize that his unannounced and unexplained departure from St. Anthony's had been a serious mistake. At the time it had seemed like the only course of action which would save him from certain humiliation at the hands of Gerald Flanagan. It hadn't taken long, however, for the folly of slipping away in the night to sink in. He now knew that what he had done had very probably convinced the church that Flanagan was right, that he did indeed have something to hide. Something which was unthinkable, yet something of which he knew he was completely innocent. But it was too late to correct his mistake. He had burned his bridges and would have to deal with the consequences.

And the consequence of most immediate importance was that he had virtually no money. He had lived a spartan life in East Moncton, but he had never lacked for the necessities. The church took care of its own. He had known what to expect when he decided to go to seminary and become a priest, and at no time had he thought of himself as poor. Quite the contrary, he had persuaded himself that doing God's work made him rich, albeit in a non-pecuniary way. But he had abandoned the security blanket that was the church, and now, months later and miles away, he was chronically in need of money.

It hadn't been so bad at first. He had decided to drive west, out of Massachusetts and into neighboring New York. Somehow, he had thought, crossing that jurisdictional border would help bring closure to a chapter in his life. He would quietly become just plain Brendan Rafferty. Or perhaps Raffy, as he had been known in years now long past. He had driven all through that first night, had breakfast at a rest stop on the New York Thruway, and eventually found himself in a small town which advertised itself as being a gateway to the Adirondack Mountains. He hadn't consulted a map, and had he done so, he still would not have had a very good idea as to where he was headed. But when he stopped for gas in that small town, he saw a help wanted notice on the wall beside the cash register.

Throughout the night as he drove west his mind had been occupied with worries about his relationship with the church. He had given almost no thought to what he was going to do. Or where. The posted ad reminded him that he had to begin thinking about those things. He knew nothing about the town where he had stopped, but then he had never focused on what kind of town, what kind of job, he might be looking for. It was possible that this town, Verona, would do as well as the next one. The man at the register turned out to be the proprietor, and he had chatted with him for a minute or two before mustering the courage to inquire about the job at the gas station.

It was apparent that the proprietor had been looking for somebody just out of high school, and was surprised that this well dressed, well spoken, and considerably older stranger needed work. Rafferty had concocted a rather vague hard luck story on the spur of the moment, and to his surprise the man on the other side of the counter offered him the job. There had been no request for references, for which he had been immensely grateful.

Two days later, with the help of a couple of phone calls from the proprietor of the gas station, he had obtained a room in a dingy former motel which was charitably described by the owner as a boarding house, even if it served no meals. The rent was cheap, even cheaper than the going rate at the nearby Motel Six where he had spent his first night in Verona. The bed springs had seen better days; the microwave was on the small side, and the mini-fridge had a large ice buildup and a sour smell. But he was in no position to complain; he knew that some of his brethren in monastic orders lived in even more basic conditions.

He had shopped at a local Wal-Mart and purchased clothes which were better suited to pumping gas than those he had brought with him from the rectory. By the end of the week he was putting in a nine-hour day, making a conscientious effort to pick up the lingo that people who spent time around cars tossed off so casually. The job gave him ample opportunity to think, and the thought that he had most trouble banishing from his mind was that one day he would find himself filling the tank of a customer he had known back in East Moncton. What if that customer turned out to be Gerald Flanagan? Unlikely, he knew, but it made him nervous.

Brendan Rafferty's existence could best be described as boring, and he knew he should do something about it. Something like making a plan, a plan which would get him out of this dead-end job and into a new life more suited to his abilities. But he found himself procrastinating, always telling himself that he'd make a new start next week. Then one day when his cash reserves were low and his mood was dangerously close to self-pity, he and Mark Cahill, a casual acquaintance, were having a cup of coffee at a local diner.

"What is it that keeps you going?" he asked. He didn't really expect an answer to his question. It had been more a way to express his own unhappiness.

"Turning Stone," Mark said. "Ever tried it?"

"Are you kidding? I'm not in that league."

He knew that Turning Stone Casino, pride of the Oneida Indian Nation and one of New York State's most popular tourist attractions, was a posh place. Las Vegas of the East, he'd heard someone call it. It was within just a few miles of where he was staying, but he had never been there. Nor had he even considering going. It was both a matter of money and the belief that gambling was of doubtful morality. The church did not regard it as a sin per se, but it was troubled by the possibility that the gambler might become addicted to it to the detriment of his responsibility to himself and society.

Cahill laughed.

"You don't have to have a big bank account. Hell, I've never stayed at any of their hotels—don't have that kind of money.

You go for the tables. Bingo, if that's your thing. All kinds of poker. Keno. You know, just about anything you want."

"Lose much money?"

"I suppose you could, but I set myself limits. I've done pretty well. Anyway, it's the atmosphere, the excitement after a dull day. You asked what keeps me going, and I suppose I should've said the job, my dog. But I don't have a dog. So it's Turning Stone. Great place."

Nothing came of this conversation for several days. Then one evening after work he was taking stock of his resources. He knew that he was low on cash, but until he counted out the bills in his wallet and checked the status of his bank account he had no idea how close to broke he really was.

His thoughts turned to what Mark Cahill had told him about Turning Stone, but he quickly dismissed the idea. Or tried to. He needed money, but he also needed the jolt that an evening out might provide After ten minutes of Hamlet-like indecision, he got into his car and headed for the casino.

As he drove he recalled a discussion he had had with a young man who came to him one day at St. Anthony's. He had listened to a sad tale of a gambling habit which was ruining the man's marriage, and he had counseled temperance. He remembered comparing it with smoking. It's like smoking two packs a day, he had said. You just cut back gradually to one pack, then eventually to a couple of cigarettes, and one day you'll be free of the habit. Of course he had never been a smoker, and he didn't know if smoking and gambling were really comparable. But he was expected to be a sympathetic priest, to preach that every human being has the capacity to overcome weakness. And so he had. He had no idea whether that young man had solved his gambling problem. Or saved his marriage. In any event, he was confident that he would not fall into the same trap.

That first night in the casino was an eye opener. It also ended with more than two hundred more dollars in his pocket than had been there when he left the boarding house. And he had done it without trying some of what he considered to be the morally borderline games like baccarat.

His next visit to the casino came three days later, and had less to do with a lack of money than it did to a feeling that it just might be fun. Nothing that had happened on his first visit had seemed immoral or beneath the dignity of a priest. Or an ex-priest. Why not do it again, stay maybe an hour, no more?

This time he did not win anything, but his losses were nominal. He still had most of what he had won the first time. He could afford a small bump in the road.

By the time a month had passed, he had settled into a routine which included at least three nights a week at the casino. Invariably he found it exciting. But increasingly he found himself losing money. There was the occasional good night, but the trend was decidedly negative. Then came a day when the bank called to inform him that he was overdrawn. That day was a full two weeks before he was due his next paycheck from the gas station.

That first time, the proprietor had helped him out. But not the second. Cahill thought he knew of someone who might lend him some money.

"Sadowsky's the name. You see him around the casino a lot. Short guy, bald, sort of heavyset. Always seems to be wearing a red vest under his jacket. I used to think maybe he was a bouncer or something, but I guess he's not employed by the casino. A guy I know told me he helps out, off payroll of course, by lending people cash. Keeps them coming back."

Sadowsky had not been hard to find. Cahill's description made it easy. They had their first conversation over a whiskey and soda on an evening in early April. When he walked out of the casino that evening, he had five new one hundred dollar bills in his wallet and a lecture on his obligations to mull over on the way home.

That had been almost two months ago. Things had gotten progressively worse in the interim. There had been fewer and fewer "good" nights at the casino. To compensate for the bad nights, he had gone there more often. But that had only produced more bad nights. And more visits with Mr. Sadowsky, whose lectures about obligation had become increasingly stern, even when he had left with the money he had asked for.

Now he had just been on the receiving end of the last in this series of lectures. It had come, not at the casino, but over the phone. And this time it had come without what had made it palatable in the past, more money. There would be no more money from Sadowsky. Instead, he would be paying Sadowsky. Or he would if he had the money with which to pay him. There was no point in taking another inventory of his dwindling resources. He knew exactly what he had, and it was but a tiny fraction of the twenty-two thousand dollars he was expected to turn over to his benefactor on Saturday.

He knew he couldn't go to the casino and beg for more time. What would Sadowsky do when he didn't show up at the noon deadline he had been given? The knot which he felt in his stomach was familiar. He had experienced it on his last day at St. Anthony's, the day that Gerald Flanagan had accused him of molesting his son. His present dilemma might be even more serious than the one he had faced when Flanagan had stormed out of the rectory. The angry father could have ruined his reputation with charges of pedophilia. The angry money lender might kill him.

Was that what people like Sadowsky did to men who didn't pay their debts? Rafferty didn't know much about such things. Maybe they broke their kneecaps. The very thought made him wince. He had been grateful that the man had been willing to help him in a time of need. Grateful to a man who might well be in league with the mob, capable of doing terrible things to those who crossed him. What a sheltered life he had led. How ill prepared he was to deal with the harsh realities of real life.

By day's end, he had for the second time made up his mind to flee, to run away from a personal crisis. First East Moncton. Now Verona. And once again he would say nothing to anyone. Sadowsky had told him not to skip town, that he would track him down. Had said it in a cold voice, full of menace. But tracking him down if he stayed at the gas station and the boarding house would be far easier than if he moved to some other town. He had no idea where that other town would be. How could Sadowsky know? In any event, he would be buying time. Time in which to burrow into a safe haven, secure from the Sadowskys and Flanagans of the world.

CHAPTER 3

Thirteen Days Earlier

The sliver of moon that had been visible earlier was now behind clouds, and a light rain had begun to fall. Brendan Rafferty turned on his windshield wipers and silently cursed himself for being so careless. It wasn't that he had other plans for the evening, but he begrudged the need to take the long drive from Clarksburg back to the winery at this late hour. More importantly, he was worried that someone might have come across the notebook and out of curiosity had read some of his entries. Not that they would have told the reader much. He was always careful not to use names and to avoid references to specific events and dates. Nonetheless, those entries, opaque as they were, might pique the interest of the reader and lead to questions which he did not wish to answer.

And what if the notebook was not at the winery? He could not recall an occasion when it had not been either on his person or locked in his flat. But when he had arrived home after work, it was neither in any of his pockets nor in its usual place on the bedside stand. He had searched the flat and gone back to the car to see if it had fallen out there, but it was nowhere to be found. Which left the winery.

The clock on the dashboard read 10:41 when he turned off the upper lake road and pulled into the Random Harvest parking lot. Everything was quiet. And dark. He circled around the cluster of buildings until he came to a ramp which gave access to a part of the winery where cellar associates like himself worked. He had no key, but the lock on an old door next to the ramp should be no impediment to his gaining access. Just lift up on the handle, turn it counterclockwise, and push hard was what he had heard one of the men saying. The door opened as he expected, and four minutes after leaving his car, he had located the notebook with the aid of a flashlight. It had apparently fallen out of his pocket and been accidentally kicked into a corner by one of the workers. Perhaps he had kicked it there himself. No matter. What was important was that it was back in his possession and had apparently not been read by anyone else.

He knew he could walk back through the winery and let himself out the main entrance. The door would lock automatically behind him. The pale beam of his flashlight led him up a short flight of stairs from the cellar into an adjacent building, and then onto a corridor that passed a series of offices. It was when he turned a corner that he first saw the patch of light on the floor a dozen yards ahead of him. Someone must have forgotten to flick the switch when he left. But when he reached that part of the corridor, he quickly stopped and stepped back away from the glass panel on the wall through which the light was shining. Someone was in the office, his back to the corridor, doing something to a cabinet in the corner of the room. And he was wearing gloves.

This was not a part of the winery with which Rafferty was familiar. But he could see from the name in block letters on the door that he was looking into the office of someone named Parker Jameson. Rafferty had heard of Jameson, an accountant or something like that. He leaned forward, the better to see what the man was doing. At that moment the man turned around to put what looked like file folders on the desk. That he had not expected to see anyone in the hall was immediately apparent from the shocked expression on his face.

"Who are you? What are you doing here?" Jameson quickly opened the door and stepped into the corridor. He looked as if he were seeing a ghost.

"I didn't mean to bother you," Rafferty said, defensively. "I'd left something at the winery this afternoon, and came back to get it."

"You work here?"

The man was obviously nervous. His hands disappeared behind his back and stayed there.

"Yes, but I was just on my way out. I didn't think anybody would be here at this hour."

"Well, I've been catching up on some work. It's our busiest time of the year. I suppose you know that."

Why the need to explain himself? What else would the man be doing there? But something was wrong. Things didn't look right. Especially the gloves. The gloves that were now out of sight.

"Are your hands all right? I mean, I see that you're wearing gloves."

He couldn't believe he had asked the question. If the man were Mr. Jameson, he would surely take offense at such an impertinence.

The man did take offense at what he saw as an impertinent question.

"Now you just wait a minute, mister," the man said. "I don't take kindly to someone who shouldn't even be in the building barging in here and asking me questions. My hands are none of your business, but if you must know, I've got a very bad skin rash and have to wear gloves. Now get out of here, or I'll report you to Mr. Drake."

"Of course. I'm on my way."

Rafferty hurried down the corridor, through the entrance foyer, and on out into the parking lot.

The drive back to Clarksburg gave him time to reflect on what he had seen at the winery. What had Mr. Jameson been doing? Maybe he always worked late. Maybe he'd fallen behind on some important task and had to put in extra hours. He remembered days like that at St. Anthony's, days when his sermon wasn't taking shape as quickly as it should, or when his tendency to procrastinate had put him in a bind. But Jameson had not looked harried; he had looked as if he had been caught doing something he should not have been doing. Had he even looked scared, or was that simply his imagination? And then there were the gloves. And the way in which Jameson had tried to hide the fact that he was wearing them.

During the years when he was Father Brendan Rafferty, he had frequently observed a member of his flock, troubled by some real or imagined transgression, try to dissemble before he was able to coax from him a candid confession. But he was no longer a priest. He was a low level employee of Random Harvest Vineyards, and there was no way he could persuade Mr. Jameson to explain what he had been doing at the winery that night. Better just to put it out of his mind and be grateful that he had found his notebook.

———

Rafferty had not slept well, and the reason came into focus over breakfast the next morning. It was the unexpected encounter with Parker Jameson that was responsible. For the first time in many months he found himself thinking like a priest. And not just any priest. He was thinking like Father Brown, or like he imagined Father Brown thought. He had always been fond of G. K. Chesterton's little fictional priest, a quiet, unassuming man of the cloth who solved crimes because he understood how the criminal mind works.

Try as he had, he couldn't shake the conviction that Jameson was up to no good. Just what he was guilty of, he didn't know, but the man had acted as if he were guilty. And people don't act guilty without a reason. As Rafferty drove to work the next day, he resolved that he would try to find out what that reason was. The thought of doing so actually gave him a lift. Not since he had left East Moncton and St. Anthony's had he felt such a sense of purpose in his life.

He decided to stop by Mary Rizzo's office before clocking in. He didn't know her well. She had seemed to take an interest in him, or at least a desire to be friendly. But he had consciously sought to maintain a low profile at the winery, to discourage friendships. The less people knew about him, the safer he felt. But Ms. Rizzo did not seem to be the sort of person who would hold a grudge because he had been standoffish. More importantly, she was likely to know something about Jameson, and he felt reasonably sure she would share that knowledge with him.

"Mr. Rafferty!" she exclaimed when he entered her office. "I haven't seen you in ages. How have you been?"

This was exactly the kind of conversation Rafferty didn't wish to engage in. But he did exchange a few pleasant words before bringing up the reason for his presence in front of her desk.

"I'm afraid I don't know nearly as much about this winery as I should. Considering that I've worked here for over two months. I was thinking about the management. I ran into Mr. Jameson yesterday, and I was embarrassed that I didn't have a clue what he does here. I figured maybe you could tell me."

"Sure. I'd guess you'd say he's the winery's bookkeeper. He handles the accounts, the money. You know, the important stuff." She chuckled. "We'd never get paid without Mr. Jameson."

"I thought it was something like that, but I wasn't sure," he said. "Poor man. He's got some kind of a bad rash on his hands. Has to wear gloves."

"He does?" She seemed surprised. "I said hello to him this morning, and he didn't have gloves on."

"That's good. The rash must have cleared up."

So much for that story, Rafferty thought. But as he said it, he had another thought.

"Let me back up a minute. About Mr. Jameson. What does he look like?"

Mary Rizzo was puzzled by the question. Mr. Rafferty had just said that he'd been talking to Mr. Jameson. How could he not know what he looked like?

"Why, he's, you know, average height. He has hair that's a sort of salt and pepper gray. I'd guess he's in his sixties."

The man in Jameson's office had not been Jameson. Rafferty now remembered that he had never said he was.

"I must have had him mixed up with someone else," he said. "The man I thought might be Mr. Jameson is well over six-foot tall, much younger, and he's got red hair. Really bright red."

"Oh, you mean Joe Clifford. He's an assistant to Mr. Drake." She laughed. "He and Jameson sure don't look alike."

So, he thought, the man I had encountered the previous night, the man with the gloves, would have had no reason to be working late in Parker Jameson's office. He chatted for another minute, thanked her, and set off for the cellar.

He had a difficult time throughout the day keeping his mind on his job. If this man Clifford had been pulling files late at night wearing gloves, it was possible that he was engaged in some scheme to defraud the winery. There could be other explanations for what he had witnessed, but he couldn't think what they might be. Not in view of the panicked look on his face when he saw him through the office window. Not in view of the gloves.

He tried to analyze his own thinking. Was he jumping to this conclusion because of his recent experience with Sadowsky? No, the two situations were very different, alike only in that both might involve ill-gotten money.

How would Father Brown assess the situation? What intuition gained from his years as a priest would help him to understand Clifford? He had long ago memorized one of Chesterton's most famous lines, spoken by Father Brown to a master criminal: "Has it never struck you that a man who does next to nothing but hear men's real sins is not likely to be unaware of human evil?" He had been no Father Brown, but he thought he knew something about evil. Of course, he would never be able to hear Joe Clifford's confession. He didn't even know whether the man was Catholic, and if so whether he ever went to confession. But he thought he knew that Clifford had not been in someone else's office the previous night to catch up on back work during this busiest of all seasons for wineries.

By day's end, Brendan Rafferty had made up his mind that he would have to make an effort to get to know this man who wore gloves in a white-collar job.

It was two days later that he screwed up his courage and made the trip from the cellar to the floor where the main offices were located.

He rapped on the door bearing Clifford's name, and the red-haired assistant to the president looked up. His face registered instant recognition. The man shook his head and turned his attention back to the papers he had been studying. Rafferty rapped again. This time Clifford got up and came to the door. He was obviously not happy to be interrupted, and said so when he opened the door. The gloves were nowhere in sight.

"Once again, Mr. Clifford, I'm sorry to be bothering you. I know you have a lot to do, like you told me the other night. But I really need to talk with you."

"What did you say your name was?" Jameson asked, his temper barely under control.

"I don't believe I did. But it's Brendan Rafferty. I'm a cellar associate here. Mostly the tanks, monitoring temperature, things like that. It's a good job. I like it. Anyway, that isn't why I'm here."

"And just why are you here? I'm a busy man."

"Yes, I'm sure you are. But it's about the other night. When I was trying to find something I'd left at the winery, and you were working late. In another office down the hall. What worried me were your hands, that bad rash you have. The gloves, remember?"

Clifford was still angry, but he was suddenly more guarded. His face showed it. He was now weighing his words.

"I appreciate your concern, but I'm all right. Now can I get back to work?"

"Of course. But first, let me say that there's something I don't seem to understand. The rash was so bad you had to wear gloves. Now you have discarded the gloves, and I don't see any sign of a rash. How did you do it? I mean, what miracle medication did you use?"

"Mr. Rafferty, I'm afraid I don't see why this is of any interest to you. I had a problem. It went away. End of story. I'm sure you have things to take care of downstairs, things that are more important than my rash."

It was at this point that Rafferty did perhaps the most brazen thing he had done in a very long time. He took a seat in the chair that faced Joe Clifford's desk.

"Before you call for security, I wish you'd let me tell you what's bothering me. I think you may need some help, and I think I can help you."

If I'm wrong, Rafferty thought, I'll be hitting the road again, looking for another job, another place to live. If, that is, I don't have to face a charge of defamation of character.

But Clifford sat down. He was making a conscious effort to put on a blank face. It wasn't working.

"I don't know quite why I'm humoring you, but why don't you tell me why you think I need help."

"What I think, Mr. Clifford, is that you weren't wearing gloves when we first met because you had a skin rash. It is my guess that you were fiddling the books, as they say. And you were doing it in Parker Jameson's office, which is where those books are. I don't pretend to know exactly how you were doing it, or how much you were planning to steal from Random Harvest. But I think the gloves were to keep your prints off something which might give the game away."

"That's crazy," Clifford said, color rising in his face. "You have no idea what you're talking about."

"Perhaps not, but I like to think I'm a fairly good judge of people. I believe that you have some kind of problem, a problem which has cast a shadow over your life. Otherwise I doubt that you would have been in Mr. Jameson's office late one night, long after the winery had closed, going through his files. I'm sure you are cursing your bad luck that I happened along. But I think you should be grateful, because you will now have an opportunity to save yourself from serious trouble and put your life back together."

Clifford began to interrupt, but Rafferty waved him off, now well past the point of no return in his impromptu imitation of Father Brown.

"What you need to do is return anything you have taken from Mr. Jameson's office and the winery. It isn't my place to advise you how to do it, but you will find a way. That done, I give you my solemn word that I shall not say a word of this matter to Mr. Jameson or to Mr. Drake. Indeed, I shall not say anything to anyone about it. Your conscience will then be clear. Indeed, you may well have saved your very soul."

For a long moment no other word passed between the two men. Clifford stared in silence at his accuser. Rafferty looked away, as if embarrassed to meet the other man's gaze. It was Clifford who finally spoke.

"You don't know me, Mr. Rafferty. My soul doesn't need saving. But I'll give some serious thought to what you have said. You have my word on that. Do I have yours?"

"You do. No one will ever know what happened. Because nothing will have happened."

It was time to go. The former priest, Brendan Rafferty, stood, nodded to the man seated across the desk, and left the room. He hoped it wasn't obvious to Clifford, but he was shaking.

The two men did not see each other the following day. More importantly, there was no hint around the winery that anything was amiss. No gossip about a theft from Parker Jameson's office. No tightening of security.

Rafferty began to breathe more easily.

But the next day they nearly ran into each other. It occurred in the parking lot at the end of the workday. They were not the only people heading for their cars, but it is doubtful if anyone noticed the look they exchanged. Rafferty seemed initially surprised to see the man whom he had so recently accused of theft; then he favored him with a brief smile. But if looks could kill, Clifford's did. At least that is the way the former priest saw it.

Back at his flat, Brendan Rafferty sank into a chair with a beer he had just uncapped. It seemed to have gone so well. Much better than he had dared to hope. But now he was experiencing a familiar feeling. He was once more afraid.

He hadn't expected Clifford to think kindly of him for interfering with his plan. But he had expected him to be grateful for his promise not to tell anyone about it. What if he were wrong?

What if the man doubted his word? He had seen the look on his face in the parking lot. The more he thought about it, the more he worried that Clifford didn't trust him. Which would create a serious problem for the young assistant to the president of the winery. If what he was doing became known, he would lose his job and quite possibly go to jail. Whatever the personal crisis which had prompted his action, it could hardly be worse than that. So what would Clifford do? Might he try to silence his accuser before he talked?

Brendan Rafferty felt a familiar sense of panic rising in his chest.

CHAPTER 4

Thirteen Hours Earlier

He crossed himself and slowly got up off his knees. Brendan Rafferty had made prayer an integral part of his life for as long as he could remember. But the focus of his prayers had undergone a change over the last year. During the time when he had been a parish priest, he had recited the ritual prayers of the church on thousands of occasions. And of course he had prayed for guidance in the conduct of his own life. In recent months, however, his prayers, with increasing frequency, had reflected the anxiety he had felt since his spur of the moment decision to leave St. Anthony's.

First there had been the feeling that he was in danger from Gerald Flanagan, a man driven by hatred. Then, after an interlude of several months, there had been the growing danger posed by Sadowsky, a man motivated by greed. And now, more than a year after he had become a man on the run, he had started to feel that he might be in danger from Joe Clifford. In his case, the motive would be fear.

Perhaps he was wrong about Flanagan. It had been thirteen months since that terrible day when the angry father had accused him of molesting his son, of turning him into a homosexual. He found it hard to believe that Flanagan knew where he lived. It was even possible that his anger had abated over time. He hoped that he had come to terms with his son's sexual orientation. But whenever he began to feel that he had finally put the problem behind him for good, some inner voice would say "what if." What if the man had never forgiven him his imagined transgression and had single-mindedly made it his mission to track him down? Then he would still be in danger, possibly mortal danger.

He was even less sure he could be wrong about Sadowsky. Hatred might fade with time. But a debt of more than twenty thousand dollars was something else. What is more, that debt had been incurred more recently. And it was owed to a man who was in the business of getting his hooks into vulnerable people and profiting from their gambling addiction. Like Flanagan, Sadowsky probably did not know where he lived. After all, he had heard nothing from him since he left Verona. But the man would be tenacious, and would be unlikely to give up until he found him. Here, too, he could be in mortal danger.

However, it was Clifford he was now most worried about. He knew much less about him. He had no idea what it was that had prompted him to try to steal from Random Harvest. It was presumably some personal problem. But he didn't know that. For all he knew, Clifford was an habitual thief, the winery only his latest victim. Whatever the real explanation, he had been caught and had been told that no one would ever learn of his crime if he returned whatever he had taken from Mr. Jameson's office. But why should this promise be believed? He was as little known to Clifford as Clifford was to him. He could readily imagine that the man was at that very moment living in fear. Fear that his nighttime act of theft would be revealed to the owner of the winery. Or that he might soon be facing the threat of blackmail. A man fearing such threats might feel compelled to resort to violence. And in Clifford's case, time was of the essence. Danger, even mortal danger, could be imminent.

Rafferty wasn't physically tired, but he was emotionally exhausted. He stretched out on his bed, still in his work clothes. He knew he would have trouble getting to sleep, and that once asleep his efforts to shut out disturbing thoughts and avoid frightening dreams would be futile. He practiced deep breathing to calm his nerves. That didn't work, so he turned on a light and tried to read a passage in a book he had recently purchased, Richard Dawkins' controversial advocacy of atheism.

He wasn't sure why he had bought the book. He had been too good a Catholic to be sympathetic to even a rational, scientific defense of what Dawkins called "the God delusion." He had told himself that he ought to be conversant with the argument, the better to refute it. Perhaps his reason had something to do with the fact that his recent experiences with the human condition had been depressing and that his faith was being tested. Whatever the reason, the book failed to engage his attention. He set it aside, turned off the light, and lay back on the bed.

It was a chilly night, and a wind had come up which rattled the windows of the old house. He really should be putting on his pajamas, but it seemed like too much trouble. He pulled the blanket and comforter over his head, seeking more warmth and hoping to block out the noise made by the wind around the window. Had he not done so, he might have seen a brief flash of light in the narrow space between the windowsill and the bottom of the shade. The light quickly disappeared, then reappeared, closer this time. A moment later it was gone, only to be followed by a low, barely audible grating sound. The bed covers muffled the sound. To Brendan Rafferty it was indistinguishable from the wind. Suddenly it seemed colder in the room, the wind louder.

The sound which next penetrated the cocoon of blankets he had made for himself was not caused by a strong gust of wind or by the window rattling in the casement. It was a human voice, low but audible.

"Good night, Rafferty."

CHAPTER 5

Damn! Carol Kelleher said it to herself, under her breath. She had just replaced the phone, bringing to an end a brief conversation with someone at Random Harvest Vineyards. The news had not been good news.

Carol had been the sheriff of Cumberland County for only four years, but she had been born and grew up in the area, and one of her favorite times of the year had always been early autumn. Summer residents would have vacated their cottages on Crooked Lake on Labor Day, but visitors flocked back to the lake and its vineyards in September and October to enjoy the harvest season and the festivals which accompanied it at local wineries. If the region was fortunate enough to be blessed by so-called Indian summer weather, the wine trail around the lake typically became a caravan of leaf peepers and wine tasters. As a young woman, Carol had often joined that caravan. As county sheriff, she had made it a point to drive through the vineyards, stopping at the wineries to chat with the tourists and experience vicariously their enjoyment of the season.

Today, in the middle of a grape harvest that had been a bonanza for the wineries, the caller from Random Harvest had reported that a dead man had been found in one of its vineyards. A man who was not only dead but who had been strung up to resemble a scarecrow. And apparently an impressive enough scarecrow to attract the attention of a passing motorist, who had dutifully notified the winery.

It was unlikely that word of this macabre discovery would have the negative effect of discouraging visitors. With Halloween approaching, it might even have quite the opposite result. But Carol knew all too well what the faux scarecrow in the vineyard could mean for her department, always understaffed and more familiar with traffic and assorted misdemeanors than with murder. Of course it might not be a case of murder. The man reporting the matter had no idea what had caused the human scarecrow's death. But it seemed inconceivable—indeed physically impossible—for this to be a suicide, and Carol could not imagine that it had been a dying man's last wish that someone fix him up like a scarecrow and leave him in a Crooked Lake vineyard. They would know soon enough how the man had died. At least she hoped they would. But she was already assuming it had been murder.

Carol estimated that it would take her at least half an hour to get to Random Harvest. A quick check of the roster board told her that her deputy sheriff, Sam Bridges, was in the tiny village of Linton, no more than three miles from the winery. She didn't hesitate.

"Sam," she said when he answered her call, "we seem to have a problem over at Random Harvest. You're close. Just drop what you're doing and get over there. There's supposed to be a dead man in one of their vineyards, and the circumstances look suspicious. Very suspicious. Something about him looking like a scarecrow. The man who called me says the body's in a vineyard on the east side of the upper lake road about a mile and a half south of the winery. I'm sure there will be people there, milling around, gawking. Clear them out. Keep everyone away from the body. I'll get there as fast as I can."

———

Bridges turned onto the upper lake road and headed toward the winery, his car exceeding the posted speed limit by ten, then fifteen, and ultimately twenty miles per hour. There were relatively few cars on that stretch of the road, so there was no need for either the siren or the revolving red light on the car's roof. It was when he crested the hill north of Random Harvest Vineyards that he saw a small cluster of cars and pickup trucks on the shoulder of the road a few hundred yards ahead of him. It appeared that the scarecrow in the vineyard had attracted an audience.

When Sam pulled off the road, it was immediately apparent that none of the two cars and two pickups was occupied. But there was a small crowd of people some distance down into the vineyard, and Sam set off to join them, following the path that Brad Robinson had taken earlier that afternoon.

"Excuse me," he said, announcing his presence, "but I represent the sheriff and I'm going to have to ask all of you what's going on here."

He had seen the body on the crude cross, and he had no doubt that it was both human and dead.

The people who had gathered around the scarecrow—and there were seven of them, six men and a woman—stepped back to let him into their small circle.

"Jerry Copeland," a stocky man with a ruddy face and a large mustache said, extending his hand. "I'm a manager up at the winery, and I guess you'd say I'm in charge. At least I'm the one who came down when Mr. Robinson here told us about that man there. Me and Bill Jenkins."

The man Jenkins introduced himself.

"Okay, so you represent the winery. Now what about you? Robinson, is it?"

"Yes, sir. And this is my wife. We'd been at the winery for a tasting. We hadn't been on the road but for a minute, maybe two, when we saw the scarecrow and wanted to get a closer look."

"And the rest of you?" Sam turned to the other men. Two of them looked to be only recently out of high school, the third somewhat older and better dressed.

"We all work for Random Harvest," the latter said. "I run the sales office. Name's Lew Grabner. These guys are just here for the harvesting work, I think."

The two grape pickers, whose names turned out to be Seth Toomey and Vincent Collins, nodded. It was quickly established that Copeland and Jenkins had been asked to see what had happened down in the vineyard and that Robinson had remained out of an understandable curiosity. Grabner, Toomey, and Collins had caught wind of some excitement in the vineyards, and had simply come down to check it out.

"Do any of you know who this man is?" Sam asked, referring to the scarecrow.

The consensus was that no one knew him. Don't think I ever saw him before was the way Copeland put it. Jenkins and Grabner both said they thought he looked familiar, that he might have a part-time job at the winery, but that they couldn't be sure. The young grape pickers shook their heads and said nothing.

"How's it happen that nobody saw the body on the cross here until Mr. Robinson spotted it? That had to be less than an hour ago. Why didn't one of the pickers realize that something was funny and say something? I don't see how they could have missed it. And by the way, where are they?"

There didn't appear to be anyone else in the vineyard. No hand pickers. No mechanical harvester.

"There haven't been any pickers in this field," Jenkins said. "These are ice wine grapes. They don't get harvested until much later, after the grapes freeze."

Sam didn't know much about ice wine grapes. Frustrated by the information that no pickers had been active near the scarecrow, he turned his attention to another problem.

"Look, the sheriff will be along momentarily. We're going to have to take that man down off the post, see if we can figure out how he died, and then get his body moved out of here. I'd like all of you except for the Robinsons and Mr. Copeland to go back to the winery, give us some room here. It's kinda crowded."

Indeed it was crowded. There were, to Sam's way of thinking, too many people around the scarecrow. If there was a chance that the condition of the ground might offer a clue to what had happened, it was fast disappearing under the assembled feet.

Jenkins, Grabner, and the two part-time grape pickers made their way reluctantly back to their vehicles. Sam motioned to Robinson.

"Tell me just what you saw and what you did," he said, and the man who had discovered the corpse on the cross and alerted Random Harvest told the deputy sheriff what he had previously told Copeland. It was a brief and straightforward story, and Sam thought it had the ring of truth. What motive, after all, would a couple who had decided to spend a beautiful autumn day wine tasting at Crooked Lake's hillside wineries have for lying about what they had done and why?

"One more question," he said. "Did you, at any time, see anybody else here in the vineyard? Anywhere in the vineyard?"

"No, I didn't, although to be honest about it I wasn't looking for anyone. My mind was on the scarecrow—you know, that man there."

Sam made a note of the Robinsons' names, their address, and a phone number where they could be reached, then wished them a good day, one free of any more shocking discoveries like the one they had just experienced. He knew that the sheriff would probably want to talk with them herself. If she did, they lived not far away and it should be easy to get in touch.

Deputy Sheriff Bridges and the Random Harvest official were alone for only a few minutes before another car pulled off the road above them, creating a small dust storm as it braked to a stop. The sheriff and Jim Barrett, one of her younger officers, climbed out of the car and hurried down the path to join them.

Introductions over, Carol turned toward the man on the makeshift cross.

"What have you learned about him? A name, for starters?"

She addressed the question to Sam, but it was Copeland who answered.

"I'm sorry, Sheriff, but I don't recognize him. None of the others seemed to know who he is either."

"The others?"

"There were a few other men from the winery here when I arrived," Sam said. "They didn't recognize him."

"Where are these other men?"

Sam suddenly had the feeling that perhaps he shouldn't have dismissed Jenkins and Grabner and those young grape pickers.

"They went back to their jobs. I think they'd just come down here out of curiosity. Unlike Mr. Copeland. He's here in his official capacity."

The thought crossed Carol's mind that one of those men might have had another reason for coming down to the vineyard upon hearing that a body had been discovered there. What if one of them knew something about the scarecrow in the vineyard? What if a worker knew something about how he had come to be there? Unlikely, she thought. Highly unlikely. But not impossible. She'd get their names and talk with them. All of them.

"Jim," she said to Officer Barrett, "let's get some pictures before we do anything else. It's a good bet he's not been hanging there very long. He still looks fairly fresh."

Carol didn't know why the word that had come to mind was fresh. It made it sound as if she were comparing the dead man to a piece of meat, something she had not intended to do.

Sam knew what she meant.

"I know," he said. "It's cool, but there's lots of sun. On the other hand, I'll bet he's been here since last night. Hard to imagine anybody putting him up there today, out here in plain sight."

"But if he's been there all day," Barrett suggested, "I can't believe *somebody* didn't see him."

"Somebody did," Copeland said. "A guy named Robinson. He came up to the winery to tell us we had a problem down in the vineyards."

Carol shook her head.

"I know that. But there must have been dozens of cars on that road throughout the day. Seems like someone would have noticed, a lot earlier than the man who reported it."

"Oh, I bet lots of people did see the scarecrow." It was Copeland. "Trouble is, that's all they saw—a scarecrow. From the road it would have been hard to know it was a man. Robinson, he didn't come down here because he was suspicious. He just thought it was a damned good scarecrow, wanted to take some pictures."

"I guess it makes sense," Carol said. She was mildly annoyed with herself. She knew it wasn't a scarecrow because she'd been told before she saw it. "We see what we expect to see, don't we, and drivers passing by would have expected to see a scarecrow, not a dead man trussed up on a pole."

These thoughts suggested that more pictures might be helpful.

"Jim, why don't you go up to the road and take a couple of pictures of it. They'll show us what anybody passing by would have seen."

Carol was studying the crime scene, and there was no question about it. It was a crime scene. The body looked to be tightly bound to the wooden crossbar, its feet barely touching the ground. The post against which it stood looked old but still sturdy enough to support the man's weight.

"It doesn't look as if the winery makes much use of scarecrows," she said, directing the observation to Copeland.

"It's not my responsibility, Sheriff, but I think you're right. There certainly aren't any other scarecrows in this field. Now it's mostly just those balloons."

"Would you know if there had been a scarecrow on this post? I mean a real one, before somebody substituted the body."

"No idea," Copeland replied. "I'd have to ask Mason. That's Dick Mason. I think he'd be the one to know."

"Okay, I'll want to talk with Mason. We'll go up to the winery and do it today, if he's there. As soon as we've finished with things here, that is."

Bridges was kneeling beside the post, only inches away from the feet of the corpse.

"I wouldn't know whether there used to be a scarecrow on this post," he said, "but I'm pretty sure the post itself has been here for quite awhile. Whoever put this guy up on it didn't have to dig a post hole or lug a post in. Look here."

There was no fresh earth around the post, only old weeds, now brown, and a few pieces of straw.

Carol nodded her agreement with her deputy's opinion. She then walked up to the body and began gently to prod it.

"I can't be certain he's been here all day, but it's been a good many hours. Rigor is firm, probably complete. We'll get an official verdict as soon as Liberti and his crew get here, but it does look like he died last night."

"Any sign of a bullet wound? Or maybe it was a knife." Sam had been aware from the minute he arrived on the scene that there was dried blood around the nose and mouth. But it looked more like residue from a nosebleed than the result of a wound.

"No. But I don't think we're going to learn much until we get him off that pole."

Carol had started to say cross, but made a conscious decision not to. She, like the others, had been struck by the similarity to a crucifixion. Whether her Catholic upbringing had somehow conditioned her to avoid the use of the term in other than its Christian context, she didn't know. But the fact that what she saw clearly resembled a caricature of the crucifixion gave her pause. Why had someone gone to the trouble of hoisting the man onto the crude cross and lashing him into place there, when it would have been far easier to simply leave him on the ground? So he'd be discovered sooner? But if that was the reason, there would have been many other places where discovery would have been easy and depositing the body even easier. She'd think about it later.

She took out a pair of white gloves and slipped them on. Carefully lifting the work shirt, she thrust a hand down into the back pocket of the man's jeans. It was a tight fit, but she was finally able to extract an old black wallet.

"We may be in luck here," she said. She squatted down and with practiced fingers opened the wallet and sorted through its contents. "It looks as if his name is—or was—Brendan Rafferty. Not much here other than a driver's license and some stuff that doesn't tell us much by itself. Seems he lived over in Clarksburg."

She dropped the wallet into a zip-lock bag which Barrett had produced and turned to Copeland.

"Does the name Rafferty mean anything to you?"

"I'm afraid not. There's no reason to assume he had anything to do with our winery, is there? He could have just been somebody hiking along the road, taking in the scenery."

"I suppose it's possible, a casual hiker running into a killer on one of these back roads. But why the scarecrow business? No, I think this isn't just the tragic outcome of a chance meeting in your vineyards."

The first weeks of autumn had passed without any problem more serious than a few cases of reckless driving. Carol had even been able to close up her office at a civilized hour on most afternoons. It looked as if the call from Random Harvest at 3:45 on this beautiful October afternoon was going to change all that. Unless, of course, they found a trail of evidence that led quickly to whoever was responsible for the death of the human scarecrow. The sheriff was not sanguine that it would prove that easy.

Not for the first time Carol found herself wishing that Cumberland County would do away with its division of responsibility for cases like this, a division of responsibility which at the moment had her waiting impatiently for the arrival of the coroner. She was no expert, but neither was Tom Liberti. She was reasonably certain that she herself would be able to ascertain the cause of death and the approximate time at which it had occurred. If not, her old friend Doc Crawford, the chief medical examiner, would be able to do so, if not when he first saw the body, at least when he had completed the autopsy. For now, however, she was constrained to follow protocol. The body would remain on the post until Liberti arrived and did his thing.

What bothered her more, however, was that she would be undertaking this investigation of a murder on Crooked Lake without the support of Kevin Whitman. For three summers their lives had been affected by a rare rash of violent deaths in this normally peaceful part of the country. Their relationship had begun early one August morning when he had discovered a dead man on his dock; initially a suspect, he had gradually become her partner in the investigation and, with its denouement, her lover. In the years that followed, that relationship had blossomed over the summers which he spent at the lake and withered during the winters when he returned to the city to resume his job as a professor of music. Moreover, Kevin had proved to be an invaluable accomplice as she had wrestled with two more shocking murders. She realized that she had come to count on his creative imagination and problem-solving skills. But now he was once more many miles away, and there was little prospect that he would be able to abandon his professional responsibilities and join her in the search for the killer of the scarecrow in the vineyard.

Kevin, I wish you were here, she said to herself, as she contemplated the unknown man on the makeshift cross.

CHAPTER 6

Forty-five minutes later, Carol was sitting in the office of Earl Drake, the owner and president of Random Harvest Vineyards. She was flanked by Sam Bridges and Jim Barrett, both of whom looked ill at ease. As well they might have been. Drake was not in a good mood. He glowered at the trio who sat across the desk from him as he peppered them with questions. From the tone of his voice and the angry look on his face, one might have been forgiven for thinking that he blamed the sheriff's department for what had taken place in the vineyard where his ice grapes were growing.

"But this is intolerable. Some fool gets himself killed in my vineyards, word gets out, and the wine-tasting crowd will drive on by, go to Rockledge or Silver Leaf."

"I'm sure nothing like that will happen," Carol said, her voice level and, she hoped, appropriately soothing. "This is a crime which just happened to have taken place on your property. Anyway, most people won't know anything about it, and if they do, it will only make them more interested in stopping here. A mystery to go with the wine. It's the Halloween season, perfect timing."

"Humph!" Drake was conspicuously unconvinced. "You've got to get this taken care of. Right away. I can't have my vineyards turned into a media circus. Or have policemen running around here 24/7."

The owner of Random Harvest stopped in mid-rant and lowered his voice.

"When *do* you expect to close the case?"

"I would like to tell you we'll have made an arrest by the weekend, but that would not be an honest answer. We heard about what had happened less than two hours ago. All I know is that a man named Rafferty was killed sometime last night. And that he was strung up like a scarecrow on an old post in one of your vineyards, probably last night. Beyond that, we don't know much of anything. Maybe we could make some progress if we could ask you and your personnel some questions. That's why my colleagues and I are here."

They had come up to the winery as soon as the coroner had made his appearance, the body had been taken down from the cross, and a cursory examination had revealed that the balding man with the dark blue work shirt had apparently died of a gunshot wound to the back of the head. He had been dead for somewhere between 12 and 16 hours.

The late Brendan Rafferty had departed for the morgue. The ice grape vineyard was now deserted except for several inflated balloons, which had apparently become the twenty-first century's version of a scarecrow. The sun was now low in the western sky, the hillside on which Random Harvest nestled almost entirely in shadow. The last of the day's wine tasters were departing, many of them with a bottle or two or even a case of wine.

Earl Drake, his anger if not his frustration at least temporarily exhausted, shrank back into his chair, and waited for the sheriff to ask what he assumed would be many questions.

"We believe we know the name of the victim," Carol began. "It's Brendan Rafferty. Does someone with that name work for you here at Random Harvest?"

"I don't begin to know the names of all my employees," Drake said, his tone of voice suggesting that he might be reverting to his earlier belligerence. "Why should you assume that this man worked for me?"

"We don't assume that Mr. Rafferty worked for you. But it's a strong possibility. After all, he was found in one of your vineyards, and quite close to the winery. I'm simply starting to form a picture of Mr. Rafferty—who he was, who knew him. If he worked here, I'd like to talk to people he worked with, get an impression of the man."

Carol knew that Rafferty lived in Clarksburg, which was only about twenty-five miles away. Unless, of course, the wallet and the driver's license were not his. She'd have to pay a visit to the address in Clarksburg. But at the moment she was interested in establishing what if any connection there was between the dead man and the winery.

"You'll have to talk with Doug Francis. He usually does the hiring, especially the labor-intensive jobs, the part-timers, the ones where there's more turnover. I'm sure there's no one on my top staff named Rafferty."

"Where can we find Francis?" Carol asked.

"His office is downstairs. Just ask whoever's on the information desk. Down there."

"Okay, we'll do that. And while we're at it, what about a Dick Mason? Where can we find him?"

"Why're you interested in Mason?"

The question surprised Carol.

"Your man Copeland thought he could tell us something about what you use to discourage the birds in the vineyards. Something about scarecrows, like the one Mr. Rafferty seems to have been impersonating."

"Oh." Drake seemed to be considering this innocuous answer. "Well, he'll probably tell you we need to go in for netting. Too expensive. I'll stick to those terror eyes balloons."

"But is he here, in this building?"

"Sure. You can ask at the desk about him, too."

"Look, Mr. Drake, I'm sorry this happened. And I appreciate your help. It looks like closing time, and I'd like to see if I can catch Mr. Francis, maybe Mr. Mason, before they go. I'm sure we'll be talking again, but right now I'd like to head downstairs. Again, thanks for your help."

Earl Drake's help had been limited and grudging, and Carol doubted that he would be of much assistance, even if he were in a more cooperative mood. Hopefully, Francis would be a different story.

As it happened, Francis was not in, hadn't been in all that day. Carol was explaining to a young woman in his office why she wanted to speak with him.

"Oh, you want to know about Mr. Rafferty," the woman said, obviously pleased to be of help. "Yes, he works here."

"Good," Carol said. "Maybe you can answer my questions."

She sent Bridges and Barrett off in search of Mason, and turned back to Francis's assistant.

"I wonder if you can describe Mr. Rafferty, Miss—I'm sorry, I didn't get your name."

"It's Rizzo. Mary Rizzo. But is there some problem? I mean is Mr. Rafferty okay?"

"That's what I hope to find out. You were going to tell me what he looks like."

"I really don't know him. No one does, really. He's what you'd call a loner. Awfully quiet."

"That's very interesting, Ms. Rizzo. But what does he look like?"

The young woman seemed to find the simple question hard to answer.

"Well," she said, searching for the right words, "I guess you'd say sort of plain. Not very tall, say about five foot six or seven. A little thin. Brown hair, but he's started to go bald on top."

Carol was not yet ready to show her the pictures on Barrett's camera, which she had in her pocket. But the description, such as it was, tended to confirm that the man on the cross in the vineyard was almost certainly Rafferty.

"And about how old would you say he is?"

"It's just a guess, but I'd say he's in his forties, maybe fifty."

"You've said that Mr. Rafferty is a loner. That you don't really know him. But you do seem to know something about him. How is that? Is it part of your job to be familiar with the employees of the winery?"

Mary Rizzo smiled a self-conscious smile.

"Well, not exactly. It isn't all that big a place, maybe thirty-five, forty people. Plus they take on extra pickers in the fall. But I like people, so I suppose I try a little extra hard to be nice to them. Especially when, like Mr. Rafferty, they don't seem to be very happy."

"What does he seem to be unhappy about?"

"He's never said. Maybe I'm wrong. But he always has such a long face. I don't think he gets along with the rest of the people here. Like I said, he's a real loner."

"Let's talk about him not getting along with the others. Does there seem to be some special reason why?"

"I wouldn't know, and of course I wouldn't dream of asking him. It's just that he's sort of off in a world of his own. I didn't mean that people treat him badly, just that he doesn't seem to welcome their friendship, so they more or less leave him alone."

"Does he talk with you, share what's on his mind? Has he ever said anything about personal problems?"

"Not really. I think he's grateful that I care, but he doesn't open up to me. In fact, something he said a couple of weeks ago makes me think he'd rather I not ask him questions. I guess he's always going to be a sad man."

I'm afraid his days as a sad man are over, Carol thought to herself. Probably sad right up until the end. Unless sadness gave way to fear if he saw death coming.

"What is his job here?" Carol asked.

"He works with the tanks. They move people around a bit, so he's had a hand in other things, like bottling, but it's mostly in making the wine."

"Has he been here long?"

"Only about two or three months, I think. Let me look." She stepped back into an anteroom off the office, was gone for less than a minute, and reappeared with a smile that said she was glad to be able to provide a specific answer to the sheriff's question.

"We hired him back in late July. I think he'd just moved to this area."

A frown suddenly crossed Mary Rizzo's face.

"I'm not sure Mr. Rafferty would like me to be talking about him like this. It might be best for you to talk with him yourself. He may have gone home for the day, but he's usually back in Building B. Here, let me show you."

She started for the door, but Carol stopped her.

"I'll be visiting Building B. But right now, I'd like you to look at a picture, see if you can confirm that it's Mr. Rafferty."

Carol fished Barrett's camera from her pocket, scanned for a close-up picture he had taken of the body on the cross, and showed it to the woman.

"Is this Mr. Rafferty?"

"Yes, but he doesn't look right. What's he doing?"

"He doesn't look right, Ms. Rizzo, because he's dead. He was found in one of your vineyards this afternoon, found just as you see him in the picture. That's why I'm here. But we weren't sure it was Mr. Rafferty, which is why I've been asking you these questions."

"Oh, my god," Rizzo said, her voice barely a whisper.

It was obvious that she hadn't heard the news about the discovery of a dead man in the vineyard. Which surprised the sheriff. She had assumed that something so unusual would have quickly become common knowledge at the winery, certainly within an hour. Perhaps Ms. Rizzo had been closeted in the inner office and talked with no one during the late afternoon. Or perhaps Mr. Drake had issued instructions that nothing was to be said about the matter. He certainly would not have wanted any of his guests at the wine-tasting bar to hear of it. But Carol doubted that such instructions would have reached all of his employees, much less ensured their silence.

Ms. Rizzo could not imagine that anyone—at least anyone from the winery—would have had a reason to kill Rafferty. Carol did not find this particularly helpful. All it told her was that in spite of Rizzo's efforts to be nice to Rafferty, she didn't really know very much about him, including the nature and extent of his relationships with other Random Harvest employees. He might be a loner, but that did not preclude the possibility that there had been someone at the winery who knew him much better than Rizzo did. Someone who harbored some grudge against him. Someone who had a reason to kill him.

Before heading back to Cumberland, Carol once more stopped by the office of the anxious owner of Random Harvest Vineyards and diplomatically but firmly shared a list of things she wanted him to do or, more importantly, things she didn't want him to do. She knew that she would be coming back to the winery. Soon. And, in all probability, many times. She had already begun to rethink her agenda for that evening and for the next day. She would first have to pay a visit to the address on Brendan Rafferty's driver's license, and then start questioning the man's co-workers at Random Harvest.

CHAPTER 7

"And what did *you* learn?"

The sheriff had been filling Officer Barrett in on what Mary Rizzo had to say about the late Brendan Rafferty. Bridges had left the winery in his own patrol car, and Barrett was driving back to Cumberland, Carol slumped beside him in the passenger seat.

"Well," he began, "it seems that this guy Mason has some kind of supervisory job where the vineyards are concerned. Anyway, he confirmed what Copeland had said—they don't really use scarecrows anymore. But it seems that there are still a few around, here and there. I think Mason hates to phase them out altogether. According to him, the one closest to the winery is in that field where we found Rafferty. And he's sure there was only that one down there."

"Which means that somebody removed the scarecrow and substituted Rafferty's body."

"Has to be," Barrett said. "Mason even remembered what the scarecrow looked like. Said it was pretty old and weathered. Thinks it was made several years ago by a Mrs. Packer for a Halloween display. Her husband—he works for Random Harvest—he gave it to the winery where it's been ever since."

"Did Mason describe the scarecrow?"

"Yeah. He said it had a pair of old jeans, hole in one of the knees, a work shirt, and a rather battered straw hat. He thought the straw had settled, so the legs looked thicker than the torso. No shoes—in fact, no feet. And he said there weren't really any features on the face. Maybe there had been, but when he saw it last they were just smudges. Probably had been done in charcoal or something, not paint."

"Which means that somewhere in the vicinity there's a scarecrow lying around. Or what's left of one. Unless, of course, whoever killed Rafferty and put him up on that post has already disposed of the original."

Carol was thinking about the scarecrow, the scarecrow that had to be taken down from the post to make room for Rafferty. She couldn't think of a reason why the killer would need to hide it. Yet it appeared to have been removed from the vineyard. Or had it? Perhaps it had been dumped somewhere else. After all, the vineyard extended over several acres, and they had made no effort to search it. There had seemed no reason to do so. But she knew they would have to look for the old scarecrow. And while they were at it, for anything else that might have something to do with the murder of the late Brendan Rafferty.

"Had Mason heard about what had happened down in the vineyard?"

"He knew that a body had been found, but nothing about the scarecrow."

"How did he react when you told him about it?"

"Surprised, I guess you'd say. Who wouldn't be? He said something like 'that's crazy.'"

Carol was wishing she had been the one to question Mason, the one to observe his face as he absorbed this information. He was the resident expert at Random Harvest on scarecrows, the one who presumably knew most about the one that guarded the ice grape vineyard. Was it possible that he had had something to do with what happened there? Carol knew that she was projecting, and doing so without a shred of evidence that Mason, a man she had not even met, was in any way involved in the death of Brendan Rafferty. No, she thought, let's not go there.

It was almost 6:30 when Barrett dropped Carol off in the parking lot of the Cumberland County Sheriff's Department. The end of daylight savings time was still a couple of weeks away, and it was nearly dark. No lights shown from the windows. Bridges' car was not there, meaning he had gone straight home to dinner after leaving Random Harvest. But Carol's supper would have to wait.

She climbed into her car and punched in 411 on her cell phone. It took less than a minute to learn that there was no phone listing for Brendan Rafferty at the driver's license address on 125 Maple Lane or anywhere else in Clarksburg. So, she said to herself, he doesn't have a landline. And damned if I know his cell phone number. Not that he would be there to take her call, but there might be a wife or some live-in companion.

Carol had known that a trip to Clarksburg that evening might well be a wild goose chase. It would probably be better to wait for morning. But she also knew that she had to check out the Maple Lane address, and that she had to do it that night. She couldn't explain the sense of urgency she felt, even to herself. Maybe supper would taste better. Maybe she'd sleep better.

It was dark well before she got to Clarksburg. The roller coaster road from the west arm of Crooked Lake had been all but deserted. Uncertain where Maple Lane was, Carol pulled into a service station at the edge of town and got instructions. It turned out to be only a quarter of a mile away, a short street that for all practical purposes marked the boundary between town and country. Number 125 was a rambler, third from the corner. She was relieved to see lights through the windows and a pickup truck in the driveway.

Okay, Carol said to herself, let's see if we can find out just who this Brendan Rafferty is. Or was.

The woman who opened the door was obviously not his wife. Not, that is, unless he had married someone much older than himself. His mother?

"Good evening," Carol began. "I'm looking for Brendan Rafferty and I understand that he lives here."

"Oh, dear, I didn't mean for Stan to make a big thing of this."

Carol had given some thought to the course a conversation with whomever answered the door at 125 Maple Lane might take. But she had not imagined anything like this.

"I'm sorry, Mrs.—" She paused, waiting for the woman to introduce herself.

"Mrs. Stafford. I'm Jenny Stafford."

"Glad to meet you Mrs. Stafford. I'm Sheriff Kelleher. But I'm afraid I don't know what you're talking about. Who is Stan?"

"Stan Evans. You know, our police chief. Didn't he talk to you?"

"No. Well, not about you." She decided to put the conversation she had planned to have on hold and let Mrs. Stafford explain herself.

"I told him Mr. Rafferty hadn't paid his rent in two months, asked what he thought I should do. Didn't he tell you that?"

"I'm afraid not. I haven't talked with Stan in several months. I take it Mr. Rafferty lives here. And that you have a problem with him."

"Indeed I do. Like I said, he owes me rent." It was at this point that it dawned on Mrs. Stafford that if the sheriff wasn't at the door to discuss Rafferty's failure to pay his rent, there must be another reason for her visit.

"You didn't come to discuss the rent, did you, Sheriff?"

"No. In fact, I didn't even know that Mr. Rafferty rented from you. Do you mind if I come in?"

Carol did not exactly barge past Mrs. Stafford, but she eased past her into the foyer, employing her best smile.

After an awkward moment, the two women took seats in what was presumably the living room. It was decorated in what Carol thought was execrable taste, but she wasn't there to pass judgment on the decor.

"I don't know Mr. Rafferty," she said, "but I am here because I hope you will be able to help me. He has listed this as his address, but I now realize that it isn't his house. He apparently rents from you. When did he move in?"

"It was back in the summer, near the end of July. I should have asked for a long-term deposit, but all I got was the first month's rent. Believe me, I'll never make that mistake again."

"So he has a room here, right?"

"More than a room. Frank—that's my late husband—he did a little remodeling a few years ago, added a kitchenette, made a sort of apartment back there. We thought our daughter would be moving in. Her marriage had broken up; her kids were grown, and she seemed to be at loose ends. But it didn't happen. I put up an 'apartment for rent' sign back in June and one day Mr. Rafferty came along."

"I take it you didn't know him. Or anything about him."

"No. I wished I'd asked around, got some references."

"Do you know where he came from?"

"No again. I asked a few questions, but he was tight lipped. You know, one of those people who like their privacy. He didn't tell me anything about himself. At first I didn't think he even wanted to give me his name."

"You do know where he works, though." It was a question.

"I think it's at one of the wineries over on Crooked Lake, but I'm not even a hundred percent sure of that."

"Do you ever talk with Mr. Rafferty? More than just hello, that sort of thing. I'm wondering whether you can tell me anything about him. Does he ever have company? Does he have an unlisted phone, or ever use yours? You understand, I'm trying to form a picture of him, just who he is, what his habits are."

Jenny Stafford leaned forward on the couch.

"Would you like a cup of tea, Sheriff?"

It appeared that there might be something the woman would like to say about her tenant, something that might take more than a few minutes.

"That's very kind of you."

The teapot must have been hot, because Mrs. Stafford was back with two cups in just over a minute. Carol said no to sugar and cream.

"May I ask why you're asking me all of these questions, Sheriff?"

"Of course," Carol said, and proceeded to be less than honest as she explained her presence in the Stafford living room. "There is a possibility that something has happened to him. We aren't sure yet. But it seems that, like you, nobody really knows much about him. I hope that with your help we might be able to find out just what has happened to him. Right now we're groping in the dark—in a manner of speaking."

"Gone missing, has he? Probably skipping out on me without paying the rent he owes."

"That's possible, but I suspect that it may be more serious than that."

"Is he dead?"

"That's what we're investigating." Carol had decided that a bit of calculated ambiguity was better than a forthright admission that the man was dead. It might produce more candid answers to her questions. "So why don't you tell me what you can about Mr. Rafferty?"

"Well, it's like I said. He doesn't say much. I don't even see much of him. Days at a time go by without my seeing hide nor hair of the man. He's a funny duck, that's for sure."

"Funny duck. Can you tell me just what you mean?"

"It's like he doesn't want me to see him. Or hear him. He kind of sneaks around. I think he waits until I'm out on an errand, or back in the kitchen, before he leaves the house. He doesn't even park near the house, at least not most of the time. Just the other day I suddenly heard a pot or something drop in his apartment. Just about jumped out of my skin, I did. I never knew he was home—never heard him drive up, come in, nothing. Then this big clatter."

Rafferty's car. She had never given it a thought while she was at the winery.

"Did he ever say anything about where he parks the car? Or why he doesn't park in front of the house?"

Mrs. Stafford laughed. It wasn't a pleasant laugh.

"I remember telling him once that he didn't need to park around the corner or wherever it was he was in the habit of parking. All he said was for me not to worry. As if I really cared."

"What you've been telling me is that Mr. Rafferty wanted to be left alone and went out of his way to protect his privacy."

"He sure did. It was almost as if he was hiding something. Or hiding from someone."

"That's interesting. What makes you think so?"

It was then that Mrs. Stafford got around to what had prompted her to offer the sheriff a cup of tea.

"There were a couple of things. Now mind you, I'm not a nosy person. But there was a day, maybe three weeks ago, when I decided to take a look in his apartment. He'd told me way back when he first moved in that he'd take care of his own apartment. Didn't want me to feel I should vacuum his room or dust or anything like that. Well, of course I didn't. After all, I'm not a housekeeper. But his behavior was so strange that I got to thinking maybe I should see what he'd done to the place. I mean, what if he was a pack rat? What if he'd junked up my apartment, made a real mess of it?

"Anyway, I let myself in with my key—he always kept it locked, you know. Well, I was surprised. It was neat as a pin. Just about like it was when I rented it to him. Only thing really different was a crucifix over the bed. A big one. Frank and I were never very religious, but I always respect a person who is. Like I said, I wasn't being nosy, but some things you couldn't miss. There was a Bible on his bedside table. It had some things stuck in it—newspaper clippings, photos, things like that. But one of those things was a note. I wasn't trying to be nosy, but it was a short note and you couldn't help but see it. I don't remember the exact words, but it was something about the writer having found him at last. There wasn't any signature. Don't you think that's peculiar?"

Carol was suddenly very pleased that Mrs. Stafford was in fact nosy, in spite of her repeated protestations to the contrary.

"Maybe the things you found in the Bible could just have been there to mark passages of scripture he was fond of. But the note is interesting. Do you know if the Bible is still in his apartment?"

"I wouldn't know. I only went in that once."

"Why don't we take a look? Right now. Like I told you, I don't know much of anything about Mr. Rafferty, and it's important that I learn whatever I can about him. That Bible may be of more help than we know."

"But what if he comes back while we're snooping in his room?"

"Mrs. Stafford, I feel quite certain that Mr. Rafferty will not be coming back to your house tonight. Trust me. I'm conducting an investigation, and I'm the one responsible. You will have done nothing wrong. If anyone is at fault, it will be me. Remember, I'm the sheriff."

Carol was convinced that the woman's curiosity was much stronger than any fear that her tenant might walk in on them. Twenty seconds later they were inside the bedroom of Brendan Rafferty's apartment. The bed was unmade.

"Now, why don't you just sit over there while I take a look around," Carol said, motioning toward the bed. Mrs. Stafford stepped back, but chose to remain standing.

The room was small and sparely furnished. The Bible was still on the bedside stand, next to a lamp and an alarm clock. On a shelf below were three books: a well-worn copy of St. Augustine's *The City of God*, a brand-new copy of Richard Dawkins' *The God Delusion*, and the old Penguin edition of G. K. Chesterton's Father Brown mysteries. Carol slipped on her white gloves and opened the single drawer in the stand. In it were a set of rosary beads which appeared to be made of hematite and a small brown notebook. A quick glance told her that the notebook contained a number of jottings that might be fragments of a diary. There did not appear to be any names or phone numbers, but a more careful perusal of the jottings might reveal one or more. She pocketed the notebook.

It was quickly apparent that Mr. Rafferty had possessed a very modest wardrobe. And an unusual one. The clothes closet, its door standing open, was no more than half full. What interested Carol most was a cassock, almost hidden behind a winter jacket and several hangers full of work clothes. Only two of the three drawers in a chest against the opposite wall were being used. One contained underwear, socks, three neatly folded shirts, a sweater, and a few other basic items. The second confirmed the impression left by the presence of the cassock in the closet. There, carefully arranged, were what her Catholic education told her were a chasuble, a surplice, and a Roman collar. An employee of a Crooked Lake winery would not be needing any of these items. They belonged to a priest.

A quick tour of the rest of the apartment turned up nothing that seemed worth taking with her. She'd have one of her men give it a more thorough going-over the next day. Carol switched off the light, picked up the Bible and the other three books, and followed Mrs. Stafford out the door.

It was time to leave, but she had one more question.

"You said there were two things you thought I should know about. One was the note in the Bible. What was the other thing?"

"Oh, yes. It was about the rent. Mr. Rafferty never wanted to talk about the rent. He always tried to avoid me. When I asked, he'd say something like 'don't worry, I'll see you get your money.' But just a few days ago he actually came to my door. Said he had good news. He said how sorry he was, being behind in the rent and all, and that he should be able to pay me in full very soon. It was like he'd won the lottery or something."

"But he hasn't paid you yet, right?"

"No," she replied, now worried that the promised payment might not come through.

"Look, Mrs. Stafford, I really appreciate your cooperation tonight. And I want to be honest with you. You asked me if Mr. Rafferty is dead. I believe that he is. I've got to run now, let you get back to whatever you were doing. But one of my colleagues will be coming by to go over the apartment more carefully. I'd like to get it done tomorrow. Let's say eight o'clock."

Jenny Stafford did not seem shocked by the admission that her tenant was dead; she had apparently assumed as much from the questions the sheriff had been asking. Whether she wanted to be up and about at eight the next morning, she mumbled that it would be okay. The sheriff thanked her, locked the door to the flat and pocketed the key, and made it clear that Rafferty's rooms were not to be disturbed until the officer had given his permission. Then she took her leave of 125 Maple Lane for the drive back to Cumberland.

What did she now know about the human scarecrow in the vineyard? He was obsessively private. He was in financial trouble. Strangest of all, it looked very much as if he was a Roman Catholic priest. But for a priest he had unusual and, it would seem, contradictory reading habits. There, side by side on his bedside table, had been a book by one of the greatest of Catholic philosophers and another by one of the most articulate of modern-day atheists.

Perhaps more important than any of this, there was the note from someone who had been looking for him and had apparently finally found him. Assuming, that is, that the note tucked into the Bible was recent. The more Carol thought about it, the less certain she was that the message would turn out to be meaningful. Even if it was, she was not sure what she should make of it.

It was after 9:30 when she pulled up in front of her apartment building in Cumberland. She was too tired to make supper, so she settled for yogurt and a peanut butter sandwich and turned her attention to Brendan Rafferty's notebook and Bible. And the odds and ends that he had stuck in it—the photos, the newspaper clippings, the unsigned note. She hoped that among them there would be a clue as to who he was. Or who he had been and what might explain his bizarre death.

CHAPTER 8

When the sheriff finally set aside the Bible and the notebook, it was getting close to midnight. She knew that what she had read might be important. But she felt as if she were doing a jigsaw puzzle, more than half of whose pieces were missing. Moreover, she feared that many of those missing pieces would be extremely hard to find. Some of them might never show up. And if they didn't, she might never find Brendan Rafferty's murderer.

The odds and ends which had been placed in the Bible were too few and too diverse to tell her much. The note was particularly frustrating. It wasn't dated, so there was no way of knowing when it had been sent, much less when Rafferty had received it. It lacked both a salutation and a signature, so she could not even be absolutely sure it had been intended for Rafferty. But common sense said that it must have been. It was a mere 26 words in length.

> Surprised to hear from me, aren't you? It has taken me awhile, but I always knew I would find you. Expect a visit from me soon.

It was not a note which would have given the recipient pleasure at the prospect of the meeting. Instead, it suggested that Rafferty may have tried to disappear and that the writer of the note had been determined not to let that happen. She tried to imagine Rafferty's reaction when he received the note. Had he been angry? Had he been afraid? She fast-forwarded in her mind to the fact of Rafferty's murder. Had the person who wrote the note visited him as he had promised? Visited him and killed him?

Unfortunately, but not surprisingly, there was no address. There were just those 26 words, penned in a barely legible scrawl.

Carol had set the note aside and turned to the newspaper clippings. One was a picture of a somewhat younger Rafferty, together with an older woman and a man who looked to be about his age. The three of them were smiling. Rafferty was dressed in the robes of a priest, and the caption indicated that he just been ordained and that the woman was his mother and the man his brother. The photograph confirmed what the garments in his bedroom had told her, that he was a Catholic priest. Or had been. She had never heard of an order whose members worked in wineries. She knew, or thought she knew, that the Benedictine Order had something to do with the making of Bénédictine liqueur and the Carthusian Order with the making of Chartreuse. But those were monastic orders, and Rafferty clearly did not belong to a monastic order.

The clipping had been cut out in such a way that the newspaper's name was missing, along with the date of publication. As a result, it was almost as unhelpful as the unsigned note. There was a second clipping; it was very brief, with neither a headline nor byline. Like the one with the photo of the newly ordinated priest, it lacked information about the paper, where it was published, and when. Its subject matter, however, was interesting if frustratingly general. Apparently, there had been a demonstration at an abortion clinic that had started to turn violent before police intervened. No names were mentioned in the article. Where and when had this demonstration taken place? Had Rafferty had anything to do with it? Why had he saved the clipping in his Bible?

Unable to guess at the answers to any of these questions, Carol had turned to the photographs. One was a duplicate of the picture in the newspaper clipping. Another was of a young man in a basketball uniform. Probably Rafferty, probably still in high school. His uniform shirt said he played for the Hawks, but not what school the Hawks represented. The third photo was more recent and was definitely of Rafferty. He was sitting at what looked like a gaming table of some sort, talking to a short, round, balding man who wore a big smile. She turned the photo over, hoping it might identify the location, the date, anything that would help her to fit one more piece into the puzzle of Brendan Rafferty's life. And death. The back of the photo was blank.

It was possible that she had learned something of importance from these bits of memorabilia in the Bible, but she couldn't imagine what it could be. Perhaps the Bible itself held a clue. She had been careful to replace the clippings and photos exactly where she had found them. But a quick reading of those passages told her nothing, and she reached a tentative conclusion that Rafferty had tucked things into his Bible at random.

Carol held higher hopes for the notebook, but quickly discovered that all of the entries were frustratingly vague or employed shorthand which she couldn't understand. The notebook had been little used. She counted only twenty-one entries, none of them dated. Logic said that they must be in chronological order, but even that was not certain. Unlike the brief note in the Bible, all of the entries in the notebook were in a neat, legible hand, all presumably made by the same person. She assumed that that person had been Rafferty.

One by one she read those twenty-one entries, her disappointment mounting as she did so. Four times she came across a reference to "gf," apparently a man of Rafferty's acquaintance. But the entries reflected only the fact that something had reminded him of "gf." Never did they offer a clue as to who "gf" was or why he might be on his mind. Was he the person who had been looking for Rafferty and finally found him? Then there was the equally mysterious "ts." That pair of initials appeared in three of the notebook entries. In context, it looked as if "ts" was more likely to be a place than a person. A place where something was happening. Sometimes that something seemed to be positive, sometimes negative. Then there was someone identified by a single letter, "s." Perhaps he was the writer of the note, but there was nothing in the entries referring to "s" which made that more than a guess. There had been one mention of "mc," and the last of the twenty-one entries introduced a new person, identified only by the shorthand of "jc." Jesus Christ? That thought occurred to Carol only because she now knew that Rafferty had been—still was?—a priest. But the notebook entry didn't seem to have anything to do with religion.

When she had finished reading the notebook—and it had only taken her a couple of minutes, she knew nothing she hadn't known when she opened it. No, she thought, there had been one common thread. Rafferty had been worried. At no point in the notebook had he actually said so, but there was an undercurrent of anxiety throughout the notebook. There was no clue as to why he was worried, but subsequent events had proved that he had good reason. Did that account for the fact that his jottings were so vague, so lacking in specifics? Why the aversion to naming names? The repeated use of initials, and lower-case initials at that? Did he fear that someone might gain access to the notebook? If so, why keep a notebook? It could hardly qualify as a record he could consult if and when his memory failed him.

Carol had begun the process of going through Brendan Rafferty's few possessions with high hopes of forming a better picture of the man, a picture which would help her as she began the investigation into his murder. When she set the notebook aside, those hopes were fading fast.

What remained were the three books that had rested on the bedside table. It was much too late in the evening to start perusing them for clues to the man who had become the scarecrow in the vineyard. She was tired. Moreover, she knew she wouldn't be reading the books. What would they tell her? Back in college she had read *The City of God*. No, that wasn't quite true. It had been assigned in a political philosophy course and she had skimmed it. She remembered nothing of it except that Augustine had converted to Catholicism and the book had been about his journey from paganism to the church, of which he had become a prominent saint. She knew even less about *The God Delusion*. It was supposed to be a sophisticated critique of religion by a respected Darwinian scholar, but she had little time for reading and in any event was not much drawn to the recent spate of books on atheism. As for the Father Brown stories, she thought of them as Chesterton's answer to Conan Doyle and of no relevance to the matter of Brendan Rafferty's death.

Before she retired for the night, she picked up the book about which she knew least and leafed quickly through it, trying to form a picture from the chapter titles of how the author had developed his thesis. The book fell open to a page the corner of which had been turned down. Carol sat up in her chair, suddenly wide awake. Along the margin of the right hand page someone had made notes, presumably commenting on the text. That someone was obviously Brendan Rafferty. The handwriting was identical to the handwriting in the notebook.

Carol read what Rafferty had written, then began reading what Dawkins had to say that had prompted his notation in the margin. The author was commenting on the story of Lot in the Book of Genesis. Carol's only recollection of the story was that Lot's wife had been turned into a pillar of salt for looking back on the Lord's destruction of Sodom and Gomorrah. But that was not

Dawkins' point. He focused instead on Lot's protection of the male angels who were his guests from the locals who wished to sodomize them. And on Lot's offering up of his virgin daughters to be sodomized in their stead. Had the Bible actually said this? Carol picked up Rafferty's Bible and located the passage to which Dawkins had referred. It read exactly as he had said it did.

What Rafferty had written in the margin of the book made it clear that he had been horrified by the story.

Is this the Bible I have been teaching my parishioners is the word of God?

Carol turned to the beginning of the chapter in Dawkins' book in which the story of Lot appeared. In spite of the late hour, she got caught up in his argument and the many examples from scripture which supported it. It quickly became clear that the author was claiming that the Bible was a poor guide to moral values. It looked as if Rafferty might have come to the same conclusion. Was that why he had left the clergy?

It was an interesting question. But was it an important one? Did it have any bearing on the question of why he had been murdered? And set up in a Crooked Lake vineyard to resemble a scarecrow?

CHAPTER 9

Deputy Sheriff Bridges rapped on the door at 125 Maple Lane at precisely eight o'clock. He had acquired the habit of punctuality during his years in the Marine Corps, and could not imagine being late for an appointment. He had actually arrived fifteen minutes early, and used those extra minutes to search the neighborhood for Rafferty's car. It had been easy. The old Dodge with a badly banged-up fender sat at a curb just around the corner on Harrison Street. But it was locked, and there had been no keys on the faux scarecrow in the vineyard.

Mrs. Stafford came to the door in her housecoat, sans makeup. Bridges had the impression that she was not very happy to have him in the house, interrupting her routine. But she directed him to the flat which Rafferty had occupied. He let himself in, locked the door behind him, took a quick look around, and slipped on the gloves which he would use as he gave the flat a thorough inspection.

What the hell is going on? he asked himself. This man Rafferty's death was the fifth murder in—what was it now, four years? Actually, not much more than three. You'd think someone had it in for us law-enforcement types in Cumberland County, he thought. Someone who's bent on testing us, someone who comes up with a different modus operandi every year. Sam liked that phrase—modus operandi. They used it all the time on the crime shows on TV. Trouble was, it had turned out that it was a different guy who was guilty every year. And this year it would once again be someone else, inasmuch as the man who'd strangled the star of Crooked Lake's opera the previous summer was currently doing time.

Bridges shrugged and surveyed the flat.

His first impression was similar to the sheriff's—Rafferty had been, like himself, fastidious and neat. The only exception was his bed, which had not been made. There was no pillow and the covers were not only askew, they were partially on the floor. Bridges considered this. He knew that the bed had not been slept in that night. Which meant that in all probability Rafferty had gone to bed the previous night, had gotten up sometime in the night, and, leaving the bed unmade, had gone out to meet his death in the vineyard.

Bridges retraced the steps that Carol had taken the night before, inventorying everything he found in the small rooms, the closets, the drawers, the medicine chest, the kitchen cabinets, the refrigerator. He made no puzzling discoveries, other than the vestments which announced that Rafferty was or had been a priest. But Carol had already told him that. Rafferty had obviously been a meat and potatoes man, and he had been in the habit of preparing his own meals rather than buying prepackaged products. The only medications he found were aspirin, cough lozenges, and an anti-itch cream, all of them over-the-counter items.

There was no desk in the flat, but Sam was sure that he would find Rafferty's checkbook in a drawer somewhere or in the pocket of a jacket or pair of pants. But he didn't. Nor was there a computer, which suggested that his bills had been paid with cash. Interesting. Not only had Rafferty been frugal, he had apparently lived his life as if he were living it in another, earlier, era. Had he even had a bank account? The question sent Sam on a search of places where money might have been hidden away. He found none.

Then there was the bed. It had been vacated in a hurry. Sam pulled the covers off the floor, one by one, shaking them out to see if anything had been trapped in the folds. The sheets, like the pillow, were missing. There was, however, some blood, now dried and dark, near the top of a blanket. Which reminded Sam of the fact that Rafferty had been shot in the head.

Sam drew in his breath. It looked as if Rafferty had been shot right there in his own apartment. Which meant that his killer had gotten into the room, shot him, and then carted his body many miles to the Random Harvest vineyard, taking the pillow and the sheets with him. Mrs. Stafford had said nothing to him or the sheriff about hearing a gun being fired. Perhaps she had been out. More likely, the killer had used a silencer.

But how had the killer obtained entrance to the bedroom? The blood on the blanket strongly suggested that Rafferty had been shot while he was still in bed. It was doubtful that he had heard a visitor at the door, gotten out of bed to admit him, and then climbed back into his bed to be shot. Of course the killer could have forced the lock, entered the room, and shot Rafferty while he was sleeping. He'd have to examine the lock. But his attention was drawn to the window. The shade should have been down, but it wasn't. Would Rafferty have gone to bed and to sleep with the shade up? Unlikely. And he had not been in his bedroom to raise the shade the next morning. His corpse had been impersonating a scarecrow in a vineyard.

Sam took a closer look at the window. It was not locked. In fact, the simple sash lock was unfastened. He tried to move it to the lock position, but it wouldn't budge. He slid the window up and down; it moved easily. Rafferty's killer had almost certainly come into the bedroom through the window. And presumably left the same way, lugging his victim with him.

This was, of course, guesswork, but it felt right. He raised the window and studied the sill and the window frame. Sam rarely smiled, but at that moment he allowed himself a satisfied smile. The sill looked as if it had been stepped on by someone wearing dirty shoes. He poked his head out the window and studied the ground several feet below. It had been scuffed up a bit, probably when Rafferty's killer had wrestled his body out of the window and onto the ground.

Sam closed the window and examined the hardwood floor between it and the bed, looking for traces of dirt. He found them, just as he had expected to. There was a good chance that the area around the window would also show fingerprints, and a closer examination of the ground below the window might tell them what kind of shoes the killer had worn. The sheriff would be pleased with what he had accomplished this morning.

Twenty minutes later, Deputy Sheriff Bridges had wrapped up his examination of Brendan Rafferty's flat, bagged the telltale blanket, and spoken with Officer Barrett and told him to get over to Clarksburg and take control of what had now become a crime scene.

"Mrs. Stafford," Sam said after Barrett arrived and he was preparing to leave, "I'm afraid that your tenant is not only dead. He was killed right here in your flat. I know you'll understand if we have to make ourselves at home in your house. This is going to be a busy place for a few days."

She stood in the doorway, watching him drive away and debating with herself whether she should be annoyed with losing her privacy or pleased at the prospect of the attention which was about to descend on 125 Maple Lane.

Then she returned to her living room, putting on her best smile as she offered Officer Barrett a cup of coffee.

CHAPTER 10

Sheriff Kelleher had never thought of herself as someone who was bothered by bad dreams. In fact, she didn't dream much at all, or so she believed. Either that or she forgot about them the minute she got out of bed in the morning. Last night had been an exception.

She busied herself making toast, but her mind was on the strange images that emerged as she tried to recall the dream. The figures that had seemed so vivid were proving hard to recapture in the light of day. They faded, then snapped into sharper focus, only to merge, losing their identity in an eerily faceless blur. What had she been dreaming of? When the answer came to her, it may have been because of the coffee. And then it may have been due to the sheer effort of willpower. But she finally remembered that her dream had been about the scarecrow in the vineyard and the Biblical figure of Lot. They had been having some kind of argument, an argument which had apparently not been resolved. She wasn't even sure what that argument had been about, but her dream had clearly been shaped by the murder of Brendan Rafferty. It was a reminder, as if one were needed, that a pleasant and uneventful autumn on Crooked Lake had undergone a dramatic transformation in the preceding twenty-four hours.

Carol finished her breakfast, put the dishes in the dishwasher, and started getting ready for a busy day. There were many people at Random Harvest Vineyards she had to talk with. Too many. She tried to remember their names as she showered.

There were the men who had gathered in the vineyard as soon as they had gotten wind that a body had been found there. Copeland, the manager. The company employees Bridges had dismissed. She remembered the name of one of them: Grabner. She'd made a list of the others, and would seek them out as well. Then there was Mason, who seemed to be something of an expert on scarecrows. Perhaps he knew more than he had let on to

Bridges and Barrett the day before. She also wanted to speak with Francis, Ms. Rizzo's boss. She hoped he could explain how he had happened to hire an ex-priest to work at the winery. Finally, there were other employees whose names she didn't know, employees who worked with Rafferty and might know something more about the man than any of the people she had talked with thus far.

The trouble was that she wanted to be the one to interview all of these people. Not Bridges, not any of her fellow officers. She was, she realized, a poor delegator. Now if Kevin were at the lake, she'd be willing to let him tackle some of the winery people. But he wasn't. Nor was he likely to be able to make the trip from the city to help in the investigation. She'd either have to rely on her colleagues' judgment of people's veracity or face up to the fact that her interview schedule would keep her busy for quite awhile. That thought didn't make her happy. She was impatient to round out her picture of the late Brendan Rafferty.

It was 9:15 when she paid a courtesy call on the winery's president to tell him she would be talking with several of his employees over the next day or two. Drake was still anxious about adverse publicity, but made no attempt to interfere with or participate in her investigation.

It was while Carol was en route to Doug Francis's office that her cell phone rang. It was Bridges. She ducked out onto a patio outside the tasting room to let him fill her in on what he had learned or not learned in Clarksburg. The call took ten minutes. The information her deputy passed on to her was well worth the slight delay in starting the rounds of Random Harvest employees. She could proceed in the knowledge that whoever had killed Rafferty knew where he lived and that his murder had almost certainly taken place there. She asked Sam to come on over to the winery and start a search of the ice grape vineyard for the recently deposed scarecrow. And, if there was time, he could also interview the two pickers he had so abruptly dismissed the day before. She would handle the more senior Random Harvest people herself.

"Ah, Mr. Francis," she said, accepting his hand, "I'm sure you know I'm here about what happened yesterday in your vineyards. The death of Brendan Rafferty, one of your workers."

"So it really was Rafferty," he said, as if a rumor had been confirmed. "Unbelievable, isn't it? I simply can't imagine why anybody would have wanted to kill him. And here, at Random Harvest. What had he ever done to anybody?"

"That's what we intend to find out," Carol said. "I wanted to talk with you because Mr. Drake says you are the person who would have hired Mr. Rafferty. I'm hoping you may know something about him, something about what prompted him to apply for a position at the winery. And maybe about how he has worked out since he was hired."

Francis looked slightly uncomfortable.

"Of course. He's one of our most recent hires. Other than part-time help we take on from time to time. Like now, when we need extra pickers. Actually, Mr. Rafferty was technically part time himself. I mean we never gave him a permanent job. But he seemed to be a quick study. The word was that he was efficient. So I guess you'd say he's sort of semi-permanent."

Carol did not correct Francis's use of the present tense.

"Were you short handed when you hired him?" she asked.

"At the moment, yes, or we wouldn't have offered him a job."

"Had he had experience in your business?"

"Let me take a look at his file," Francis said.

Carol had the distinct feeling he was stalling, that in all probability he had a pretty fair recollection of Rafferty. It wouldn't be all that often that an ex-priest would be inquiring about a menial job with a winery.

"Now let's see," he said as he resumed his seat and opened a thin folder. "It doesn't really say. My note indicates that he sounded like an intelligent man who could do what we needed done."

"So you didn't ask him about his background?"

"I may have. It's just that the file doesn't say anything about his background."

"Do you usually ask for references?" Carol persevered.

Random Harvest's man in charge of personnel decided that he should explain the business to the sheriff.

"It's like this, Sheriff. Random Harvest—like all of the wineries around the lake—doesn't have a large permanent staff of what you'd think of as professionals. Of course there are a few people who are real winemakers, enology degrees and all that. They have to know a lot about grape varietals, have all the requisite technical skills. I mean I couldn't just step in and run that part of the business; hell, I'm just an ex-liberal arts major. But like I said, that's just a few of our people, and Mr. Drake likes to oversee those jobs himself. Most everybody here who's actually involved in making wine is either part time or what we call a cellar associate. I think Rafferty might have been on track to be a cellar associate."

"That's interesting, Mr. Francis, but I don't think you answered my question. Did Mr. Rafferty provide you with references?"

"I don't see any in his file here. So probably not. With the part-timers, what we care about is whether someone sounds like he could catch on quick to the routines. Wine making is mostly about routines. As I remember, Mr. Rafferty seemed like a bright guy. You know, well spoken. We tend to get a lot of itinerant workers. Don't get me wrong, they usually work out just fine, but Mr. Rafferty, well, he was different."

I'm sure he was, Carol thought. Didn't you wonder about that?

"Were you surprised that he would be wanting a job like this? Ever wonder what he'd done with his life before he walked in here?"

"A little, I guess. I probably should have asked." Francis looked very much as if he had failed the sheriff's test.

"Did you know that Mr. Rafferty had probably been a Catholic priest in a former incarnation?"

This news obviously came as a surprise to Francis.

"I'll be damned," he said.

"Well, that's another story," Carol said, changing the subject. "Did you have any contact with Rafferty after he came aboard?"

"No, afraid not. Our jobs were in different parts of the plant. Anyway, word was that he didn't mix much."

Nor did you, she thought. In any event, Francis had reinforced the impression she had gotten from his assistant: Brendan Rafferty was a loner.

Her next stop was with the man in charge of marketing, Lew Grabner. He was one of the men who had hurried down to the vineyard when word reached the winery that there was a dead man there. One of the men Bridges had dismissed before she had arrived. Had his reason for going to the vineyard had to do with more than natural curiosity? Carol hadn't expected him to say it had, and he didn't. In fact, his explanation of his being there was quite straightforward. He just happened to be in the entrance foyer when Robinson, the man who had found the body, came rushing in with the news. It was Grabner who had escorted Robinson to Copeland's office and then, after telling his secretary to hold his calls, set out to see what had happened.

Copeland's story dovetailed neatly with Grabner's. Upon hearing from Robinson that something was amiss in the vineyard, he had called Earl Drake, the owner of the winery. Drake had told him to go see what was going on, and he had promptly set about doing so, taking Jenkins along with him. Like Drake and Grabner, he didn't know Rafferty and doubted that he'd ever set eyes on him.

The two grape pickers who had also rushed down to see the scarecrow were currently out doing what they had been hired to do, and Jenkins, who had accompanied Copeland to the scene of the crime, had taken a sick day. Which left the two men she associated with scarecrows, Mason and Packer, and all of the cellar associates who had worked with Rafferty.

Bridges was at that very moment searching for the original scarecrow. She decided to concentrate on the cellar associates, or cellar rats, as she'd heard them called.

Carol had expected to see a dozen or more busy men in Building B, checking temperature gauges, inspecting vats of fermenting wine, doing whatever cellar rats do. She found three men, standing in the corner of a large room full of unfamiliar equipment, talking among themselves.

"Hello, I'm Sheriff Kelleher. I'd like to talk with you men if you have a few minutes." They would have a few minutes, of that she was sure.

"You're here to discuss Rafferty, right?" one of them said. "That's what we've been doing."

"I'm sure you know that your colleague is dead and that his body was found in one of Random Harvest's vineyards," she said, doing a little stage setting. "I'm here to talk with people who knew him, to see what we can learn that may help us find out why he was killed. And, of course, who killed him. You men worked with him. What can you tell me about him?"

One by one the men introduced themselves. They all seemed excited to be part of the sheriff's investigation. No long faces over losing a fellow worker, only an eagerness to tell her what they could.

"Funny duck, he was," a man with bulging biceps and dark curly hair volunteered. It was the second time in less than 24 hours that Carol had heard Rafferty described that way.

"How so?" she asked.

"Well, to begin with, he never talked. Hardly ever, anyway. Ask him a question, he'd give you a one-word answer, maybe two. 'Don't know,' 'yes,' 'maybe,' things like that. I figure I know about as much about him today as I did when he first showed up. Except, of course, that he's dead. Maybe somebody got fed up with trying to get him to talk."

"That's not funny, Jake," one of the other men said, although he said it with a smile. "But he's right. The guy was the original clam. He did his work though. Didn't know a damned thing when he came on, but he caught on fast. Never missed a day. I guess he'd had some bad luck—the missus left him or something, and he just tuned everyone out."

The third man, taller than the other two and obviously older, interrupted to set the record straight.

"I remember once," he said, "maybe three weeks ago, out of the blue he asked me if I knew of any casinos in the area. You know, a place where a guy could pick up some money playing the slots, maybe poker. Funny question, considering we'd never talked about anything but the job here. Not much of that either. Anyway, I suggested a place over near Utica. Turning Stone it's called. 'Too far away,' he said, and that was the end of our conversation."

"Yeah, we had a good laugh about that," the man named Jake said. "Figured he was down on his luck, needed some quick cash. If he'd gone to Turning Stone, he'd have more likely lost his shirt."

Carol had expected to hear more about Rafferty the loner, Rafferty the man who kept to himself. And these men had reinforced that impression. But they had given her something else, something which could prove to be important. His landlady had reported that he was behind in his rent. And that he had recently told her that he expected to be able to pay what he owed very soon. Suppose he had decided to try his luck at Turning Stone or some other casino and had made a bundle. Or was optimistic enough to believe he would be making a bundle one day soon.

"Did Mr. Rafferty ever say anything to any one of you about whether he had found himself a casino? Whether he had been lucky?"

All three of them nodded in the negative.

"He never brought it up again," the older man said. "In fact, that conversation I had with him about casinos was the only time he ever loosened up, at least with me."

"What about the other men who work here in the cellar?" Carol asked. "Have you ever heard any of them talk about Mr. Rafferty?"

"There aren't that many of us. Bernie and Don, they're around somewhere. Manuel. But he's like Rafferty, doesn't talk much. His English is pretty poor. I suppose you'd have to ask them, but no, I don't think any of us knew anything about Rafferty. Bernie always called him our resident stranger."

Carol made notes of the names of the men she'd been talking to and told them she would probably be seeing them again. Before she left the winery that day she had found Bernie and Manuel. Nothing they told her altered what was obviously the consensus picture of Brendan Rafferty. Bernie Stolnitz, something of the self-proclaimed Random Harvest wit, didn't disappoint Carol or let his colleagues down. When she asked him about Rafferty, he had said, "Oh, you mean our resident stranger."

On the spur of the moment she decided to postpone her conversation with Mason until the next day. She called Bridges before taking her leave of the winery, only to learn that he still hadn't found the original scarecrow. She briefly debated questioning staff in the wine-tasting room before heading back to Cumberland, but the crowd there was three deep at the bar. Earl Drake would be pleased. News of a murder in his ice grape vineyard had not had a negative effect on business.

CHAPTER 11

It had been only a little more than twenty-eight hours since she had first heard about the dead man in the Random Harvest Vineyards. All things considered, Carol had learned quite a bit since then. She knew who he was, that he had almost certainly once been a priest, held a menial job at a local winery, was taciturn in the extreme, seemed to have no friends and little money, kept a mysteriously vague notebook and had strange reading habits, and just might be into gambling. That knowledge, however, was balanced by the fact that she had absolutely no idea why he had left the priesthood, why he had sought work in a winery, and, more importantly, who might have disliked him enough to kill him. And not only kill him, but leave his body lashed to a pole in a vineyard, where he appeared to be recreating the crucifixion.

Mister Cellophane, she thought as she drove, recalling a favorite song from *Chicago*. Most of the employees at the winery had looked right through the former priest and walked right by him without ever knowing he was there, just like the character in the musical. Had Brendan Rafferty been a Mr. Cellophane? Well, probably not, if the truth were known. There was obviously much more to his life—and his death—that she did not know. But it had only been twenty-eight hours.

When she got home, she headed for the kitchen, wondering what there might be for dinner. She hadn't been shopping for nearly a week, hadn't had a decent meal for two nights, and was in no mood to settle for yogurt as she had the night before. The cupboard was bare.

She briefly considered a quick shower and then a drive out to The Cedar Post. Just as quickly she canceled the idea. The Post was her favorite area restaurant, but it was her favorite because it had become the place where she and Kevin had dinner when they were enjoying the challenge of trying to solve a crime. And Kevin wasn't at his lake cottage. He was far away in the city, living a bachelor's life and attending to his students' intellectual needs. At least that was what she hoped he was doing. At that moment, going to The Cedar Post didn't feel like a very good idea.

But just as quickly as she had changed her mind about The Cedar Post, she decided that she had to talk with Kevin. He'd want to hear about this latest murder on Crooked Lake. She wanted him to hear about it. She hated that another murder had occurred in her backyard, the fifth in just over three years. But if it had to happen, she wished it had happened back in the summer when Kevin was still staying in his cottage down on the lake.

Carol wasn't sure he'd be back to his apartment yet. She didn't know just what his teaching schedule was like, or what other obligations might keep him at the college. Which meant that it would be better to try calling him later in the evening. In the meanwhile, she'd make do with some wine and whatever she could scrounge from the refrigerator. And enjoy conjuring up pleasant pictures of Kevin and their time together.

It gave her a warm feeling just to forget about Brendan Rafferty for the time being and focus on the man she loved, even if geography made being in love with him difficult.

He was smart, but not a Mensa genius. He was talented, but not self impressed. He was attractive, but he'd never be considered for *People* magazine's hundred greatest hunks. He had a good sense of humor, but his humor was never cruel. He was sensitive, but in no way wimpish. He was a wonderful lover, but not, thank goodness, narcissistic. Carol was just getting warmed up with her inventory of Kevin's attractive features when the phone rang.

Annoyed at the interruption, she answered the phone. Her "hello" gave away her annoyance.

"Carol, it's me. You okay?"

"Kevin! You beat me to it by about two hours. I was going to call, but figured you might not be home yet."

"I'm home. And lonesome. You sounded upset."

"I was," she said. "I was daydreaming about you, and didn't like the interruption. You're forgiven. Now I can daydream out loud."

"It's been almost two weeks. I needed to hear your voice, see how things are going."

"I was going to tell you how things are going, but mostly I just needed to share some of the evening with you."

"Still think I'm okay?"

"That's easy. Much more than okay."

Carol decided to end this exchange of mutual assurances of love and affection and tell Kevin about her newest case and why it made her want him at her side.

"Look, I've got news, and I know you won't believe it." For a fleeting instant it occurred to her that he might think she was pregnant. She hurried on, getting right to the point.

"We've had another murder up here. It happened just yesterday. At least that's when we found the body."

"Come on, Carol. Is this some kind of joke? We just wrapped up the last murder less than two months ago."

And well might he have thought she was joking. The murder which had put an end to Kevin's plan to stage an opera on the lake at Brae Loch College had not produced a confession until just before the Labor Day weekend and his return to the city for the new academic year.

"Don't I know," Carol said in a tone that said she had given up on any expectation that Crooked Lake would soon be returning to its traditionally peaceful calm. "But it's no joke. You know the Random Harvest Vineyards, don't you? Well, one of their employees was found dead there, murdered. And strung up like a scarecrow to boot."

"I don't suppose you were going to call to tell me you've nabbed the killer."

"The victim hasn't been dead more than a day and a half, Kevin. We're lucky even to know who he is."

"Then you're going to tell me I'm needed up there to solve the case. Right?"

Much as Carol appreciated his help in bringing to close her investigations into Crooked Lake's recent rash of murders, she didn't expect him to come rushing back to the lake. The Rafferty murder was her problem, not his.

"Wrong. I'm the sheriff, remember? I just wanted to tell you about it—thought you'd find it interesting. Not to mention unusual."

"So what's this about a scarecrow?"

Carol proceeded to fill him in on the bizarre developments at Random Harvest and the mystery of an ex-priest turned cellar rat and murder victim. It took awhile, during which time Kevin listened attentively, punctuating her story occasionally with words like "really" and "no kidding."

When she paused, he asked her if she could be sure that the victim had really once been a priest.

"All you have," he said, "is his church vestments or whatever they're called. It doesn't sound as if he ever told anyone. At least not the people you've talked to. I mean, couldn't anybody buy those things? Maybe he's got some kind of strange clothes fetish. Like a guy who dresses up in women's clothes."

"No, that's a transvestite. As far as I know, Rafferty always dressed as a man."

"I didn't mean he was a transvestite," Kevin said. "But what if he got a kick out of putting on a priest's robes in the privacy of his room? Who knows what people do behind closed doors."

"That's a pretty weird theory. Anyway, I'm sure he had been a priest. He practically said as much in some notes he made in the margin of his Bible."

"You're probably right. But maybe he was all mixed up about his faith. A Dawkins-like atheist one day, then a God-fearing Catholic the next. What do they call those people with dual personalities? Maybe they have to have two wardrobes."

"I think you're getting into something you don't know anything about, Kevin. I'm sticking to the evidence; he's an ex-priest."

"You're right. I don't know anything about it. But I think you told me once that I'm most helpful when I think outside the box."

"I did?"

"If you didn't, you should have. Anyway, it sounds like I should find a way to get up there. This sounds like a job for the Kevin-Carol team."

"You're very sweet. But I really can take care of it myself. It's what I'm paid to do, and so far I don't hear a pack of unhappy citizens demanding my resignation. Besides, it's midway through your fall semester, so you must have a bunch of needful students to take care of. Not to mention a dean who thinks you should be publishing things. About opera, not crime."

"Ah, but I think I can have the best of both worlds. I planned my teaching schedule pretty well. All my classes come between Tuesday and Thursday. Which means I can get away late Thursday and not have to be back until Tuesday morning. Remember, that's how I was able to spend that long weekend with you in September."

She remembered. It had been a great weekend, a nice coda to the summer season. But she hadn't seen it as something which could be repeated at will.

"Look, don't get me wrong. You know I'd love to have you here at the lake all the time. But that's not going to happen. I really don't want you to jeopardize your job, and I worry that you tend to get irresponsible when you start playing detective. So let me handle this one."

"If I were a little more sensitive," Kevin said, "I'd take that to mean that you don't care to see me."

Carol had no intention of letting him get away with that.

"So tell me when it is that you plan to spend your next long weekend up here. I'll change the sheets and make a reservation at The Cedar Post. Just be prepared to tell me that you've graded all your papers and finished that article you've been writing for the past year."

"Consider it done. I'll be there Thursday night. If you don't have your calendar handy, that's tomorrow."

Carol brushed aside a moment of panic as she tried to recall what she had to do tomorrow. Somehow she'd squeeze in the time to pack her overnight bag, open Kevin's cottage, and pick him up at the airport at the usual time. She didn't need his help on the case, but she was thrilled at the prospect of spending the weekend with him. Maybe they'd find a few minutes to talk about the investigation of Brendan Rafferty's murder.

CHAPTER 12

The new day, the day when she'd again have the pleasure of Kevin's company, began with the insistent ringing of Carol's alarm clock. She'd set it for an earlier than usual hour because she wanted to be at the office before her officers arrived. Sam Bridges would be first on the job as always, and she needed to talk with him before the others clocked in.

It had become apparent to Carol over the previous summer that Sam didn't like the fact that his boss was spending so much time with the professor. It wasn't that he disapproved of her having an affair with Whitman. She could do whatever she wished in her personal life. In fact, she ought to be considering marriage. What was bothering him was the fact that the professor was becoming, indeed had already become, the sheriff's go-to person in her investigation of crime on Crooked Lake. Sam didn't have an oversized ego, but he did take pride in his title, Deputy Sheriff of Cumberland County. Which meant that she should be brainstorming investigative strategy with him, not with some vacationing academic.

Carol had tried to assuage what she saw as Sam's bruised feelings by the assignments she had given him, but she had never discussed with him the real issue. And the real issue was Kevin Whitman and what her deputy imagined to be pillow talk with him about the latest murder investigation. Today, she thought, I'll be more direct.

When Bridges arrived, Carol had already made coffee, a task normally handled by Diane Franks, her young secretary. Ms. Franks would be along in another five or ten minutes, but Carol wanted to create what she hoped was a relaxing environment for her little tête-à-tête with Sam.

"Everything all right?" he asked, his voice registering his surprise at the fact that the sheriff was already at her desk, sipping coffee.

"Everything except the fact that a murderer is loose again. What's the matter, Sam? Is it something in the water up here?"

The deputy sheriff produced a wan smile.

"No idea. This one looks like a real doozy."

"That's what I wanted to talk with you about," Carol said. "I'm putting you in charge of things today. Let's say today and tomorrow. Oh, I'll be around, but I've got some other things to tend to. My friend Whitman is coming up today, and I guess you know that means I'll be tied up evenings."

Sam chose not to comment.

"I'm aware that the men have mixed feelings about my relationship with Whitman. Understandable." Carol was careful not to single out Sam. "You all know that he weighed in a couple of times with ideas about the Gerlach case this summer. He's got a good head on his shoulders. But he's not a policeman, doesn't know anything about the stuff we do. So I wanted you to know he's not coming up this weekend to get involved in the Rafferty case. It's just personal. He wants to see me. If you were in my shoes, you'd want to see him, too. He's a great guy. Anyway, I know you can keep everyone busy, take emergency calls, whatever needs to be done."

She knew that Sam would interpret this as her need to spend time alone with Kevin without phone calls at ten p.m. or six a.m. Let him make of that what he would. She also hoped that it would reassure him that he was her second in command, not Kevin.

"Not to worry, I'll mind the store." It wasn't clear from his brief response whether he believed the part about Kevin being sidelined during the Rafferty investigation. It was clear, however, that he didn't want to talk about it.

Better to leave it at that, Carol thought, and get on to the business of the day.

"Thanks. And while you're minding the store, I'd appreciate it if you'd do something about Rafferty's car. Or put Barrett or Byrnes or one of the other men on it. Anyway, we don't have his keys. They weren't on the body, and you'd have found them in the apartment if they'd been there. We have to assume that his killer took them with him. Heaven knows why. But I want the car moved over here from Clarksburg. You'll find a way to do it. Chances are, it'll tell us nothing, but I want to go through it, see if he's left something in it that can help us get a better handle on the guy.

"Oh, and another thing. That damned scarecrow, or what's left of it. The one that got taken down to make room for Rafferty. I hate to keep you tromping up and down the Random Harvest Vineyards, but we've got to find it. I can't imagine why the killer had to cart it away, but it looks like he did. And if he did, he probably had his reasons. So put one of the men on that one, too."

Carol had been planning on talking with Mason that morning, but was having second thoughts.

"You're pretty sure Mason knows nothing about this business of switching scarecrows?"

"Positive." Sam caught the skeptical look in the sheriff's eyes, and backed off a bit. "Okay, maybe he's a damned good actor. But why? He struck me as a straightforward guy, committed to making sure the grapes get tended to. He says he's always after the owner to invest in netting. Thinks those terror eyes balloons aren't very effective. But he has a thing about scarecrows, the old-fashioned kind. He was properly horrified by news of Rafferty's murder, but I've got a hunch he was almost as upset by the thought that the scarecrow the Packer woman had given the winery might be missing."

Ms. Franks arrived at that moment, followed shortly by a couple of the officers. It was nearly time for the morning's staff meeting.

"Let me have a word with them," Carol said to Sam, "then you take over. Just focus on the car, the scarecrow, and, while you're at it, those two young pickers you met in the vineyard. Push them on what they know or have heard about Rafferty. I'm beginning to get the feeling that we may have to interview all of the winery people."

———

It had occurred to her on her way to the office that morning that it might be a good idea to talk with the priest at St. Leo's church in Clarksburg. So having left Sam in charge, she had a brief word with Ms. Franks and then headed out into the parking lot. Two minutes later she was on her way to the village where the late Brendan Rafferty had lived.

St. Leo's had long served the Catholic residents of Clarksburg and the rural hinterland surrounding it in the northern part of the county. It was not the church she attended when she attended church, which had been infrequently of late. But she had a clear picture in her mind of just where it was. And she knew that the priest was one Father Dietrich Kraus. She had met him several years earlier when her father died. He had kindly called to offer his condolences. Father Kraus had not known her father personally, but, like most people in the area, he had thought highly of Big Bill Kelleher, the beloved longtime sheriff of Cumberland County. When Carol succeeded her father in that post, the priest had been among the first to extend his best wishes to her. She remembered him as a sad-faced, soft-spoken man of indeterminate age, someone whose sermons would be unlikely to stir the hearts of his parishioners.

If Brendan Rafferty had indeed been a priest and not, as Kevin had suggested, a man who had a clothes fetish, it was possible, even probable, that he had attended services at St. Leo's. Perhaps he and Father Kraus had become well acquainted. If not, she would have wasted an hour.

Carol was not familiar with Father Kraus's living arrangement, but assumed that if it was not at the church there would be someone who could direct her. Father Kraus was at the church, however, and recognition was instant.

"Sheriff Kelleher," he said, "how very nice to see you again. How have you been? I've read a thing or two in the papers about what you have been doing to keep us safe from undesirable types."

They shook hands as Carol assured him that she was fine and that undesirable types were unfortunately still at large in Cumberland County. He steered her to a chair and they exchanged pleasantries for a minute or two before she came to the point of her visit.

"Father Kraus, do you by chance know a man named Brendan Rafferty?"

"Mr. Rafferty," he said. The smile he had been wearing vanished from his face for the briefest second before returning. "Yes, he is a member of my parish, a recent addition to the small flock here at St. Leo's. How do you happen to know Mr. Rafferty?"

This was not an occasion to approach the matter by indirection.

"He was killed two days ago. It happened at a winery on Crooked Lake where he was working."

"How terrible," he said, shaking his head. The smile disappeared for good this time. "Was it an accident at the winery?"

"No, Father," she replied. "He was murdered."

The priest closed his eyes and took a deep breath.

"This is dreadful news. Who would—" Father Kraus seemed to choke up. "Excuse me, I need some water."

He disappeared into the hall for a minute. When he returned, it looked as if he had been crying.

"Please excuse me. I used to take word of personal tragedies better than I do now." He dabbed at his eye with a large handkerchief. "The poor man was new to our parish. He was just beginning to make a life for himself here. Do you know who did this terrible thing?"

"No, and that is why I've come to talk with you," Carol said. "When I visited his apartment here in Clarksburg, there were things that suggested he might be Catholic. It occurred to me that if he was a practicing Catholic, he could have been attending your church, and maybe you could tell me something about him. Something that might help us discover who is responsible for his death."

Father Kraus considered this invitation to talk about Rafferty. It was apparent that he was reluctant to do so.

"I'm afraid I didn't really know him very well," he said. "He hadn't been here long, as I suppose you know. I saw him quite regularly on Sunday morning, but we only spoke a few times outside of church. He was a private man."

"That's what I'm hearing. I was hoping, though, that he may have opened up to you a bit. Did he ever say anything about his life before he came here? Where he lived, what he did?"

"I don't think I can be of any help."

Once again, Carol had the feeling that Father Kraus was uncomfortable. She thought she understood why. He had become Rafferty's confessor and believed himself bound by the confidentiality of the confessor-penitent relationship. She knew she was only guessing. Better to be sure.

"Father," she said, "were you Brendan Rafferty's confessor?"

"Yes, I was," he replied. "Briefly, of course."

"And did he say things to you which you feel you cannot share with me?"

"I'm sorry, Sheriff Kelleher. I know this is difficult for both of us. But I'm sure you understand my responsibility."

"I do, but Mr. Rafferty is now dead. He died a violent death at the hands of someone who certainly deserves to be apprehended and brought to trial for his crime. I can assure you that Mr. Rafferty was not an accidental victim. His murder was well planned. Whoever killed him had what in his mind was a compelling reason for doing so. That suggests that the killer knew his victim, that their paths had crossed before. But we know next to nothing about Mr. Rafferty, so we can't even begin to speculate as to who that killer might be or where their paths may have crossed."

Carol paused, hoping Father Kraus would choose to offer more information. He didn't.

"I'm sure you can see how it looks to me, Father," she said. "We wouldn't be having a problem if Mr. Rafferty had confessed to failing to attend mass or simply harboring unkind thoughts about an acquaintance or neighbor. But if he had confessed to committing a crime or threatening an acquaintance or neighbor, then you would indeed have a moral dilemma. The fact that you are not prepared to tell me anything about Mr. Rafferty's past—even such innocuous things as where he lived and what he did for a living—strongly suggests that he may have confessed to doing something illegal. And that by answering those innocuous questions you would have given me the keys to something he shared with you in a privileged confession. Do you see *my* dilemma?"

"I do, and it troubles me more than you know. But I don't think I can say more."

"I appreciate your position, Father," Carol said. "Let me ask a different question. What do you know about Mr. Rafferty's friends? Maybe I should say acquaintances. Did he seem to talk with any of your other parishioners?"

"You'd like to know if there are other people here in Clarksburg who could answer the questions I can't answer. Is that right?"

"I'm trying to understand a man I never met when he was alive. A man I'd never heard of until he was killed. So far I've only had a chance to speak with his fellow workers at the winery. Maybe somebody he knows through church, some non-work acquaintance, will be able to help me. I don't have any preconceived agenda, Father. I'm only trying to solve a crime. A very serious crime."

The priest nodded, as if in acknowledgment that the sheriff's question was a reasonable one.

"Like I said before, Mr. Rafferty was a private man. I don't have the sense that he socialized much. In fact, I can only think offhand of two people I've seen him talking with. After church, that is, those times when people are just standing around. Probably criticizing my sermon."

It was the first hint that Father Kraus had a sense of humor.

"Anyway, he occasionally chats a bit with a man named Rucker. John Rucker. He's a contractor. I think his business is down, what with credit tight, people not spending much. I don't have any idea whether he and Mr. Rafferty did things together, but they seemed to get along. The other person he talked some with is Esther Rhodes. In that case, I think she was the one who took the initiative."

"Initiative?"

"Well, she's single. She lost her husband several years ago. A sad story. Anyway, you know how it is in a small town. People think she's angling to get married, and along comes a single man. Probably nothing to it, but she did make it a point to seek him out after church. And I heard that she did have him over to her house once for supper. Maybe it was twice. Somehow I don't think anything was going to come of it. Of course, we'll never know now, will we?"

Carol had the impression that Father Kraus might actually have enjoyed the gossip. He, too, after all, was a longtime denizen of a small town.

When she left St. Leo's, she considered paying a call on Mr. Rucker and Ms. Rhodes. It hadn't seemed appropriate to ask the priest for their addresses, but it wouldn't have taken long to find where they lived. She decided against it. They would probably be at work, and in any event she was anxious to get back to Cumberland.

She had learned nothing about Brendan Rafferty that she hadn't known before. Nothing, that is, but for the fact that he had very probably confessed something to Father Dietrich Kraus about a blot on his life before he had moved to the area. Something which might explain why he had been murdered. And why he had then been strung up as a scarecrow in a Crooked Lake vineyard.

CHAPTER 13

Carol debated whether to stop for lunch first or swing by the office to see what Bridges had accomplished in his search for the missing scarecrow. She opted for the latter, and ran into Sam in the parking lot just as he was about to leave.

"Any luck?"

"No. The damned thing's just disappeared. The nearest thing to a scarecrow is some pieces of straw in the trunk of the car. Actually, quite a bit of straw. Which suggests that the scarecrow was in the trunk for awhile. It looks like the killer put it into the car, drove off somewhere with it, and then dumped it. Heaven knows where that somewhere is."

"It doesn't make much sense, does it?"

There had to be an explanation, but Carol had no idea what it could be. She still couldn't understand why Rafferty had to be put up on his cross instead of left where he had been killed. Or why the real scarecrow had to be hidden instead of being left in the vineyard.

"I think the guy's just playing mind games with us," Sam said, expressing his frustration.

"I take it you didn't find anything of interest in the car? Anything, that is, except some straw."

"Well, yes, we did. We've been assuming that the killer took Rafferty's keys. He didn't. They were in the trunk, along with a pillow and bed sheets. I'm sure they're Rafferty's, the ones he'd been sleeping on. They have bloodstains. The killer probably used the pillow to help deaden the sound when he shot Rafferty."

Carol thought of Alice's observation in wonderland: curiouser and curiouser.

"See that Doc Crawford gets the bedding. Anything else?"

"Not yet. They're still going through the car. But no clues in the glove-box stuff—nothing to tell us who Rafferty is. I mean was."

"Okay. Now how about those two grape pickers you met down in the vineyard the day the body was discovered."

"I tracked them down this morning. There's nothing new there. They said pretty much what they said when we first met. I don't believe they're hiding anything. Just a couple of kids who've got a part-time job with the winery, happened to hear about the scarecrow that day, went rushing down to the vineyard out of curiosity."

"Where are they from? Either one live in Clarksburg by any chance?"

"I didn't ask for addresses," Sam confessed, "but when I asked how it was they were working for Random Harvest, they both said they'd just graduated from Southport High School and hadn't made any plans yet. One of them, guy named Toomey, talked about maybe going to community college. So, no, I'm pretty sure they don't live in Clarksburg, not if they went to school in Southport."

It probably didn't matter. But Carol found herself wondering whether any of the other Random Harvest employees were from Clarksburg and might have known Rafferty from church. She'd have to get the addresses for all of the winery personnel.

After a hasty lunch, Carol put a call through to Doc Crawford, who served as chief medical examiner for the county. He probably hadn't completed the autopsy on Rafferty or he would have called to say he had. But she was impatient.

It took a few minutes, but Crawford finally came to the phone.

"Couldn't wait for my report, huh?" he said in his rich bass voice. "By the way, thanks for the business you keep sending my way."

She had known him since back in the day when her father had been sheriff, and his wry sense of humor had always been one of the things that endeared him to her.

"I'd be very happy to send you off into permanent retirement, Doc, but we can't seem to stop this latest crime wave. So, what do you have for me?"

"This one was easy. Not like that woman in the ravine. Remember her? The official report should be in your hands tomorrow, but let me give you a preliminary *Reader's Digest* version. The man was killed by a bullet to the back of the head.

Death almost certainly instantaneous. Otherwise he was in good shape. No evidence of bad habits. If your killer hadn't had other ideas, he'd probably have lived to a ripe old age."

"How about time of death?"

After a short lecture on the inexactitude of medical science, Crawford settled on somewhere between midnight and two a.m.

"What kind of gun was used?"

"Small revolver, like maybe a Smith & Wesson model. Your man was shot at close range..."

"Would the wound have bled a lot?"

"There's a good likelihood that he bled a fair amount from the nose and mouth."

"I wonder how much noise a shot like that would have made."

Doc Crawford sighed audibly.

"I'm sorry, Carol, but I'm not a ballistics expert. Silencers are illegal, you know. But it's my understanding that they're not hard to come by if you're determined to get your hands on one. If not, you can always make one yourself. Crude, and not necessarily very effective. The truth is, I can't tell you how much noise the gunshot made. Or whether the killer used a silencer to soften the bang."

Carol smiled to herself. Her question had been rhetorical. She knew Crawford's expertise lay in another area. But she was facing the probability that Rafferty had been shot to death in his own bedroom, separated only by thin walls and not more than twenty yards from where Mrs. Stafford was presumably sleeping or reading or watching television. The woman had said nothing about hearing a gunshot in the night. And like the good doctor, Carol knew that silencers were not all that effective on small handguns.

"Bridges will be dropping off a bloody sheet and pillow. I'm sure the blood is from the victim. I'll be wanting the bullet, Doc. Send it along with the report. "

"Of course," he said, and rang off after wishing her well in what promised to be a challenging investigation.

———

It had not been a particularly productive afternoon. Sam's report had only added to her feeling that almost nothing about the Rafferty case made much sense. Doc Crawford's report had told her almost nothing she hadn't already known. She had fiddled with a batch of papers in her in-basket, taken a couple of phone calls, and consumed too much coffee. But her mind was on Kevin's arrival, and she was privately pleased when at five o'clock she could clear off her desk and head for the airport to pick him up.

After a sunny morning, clouds had built up and a light rain had begun to fall. As Carol reached the long downhill stretch of the road between Cumberland and Crooked Lake, the sun reappeared behind her in the western sky. Ahead of her the sky was still dark. The rain continued to fall. As if by magic, a rainbow began to take shape and in a matter of seconds it formed a perfect arc across the lake and against the backdrop of the bluff. Had there been a place to pull off the road, she would have stopped. It was a beautiful sight, a reminder of the way in which nature at its best could wash away worry and restore a sense of optimism. She had been preoccupied with the harsh fact that for the fifth time in only three years Crooked Lake had become the scene of an ugly murder. The rainbow buoyed her spirits. No amount of human evil could spoil her enjoyment of the lake or dull the memory of the pleasures it had given her since she was a little girl.

Now she was on her way to meet a man who shared her love of the lake. Brendan Rafferty's inexplicable murder in the Random Harvest vineyard could be put on hold for awhile. The weekend belonged to Kevin and her.

CHAPTER 14

"Excuse the formal attire," Kevin said as they settled into their chairs at a corner table for two at The Cedar Post.

"No apologies necessary. I was about to tell you that the coat and tie are an improvement."

"Over what?" Kevin was smiling. He took off his tie and stuffed it into the pocket of his sports jacket. "If I'd tried to change after class, I'd have missed my plane."

"I thought all the young profs today wore blue jeans and sweatshirts. Sloppy casual, or something like that."

"Most of them do. But somebody has to be old school. Why not me? You're in uniform, I've noticed."

"Like you, I didn't have time to change," Carol said. "By the way, why don't you tell me how it happens that you can run out on your students like this. I mean, classes only on Tuesday through Thursday. What kind of a boondoggle is that? Most people I know put in a five-day week, minimum, more often Saturdays, too."

"I thought you'd be pleased to see me," Kevin said in self-defense.

"I am, and you know it. But how do you academic types justify these short workweeks?"

"Actually, we work all the time, not just when we're standing in front of a class. My mind is in high gear at this very moment."

"You're thinking about your students?"

"No, I'm thinking about you," he replied, feeling good about himself and his partner across the table.

Carol was, of course, well aware from similar conversations with Kevin that the academic life entailed many hours of course preparation, the grading of papers and theses, university committees, and research and writing. Teasing him about the flexibility in his schedule had become a part of their relationship.

"Seriously, though," she said, "did you bring some work with you?"

"Just a set of papers from my 'Music Appreciation' course. But I thought I could put in a couple of hours on Sunday morning while you went to church."

Carol had not given any thought to church, but it suddenly occurred to her that it might be a good idea to attend mass at St. Leo's. She might be able to corner Esther Rhodes or the man named Rucker, the people Father Kraus had identified as acquaintances of the late Brendan Rafferty.

"Well, if you have to do some grading, I suppose I could absent myself for awhile."

"Thank you. Offer accepted. As long, that is, as you're back in time for lunch."

The waitress took their orders, brought them a couple of beers, and left them to enjoy the unexpected pleasure of each other's company on a Thursday evening in October.

Neither of them wanted to talk about the murder du jour. It was only the second time they had seen each other since Labor Day, and while the atmosphere in the crowded Cedar Post could hardly be described as romantic, Kevin and Carol were in a romantic mood. He reached across the table and took her hand.

"Why don't we do this more often?" he said.

"Could you? I don't want to sound greedy. I mean, every week is probably a bit much, but what about every couple of weeks?"

Both of them realized that they were edging toward the discussion they had been assiduously avoiding. Marriage. Or something very much like it. Summers had been different. It was one thing to share the cottage on Crooked Lake where he spent the months between his spring and fall semesters down in the city. But it was quite a different matter from September to May, when their geographical separation complicated their relationship and made marriage problematic.

Carol fiddled with her fork, not quite sure whether she really wanted to pursue the issue.

But Kevin seized on her question as if it had been an invitation.

"I'll do it!" he said, almost knocking over Carol's beer as he leaned across the table to kiss her. "Well, maybe not *every* second week. I don't control the scheduling of faculty meetings, and other things could come up now and then. But let's plan on twice a month, Thursday till Monday. At the cottage."

She started to ask him if he could really do it and not antagonize his dean in the process. But she thought better of it. After all, it was his responsibility, and the more doubts she raised, the more likely he was to reconsider. She wanted to live with him the year around. All summer plus three or four days twice a month for the rest of the semester wouldn't be perfect, but it would be a huge step in the right direction. It was then that something else occurred to her.

"You aren't saying this because you want to get involved in another murder investigation, are you?"

A wicked smile crossed Kevin's face.

"That just makes it a twofer—I can spend my time here because I love you and because it gives me an opportunity to play Sherlock Holmes."

Suddenly afraid that Carol would misinterpret his attempt at humor, he took her hand again.

"All kidding aside, I'd spend every day I possibly could up here even if crime took a holiday. No murders. Nada. Just you and me and the lake. All four seasons, not just one."

The moment passed without either of them venturing further into "what if." The word marriage wasn't spoken. But it was on both of their minds.

Dinner arrived, and after the steak sandwiches they took the plunge and went for The Cedar Post's famous pecan pie. It was while they were finishing the pie and coffee that Carol finally brought up the Rafferty case.

"Want to talk about our latest murder for a few minutes?"

"I thought you'd never ask."

"I gave you all the salient details over the phone. At least the ones we know about. But I can't see us solving this one until we learn a helluva lot more about the victim. He's either a near-complete cypher or he's been doing his best to conceal a checkered past. To listen to people he worked with, he's the cypher—dull, uncommunicative, a real loner. But if that's true, why was he killed? It sure wasn't an accident. Anyway, there's something I'd like you to do. I know, I told you this is my case.

But before you butt out, I'd be interested in what you make of a diary this guy Rafferty was keeping. I've got to be on the job tomorrow—it's only Friday, and up here we work a full week. What I'm proposing is that after I go back to the office, you hole up in that study of yours and concentrate on the diary. And tell me what it means when I drag my tired bones back to the cottage tomorrow night."

"What's so puzzling about the diary?" Kevin wanted to know.

"Well, in the first place, it's a pretty sorry excuse for a diary. No dates. Not many entries. Plus a strange kind of shorthand. It doesn't have a single name. It's obvious Rafferty was referring to people he knew. Same with places. But they're always referred to by initials, and the initials are invariably in lower case. Why not name names? And if you were using someone's initials, wouldn't you just automatically use capital letters?"

"Maybe he was using some kind of a code," Kevin suggested.

"I don't think so, but you'll have to read the diary and form your own opinion. I'm not going to say anything more about it. I want to hear what you think, not what you think I'm thinking."

"It sounds like you aren't planning to call in sick or something so we can spend the day together, so what choice do I have? Sure, I'll look at it. It sounds interesting. More evidence, I'd bet, that your scarecrow man was hiding something. Now, what else were you going to tell me about the case?"

"On second thought, nothing. Not tonight. Why don't we pay up and head home? I'd like some dessert."

"We've just finished dessert, Carol," he said, waving a hand toward the empty pie plates on the table.

"I had something else in mind," she said, her tone of voice betraying her thoughts.

CHAPTER 15

When Kevin awoke the next morning, he experienced a moment of disorientation before he remembered that he was at the cottage and that Carol was in the bed beside him. He rolled over only to find that she wasn't there.

"Carol?" He could smell the coffee.

No answer.

He climbed out of bed, pulled on his robe, and went to the kitchen. No Carol, but a note was on the counter next to the coffee pot.

Hi. You were really out of it this morning, and I couldn't bring myself to wake you.

Enjoyed last night. Loved dessert—both of them!

I'm leaving the shopping and cooking to you. Nothing fancy, please. I'll be back around six unless you hear from me.

The diary is on your desk. See what you make of it. In spite of a frustrating lack of clarity, I hope it may offer useful clues to who he was and what was going on in his life.

Love, Me.

Kevin poured himself coffee and went out onto the deck. It was a chilly morning, but the rain had stopped overnight and the sky had cleared. There didn't seem to be anyone else about. Several of his immediate neighbors were year-round residents and had presumably, like Carol, gone to work. On impulse he left the deck and headed down to the water where his dock now rested in sections on the beach. Most people on Blue Water Point had left their docks in the lake, protected by bubblers from the effect of ice buildup over the winter. Maybe he'd follow suit. Next year.

He tightened the sash on his bathrobe and walked along the beach, admiring the changing colors on the trees. The transformation since he had last been at the cottage was remarkable. It had been an excellent season for colorful autumn foliage, mostly sunny and dry, the nights cool.

Someone else was enjoying this beautiful morning. It was Edna Morgan, a longtime neighbor and an inveterate reader with whom Kevin had swapped books over many summers. They exchanged pleasantries, and he satisfied her curiosity as to whether the sheriff would be staying over. He had never been quite sure how Edna and her husband George viewed his relationship with Carol, but if they disapproved they kept it to themselves.

It was nearly 9:30 when he finally settled down to breakfast. Over a third cup of coffee, one more than his usual quota, he made out a list of the things he'd need to pick up for the weekend's meals. Anxious as he was to study the notebook which Carol had left for his perusal, he decided to get the shopping out of the way first. He would have preferred to be using Carol's Buick for the trip, but it was still over in Cumberland. So he made arrangements to borrow the Morgans' car.

By noon he had done the shopping, put away the groceries, and had a bite of lunch. It was time to tackle Brendan Rafferty's thin little pocket notebook, the notebook which contained twenty-one entries, none dated, all brief, all, according to Carol, frustratingly opaque.

The notebook was nothing more than an inexpensive item one could purchase at any multipurpose pharmacy. It didn't look old, but it had lost some of its shape from time spent in the owner's pocket. There was no legend announcing that it belonged to Rafferty. What had been written in it covered no more than a quarter of its pages. There seemed to be no rhyme or reason to the way the notebook had been used. Some of the entries had been made two to a page, while others had a page to themselves, leaving much of it blank. Occasionally a blank page appeared between two pages that had been written on. As Carol had warned him, none of the entries had been dated. The only sign that any special care had been taken in the notebook's use was the neat, precise handwriting which characterized all of the entries.

Kevin decided to read all of the entries, from first to last, before focusing on them individually. He would be looking for the writer's voice, for a unifying thread. He settled back in his chair and started at the beginning.

What am I doing here? Have I made a mistake? Was it wrong of me to judge him? Judge not, He taught, that ye be not judged. But surely he was wrong, wrong to judge his son and wrong to judge me. I can still kneel and pray, but it is so very difficult. I feel empty.

I dreamed about gf last night. Nightmare is a better word. A terrifying nightmare. He was a demon with horns, yet he was the man I knew. I am reminded of the devils in Signorelli's frescoes in Orvieto, the devils tormenting the damned in hell. Was I one of the damned in hell? It felt that way.

This place deadens the spirit. There is no joy, nothing that is uplifting. It should be my task to create joy, but how can I presume to take it on?

I wonder what gf is doing today. Maybe he's just going to work like I am. That is what men do. So why do I have a premonition of trouble.

So this is what it is like to be poor. Why did I think it would be easy? The problem is that I didn't think. I know He told us that life is more than the food we eat and the body more than what we wear. But I hope it is not blasphemous to disagree with the notion that God will provide.

A man drove in today who looked like gf. I mustn't panic, but today I did. Without thinking, I took refuge in the men's room. So very foolish. What if he had wanted to use it, too? I thanked God that he didn't, that I had survived another day. Why thank God? Why should He protect me?

Last night I visited ts on the recommendation of mc. It is a whole new world, and I think a bad one. What was a God-fearing man like me doing there? Or maybe in some strange way, God is there. I shall pray for guidance.

I agonized all day about ts. It has been a weight on my mind for a week now. This is what the scriptures mean when they speak of temptation. But is it evil? Can that which is necessary be evil? I want to say no, but if I am honest, I must admit that my own actions have made it necessary.

Kevin put the notebook down on his desk and got up to get himself a glass of water. What a strange, disjointed diary this is. Rafferty had obviously been a troubled man. Troubled about what? About whom? Glass in hand, he returned to the study, pushing aside these questions until he had finished reading the rest of the notebook entries. He found his place and immediately encountered more evidence that Rafferty had been a troubled man.

I wish I had never heard of ts. At first I worried that I had made a pact with the devil. Now my worries are much less matters of theology and much more immediate and worldly. I pray, but why should God listen to me?

For the first time in months I considered going back. How do they handle things like this? Would I be welcome? What if gf had poisoned the well? I hope and pray that he has found peace with his son.

I am tempted to say that the man in the red vest is my savior. Of course I cannot do that. Jesus is my savior. But disaster has been averted, and I can spare a word of thanks for the man in the red vest.

This was a bad day, but s rescued me. I should leave while I am ahead. But am I ahead? Where would I go? No, I can't do that.

When I look around me and take stock of the life I have made for myself, I realize that I have no friends. Have I ever had real friends since college? I need one now, but it isn't possible. One must trust friends. Whom could I trust?

Why is it so hard to examine my conscience? I wanted to make an act of contrition, but my failures all seemed to be very old and very tired. Each night is like every other.

I fear that s has run out of patience, and I cannot say that I blame him. What am I to do? I need a miracle, but I do not deserve one. Prayer won't make things better. Nothing will make things better.

So once again I am on the road, running, always running. I have spent my life telling people that they are not alone, that God is with them. Today that feels like a lie.

So little money, yet I spent some today on a book. *The God Delusion.* Why did I do that? To repair my faith? To test it against the counsel of a non-believer? What if the argument is compelling? Is it a sin to contemplate the non-existence of God?

This place is strange. The only comfort is that I may again be safe. I'm sure s would never find me here, nor would gf. But what if they wouldn't rest until they found me? Is that what people mean when they speak of paranoia? At least I slept last night, a rare occurrence. Blessed sleep without a dream.

So many questions. People here are kind. They want to know me. But I turn them away, and they will never understand that this isn't me.

Tonight I became Father Brown. Or tried to. Have I ever saved a soul? I doubt that I shall ever know. But it was the right thing to do. If nothing else, this man's conscience will be clear.

Is not pride one of the seven deadly sins? Pride. I imagined that I could save jc, but have I not been guilty of hubris? Was I not more interested in burnishing my own self image than I was in helping jc? I do not even know if he wants to be helped. Father, I have sinned.

In some strange way, reading the notebook had been exhausting. It had been like slogging through ankle-deep mud, struggling to place one foot ahead of the other. What had he learned for certain? Nothing, or at most very little. But he had tentatively formed a number of fairly strong impressions.

Kevin took out a yellow pad from his desk drawer and began to make notes, using bullets to identify his impressions.

The man was religious; that was quite clear. Of course Carol had told him about the priestly garments they had found in his flat, garments that strongly suggested that he had been a Catholic priest. The fact that he had been attending St. Leo's strengthened the conviction that he was Roman Catholic. But the notebook was also a testament to his faith, albeit an unusual one. Rafferty had mentioned God as many as nine times. He had spoken of prayer nearly as often. And he had cited scripture, beginning in his very first entry and then paraphrasing another verse from the Sermon on the Mount only four entries later.

But Rafferty's faith was under siege. Or at least the notebook could be interpreted that way. Why would a good Catholic, in all likelihood a priest, be reading a book on atheism? He had written that he might have been doing it to test his faith. The notebook contained passages which expressed the man's doubt. And that doubt seemed to have grown as time went on. Did he believe that God might not listen to our prayers? That we may be alone, bereft of God's company? That there may be no God? He had, in effect, said these things, never as truth, but as a frightening possibility.

Kevin pushed the yellow pad aside and let his mind wander. What was the relationship between Rafferty's religion and the problems he wrestled with so inconclusively throughout the notebook? What were those problems? He spoke of being poor. Priests were not supposed to be wealthy, but the impression he had gotten from the diary was that his lack of money was unrelated to his role in the church. He seemed not to have had the means to function in the real and presumably harsh world. And that was apparently the world in which he had been living since he started keeping a diary. Kevin read again the very first line that Rafferty had written: "What am I doing here?" He didn't think that "here" referred to a church. Later he would speak of running. Always running. The picture that emerged was not of running to something, but away from something. The church? If so, why?

He picked up his pen again and added another bullet. What he wrote after the bullet, and then underlined, was something to the effect that Brendan Rafferty had been afraid. He ran because he was afraid. It wasn't the church that he was afraid of. He had been afraid of people. People whose initials were gf? ts? mc? jc? even just plain s? No, not all of those. In context ts was apparently a place, a place of temptation, a place which he thought of as bad but at the same time a place which exerted a strong pull on him.

Rafferty had agonized over everything. At least everything he deemed important enough to mention in the diary. He not only agonized during his waking hours, he seemed to have spent restless nights as well. He had been a haunted man, and the troubles he had chosen to comment on in the notebook had begun with some kind of altercation with a man. A man who had a son, a man Rafferty had later prayed would find peace with that son. Who was that man? Was he gf? Those were the first initials used in the diary, coming in the second entry, the one which recounted his horrific nightmare.

Kevin turned from gf to ts, s, and the man in the red vest. He couldn't be certain of this, but the diary seemed on reflection to fall into sections. They overlapped, but their focus changed. The second section was mostly about ts, whatever and wherever that was. And it was there—and then—that the man in the red vest appeared. Red vest and s. Were they one and the same? Rafferty had never said that they were, but in context they might well have been. In any event, s had lost patience with Rafferty and almost immediately thereafter the priest was again on the run, this time presumably from s. Were s and gf united in some common grievance? Or were they simply way stations on Rafferty's flight?

Then there was a third section. There had, of course, been no clear line of demarcation, but the last several entries had a different tone. The place was strange, but the people were kind. And Rafferty had actually reached out to someone, someone he referred to as jc. Kevin found the reference to Father Brown puzzling. He had read some of the Chesterton stories about the little Catholic priest many years ago, but had never thought of him as one of his favorite detectives. The anti-Holmes he had called him, his methods less interesting than those of Conan Doyle's sleuth. Why would Rafferty be trying to emulate Father Brown? Both were priests. Both were in the business of saving souls. From what did jc need to be saved, and why would Rafferty, normally wary of human contacts, choose to reach out to help this man?

As Kevin reflected on these things, he was acutely conscious of the fact that reading the diary had generated far more questions than it had answers. Brendan Rafferty remained an enigma. There was nothing in the notebook which explained his presence on Crooked Lake. What had brought him there? Was it just chance that had led him to a menial job at Random Harvest Vineyards? He had apparently sought a place where he could burrow into the landscape, where he hoped to remain hidden from his pursuers, whoever they were and whatever the reasons for their pursuit. Crooked Lake had become that place, but it had not served him well.

Kevin was feeling frustrated. Frustration led to an unreasoning irritation with the author of the diary. Why could he not have been more specific? Any normal human being would have specified dates. Names would have been named—at least people would have been called Jim or Jane, something that hinted at a three-dimensional personality. The only person whose name Rafferty had used in the entire notebook was Father Brown, a fictitious character in a bunch of short stories. If it hadn't been for the fact that Carol had asked for his help in trying to understand the reason Rafferty had ended his life as a scarecrow in a Crooked Lake vineyard, he'd have said the hell with it.

It would still be several hours before Carol arrived back at the cottage. No need to spend those hours worrying about this latest murder to roil the normally placid waters of Crooked Lake. Kevin decided to put in some time thinking about an article on the *King Lear* opera that Verdi had contemplated but never composed. He had imagined what such an opera might be like off and on for several years. It was time to put those thoughts on paper. There would be time after dinner to share with Carol his impressions of Rafferty's diary, such as they were.

CHAPTER 16

Happy as she was to have Kevin back at the lake and to be sleeping at the cottage rather than her own apartment, Carol was forcing herself to concentrate on the investigation of Brendan Rafferty's murder. The first order of business on the Friday after the discovery of Rafferty's body in the Random Harvest vineyard was to forego a leisurely breakfast with Kevin and hurry back to Cumberland. It had been easier than she had expected because Kevin was sound asleep when she woke up and showed no sign of being ready to face the new day.

Carol had arranged for Deputy Sheriff Bridges to take the morning briefing, but she had decided that she should be there rather than stir up further talk about her priorities when the professor was around.

She slipped into the briefing room just as the meeting was about to start and took a seat in the back row. Sam acknowledged her presence with a nod of his head, but made no effort to turn the meeting over to her. Good for him, she thought. Twelve minutes later the men scattered, on their way to the assignments Sam had given them. Carol stopped her deputy on his way out the door, thanked him, and told him where she would be and what she would be doing.

Where she would be was Rafferty's flat on Maple Lane in Clarksburg, and what she would be doing was taking a closer look at his rooms. She had no doubt that Bridges had been thorough, but she wanted to see everything for herself, and she knew her own visit to the house had been quick and superficial. Armed with Sam's notes and following a phone call to Mrs. Stafford, she set off for Clarksburg.

Before tackling the flat, Carol asked if she might have a cup of coffee and then launched into a discussion of a few matters which still puzzled her.

"You told me that Mr. Rafferty owed you rent," she began. "But you also said that he had paid a deposit when he became your tenant. Do you by any chance remember the name of the bank the check was written on?"

"He paid me in cash."

"Really." Carol was surprised to hear this, but then immediately decided that perhaps she shouldn't have been. "Do you remember questioning him about it? Why cash, not a check?"

"I'm sure I didn't. I suppose I was glad to have the cash. No possibility of a check bouncing."

"Do you know if he had a bank?"

"No, and why would I? Like I said, he paid in cash that once and he never paid me again. Anyway, there's only the one bank here in town, Lake Country."

"I know the rent he owed is a sore subject, but I need to go back to that for a moment," Carol said. "You told me that he came to you fairly recently, said that he'd be paying up soon. I'd like you to think hard about that conversation. Did he say anything about when? Or about what had to happen before he could pay? Anything that might help us get a better picture of his finances?"

"I'm afraid not," Mrs. Stafford said. "I tried to pin him down, but all he'd say was I'd get the money soon."

"Okay. Let's talk a bit more about his acquaintances. We know he was a loner. But he must have known other people. Do you remember ever seeing him with anyone? Anybody ever come to his flat that you know of?"

"If he had company, it must have been when I was out of the house."

"Do you know a man here in Clarksburg named Rucker? John Rucker. I think he's a contractor."

"I know who he is, but I don't really know him. This is a small town, Sheriff. Actually, tiny might be a better word. But Mr. Rucker and I aren't close."

Was there just a hint of disapproval of the man in Mrs. Stafford's voice?

"Do you know if he and Mr. Rafferty knew each other?"

"No idea." It was clear that she neither knew nor cared.

"It doesn't matter," Carol said, although it was possible that it did. "All I'm doing is trying to locate people who could tell me something about Mr. Rafferty, and I'd heard it mentioned that maybe this man Rucker might be of some help. Let me try another name. Esther Rhodes."

"Sure, I know Esther. Everybody in Clarksburg knows Esther."

"So, did she know Mr. Rafferty?"

"I think so. It wouldn't surprise me if they've spent some time together."

"Why is that?"

"Well, Esther doesn't have a man. Neither do I, of course, not since Frank died. But I accept it. Esther doesn't. She lost her husband when a backhoe fell over and crushed him. It was a long time ago, but Esther's been looking for another man ever since."

"And you think she might have seen Mr. Rafferty as a promising candidate?"

"It wouldn't surprise me. The woman has a reputation around here, always talking about men. She's all of 55 and no beauty, but that don't stop her. What she should do is move to a bigger place. Heck, there can't be more than half a dozen single men past high school in this little god-forsaken town."

Carol decided that she didn't like Mrs. Stafford very much. But she was seeking information, not passing judgment on her qualities as a human being.

"Have you ever seen the Rhodes woman with Mr. Rafferty?"

"Once. Not here at the house, of course, but downtown. I might have seen her getting out of his car."

"Why don't you tell me about it?"

"There isn't much to tell. Maybe I'm wrong. It was way down the block, over by Cassidy's. But it looked like her."

"Cassidy's?" Carol didn't know much about downtown Clarksburg.

"You know, the general store on Vine Street."

Carol had every intention of talking with the Rhodes woman, and what Mrs. Stafford had told her might open up a line of conversation. But there didn't seem to be much point in pursuing the matter right then. She changed the subject.

"The other night when I stopped by to talk about Mr. Rafferty, you told me that you had been inside his flat about three weeks ago. I got the impression that that was the only time you'd been there since he'd moved in. Perhaps I'm wrong. Had you been in the flat on other occasions?"

Color rose visibly in the landlady's face.

"Like I told you, I didn't make it a practice to sneak into his rooms."

"I'm sure you didn't. I'm asking only because we need any information we can gather that might help us find out why Mr. Rafferty was killed. Little things which may seem unimportant at the time often turn out to be critical. So I'd appreciate it if you could tell us anything you can about him. About what you may have seen in his room, anything at all out of the ordinary. Anything which struck you as unusual."

Mrs. Stafford shook her head slowly.

"I'd like to help, but I can't think of anything."

"Don't worry," Carol said. "But if you do, please give me a call. Now I need to take another look at the flat, so if you'll excuse me, I'll do that."

She got up and fished the key to the flat from her pocket. Mrs. Stafford stepped aside, but not without asking a question which had been bothering her.

"Do you suspect Esther Rhodes of killing Mr. Rafferty?"

"No, I do not," Carol said sternly. "There is no reason to think she had anything to do with it. I mentioned her, along with Mr. Rucker, only because they might be able to tell me something about him. They went to his church, St. Leo's."

It took her the better part of half an hour to do what she wanted to do in what had been Rafferty's flat. Sam and Barrett had done a thorough job, and she could find only one thing which they had overlooked. Not Sam's fault, she said to herself. Looking for it hadn't occurred to her until she started going through the clothes in the closet and the dresser drawers one more time. There were labels, sewn into the cassock, the chasuble, and the surplice, bearing the name of the store from which they had been purchased.

The store, Christopher Vestments, was unfamiliar to Carol, but the label indicated that it was located in Boston. She had planned to follow up her visit with Mrs. Stafford by going back to Random Harvest to have another chat with Earl Drake, the winery's owner. But that trip could be deferred. It was much more important that she contact Christopher Vestments and see if they remembered the late Brendan Rafferty as a former customer.

―――

Back at the office, Carol asked Ms. Franks to get the phone number and put her through to Christopher Vestments in Boston. It seemed to be taking longer than she had expected, and she was becoming impatient. There were other things to do, but the only thing that mattered at the moment was the enhanced prospect of locating the address of Rafferty's church when he was still a priest, not a cellar rat on Crooked Lake.

"They're on the line," Ms. Franks finally announced over the intercom.

Carol assumed the phone manner she had adopted when seeking information to which she felt entitled as an officer of the law.

"Good afternoon. This is Sheriff Kelleher calling from Cumberland County in New York State. I believe that in the past you have supplied vestments to a priest named Brendan Rafferty. I'm not sure when you last filled an order of his, but I'm sure you have a record. He recently passed away, and we need to have an address. I'd appreciate it if you could help us."

She did not like the "passed away" euphemism, but thought it would do in the circumstances. She'd change the verb to "was killed" only if she had to.

"I'm sorry, but I'm not sure I got that. You are a sheriff?"

"Yes," she repeated, "I'm the sheriff of Cumberland County in upstate New York. Father Rafferty has died, and it is very important that I have his address. The label in his cassock and chasuble tell us that he bought them from Christopher Vestments, which is why I'm asking you for his address. Unfortunately, I do not have it."

"I see. I'll have to consult the manager. We do have a lot of customers, but he may have the information you want."

The clerk left the phone to track down someone who could be of help. Carol could not imagine that information as to the ex-priest's address and other pertinent data was not readily available in their records. It took a few minutes, but eventually a man with a deep, husky voice came to the phone.

"Hello. I understand that you are interested in a Father Rafferty. That is a fairly common name out here. Perhaps you can tell me what parish he served."

"That is what I don't know," Carol said. "The name is Brendan Rafferty."

"Just a minute," the husky voice said. She could picture him scrolling through a host of Raffertys on his computer.

"Ah, here it is," he announced, as if pleased to find a Rafferty named Brendan among the many customers of Christopher Vestments. "Brendan Rafferty. St. Anthony's Church, 217 West Lexington Street, East Moncton, Massachusetts. If you need the zip code there, it is 01754. I understand that Father Rafferty has died. I'm so sorry to hear that."

"Did you know him well?" Carol asked, suddenly hopeful that the husky voice might add to the limited picture she had of the ex-priest.

"No, I'm afraid not. I never met him, but it appears that he availed himself of our services on a number of occasions."

Carol asked that the address be repeated, learned that East Moncton was somewhere not that far west of Boston's city limits, and thanked the manager for his time and his assistance.

Another important piece of the jigsaw puzzle of Brendan Rafferty's life was now in her possession. But she still had no idea whether St. Anthony's was where the travels and travails laid out in his notebook diary had begun. Or whether it was the place where he had met the man who would later visit him in a nightmare. The man he referred to as gf.

CHAPTER 17

"There's a cold beer waiting for you," Kevin said as he released Carol from his embrace at the kitchen door.

"Good. And a warm professor. A perfect combination."

She went to the fridge, got her beer, and went on into the living room, dropping her jacket onto a chair in the corner.

The solstice was now weeks in the past, and the sun was setting earlier and earlier each day. It was only a little after six, but night was approaching and it was too cool to sit on the deck. Kevin had laid a fire in the fireplace, a fire which both took the chill off the air and created a more romantic atmosphere. It was the latter which had been on his mind when he lit the match.

"How did you like the notebook?" Carol asked as she curled up on the couch.

"It's a bit frustrating. I actually had more fun with my notes on the Verdi article."

"You actually worked on your article?"

"After I finished with the diary, I remembered I didn't have a car. I didn't want to take further advantage of the Morgans and their car, so I stayed here and tackled the *Opera News* piece. By the way, just how do you propose to put me into your Buick?"

"I thought we'd drive over to my place in the morning, then take the two cars and make a circuit of the wineries. Are you up to a wine-tasting trip?"

"I'd love it. You're on."

"I want to hear about the diary, but I'm curious about the article. You've done a pretty good job of procrastinating—lots of talk about writing, but nothing to show for it. Want to tell me?"

"I'm still at an early stage, but what I'm doing—or trying to do—is imagining the opera about Shakespeare's *King Lear* that Verdi never got around to composing. There's a lot written about why he didn't do it, but I thought I might have some fun speculating about how he might have approached it if he'd gotten past writer's block or whatever got in the way. He loved Shakespeare, you know, wrote three operas based on his plays. *Otello* and *Falstaff* in his old age and *Macbeth* back in his salad days."

"I read *Lear* in college. Pretty depressing. Would it make a good opera?"

"That's what I'm trying to decide. Maybe I'll end up agreeing that Verdi was better off not doing it. But let's talk about Rafferty. Now there's a subject for an opera."

"How so?"

"In the first place," Kevin said, "the central character's a haunted man, trying to escape from his past, his life one crisis after another. Of course you'd have to create a part for a soprano. There don't seem to be any women in Rafferty's life. If there were, he never mentions them in his diary."

"Not surprising, considering that he's a priest. Vow of celibacy, you know."

"Let's forget about the operatic possibilities. It's amazing how much and yet how little your murder victim managed to say in that notebook. If I had to choose one word that best captures his state of mind, it would be fear. He never tells us whom he's afraid of, just those damned initials. But I think he didn't name names because he was afraid that someone would see his diary, figure things out, make things worse."

"But why, then, bother to keep a diary at all?"

"We'll probably never know the answer, but my guess is that he was the kind of person who was always engaged in some kind of dialogue with himself. Something in his persona compelled him to write it down. Maybe he wanted to capture it, afraid he'd lose the thread if he didn't commit it to paper. I have a colleague like that. He's got issues, and he can't bring himself to leave them alone. It's like he's forever picking at scabs, like maybe he doesn't really want them to heal."

"It looks like Brendan Rafferty had good reason to be fearful," Carol said.

"The key, I think, is what started it all. What he was running away from in the first place. Because one of the things the diary tells us is that his problems snowballed as he ran."

"Any idea of what it was?"

"Yes, but it's just another guess. The most important fact is that he was a priest. What is it that has been causing trouble for

Catholic priests recently? You read about it in the papers all the time. Pedophilia. Hardly a month goes by without a news story about charges that some priest has been molesting young boys. It isn't hard to imagine that Rafferty was caught at it and decided to leave to avoid public humiliation, even prosecution."

"The same thought occurred to me," Carol said, "but we don't know that that's what happened. Wouldn't it be more logical that the church would have intervened? That it would have moved him to a post where he wouldn't have been vulnerable to that kind of temptation?"

"Whatever action the church took, I can believe that Rafferty would have worried about the consequences of what had happened. Remember that the diary refers to a man, presumably gf, and his son. He says something about the man being wrong to judge his son. And then later he prays that the man will have found peace with his son. What does that tell us? How about that Rafferty had had a relationship with the son, and that as a result the man—let's call him gf—was angry not only with the priest but also with his own son."

Carol looked uncomfortable.

"It bothers me that we seem to be assuming that Rafferty was a pedophile. Maybe he left the parish he was serving for reasons totally unrelated to that sort of thing. Anyway, I learned something today that should help us find out why Father Rafferty left the priesthood."

Kevin looked at her with ill-concealed disbelief.

"When were you going to tell me about it? Here I am, speculating about the meaning of the stuff in the diary, and you already know more about it than I do."

"I don't know anything about what was going on in Rafferty's mind, but I do know where he was serving as a priest. His cassock and the other church garments had labels from a Boston store, so I called them and found out that his parish was St. Anthony's in East Moncton, Massachusetts."

"That puts a new light on things," Kevin said. "I say we get in touch with St. Anthony's and cut through all this guesswork. Or have you already done that, too?"

"Yes and no," Carol said, a bit sheepishly. In retrospect, she should have shared this information with Kevin before getting his reaction to the entries in the notebook.

"I called St. Anthony's. I pretended I knew nothing about him and asked for Father Rafferty. The woman I spoke with, presumably a housekeeper, said he wasn't there. Not that he had left the parish, that he was no longer their priest, just that he wasn't there. It might have been better if I'd been more straightforward, but it was too late to shift gears. So I asked when she expected him back, and again she sidestepped the question. It was obvious that she was acting on instructions to stay mum about him. I assume that someone in the diocese—whoever was handling the case of a missing priest—had passed down word that nothing was to be said until they knew more."

"Which would mean that they didn't know where he was. And maybe that they didn't know why he had disappeared."

"You're probably right," Carol said. "One thing I think we can be sure of is that they didn't know he was dead. The only way they'd know that is if his killer told them, and that's about as likely as snow in July."

"Anything in the way the housekeeper sounded that seemed funny? Did she sound curious, want to know who you were?"

"No. I expected her to tell me that Father so-and-so was now the priest, did I want to speak with him. But she never did. Just that Father Rafferty wasn't there."

"Sounds like a cover-up to me," Kevin said.

"I hope not. It's my church, Kevin, even if I'm not exactly a very conscientious Catholic. I hate to think they'd be covering up another pedophile. We'll have to see what the diocese and the police have to say."

"What I think," he said, suddenly energized, "is that we ought to take a trip to Massachusetts—to that town where St. Anthony's is—and poke around a bit. Your people can use the phone, but this calls for—what's that expression they use in the Marines—boots on the ground? I can't believe that there wouldn't be a lot of talk about a priest who disappears, a priest who's been missing for who knows how long. It isn't the kind of thing that happens every day. There's bound to be some local gossip about it, even if there hasn't been a public statement by the church. That's the kind of stuff you're likely to get only if you're there. What do you say we put that into our plans?"

Carol got up from the couch and headed for the kitchen.

"I'm getting another beer. Want one?"

"Sure. Supper can wait."

"Now please listen to me for a minute," she said as she resumed her place on the couch. "It makes sense that I find out everything I can about what has happened at St. Anthony's. But let me remind you that you have a job to do at Madison College, and I am in charge of investigating Brendan Rafferty's murder. We'd agreed that you're here for the weekend because we miss each other, because we need some quality time together. Rafferty isn't your problem; he's mine. So *we* don't need to go running off to Massachusetts. Okay?"

"Okay, I came to the lake because I love you, not because I'm needed to put Rafferty's killer behind bars. But just last night you asked me to take a good look at the diary. And tonight you asked me what I learned by reading it. You know what happens to me when I start thinking about one of your cases."

"I asked you to read the diary because I had to be at work, and didn't want you to be at loose ends all day."

"That's good, Carol, very good." Kevin laughed, enjoying the amiable sparring which had become such an important part of their relationship. "But I really do think that a trip to St. Anthony's is a good idea. I'm just volunteering my services. We've already agreed about how nice it is that I have such a flexible schedule this fall. So what's the next step? Why not see if the two of us can go out to Massachusetts? Or if your calendar is not as flexible as mine, why don't I make the trip?"

The ensuing conversation was a familiar one, half-serious, half-joking banter, the outcome of which was foreordained. The specifics could be left for another day. But Kevin would somehow become involved in the quest for more information about the priest who had become a cellar rat and then a scarecrow in the Random Harvest vineyard.

CHAPTER 18

It had been chilly for the last day or two, but when Carol and Kevin awoke on Saturday morning, it was really cold. A front had moved in and The Weather Channel promised a week of early winterlike weather. Snow was not in the forecast for upstate New York, but it hadn't been ruled out. It looked very much as if the leaf peepers and wine tasters who had flocked to the region would be staying at home. October had been a good month for the wineries, but it was about to come to an end.

"Can you believe this?" Kevin asked. "Just look at the lake."

He and Carol were standing in front of the big picture window, coffee cups in hand, looking out over the deck toward the lake, not fifty feet away. The water was a dull slate gray, the waves large and crested with white foam. Even with the door to the deck closed, they could hear the sound of the waves crashing on the beach. It was neither raining nor foggy, but the bluff across the lake lacked clarity and color, the line between water and shore indistinguishable.

"I'm not ready for this," Carol said. "All my warmer stuff is over in Cumberland. I'll have to pick something up when we get the Buick."

"I've been thinking about the car," Kevin said, "and I don't think I'm going to need it. It would have been handy yesterday, but we won't be needing both cars over the weekend, and then you'll be taking me to the airport on Monday. Let's forget the car. And I think I've got an old coat you can borrow."

"You're probably right about the car, but I want my own jacket. I don't want to be seen in the wineries looking like I'm wearing your hand-me-downs. I'm no fashion plate, but I do have my pride."

"C'mon, Carol. My coat may be old, but it isn't all that bad. Besides, you'd make any clothes look good."

"Let me take a look at it," she said skeptically.

Kevin searched the hall closet and produced a well-worn tan sheepskin coat that was a bit too big for Carol. But after examining herself in the mirror, she decided that it would do, thereby saving a trip to Cumberland and making it possible for them to start their wine-tasting excursion after breakfast.

"Are you proposing to make Random Harvest one of our stops?" Kevin asked as they tackled the bacon and eggs.

"I do," Carol said. "We're in this for the fun of it, but it won't do any harm to see what people up there are talking about. The owner's been worrying that the murder of one of his employees will hurt business. My guess is that bad weather will do more to hurt sales than Rafferty's death. Anyway, I'm going in with my ears open. And I'm more interested in what the Random Harvest people are thinking than I am in the wine tasting."

They mapped out a morning itinerary that would take them over the hill to the Gray Goose Winery, down the ridge to Random Harvest, and finally to Silver Leaf, a winery still in recovery mode after the shocking murder of a previous owner, a murder that had brought Kevin into the sheriff's life just over two years earlier.

Bundled up against the unseasonably cold weather, they set off up the West Lake Road, leaving Blue Water Point behind, its waters conspicuously not blue. The wine tasters at the Gray Goose were fewer than the staff there to serve them. Carol put on her "friendly sheriff" hat and chatted up both the employees and the visitors. By mutual agreement, they limited themselves to sampling three wines each. Good diplomat that she is, Carol praised them all. Kevin voted for the Chardonnay. He bought a bottle of it, along with a set of attractive coasters, and they took their leave, heading for Random Harvest.

En route, Carol pointed out the place in the roadside vineyard where Brendan Rafferty had been strung up to resemble a scarecrow. The post with its crosspiece was still there, but on this gray, gloomy day, it was barely visible among the serrated rows of ripening grapes. She wondered if Mason, the Random Harvest expert on scarecrows, would seek a replacement for the missing original. Or if doing so would be too much of a macabre reminder of the ex-priest's murder.

Carol made it a point to stop by Earl Drake's office to inquire as to how things had been going, hoping that the owner of the winery would be less anxious and agitated than he had been when they first met after the discovery of Rafferty's body. She insisted that Kevin accompany her. Perhaps by introducing him around she would get people used to the possibility that their sheriff might be entertaining the idea of marriage. At least Kevin wondered if that was her motive. Whether true or not, the thought pleased him.

Drake was still his grumpy self, but the reason seemed to have more to do with the change in the weather than it did to the fallout from the murder of one of his employees. He admitted that the crowd in his wine-tasting room had not fallen off as he had feared, but he was not happy about the cold snap and the prediction that it might last for several days.

Carol was determined not to become sidetracked by the opportunity to corner Random Harvest employees whom she had not yet interviewed. She and Bridges would turn to that item on her agenda on Monday. For now, they would, as planned, concentrate on sampling the fruit of the grape. She counted on Kevin to do most of the talking to the staff about the different wines. Primarily a beer drinker herself, she doubted that she would know a Pinot Noir from a Merlot.

The tasting room had a long bar, behind which several members of the Random Harvest staff poured the wine and answered questions, the smiles on their faces a testament to the fact that these people had been hired for their public relations skills. The wall in back of the bar provided a view of the lake far below out a large, wall-length panel of picture windows. On a bright sunny day, the view would have been spectacular, a fitting complement to the wine and an inducement to purchasing a few bottles of it. Today, it was hard to make out the nearest vineyard, much less the far shore of the lake.

There were a dozen tourists standing at the bar, more than at the Gray Goose but less than Earl Drake would have liked to see sampling his wines. A garrulous group of three couples was laughing, apparently at the lack of even basic knowledge about wines of one of their number. A quieter couple was standing several feet away, carefully going through the motions of swirling wine in their glasses, sniffing the aroma it should be giving off, commenting seriously on their reactions. Kevin wondered if they might, eventually, actually take a sip of the wine. The other tasters were strung out along the bar, an array of glasses in front of them. One of them was making notes.

"Hello, Pat," Carol said, recognizing a young woman who was in the process of pouring a bit of red wine into the glass of a tall, white-haired gentleman in what looked like a hunting jacket.

"Sheriff Carol!" the woman named Pat responded. "I didn't recognize you out of uniform. Give me a couple of minutes and I'll take care of you."

"That's fine. We're in no hurry."

Kevin smiled to himself as he saw Pat sizing him up, the other half of the "we" Carol had referred to.

It wasn't Pat, but another staff member, who turned to them after the people he had been serving moved away from the bar and toward the winery's gift shop.

"Hello, folks. The weather's bad, but the wine's good." He chuckled at his witticism, and started into an obviously rehearsed but appropriately informal spiel. They were welcome to sample any and all of the company's wines, but he'd suggest the whites first. Unsure whether they knew the proper drill, he explained that they weren't obligated to drink all the wine in their glasses, but could empty it into the silver bucket on the counter. He recommended a little water between wines to clean the palate and rinse the glass. Both of them had been through the tasting process many times, but they paid attention, nodding their understanding as he went through the rituals of wine tasting.

"Let me suggest we begin with a Chardonnay."

"Is it oaky or not?" Kevin asked.

"No showing off," Carol whispered in his ear after kicking him gently in the shin.

"Yes, definitely oaky, but not too much." The man, whose nameplate said his name was Bob, gave Kevin a knowing smile, as if to acknowledge that he was speaking to a fellow expert.

They sipped the Chardonnay. Kevin looked thoughtful.

"Interesting. The taste of apples is quite pronounced, but there's a hint of pear. Wouldn't you agree?"

Carol suppressed the urge to roll her eyes. She had never understood this kind of talk about wines. Indeed, she suspected it was a lot of nonsense, a game played by wine connoisseurs to demonstrate their superiority over the casual weekend drinker. She had never heard Kevin talk like this, and she doubted that he knew what he was talking about.

They continued with the tasting for another twenty minutes, trying everything from Gewurztraminer to Cabernet Sauvignon. Kevin threw in the occasional comment about "good body" or "too much tannin," and at one point insisted that he detected a strong flavor of cinnamon in a Merlot. Carol planted another kick or two on his shins before finally nudging him away from the bar and off in the direction of the gift shop.

"You're a real pain, do you know that?" she said.

"No, I'm just enjoying my day off. Bob didn't look like he'd have anything to contribute to the resolution of your murder case, so I thought I'd keep the conversation on wine and its wonderful attributes."

"How do you know what Bob knows about the murder? You kept him talking about apples and pears and cinnamon— cinnamon, for God's sake."

"Okay, I overdid it. But it was fun. Do you want to go back and talk about scarecrows?"

"No, I think Pat is free for a moment. Let's talk with her."

The small crowd had thinned out, and Pat was indeed free. She was putting things away and cleaning up her end of the bar.

"Hi, again," she said in a cheery voice. "Sorry I got caught up with that other couple."

"Pat, let me introduce Kevin Whitman. He's visiting us here on the lake, and I thought I'd treat him to a wine tasting."

"Pleased to meet you, Mr. Whitman," Pat said. He felt like a specimen under glass.

"We've had all the wine we need," Carol said, "but I was wondering what you've heard about that crisis the winery had earlier in the week."

"You mean the murder," Pat said, her eyes lighting up with excitement. "Wasn't that awful. Do you know who did it?"

"I'm afraid not. It's only on TV that crimes are solved so fast. But we're making progress. What have you heard?"

"Oh, there's a lot of gossip, even if Mr. Drake has made it clear that we're not supposed to talk about it with the customers. Sometimes it's hard. I mean a lot of these people are from the area, and they've all heard about what happened. Anyway, I don't know anything. I didn't know poor Mr. Rafferty. I saw him in here a few times, but he didn't come by to talk. He was just looking at the wine cases and the stuff in the gift shop. In fact, I didn't even know who he was until Mary Rizzo said something over lunch."

"What's the gossip?"

"Well, mostly the employees think somebody had it in for him. Not anybody from the winery, of course."

"I'm sure somebody had it in for him, as you say," Carol observed. "People don't get killed like that unless there's been some kind of bad relationship. Have you heard anybody here say anything about knowing Mr. Rafferty? About ever spending any time with him outside of the job?"

"I don't think so. Most of the talk is that he was a quiet guy. Kept to himself. But wait, there was something. Bernie Stolnitz said something about him actually acting like a normal human being one day."

Stolnitz. He was the cellar rat who had called Rafferty "our resident stranger." But he hadn't mentioned a time when the stranger had acted like a normal human being. She'd pay Stolnitz another visit.

Carol had spoken with a handful of other people at Random Harvest before they moved on to Silver Leaf Winery, but learned nothing new, only repeated expressions of shock that one of their employees had been killed and in such a horrible way.

Silver Leaf had a more elaborate wine-tasting room, but there were even fewer tourists present than there had been at Random Harvest. It was the first time Kevin had been in the winery since the summer when he had made the most shocking discovery of his life. He had returned to his cottage after an early morning swim, only to find John Britingham, the wealthy and much disliked owner of Silver Leaf, lying on the dock, dead and not by accident or by his own hand. But he remembered Silver Leaf positively because it was as a result of its owner's murder and his own role as a suspect in the subsequent investigation that he had met Carol Kelleher, the sheriff of Cumberland County.

After lunch, relaxed and happy following a morning of sipping every kind of wine known to the Crooked Lake region, they spent a lazy afternoon at the cottage. The prospect of doing it again in two weeks, and at two-week intervals thereafter, was on both of their minds. It was almost easy to forget that there was a murder to solve. A murder for which there was no apparent suspect.

CHAPTER 19

Carol's enthusiasm for going to mass at St. Leo's had abated considerably by Sunday morning. Kevin found himself in the unusual position of trying to persuade her that it was still a good idea.

"Much as I'd like to have your company, I think you'd feel better if you took advantage of the opportunity to catch those people after the church service. The ones the good Father identified as acquaintances of Rafferty."

"You're supposed to argue that you don't want me to leave you," Carol said.

"I know, but I'm capable of being responsible. Some of the time, anyway. Besides, I do have those papers to grade. You told me so yourself."

"Okay, you win. But I'm doing it under protest."

Carol disappeared into the bathroom to take a shower, while Kevin started to clean up the breakfast dishes.

"I've no idea how long I'll be," she said half an hour later as she prepared to leave. "The service won't be long, but I don't know what to expect with the Rhodes woman. Or the contractor, for that matter. Frankly, I'm not optimistic that I'll learn much from either one of them. There's no reason to think they were any closer to Rafferty than the people at the winery."

"You're probably right, but one of these times you'll be surprised. I hope it's today."

He gave her a peck on the cheek, and she stepped out the back door into another cold and blustery morning.

As she had expected, Father Kraus was wholly lacking in charisma, a fact which probably accounted for the many empty pews at St. Leo's that morning. Those who were in attendance were testimony to the triumph of faith and habit. It was doubtful that they were there because they anticipated an intellectually or emotionally uplifting experience.

Carol hastened to the vestibule immediately after the service, anxious to have a word with Father Kraus before he became engaged in saying good-bye to his departing parishioners. He expressed his pleasure at seeing her again and identified for her the woman named Rhodes. Rucker actually materialized beside her while she and Father Kraus were talking, and they were introduced to each other before the priest turned to the next person in the queue that was forming.

"Mr. Rucker," Carol said as they drifted away from the receiving line, "I'm glad to meet you. In fact, I came to mass this morning hoping that I might have a chance to talk with you. Can you spare me a few minutes?"

"Of course," he said, looking puzzled. "Father said you're our sheriff. Is there some problem?"

"No, no. Nothing involving you. Why don't we sit over there?"

She steered him to a bench along the foyer wall next to a rack containing Catholic literature and flyers.

"I don't propose to keep you but for a very few minutes," she said, and then got right to the point. "I'm sure you've heard about the untimely death of Brendan Rafferty. It's my understanding that you knew him. Through the church, I presume. I didn't know him at all. In fact most of the people I've talked to didn't know him. We need to learn more about him in order to find out why he was killed, and I thought you might help us. What can you tell us about Mr. Rafferty?"

John Rucker was still looking puzzled.

"There really isn't much I can say," he began. "I hardly knew him. I mean we never did more than talk after church. He was new here, and I had the impression that he was sort of down on his luck. Things weren't going too good for me, either, what with the economy in bad shape. Didn't have the jobs I did a year or two ago. Anyway, we talked about it a bit."

"How did you know he was down on his luck?"

"I think he saw me getting into my pickup after church one day. It's got the name of my little company on the door. As I remember it, he asked how the construction business was doing, and I said not so good. We didn't talk long, but he mentioned he had a job that didn't pay too good at one of the wineries. He wasn't very specific, but I got the idea he'd had better times."

"You say he wasn't very specific. But did he say anything about what he'd been doing before he moved here? Anything more about his financial situation?"

"No, he obviously didn't want to talk about his past. But he was worried about money. He said that much. One Sunday, a week or so after our first conversation, he asked if I knew of any place around here where he could maybe pick up some money gambling. Or gaming. Actually, he didn't use either of those words. I got the impression he thought I'd think less of him if I knew he did that kind of thing. But that's what he meant, I'm sure. Well, it happens I'd been to a few places where you can try your luck, so I mentioned them. He acted as if he'd been kidding, that he wasn't really interested. But I think he was, although I don't know if he ever gave it a try."

Carol was now very interested in John Rucker's casual, nonspecific conversations with Brendan Rafferty.

"Do you remember the names of the places you mentioned to him? The places where he might try his luck?"

"Sure, because I'd tried them all. There's the Oneida Indian Casino in Verona and a Seneca Indian Casino in Salamanca. The Verona one, Turning Stone, is a real show place. Then there are racing tracks at Batavia Downs and Finger Lakes in Farmington. Lots of slots at both of them. None of them is real close, but it's not too bad a drive."

"But he didn't take you up on any of these suggestions?"

"It's like I said, Sheriff. He never told me whether he did or didn't. I'll bet he did, but that's just a guess. I probably shouldn't have encouraged him. You can't win at those places. At least I never did."

Carol thanked Rucker for his help and considered what she'd learned as he left the church. It wasn't much, other than confirmation of what she already knew from Rafferty's diary. The man had been in difficult financial straits.

While she was talking with Rucker, she had tried to keep an eye on Esther Rhodes. One minute she was engaged in conversation with two other women across the foyer. The next she had disappeared. Carol quickly got to her feet and hurried out into a spitting rain that had started to fall. She spotted Rhodes, walking briskly away from St. Leo's.

"Mrs. Rhodes?" she called out to the woman as she closed the distance between them. "Could you wait a minute, please?"

Esther Rhodes looked back. It was clear that she didn't know the woman who was approaching her.

"Excuse me for startling you like that," Carol said as she caught up with her quarry. "I'm Carol Kelleher, and I'm the sheriff of Cumberland County. I need to talk with you. I need some information, and I think you may be able to help me."

The Rhodes woman, like Rucker, was puzzled, as well she might have been. She pulled her coat more tightly around her, as if to protect herself from the sheriff and whatever charge she might bring against her.

"This weather is turning nasty. Maybe we could talk for a minute at your house. Is it nearby?"

"I'm just down Oak Street, about half a block. What's this about?"

"Let's talk when we get in out of the rain."

They walked at a brisk pace to a gray frame house with a wrap-around porch which, happily, was as close as Mrs. Rhodes had said it was.

"Let me slip my shoes off," Carol said. "I don't want to track into your home."

They took seats in what was presumably the living room, although it more resembled a game room. A jigsaw puzzle, no more than one-third assembled, was spread out on a card table. A second card table contained a Scrabble board and tiles; it looked as if it had been abandoned in mid game. An end table next to the couch held a stack of crossword puzzles, all neatly clipped from newspapers, plus a deck of playing cards.

Mrs. Rhodes made no attempt to explain this assorted evidence of her interests. Nor did she suggest a cup of coffee or tea.

"I must say, you took me by surprise," she said. "I didn't expect to be accosted by the sheriff."

"I didn't think of it as accosting you, Mrs. Rhodes. I'm in the process of investigating the death of someone whom I understand you knew. Brendan Rafferty. We need to gather a lot of information about him if we are going to find out who killed him and why. I thought you might help us."

Carol had assumed that Esther Rhodes knew of Rafferty's death. It would have been hard for her not to have known.

"It was a terrible thing, him being killed. I couldn't believe it." Mrs. Rhodes shook her head, as if to emphasize how terrible it was. Her face, however, betrayed no emotion.

"Yes, it certainly was a terrible thing," Carol agreed. "I can't imagine who would have wanted to kill this man. But my problem is that I know almost nothing about Mr. Rafferty. Perhaps if I get to know who he was, what he was like, it will be easier to figure who might have killed him. And why. That's why I'm here. You knew him, so I believe you can help me. I know this isn't what you thought you'd be doing after mass today, but I'd be most grateful if you'd share with me your impression of him."

"I really don't know very much about him. We only met at the church. I suppose we didn't talk but a few times."

Was this always going to be the way it was? Nobody knew much of anything about Rafferty. Nobody spoke with him but two or three times, if that. She always asked the same questions, gave the same reasons for asking them. And she always got the same answers. Well, almost always. At least Rucker was now the second person to mention Rafferty's query about gaming sites. But either Jenny Stafford was imagining things or Esther Rhodes was being less than honest. Carol decided to challenge Mrs. Rhodes.

"I've heard that you had Mr. Rafferty over to your house for dinner. Why don't you tell me about it?"

"Where on earth did you hear that?" The way she said it suggested that it was the most preposterous thing she'd ever heard.

"This is a small town, Mrs. Rhodes. It is very hard for anything anyone does to remain a secret for long. There is surely nothing wrong with inviting a newcomer in town to have dinner with you. It sounds like a very thoughtful thing to do."

The woman's face, already ruddy from the walk back from the church, took on an even redder hue.

"I'll bet it was that Jenny Stafford. She's an incorrigible gossip. Doesn't know enough to mind her own business."

"It really doesn't matter, Mrs. Rhodes. I suspect it's general knowledge. So you did have dinner with Mr. Rafferty. And presumably talked about more than the weather. I'd like to hear what you talked about. What you learned about him."

The silence that greeted Carol's invitation to share her impressions of Rafferty suggested that Mrs. Rhodes was having a debate with herself about just how candid she should be. Candor won out.

"Well," she began, somewhat uncertainly, "we didn't really talk about very much. He didn't talk. Not much anyway. Said hardly anything about himself, just asked me questions, about me, about Clarksburg, about life here in this neck of the woods. It's nice when people sound interested in you, not just go on about themselves. But it got frustrating. I mean, why not tell me where he'd come from? Why the big secret?

"I figured there was something wrong somewhere. Maybe he'd been in jail, didn't want to talk about it. He seemed kinda lonely. It made me want to help. One night we'd sat down for dinner, and I reached across and rested my hand on his. It was just a nice gesture, a way of saying I understood. Of course I didn't. He snatched his hand out from under mine as if he'd been scalded. I remember looking at him, not saying a word, just wondering what had gotten into him. He apologized for being rude, but he didn't explain himself, just pitched into his soup."

Mrs. Rhodes had decided to open up. Carol sat back and listened with growing interest as the story of this odd couple came pouring out.

"Now I'm not a touchy-feely person, Sheriff. But the next time I had him over for dinner—there was only the two times—he was looking a bit down in the mouth. What I did was pat him on the top of his head. You know, one of those little pats that don't mean anything special, just that you're there for someone. Well, he practically shouted at me. 'Don't do that,' he said. Now wouldn't you think that was weird? I got to thinking about it. And it finally dawned on me. He must be gay. Why else would a man react like that when a woman as much as touches him? I'm sure Stafford would say I was coming on to him. She's got a nasty mind. All I was doing was being kind, maybe worried he had a problem."

Esther Rhodes hitched herself forward on her chair as if to emphasize what she was about to say.

"Well, I guess he really did have a problem. And I didn't want any part of it. I don't have any patience with all this homosexual business, men wanting to marry each other. It's not what the good Lord planned for us. So I hurried through dinner, saw him out the door, and never talked to him again. As far as I'm concerned, he didn't deserve my sympathy. I should be sorry he got killed, I suppose. Nobody, bad as he is, should end up like he did. But I'd bet that he paid for his sins—probably got done in by some guy he'd met in a gay bar somewhere."

It had been a remarkable story. The woman was very probably wrong in her diagnosis. It was clear from what she had said that Rafferty had never divulged to her the fact that he was, or had been, a priest. That could explain his dismissal of what he might have construed as the woman's advances. Had he said he was a priest, Mrs. Rhodes might have been disappointed, but it is doubtful that she would have jumped so quickly to the conclusion that he was gay.

"There is no evidence that Mr. Rafferty was gay," Carol said. Whether he was or not, she hoped that Mrs. Rhodes would not be going around telling the citizens of Clarksburg that he was. "But there is one more question before I go. Were you ever in Mr. Rafferty's apartment on Maple Lane?"

"No, never," was the reply. Once again she sounded as if the idea was preposterous. "He didn't invite me, and I wouldn't have gone there if he had. It's that Stafford woman's place. We aren't on speaking terms."

No, I suppose you aren't. I only know two women in Clarksburg, Carol thought, and I don't think I care much for either of them. She knew that there were small-minded people in every imaginable setting, but was there something about small towns that actually encouraged such a mindset? When she left Esther Rhodes to her unfinished jigsaw puzzle and headed back to Crooked Lake, the always-pleasing prospect of spending the rest of the day with Kevin had acquired a new allure.

CHAPTER 20

Kevin fastened his seat belt and turned his attention to a copy of *Newsweek* which an earlier passenger had left in the pocket of the seat in front of him. It held his attention through takeoff, but as the plane gained altitude, he set it aside and settled back in his seat to think about Carol and the promise he had made to her to spend more long weekends with her at the cottage. He was pleased with himself that he had had the foresight to concentrate his teaching schedule in the middle of the week. He was less certain that flying off to Crooked Lake every other Thursday was really a responsible thing to do, in spite of his having told Carol that it posed no problem. But if he put in longer hours when he was in the city and at the college, he believed he could do it.

It was while he was occupied with anticipating more time with Carol that he found himself thinking about going up to East Moncton, Massachusetts, to find out what he could about Brendan Rafferty when he had been Father Rafferty of St. Anthony's Church. Such a trip would mean less time with Carol, but he knew that he would be doing it, even that he wanted to do it. In fact he might have to make it two or even more trips. He had no illusions about how willing church officials would be to talk about the case of the disappearing priest. And if it became necessary to talk with St. Anthony's parishioners, well then...

It was not a long flight, although Kevin knew from experience that it would take almost as much time to disembark, get a cab, and make the trip back to his apartment as it did to fly point to point. By the time he reached the apartment, he had formulated a plan. A simple plan. Perhaps too simple, especially if the church had chosen to draw a curtain of silence around the matter. It certainly had not been forthcoming when Carol had called to ask about Rafferty. But Kevin was reasonably confident that he'd find people who would talk with him about the priest.

People liked to talk about mysteries. Or, if there had been a hint of pedophilia, about crimes. It was even possible that people knew why the priest had left St. Anthony's and where he had gone, even if the church was declining to discuss the matter.

The church and the local authorities, if they had become involved, would want to know what his interest in Rafferty was, and it was for the sheriff, not for him, to tell them what had happened to the priest. They had discussed this before he left the lake, and she had not wanted to pass along this critical information just yet. After all, she did not know that Rafferty's death had anything to do with the fact that he had been the priest at St. Anthony's. There didn't seem to be any reason to bring the church into a murder investigation hundreds of miles from East Moncton and a long time after he had left that town. Better first to find out more about just what had happened there and when it had happened.

He assumed that Carol would have traced Rafferty's next of kin through the magic of the Internet, and that she would have to be in contact with the family. He remembered the now-dated photo of the proud mother and brother. Would they have known anything about what had prompted Brendan to leave St. Anthony's? Would he have been in contact with them since then? These were questions which Carol would ask when she got in touch with them to explain that Brendan was dead, that his body would need to be claimed. Kevin's task was to probe for information—both fact and rumor—from people outside of the family.

It was after he was back in his apartment, and while he was organizing his notes for his class the following morning, that something occurred to him. Something which sent him in search of his copy of the Madison College phone directory. He thumbed through it, looking for a professor in sociology named Martin. He barely knew him, and couldn't remember his first name. The one he was looking for turned out to be Lester Martin. Kevin dialed the number at a west side address.

"Martin speaking," announced a clipped voice.

"Professor Martin, this is Kevin Whitman. I believe we've met, probably at one of those meetings of the school senate. Anyway, I'm a colleague at Madison. In the music department. I think I've heard that you have a grant for a project that's studying the issue of pedophilia in the church. Do I have it right?"

"Why, yes, that's me. It involves a lot of quantitative analysis. Tracks every case we can document, how the church responds, what the outcome is, and so on."

"That's pretty much what I'd heard. Look, I'm sorry to be bothering you, but I wonder if it might be possible to sit down with you at your earliest convenience and talk about it. Actually, that's not quite the way I should put it. What I'm interested in is a particular case, or maybe I should say an alleged case. If your project covers every reported case, there's a good chance that the one I'm interested in is in there."

There was a moment's hesitation before Martin said anything.

"May I ask if you're an interested party in the case? I mean do you represent the family? Or the church?"

"Oh, no, nothing like that. It happens that I have a friend who's a sheriff. She's investigating the death of a priest who left his parish under mysterious circumstances. Neither she nor I know any of the parties. Trouble is, we don't know why or when the priest disappeared. We don't even know the parish, just its location in a town in Massachusetts. The sheriff needs information that might help identify the priest's killer."

"A murder case? My goodness. You understand I had to ask what your interest is. There are people who have a personal stake in these pedophilia cases. They don't realize that this is a statistical study. We don't name names, and we don't have a policy agenda."

"I appreciate your concern. But like I said, I'm just looking to obtain some factual information. It's quite possible that this murder doesn't have anything to do with allegations of pedophilia. So might it be possible for us to meet?"

"Of course. You've piqued my curiosity, you know. We should meet with my assistant. He handles the computerization of our records. I'll see him in the morning and get back to you. Why don't you give me a number?"

Kevin supplied both office and home numbers, thanked Martin, and finished organizing his briefcase for the following day. He hoped that Martin, his curiosity piqued, would be as anxious to meet with him as he was to meet with the sociologist. Tomorrow would be none too soon.

He set about rustling up something for supper. It was too early to call Carol and fill her in on his latest brainstorm. He'd try her in another hour, energized not only about the prospect of seeing her in less than two more weeks but also by the possibility that by then he'd have something critically important to contribute to her investigation of yet another murder on Crooked Lake.

CHAPTER 21

Either Tuesday was a slow day for Professor Martin or he was genuinely fascinated with the story Kevin had told him over the phone the previous evening. In any event, he asked Kevin to stop by that afternoon after his class. So it was that at 2:30 they were sitting in the sociologist's office in Graham Hall, along with a young man who had been introduced as Warren Hungerford, the assistant who was managing Martin's database on pedophilia.

"Tea?" Martin asked as they took seats in the cramped space around his desk. "Sorry, but I don't drink coffee. The Earl Grey's good, though. I swear by it."

Kevin waved off the offer, and once again voiced his demurrer.

"Like I told you, I don't even know if the case I'm talking about involves pedophilia. It just seemed as if such an allegation might have been the reason this priest left his parish. And why the person we contacted there didn't want to talk to us about him."

"No problem. If this is a matter that got any publicity, it's likely we'll have it in our files. Warren's a real bulldog when it comes to tracking down media coverage of such cases. It seems like any charge of child molestation, especially one involving a member of the clergy, gets the media's attention. It's not one of those issues which the public tires of hearing about."

A project like the one which Lester Martin had undertaken was far removed from the kind of research familiar to Kevin. He had no particular interest in aggregating data, subjecting it to the kinds of analysis popular among social scientists, and publishing the results in papers full of charts and mathematical equations. He was sitting in Martin's office because he hoped that the computer in front of Hungerford could be made to spit out information that would help Carol to determine who had killed Brendan Rafferty and why. He wasn't optimistic, but he saw what he was doing as a small step in what promised to be a potentially long and difficult quest for the answer to that question.

"Let's see what you've got," Kevin said to Hungerford. "In this case the priest's name is Rafferty—Father Brendan Rafferty. His church was St. Anthony's in East Moncton, Massachusetts."

The young man went to work, and it soon became apparent that he wasn't finding anything to indicate that Rafferty had been charged with molestation of a minor. In fact, neither St. Anthony's nor Brendan Rafferty came up on the screen.

"Does this mean that the priest was definitely not a pedophile?" Kevin asked.

"Not necessarily," Martin replied. "It's possible that nobody accused him. Or if there was an accusation, that it was voiced quietly to the church and taken care of out of the public eye. In other words, it never became a news story. The project only deals with cases which become public and are considered newsworthy."

"But what about the fact that Rafferty left his church suddenly? He had a strange diary which clearly implies that he was running away from something, and in context it sounded as if that something happened at his church. When I started to speculate about reasons why he did what he did, one of the first things that occurred to me was that maybe he thought he was going to be accused of being a pedophile and decided to leave before the matter became public. If that's what happened, the church might well not have been involved. The accused was gone, the church could put a new and presumably safe priest in his place, and the whole matter would blow over. Your records wouldn't show any of this, but there could still be a case of pedophilia."

"That's possible," Martin said. "In which case we try a different tack. Warren, see if you can find a clipping that deals with a missing priest."

Hungerford left the desk and went over to a set of boxes which appeared to contain files of newspaper clippings and computer printouts. They were alphabetized, and he took out one labeled Massachusetts. The research assistant had obviously been dogged in his labors, and, sure enough, he dredged out a clipping from the *Boston Globe* that reported on the disappearance of a priest in a town just west of the city. It appeared in a section of the paper devoted to local news, and only took up three inches of column space. The town was East Moncton and the church was St. Anthony's. The priest's name was given as Brendan Rafferty. The piece said that there was no evidence of foul play and that sources knew nothing which could explain the priest's disappearance. It indicated that the church had no comment on the matter and made no reference to any involvement of local authorities. The date on which the piece had been published was September 13th of the previous year, not much more than thirteen months ago.

"Nice work," Kevin said. "It doesn't answer all of the sheriff's questions, but it tells us when Rafferty vanished. And it suggests that the church was being close-mouthed from the very beginning. Of course, they might not have known anything and didn't want to speculate. But it's also possible that they were into a cover-up."

"So what are you going to do?" Martin asked.

"It's really a matter of what the sheriff's going to do. If I can help, I will."

"Forgive me for asking, but who is this sheriff?"

Kevin smiled and leaned back in his chair.

"Here at Madison everyone thinks my field is music appreciation. But I've got a secret life upstate, helping a sheriff in the Finger Lakes region solve crimes. No, that's not completely honest. The sheriff is a *she*, and I'm more than a little fond of her. So when she asks me for my ideas about a case, I'm only too happy to oblige."

The sociologist produced a smile of his own.

"And I'd be willing to bet that you are also planning to miss a faculty meeting or two in order to go rummaging around up in that town near Boston. What is it, Moncton?"

"East Moncton, I believe," Kevin said. "And the answer is yes. I find it hard to believe that a priest simply tires of his vocation and takes off one day to assume a job at a winery. Anything is possible, I suppose, but I'm sure there's something else going on here."

"Do me a favor, will you? If you learn something which should have a place in my database, let me know."

"Absolutely. And I'll be looking forward to reading the book or whatever it is that presents the results of your study. I guess you could say that we're looking at the same problem through different ends of the telescope."

Kevin thanked Martin and Hungerford and headed back across campus to his own office. But his mind was not on his next class. It was busy reviewing the things he wanted to share with Carol when he called her that evening.

CHAPTER 22

Having driven Kevin to the airport on Monday morning, Carol sat down at her desk in the Cumberland County Sheriff's Department to map out her schedule for the day. She knew that she would be much too busy to miss him, at least until evening. But she also knew that moving back to her own home would be a downer. For a few brief moments her thoughts drifted back to the conversation they had had at The Cedar Post on Thursday, the conversation which had prompted her to think about the "M" word for the first time in many long months.

Sam rapped on her door just as she was letting herself speculate as to whether it would be better to live a married life at her place or Kevin's. Carol shook her head, put Kevin out of her mind, and turned her attention to her deputy's agenda. They talked about dividing up the people at Random Harvest with whom they had not yet spoken. She asked him to focus on the white collar, salaried contingent, the group she assumed would be least likely to know Rafferty. She would tackle the others, from field hands to gift shop personnel.

The list Carol drew up began with Bernie Stolnitz. She had been intrigued with the news that he had spoken about a day when Brendan Rafferty had actually seemed quite normal. What did Stolnitz mean by normal? What had they talked about on that "normal" day? And why had he not mentioned it when she had questioned him earlier? He had enjoyed being able to use what was apparently his favorite description of Rafferty: the resident stranger.

There was something about that phrase that bothered her. It was tantalizingly familiar. Where had she heard it before? Nor that it mattered. It was just Stolnitz's way of saying that no matter how long Rafferty had worked at the winery, he still didn't fit in. But the idea that Rafferty was the resident stranger wouldn't go away. It nagged like a toothache.

It was sometime later, just as she was getting ready to drive over to the winery, that she remembered why Stolnitz's characterization of Rafferty was familiar. The phrase that suddenly popped into her mind was "the resident patient." It had a similar ring to it, even if it had a different meaning. And it was the title of one of the Sherlock Holmes stories. Would Stolnitz have been familiar with the Holmes canon and adapted a small element of it to describe Rafferty? Of course it didn't really matter, but Carol found herself thinking that if Stolnitz was familiar with Holmes, familiar enough to remember the title of one of dozens of his exploits as chronicled by Doctor Watson, he wasn't a typical winery cellar rat. Any more than the ex-priest was.

The more she thought about it, the more she was convinced that Stolnitz was indeed different from his fellow workers at the winery. She recalled the way he talked. What in retrospect seemed like a wry sense of humor. Eyes that hinted at a quick mind, sizing up the sheriff as she questioned him. Someone who could well be a reader. She wondered what in addition to Conan Doyle he read for pleasure. If, that is, he read the Holmes stories at all. If, in fact, he had ever heard of the resident patient.

Carol laughed to herself as she drove. Resident patient. Resident stranger. She was creating an image of Bernie Stolnitz based on nothing more than the possibility that he was familiar with Sherlock Holmes. In all likelihood a remote possibility. No matter. She would talk to him because he might enlighten her as to Rafferty's normal day.

After informing the owner that she would be asking questions of some of his personnel, she headed for Building B. Stolnitz was there. But she didn't want to talk with him in the presence of his co-workers. On the other hand, she didn't want those co-workers to think that the sheriff was suspicious of him. She solved that problem, or tried to, by claiming to have a cold and needing to get some fresh air.

They settled themselves on a low stone wall that extended out from the building, separating the entranceway from a small plot planted with barberry bushes. Behind them a hill covered with pine trees rose sharply toward the western sky, while below, where it was not hidden from view by the corner of the building, the lake was visible in the distance. It was a place conducive to relaxation. Carol hoped Bernie Stolnitz would relax and respond candidly to her questions.

"Are you ready to collar the guy who did it?" Stolnitz asked.

"In my dreams," Carol replied. "We're making progress, but it's a tough case. I'm still working on getting to know the victim, and that's why I want to talk with you. We didn't have but a couple of minutes the other day. I have a hunch that you're a pretty observant guy, that you can help me get a better picture of Mr. Rafferty."

Carol manufactured a slight cough, the better to back up her claim to be bothered by a cold.

"I think I told you pretty much what I know," Stolnitz said. "He wasn't a very colorful figure, if you know what I mean. Kept to himself, didn't say much, didn't seem to have friends."

"That's what everyone's been telling me." Carol pivoted on the wall until she was half facing Stolnitz. "But nobody's ever quite that one-dimensional. Was there ever a time, ever a day, when he seemed like a different person? Not suddenly all buddy-buddy, of course, but more—what shall I say—normal? More like the other guys?"

A guarded look came over Stolnitz's face.

"Normal? You mean less introspective? Someone you can get an answer out of when you ask him a question?"

"Something like that," Carol said. "I'd just like to hear someone here at Random Harvest say he'd had a real conversation with Rafferty. Someone who'd tell me what they talked about, what he'd learned about the man, his interests, his life outside of the winery. Like I said, I figured you might be that someone."

"Well, we did talk on a few occasions. Mostly about me, as it happens. Not about him. He did tell me that he found his job kind of boring. I got the impression that he didn't plan on staying here all that long."

This was not what Carol had had in mind. It was time for her to mention that Pat Collins had quoted Stolnitz in the tasting room.

"This weekend I was here for a wine tasting, and one of the staff quoted you as saying that Mr. Rafferty had actually acted like a normal human being one day. What were you referring to?"

The guarded look came back.

"Did I say that?"

"You did," Carol replied, confident that Pat, whom she considered a transparent person, was a reliable source.

"Well, I suppose it had something to do with a conversation we had about gambling. I mean that's not something a recluse like Rafferty would normally bring up with someone who was practically a stranger. And he was the one who brought it up."

"But a couple of your colleagues mentioned it, too, and I'm sure Rafferty would have thought of them as strangers."

"Yeah, you're right," Stolnitz said, sighing as he did so. "Actually, he brought the subject up more than once. One day I caught up with him as we were leaving at the end of the day and asked him if he was in any kind of trouble because of gambling debts. It seemed like a reasonable inference, and I meant to sound like I was concerned for him. I'm not sure why, but instead of telling me to bug out, he decided to share with me."

Stolnitz paused, deciding what he should say.

"He didn't talk about being in debt, like I thought he was going to. He asked me if I'd done any gambling at places around here, and when I mentioned that I had, he surprised me by asking if I'd be willing to go with him to one of the casinos or racetracks."

"When did this conversation take place?" Carol asked, aware that what she was hearing could be important.

"I don't remember the day, but it must have been about three weeks ago."

"And what was it you told him?"

"I said I'd think about it."

"And did you think about it? More importantly, did you and he ever go to one of those places?"

"Look Sheriff, this is what I didn't want to talk about. Rafferty asked me not to say anything to the other guys. He really seemed anxious to keep it between the two of us. I got the impression he might have gotten into trouble at some time or other. Anyway, we did agree to take a trip to Farmington. That's the Finger Lakes Race Track with slots up near Rochester."

"And now I think you're going to tell me that you did make that trip. When?"

Stolnitz stood up.

"Do you mind if we take a walk? Down that path over there." He was looking at a gravel walkway that skirted the parking lot and then disappeared over a small rise in the ground a hundred yards south of the winery.

"Not at all," Carol said, eager to hear what the suddenly more forthcoming Bernie Stolnitz would be telling her about his trip to one of the Empire State's gambling meccas with the ex-priest.

"This is hard for me," Stolnitz said as they followed the path beyond the parking lot. "Rafferty really didn't want me to talk about it. I got the impression he was afraid of something. Probably of someone. Now that he's dead, murdered like he was, I guess that maybe he was right to be afraid. I'd like to do whatever I can to help you, but I don't want to get involved. Do you know what I mean?"

"I do and I don't. What I think you're telling me is that if you tell me about your relationship with Mr. Rafferty, you might end up in the witness chair at a trial. And that for some reason you don't want that to happen. Am I right?"

For a long moment Stolnitz said nothing.

"It's a long story," he finally said, "and it doesn't have anything to do with Rafferty. There's no reason why it would matter to you. It's just that when I agreed to go up to the racetrack with Rafferty, I had no idea what I was getting into. I mean, who would have expected him to get himself murdered?"

"From what you've been telling me," Carol said, "it sounds as if Mr. Rafferty singled you out as a confidant. It doesn't appear that any other of the Random Harvest employees were close to him. Can you think of any reason why he might have chosen to confide in you?"

"Not that I can think of."

"It strikes me that in some way that was apparent to him you were kindred spirits. In spite of the fact that he was working at a menial job at the winery, he was obviously a well-educated man, even an intellectual. What he was doing was almost certainly not what he had been doing all his adult life. At least that's the way I see it."

Carol chose not to divulge the fact that she already knew that Brendan Rafferty had been a Catholic priest.

"And what did he see in you?" she continued. "I think he saw someone who, like himself, was a square peg in a round hole. Excuse the bad analogy, but you don't look like or sound like a man who's likely to be found working in a low-paying job watching wine ferment. Mr. Rafferty was a lonely man—everyone says so. But unless he was a total social misfit, he must have wanted *someone* he could talk to. Then he meets you."

Carol left it at that, waiting for Stolnitz to say something. She was sure she was on the right track. Hadn't he said that Rafferty was introspective? Hadn't he called him a recluse? Hadn't he said that it was a reasonable inference that Rafferty had gambling debts? Introspective, recluse, inference—not words that most people employ in a brief conversation. She was reasonably certain that Bernie Stolnitz had, at some time in the past, had a very different career. Had he been a lawyer? An educator? Had he been a corporate executive? Whatever it had been, and Carol knew she was simply guessing, Stolnitz did not wish to talk about it.

"Sorry, Sheriff," Stolnitz said. "I don't presume to know why he latched on to me. In retrospect, I wish he hadn't."

"Let's go back to the trip you took with him to the racetrack. Farmington, I think you said. I'd like to hear about it. Why don't you tell me everything you can remember about that night. It was a night, wasn't it?"

"Yes," he began, reluctantly, "it was a couple of weeks ago. I don't remember the exact day. We left in his car, right after work. Nothing much happened. He played the slots for awhile. Didn't bet on any of the races, but I thought he was interested. Asked a bunch of questions about how it worked, if I had any ideas about picking winners, that kind of thing. It may have been my imagination, but I thought he seemed nervous. It was like he was on a high all evening long."

"Did he win or lose at the machines?"

"He lost a little. Not much. I kept telling him to be careful, that the odds were against him."

"You didn't play yourself?" Carol asked.

"No," Stolnitz said, "I've been burned, including right there at Farmington. I was worried about Rafferty, though. You probably don't go to the tracks or the casinos, being in law enforcement. But I've seen a lot of guys, they get that almost feverish look about them. They lose a bit, then think they can make it up the next time. Law of averages, you know. But when it comes to gambling, there's no law of averages at work. You're as likely to lose every time as you are to lose one, win one."

"So Rafferty heeded your advice and left the place in fairly good shape?" Carol asked.

"Right. He might have stayed longer, lost more, I don't know. But something happened around nine o'clock, and he suddenly wanted to get out of there."

"Something happened? What was it?"

"I don't know. One minute he was watching the ponies, and then he came over to me and said 'let's go.'"

"How did he act? Matter of fact? Anxious?"

"Anxious. Like I said, he was nervous all evening, always looking around, as if he might see a disapproving wife behind him."

"Did he say anything about seeing someone, someone he didn't want to see him?"

"No, he didn't. I asked him the same question. He tried to pretend it was nothing. He was just tired. Time to go. I didn't believe him, but that's what he said."

"Forget what or whom *he* might have seen," Carol said. "Did *you* see anyone who looked suspicious? Anyone who'd have stood out in a crowd?"

"It's funny, but I was thinking the same thing as we drove back. There weren't that many people around, and none of them looked unusual. One guy looked as if he weighed 300 pounds, but that's not unusual these days, what with all the obesity. Another guy was wearing a gaudy red vest. Don't see many of those any more, but I doubt Rafferty would be put off by someone's sartorial style. So no, I don't think he wanted to leave because of anyone he saw. It must have been something on his mind. Maybe he was starting to worry about what he was doing, putting his money at risk."

Perhaps, thought Carol, but I don't think so. The problem, most likely, was the red vest. Or rather the man who was wearing it. She was thinking about Rafferty's diary, and the reference to someone in a red vest. It wasn't clear, but that person was probably the one Rafferty had referred to as s. What is more, the fact that a red vest had been seen at a racetrack with slots strongly suggested that Rafferty had had a gambling den in mind when he penned several of the entries in his notebook. She had already considered that possibility, taking into account his money worries and his agonizing over whether it was sinful to be visiting the place he called ts.

She would need to give the matter considerably more thought. Which meant she would have to reread the diary, very carefully, with this new information in mind. And that she or Bridges would have to take a trip to the Finger Lakes Race Track. And to ts, if she could figure out what the initials stood for.

Carol exhausted her list of questions and walked back to the winery with Stolnitz. He again expressed his concern that he may have violated his promise of confidentiality to Brendan Rafferty. She assured him that she would say nothing to anyone else at the winery, but reminded him that if it became necessary in a murder trial to call him as a witness, she would have no choice. Nor would he.

There were other people she wished to speak with, and first among them was Doug Francis, the man in charge of hiring for Random Harvest. He had admitted to seeking no references when he hired Rafferty, so he had known nothing about the man's background. She wondered if he had been similarly casual when he took on Bernie Stolnitz. She had become convinced that, like the ex-priest, Stolnitz was also hiding something in his past. It was doubtful that it had any bearing on her case, but what did she know. It was possible that Stolnitz had not told her the whole truth about the trip to the racetrack. Perhaps his whole story had been a lie. But why would he have lied, or shaded the truth? Because he had had something to do with Rafferty's death?

Carol tried to put that improbable thought out of her mind. She would, however, talk with Doug Francis.

CHAPTER 23

The efficient way to proceed was to stop by Francis's office right away and then head down to Southport for lunch. Carol decided to be inefficient. She had an urge to visit the pole on which Brendan Rafferty had been suspended, and as she thought about it she decided that she'd like to eat her lunch down in the vineyard. Communing with nature, contemplating the final resting place of the scarecrow, postponing another sterile conversation with Random Harvest's personnel manager—whatever the reason for her decision, and it had something to do with all of those things, she got into her car and headed for Southport. Her destination was a cute little sandwich shop, struggling to survive the economic downturn by offering a variety of excellent paninis to locals and tourists throughout a lunch hour which began around ten and ran until customers stopped coming in, anytime between two and four. It was now close to twelve, and Carol, for the sake of the paninis and the friendly proprietor, hoped that the place would be crowded.

It was, and it was not until 1:10 in the afternoon that she finally parked the car on the shoulder above the ice grape vineyard and walked down to where she had first encountered the recently deceased Brendan Rafferty. It had warmed up a bit since the cold snap that Kevin had brought with him from the city. Carol found a spot some dozen yards from the now-empty pole. She took off her jacket, folded it to sit on, and took the panini and a ginger ale out of their sack.

She thought about her decision to eat her lunch at a distance from the pole. She was not superstitious. Nor did she find the fact that a dead man had been on that pole less than a week before unsettling. But she was somehow more comfortable where she was. The pole was visible from where she sat, still between five and six feet of rough-hewn wood, its smaller crosspiece slightly askew, as if a strong wind had tilted it.

There was no new information to be gleaned from an examination of Rafferty's final resting place. Carol turned her attention to a sky in which altocumulus clouds stretched almost from horizon to horizon. It was a beautiful sight, almost enough to make her forget the terrible fate of the ex-priest and the problems which she knew lay ahead in her search for his killer. Kevin would have loved it. She doubted that the sight lines were nearly as good in the steel and concrete canyons where he lived. Carol let her mind wander, and by the time she got around to the panini, it was getting cold.

Francis was waiting for her when she got back to the winery. It was a conversation she didn't look forward to. She was sure of what he would say, and it would leave her with no more information than she already had plus an even less good impression of the man who did the hiring for Random Harvest.

Carol got right to the point.

"I'm here to ask you about one of your employees, Bernie Stolnitz. Do you remember him?"

"Sure. He's not exactly your typical hire in a place like this. Smart as a whip. A bit of a smart-ass, too. I always have the feeling he finds most of his co-workers amusing. Why—do you think he had something to do with Mr. Rafferty's death?"

"No, I don't, and that's not why I asked. I was wondering about where he came from. Why do you suppose he came looking for a job here?"

"I couldn't say. He walked in one day, maybe six months ago, said he'd like to get to know the business. Told me he was willing to start at the bottom. Which he did."

"So, like Rafferty, you didn't ask for references? Didn't ask him what his background was?"

Francis was not happy to be on the receiving end once again of the sheriff's criticism of his interview methods.

"I haven't heard anyone complain about how he does his job, Sheriff. Maybe he really is learning the business. He's smart enough, heaven knows."

"It strikes me that you've taken on two men recently who aren't the kind of employees you'd normally find doing what they've been doing for Random Harvest Vineyards. One of them turns out to have been a Catholic priest. Don't you wonder who Bernie Stolnitz really is? Or was?"

"Well, he's surely no priest," Francis said, apparently referring to the fact that he was probably Jewish.

"No, I suppose you're right about that." Carol wanted to ask if it had occurred to him that Stolnitz might have been in trouble with the law. That he might even have served time. But it was only a suspicion. She had no idea whether it was true, and mentioning it to Francis would be professionally improper, not to mention unfair to Stolnitz. She decided to let it go.

On her way out of the winery she ran into Parker Jameson, Random Harvest's accountant. Or rather Jameson ran into her. He was hurrying through the entrance foyer, a sheaf of papers in his hand, looking agitated and paying no attention to others around him. The collision was not serious, but it served to spin the bookkeeper halfway around.

He found himself staring at the sheriff, looking momentarily confused.

"I'm sorry. I wasn't watching where I was going," he said, and almost immediately his eyes widened and he started to stutter. "You're the sheriff! I—I—oh, my God, I—it's going to be all right. I have to talk with Drake—there's no need—can I see you later? Please, we mustn't—look, I have to see Drake."

Parker Jameson seemed completely unhinged. It was obvious that he was deeply disturbed about something, but it was not at all obvious what that something was. He went stumbling off in the direction of the owner's office, leaving Carol to wonder just what new problem had materialized at Random Harvest Vineyards.

It was not until she was halfway back to her office in Cumberland that it occurred to Carol that her encounter with Parker Jameson might have more significance than she had given it at the time. It was not just that he was apologetic for having bumped into her, or that he seemed to be in a state of heightened anxiety. What seemed most interesting on reflection was the fact that he had completely lost his composure when he realized that he had come face to face with the sheriff. Jameson had been afraid. He had been overcome by fear that her presence at the winery had something to do with him and whatever it was that was on his mind at that moment.

Carol had no idea what had happened, much less whether it had anything to do with the Rafferty case. But she was determined to find out.

CHAPTER 24

Much as she had wanted to be quizzing more of the Random Harvest employees about Brendan Rafferty, Carol had gone back to her office that afternoon because she was feeling guilty about having neglected other matters awaiting the attention of the Cumberland County Sheriff's Department. The scarecrow in the vineyard had preempted much of her time and that of key members of her team, but if she were completely honest with herself she would have to lay some of the blame on Kevin's presence over the long weekend. They had enjoyed themselves, and she had no regrets on that score. It was time, however, to clear off her desk and make sure that there were no unpleasant surprises waiting for her in her in-basket.

What she discovered were two problems, neither of which seemed likely to replace the Rafferty case as priority number one, but both of which held the promise of trouble. The first involved a property-line dispute in which one of the parties had started building on what the other considered his land. This was not an issue which fell within her jurisdiction, but both owners were hotheaded and she knew that she might have to intervene. The second was the result of a report by a young high school student named Kemper that he had seen somebody dumping a body out of a boat somewhere out in the lake south of West Branch. The boy's report had been contradicted by his mother, who apologized, claiming that her son was always making things up.

Carol did the only thing she could do about the property matter, referring it to the proper department while knowing full well that she had not heard the end of it. She decided to turn the Kemper boy's story over to Bill Parsons, her colleague who spent most of his time patrolling Crooked Lake's waters. It was while she was waiting for Parsons' call back, though, that she realized from the date and hour on Ms. Frank's message that the boy's report had come in the day Rafferty's body had been discovered.

She was angry with herself that nothing had been done about the matter for the better part of a week. Terrible public relations, she thought, even if the matter was inconsequential.

Anxious to restore the credibility of her office, Carol had Ms. Franks call the Kemper home.

"Hi." It was a male voice, out of breath.

"Hello, this is Sheriff Kelleher. I'm trying to reach Mr. Kemper."

"Me or my dad?"

"That depends. Are you the one who called my office last week?"

"That's me. I'm Donnie. Don, Junior, to my dad."

"Then you're the one I want to talk to. In the first place, I want to apologize for being so slow to get back in touch with you. There's really no excuse, but we've been unusually busy these last few days. I'd like you to tell me more about what you reported. Okay?"

"Sure, Sheriff, but can you wait until I get rid of my backpack? I just got off the school bus."

Carol waited while the young man caught his breath and unloaded what she imagined to be the typical overstuffed backpack that kids carried these days.

"I'm here," he announced. "I know my mom told you to pay no attention to me. But she's wrong. I saw what I saw."

"Let's go over it one step at a time, Mr. Kemper. You said you saw a boat with a man in it, and that he was putting what you thought was a body overboard. That was last Tuesday morning. What time was it?"

"Early. The school bus comes by at an awful hour, like 6:45. It was before that, at least half an hour before. I'd gone out to get some wood for the fireplace. I saw this boat and what the man was doing. I called your office after school because it seemed kinda strange."

"If you saw what you say you saw, it would indeed have been strange," Carol said. "But you'll have to admit it seems pretty unlikely. I mean people aren't in the habit of dumping other people in the lake. Except when they're horsing around, and I don't suppose anyone was horsing around that early in the morning on a chilly October day. How far out in the lake was the boat?"

"Oh, close to half of the way across. Far out, anyway. But it was a body that went in the water, and it wasn't any horsing around."

"What makes you think it was a body? After all, at that kind of distance wouldn't it be hard to tell?"

"That's what my parents said when I told them. It wasn't wearing a bathing suit. It was kinda dark, like it was wearing black or dark clothes. You could see it was a body."

"And what about the man who was doing this, the other man in the boat?"

"The same. I mean dark clothes, just like the one he shoved overboard."

"Do you know what kind of boat it was?" Carol asked.

"It looked about the size of our Four Winns, but I can't be sure what make. It was pretty early, and the light wasn't too good."

"I'm sure it wasn't. That's why I'm raising these questions. If it had been later in the morning, you could have been more certain. But at six something?"

"But I saw it, just like I'm saying." Donnie Kemper was beginning to sound agitated.

"I'm interested in what you believe you saw," Carol assured him. "I wouldn't be calling you if I wasn't concerned. Tell me, what happened to the body? Did it sink? Float? Did the other man do anything to it after he put it into the water?"

"It sank. At least I think it must have. The man poked at it with a paddle, and I didn't see it after the boat moved away."

Carol had viewed her call to the Kemper residence as a courtesy. She wanted it known that the sheriff's office took the complaints and reports of county residents seriously. She had been sure, however, that the young man was mistaken. People simply don't go around dumping bodies into the lake. But now she was not quite so sure. What if Donnie Kemper had seen someone disposing, not of a body, but of a scarecrow? The scarecrow that had to come down off its cross to make room for Brendan Rafferty. The scarecrow that had mysteriously vanished, defying the best efforts of her men to find it. It was unlikely, but it was possible.

"I don't know where you live, Mr. Kemper. Where this took place. I assume you live on the lake. What's your address?"

"You know that place south of West Branch where they've recently built a bunch of cottages across the West Lake Road from the lake? About two miles down from the Shoreline Marina? We're number 338."

"Mr. Kemper, I'd like to drive over to your place and let you tell me this again while I'm where you were when you saw it happen. Are you going to be at home, say, for the next forty-five minutes?"

"Sure," he said, obviously pleased that his report was important enough that the sheriff would make the trip to his house. "I was going over to Jimmy's, but that can wait."

"Good. I'm leaving now."

The Kemper home was not hard to find. It was a substantial but hardly elegant house on a wedge of land about four miles south of West Branch. The door to a garage for two cars was open, but no cars were in evidence. A small porch leading into what was presumably a mudroom contained a neat lineup of five pairs of shoes.

Carol walked around to the lakeside of the house. The beach was small, not more than fifty feet in width. The dock looked old, as did the Four Winns powerboat in the boat hoist on its north side. The stack of wood from which Donnie Kemper was collecting logs for the fireplace when he spotted the boat and its strange cargo was small but every bit as neat as the row of shoes on the porch.

The young man had seen the sheriff pull in, and came out to meet her on the beach.

Carol watched him as he came down the steps. Tall enough to play basketball for his high school, but skinny and unlikely to be strong enough to control the backboards for his team. Still in the process of cultivating his first real sideburns. Apparently comfortable in the chill autumn air wearing a U2 T-shirt.

She extended him her hand, and suggested that they go to wherever it was that he had been while watching the boat that morning.

"I was over by the woodpile when I saw it, but I went down to the beach to get a better look." He demonstrated, leading her to a place near the dock.

"And it was pretty much straight out from here?" she asked.

"Right. Just about there." Kemper pointed in the direction of the bluff, less than a mile away across the lake.

"Did you see where it came from and where it went after dumping the body?"

"The man was already pushing the body overboard when I first saw the boat. Afterwards, he headed down lake, but sort of toward shore."

"Let's assume he was heading back to his cottage. Do you think you can estimate where he would have come ashore?"

"I'm not sure, but it was definitely on this side of the lake, and not all that far below here. Maybe a quarter of a mile, considering the way he was going."

"Did anything else about what you saw seem strange?"

"Only that he didn't start the engine. He was using a paddle."

Carol was surprised. If the man in the boat was paddling, it meant one of two things. He couldn't start his engine, or he wanted to make as little noise as possible.

"Did you ever hear the boat? I mean were you aware of the motor at any time while you were outside?"

"No, I guess I didn't."

Donnie Kemper looked thoughtful, as if he were trying to figure out what the man in the boat was up to. Carol was thinking about the same thing. What if what Kemper had seen being dumped out of that boat was indeed the scarecrow? And what if the man driving the boat not only lived somewhere near the Kempers on the west branch of Crooked Lake but also worked at Random Harvest Vineyards? She would have to check the addresses of all of the winery's employees.

CHAPTER 25

It was late in the day when she left the Kempers' house, but she wanted to make a brief stop at the winery to pay her respects to Earl Drake. He was entitled to an update on her investigation, and she was interested in whether he had given any further thought to the violent death of one of his employees.

Drake's secretary said that he was in a conference. The query as to when he might be free elicited an answer which decided her to stick around for awhile.

"Have things settled down here?" she asked the secretary in an effort to make small talk.

The secretary, whose nameplate identified her as Melanie Thurston, looked slightly flustered. Perhaps she had been given instructions not to talk about the recent murder in the Random Harvest vineyard. Carol persevered.

"What I mean, is everyone still talking about Mr. Rafferty's death, or is the winery more or less back to normal?"

Ms. Thurston reached for the phone on her desk, but it hadn't rung, so she put her hand back in her lap and mumbled something which Carol did not understand. Apparently aware that she was looking foolish, she cleared her throat and finally answered the question. After a fashion.

"It's been a bad day, ma'am. Probably better to call it a bad week. I think you should talk to Mr. Drake."

"Yes, I'll be doing that. In just a couple of minutes, you said. I'm sure Mr. Drake will bring me up to speed on how things are going here at the winery. And I know he'll want to hear from me as well."

Something's happened here, Carol thought. Something other than the old news of the scarecrow in the vineyard. She'd hear about it soon enough, assuming that Drake's appointment ended as soon as Ms. Thurston said it would.

Less than a minute later Parker Jameson came out of Drake's office. The man looked miserable. When he saw the sheriff, he stopped dead in his tracks, obviously surprised to see her. But unlike their collision in the foyer earlier in the day, his face did not register panic.

"Nice to see you, Sheriff," he said and continued on out the door.

"Mr. Drake will see you now," his secretary said, looking relieved that she wouldn't have to field any more of the sheriff's questions.

The owner of Random Harvest Vineyards was not in a good mood.

"I don't mind telling you," he said as Carol took a seat, "I'll be a candidate for a heart attack if this keeps up. First that damned scarecrow murder, now this problem with the books. What did I do to deserve this?"

This was the first Carol had heard about the winery's books.

"I'm sorry, but I don't know anything about a problem with your books. May I ask what happened?"

"Nearly thirty thousand dollars gone missing, Sheriff," Drake said. "*Thirty thousand dollars!* It doesn't have anything to do with that murder you're investigating, not that that makes it any easier to cope with. Parker says the books don't add up. We're out thirty thousand dollars. Just like that!"

Eric Drake snapped his fingers as he said it.

"I don't understand," Carol said. She was more interested in where the money had gone than she was sorry for the winery's owner. Probably the reflex of a law enforcement officer.

"Neither do I," Drake said. "Parker's been in here three times today, going over everything we can think of. By the way, he told me he thought you were at the winery to arrest him. Only laugh I've had all day. Parker's a good friend, has been for years. But he's disorganized. I used to think it was only kids who had that—what do they call it—attention deficit disorder? Anyway, Parker's got a middle-age version of it. His office looks like a rat's nest. Not to mention that he's not computer savvy. He uses one, but he refuses to rely on it. What matters to him are those files he keeps, all in his own meticulous handwriting."

"If he's so inefficient that he's cost you thousands of dollars, your friendship must be, shall we say, strained."

"Well, it is. I chewed him out just now. It wasn't pleasant. But he's sure there's an answer, like some stuff got misfiled, or some checks were never deposited. But where the hell are they? We're a small company, Sheriff. We're talking about pretty big money."

"You're probably going to need to hire some outside firm to go over your books."

"Why do you say that? Do you think Jameson's screwing me? You're wrong, dead wrong."

"Mr. Drake, I'm here only because a murder has been committed on your property and the murdered man was one of your employees. I don't propose to get involved in your financial problems. Unless, that is, the disappearance of all that money has something to do with the murder. And offhand I can't think of a reason why it would. I mentioned bringing in an auditor to go over the books because it's what I would do. But I don't know Mr. Jameson, and I'm happy to take your word that he would never do something like this to you."

"So what do you think could have happened to the money?"

"I haven't had any experience with cases like this, so I'm in no position to speculate. On the other hand, I have never put much stock in coincidences. And now we have one: an employee of yours is murdered and then the very next week you discover that you're out a lot of money. That's sort of like lightning striking twice in the same place, don't you think?"

Drake ran his hand across his chin, thinking about what the sheriff had said.

"Maybe someone is defrauding Random Harvest," he said. But almost as quickly, he brushed the thought aside. "No, that can't be. We're a team here. My handpicked people."

"Mr. Rafferty wasn't one of your handpicked people, Mr. Drake."

"Oh, that," he said, dismissively. "I'm talking about the people who would have access to the company's finances—the books, the files, the bank accounts."

"You mean who have access to Mr. Jameson's office."

"Right."

"Who are these people? Who beside Mr. Jameson would have access to his office and hence to everything in there—to everything in what you call Mr. Jameson's rat's nest?"

"That's easy. It's a short list. I do. So does Grabner—he's head of marketing—and Francis. I think you met him. He handles personnel."

"That makes four keys," Carol said, doing the simple arithmetic. "How about a custodian? What about spare keys?"

"Oh, sure. There would be a couple of others. Ask Ms. Thurston when you leave. She'll show you where they're kept."

"I'm afraid that you really do have a problem, Mr. Drake. First you tell me that Mr. Jameson is afflicted with attention deficit disorder, and now you're saying that there may be as many as six or more keys to the office where the company's books are kept."

"Good God, Sheriff. You're implying that one of my people is fixing the books. If not Jameson, somebody else. We're tight here. Like family. I don't want to have to start suspecting my friends."

"I don't blame you. But you tell me you're out close to thirty thousand dollars, and it's going to take quite a few cases of wine to make up the loss. I'd still hire an auditor."

"I'll think about it, but Parker will probably remember something he's forgotten. Anyway, you didn't come in here to talk about money, did you? How's the investigation going?"

Carol was grateful that Drake's new problem had temporarily supplanted Rafferty's murder as his number-one worry.

"We're making progress. I mean we've been learning things about Mr. Rafferty which I think will lead us to his killer. In time, of course. If you're asking if I have a suspect, the answer is no. But I feel optimistic, and considering that my friends think of me as a pessimist, that's a good sign."

Drake didn't look as if he found this progress report particularly reassuring.

"You're learning things about the dead man? How's that help?"

"I think it's going to tell us why he was working for you, and who might have had a reason to kill him. Did you know that he used to be a Catholic priest?"

"A priest?" If she had said he had been a former quarterback for the Buffalo Bills, Drake could not have looked more surprised.

"Yes, a priest. I'll keep you apprised of any new developments."

When Carol left the winery, she was mulling over the day's two new developments. Random Harvest had in all likelihood been victimized by someone who had made off with quite a bit of money. And a young man living on the West Lake Road was convinced that a body had been dumped into Crooked Lake early on the morning of the day when Brendan Rafferty had been found, impersonating a scarecrow in a Random Harvest vineyard. Were either of these developments related to Rafferty's murder? It seemed unlikely, but Carol knew that she would be unable to ignore them. At least not until a simple explanation of the missing money surfaced and the Kemper boy changed his story.

CHAPTER 26

The sheriff steered the car onto the shoulder of the road next to the culvert which carried the wash from the small ravine under the road and down to the lake. The ravine ran between two cottages only a short distance down the lake from the Kemper home. Carol worked her way down the embankment to the ravine and followed it down to the shoreline. It had been a relatively dry fall, and the water in the ravine was but a trickle. She could see the Kempers' dock, a ghostly arm reaching out into the lake. The sky above the bluff had just begun to change from a dull, lifeless dark gray to a pre-sunrise milky blue. It was much too early for sunrise, but dawn was breaking.

Carol had chosen not to set up vigil on the Kemper beach. The spot on which she was standing was close enough. She looked at her watch. 5:55. According to the plan they had made the previous evening, Bill Parsons would make his appearance at the agreed location offshore at five after six and hold his position there for about five minutes. She had ten minutes to kill.

The sheriff's department's patrol boat was somewhat larger than the boat Donnie Kemper had described, but the difference in size was not so great as to make her experiment pointless. All she was trying to establish was whether it would have been possible for Kemper to see what he claimed to have seen at the time he claimed to have seen it. She had felt guilty asking her colleague to start his day at such an early hour, but Parsons was an easygoing veteran of the force. And someone she had asked little of during her tenure as sheriff.

It was another chilly morning. Some would have called it cold. Carol would have been more comfortable had she been able to keep moving, but to do so while watching for Parsons would have necessitated leaving the ravine and going onto someone's property. Inasmuch as she didn't want to have her vigil interrupted by a chance encounter with one of the Kempers' neighbors, she zipped her jacket all the way to the collar and stomped her feet to keep warm.

Right on schedule, the patrol boat appeared from the direction of West Branch. Carol was not sure whether it was a third of the way across the lake, but she had confidence in Parsons' judgment. He cut the engine and turned the boat in a tight circle as it slowed down and came to a stop roughly opposite the mouth of the ravine. They had agreed that he shouldn't wave in recognition, but she saw him and was certain that he had seen her. If Donnie Kemper was once again performing his morning chore of bringing in a few logs, he, too, would see and be seen by the boat's operator. The important question was how clearly and unmistakably an observer on the beach could see what that man was doing.

It was not dark, but neither was it very light. Daylight Saving Time would end in less than a week, after which the mornings would be lighter at this hour for awhile. But young Kemper had seen the boat on a day much like this one, much as Carol was seeing the patrol boat at that moment.

As she watched, Bill Parsons did as they agreed he would do. He lifted something out of the well of the boat and brought it over the side. He didn't let it go or try to prod it with a paddle, but otherwise he did his best to replicate what Kemper said he had seen the previous week. All of this took no more than half a minute, after which he quickly pulled whatever he had pretended to toss overboard back into the boat.

Carol had no idea what it was that Parsons had heaved overboard. She had explained to him what Kemper had said about it, but insisted that he not tell her what he would use for the "body." Having observed the pantomime closely, she still had no idea what the large dark object was. It could have been a body. But it could also have been a large sack of garbage, a bundle of wood, a partially inflated beach toy. Of course young Kemper probably had keener vision than she did; after all, he was close to twenty years her junior. But she doubted that his eyesight was that much better than hers.

To her surprise, Carol felt disappointed. She had been skeptical of the boy's story, but now that she had seen with her own eyes how hard it would be to identify a body in that light at that distance, she experienced a letdown. Had she really hoped that he had witnessed the deep-sixing of the scarecrow? Had she wanted to believe that out there, near the north end of the west arm of Crooked Lake, a straw man, weighted down by rocks, now rested at the bottom of at least a hundred feet of water?

Bill Parsons began his run back to West Branch. Carol began her trek back up the ravine to her car. She would still want to see the addresses of all the people associated with Random Harvest Vineyards. If none of them lived anywhere nearby, she would tuck Donnie Kemper's story into her file of leads that had turned out to be dead ends. If any of them did live nearby, she would, of course, keep an open mind. Or try to.

On the way back to Cumberland, she found herself wondering what it was that Bill had decided to use as the "body." She'd know before the day was over. But she also lapsed into self criticism. Why on earth, she thought, did I ever think that the killer might have chosen to bury the scarecrow in the lake? It was just about the last place any rational person would have considered. He could have burned it. He could have scattered the straw to the four winds and given the clothes to Goodwill. He could simply have left it in the vineyard, or if that was, for some strange reason, impossible, he could have dumped it in any of dozens of backwoods places where it was unlikely to have been found for months, if at all.

No, she decided, I haven't been thinking straight. I should have been polite when Kemper told me his story, but it is his mother I should have believed.

———

It had been Friday that she had learned that Brendan Rafferty had been a priest at St. Anthony's church in East Moncton, Massachusetts. Now it was Tuesday, four days later, and she had still not notified anyone that he was dead. Not his former church. Not his mother or his brother, both of whom had looked so proud of him in the picture taken at his ordination. The picture had not been dated, so she had no idea when he had entered the priesthood. It was possible that his mother was deceased, perhaps his brother as well. But she had not yet made any attempt to track down these next of kin, and that was uncharacteristically thoughtless of her. It was also possible that either the mother or the brother, if they were alive, could provide her with critical information that would facilitate her search for Rafferty's killer.

Carol examined her reasons for not immediately contacting the family. And the church. When she called St. Anthony's she had been as guilty of withholding information as the church had been. They had not admitted that Father Rafferty had abandoned his post; she had not admitted that he was dead. Why had she not said so? Was it because the person she had spoken with had not been honest with her? She had the impression that something was not quite right, and that she should try to find out what that something was before reporting Rafferty's death. But to fail to notify the family was unconscionable. Moreover, the priest's mother or brother might have information which could help her investigation. Had he been in touch with them since leaving St. Anthony's? Had he told them things which he had not recorded in his diary? Did they know who gf was? Or s? Or jc?

She first had to find them. The person to do it was Officer Byrnes. He was the most computer savvy member of her team, and she was reasonably certain that he'd be able to turn the two names on the photo into people with addresses and phone numbers. She put him to work, and by shortly after noon he had put a note on her desk with the information that Martha Rafferty was living in Portsmouth, New Hampshire, and Sean Rafferty in Waltham, Massachusetts. Addresses and phone numbers were included. Attached in addition were the names of possible persons of interest in East Moncton. Byrnes had been thorough. It's amazing, she thought, the time and trouble the Internet saves us. Things were more complicated back when my father had been the sheriff.

Carol decided she would call Sean first. She had no idea how close the brothers had been, but he might be easier to talk with than the mother. Unfortunately, he wasn't home, and the message on the answering machine said simply to call back. She decided to try him again in the evening.

Before she had a chance to do so, Kevin called, catching her in the middle of a Hamburger Helper dinner. She didn't care if her meal got cold. It was much more satisfying to hear his voice, telling her what he had been doing and that he loved her and couldn't wait to get back to the lake.

They talked about many things, including Donnie Kemper's dubious tale and the missing money at Random Harvest. But most of the conversation was devoted to Kevin's meeting with

Professor Martin and his proposal to go up to East Moncton over the upcoming weekend.

Much as she welcomed the offer of help, Carol was uneasy about the possible consequences of Kevin taking over what might be the most sensitive part of her investigation on his own. She knew that she wouldn't be able to go with him, but she had no intention of letting him freelance.

"I'll let you do this for me on one condition," she said.

"Okay. What's the condition?"

"That you do it on my terms. Understood?"

Kevin had no intention of doing otherwise, but he enjoyed the opportunity to go through the motions of argument. They bantered good-naturedly for a minute or two, then focused on just what he would do when he visited St. Anthony's, chatted with its parishioners, and otherwise took stock of the situation in East Moncton. With any luck he would ferret out the reason the priest had left the church so precipitously.

"What is it you propose to do?" Carol asked. "Assuming I give you a green light."

"I thought I'd go by the church on Saturday, pretend I used to know Rafferty, was just hoping to say hello. Whatever they tell me, I'd show up for mass on Sunday and talk to people. I'd use the same line—an old friend, sorry to hear he's no longer their priest. Hopefully somebody would have something interesting to say."

"You'd attend mass? Come on, you wouldn't know what to do."

"You underestimate me, Carol. Back in college I sat through an entire service at Notre Dame during a junior year abroad in Paris."

"That doesn't count, and you know it. You were a tourist, not a practicing Catholic. Just don't do something stupid at St. Anthony's. More important, don't say anything to anybody about Rafferty being dead. That could affect the way his old parishioners talk about him, and I want to hear the candid gossip."

"I'd be surprised if there isn't talk about Rafferty being a pedophile. He doesn't show up in Professor Martin's study, but I think he believes that that's a likely reason for his disappearance from St. Anthony's."

"If that's the gossip, it's important to know who the victim was. Or victims. I'm e-mailing you a list of the people Byrnes has identified who might be gf. See if you can link any of them to St. Anthony's. I don't have to tell you to be discrete. We can't afford to start any rumors."

For the better part of half an hour Carol and Kevin rehearsed what Kevin would do when he visited East Moncton. The sheriff was clearly anxious about how it would go. So was Kevin, although he kept reassuring her that all would be well.

"Give me a call after you talk with the people at the church. There's a new priest. Byrnes reports that his name is Merton. I don't know how large the parish is. There will be a rectory, and somebody will be there—a housekeeper in all likelihood. I'd rather my office speaks to the diocese. Same goes for the local police, in case the church ever reported Rafferty's disappearance to them. You're just keeping your ears open, trying to get a handle on what people are thinking about our man and what might have happened to him."

About halfway through their conversation it occurred to Carol that Kevin's trip to Massachusetts would mean three consecutive weekends away from the city and his academic responsibilities.

"Does this mean that you won't be able to make it back to the lake a week from Thursday?" she asked.

"Not to worry. I've already penciled you in for every other weekend between now and Christmas. I'm not going to let anything mess that up."

From there it was an easy segue into more personal matters. When Carol put the phone down at 7:50, her supper was stone cold but she was in a very good mood. She hoped that the conversation she expected to be having with Brendan Rafferty's brother wouldn't spoil that mood.

CHAPTER 27

It was not something the sheriff had had to do very often, but notifying the family that a loved one had been killed was one of the things she liked least about her job. Her call to Sean Rafferty was an unpleasant duty, made only slightly more tolerable because there was a possibility that she might learn more about Sean's brother's past life.

The person who answered at the Waltham address had a bad cold. Carol involuntarily turned away from the phone as Sean coughed his way through their exchange of hellos.

"Mr. Rafferty," she said after announcing herself as the sheriff of Cumberland County in New York State, "I believe that you are the brother of Father Brendan Rafferty. Is that correct?"

More coughing, followed by an apology for it.

"Yes, Brendan's my brother. What is this about?"

Carol came straight to the point.

"I'm afraid that I have bad news for you. Your brother is dead. I'm calling to pass along this unhappy news, and because I need very much to talk with you about your brother."

"What happened?" No expression of shock, no words saying that he couldn't believe what he was hearing. Just the predictable question: how?

"I very much wish we were sitting down someplace together, Mr. Rafferty. This is hard over the phone, very hard. Your brother was murdered. Shot. I'm sure he died instantly, if that is any consolation. I am the sheriff responsible for finding the person who did this. I hope that you feel up to talking with me, letting me ask you a few questions."

Sean Rafferty repeated his question.

"What happened, Sheriff?"

Carol wasn't about to tell him about the scarecrow in the vineyard. She'd finesse the details and move on to her questions.

"There's a lot we don't know. He was killed, as I said, by a gunshot, and it was not an accident. He was shot at point-blank range. His body was found at a winery where he was working. Random Harvest. It's located above Crooked Lake in the wine country of upstate New York. Did you know that he was working there?"

"I was afraid that something like this would happen," he said, then coughed again.

"Why is that?" Carol asked. "Had he been in touch with you recently?"

"Excuse me, please. I'd like to take this upstairs. I'm in the kitchen at the moment, and I'd rather be in the bedroom."

Carol waited while Sean Rafferty moved to another room, possibly to find a more comfortable chair. Perhaps to consult a calendar?

"Hello, Sheriff," he said, resuming the conversation. "You want to know why I expected news like this. May I start at the beginning?"

"I wish you would. Please take your time."

Carol was encouraged. It appeared that Rafferty had something to tell her, something that might shed light on his brother's death.

"I don't know how you located me, but I gather that you already know that my brother was a Catholic priest. You referred to him as Father Rafferty. You probably know that he left his parish over a year ago. Is that right?"

"I don't know exactly when he left, but I do know that something happened which prompted him to leave not only St. Anthony's in East Moncton but also his vocation as a priest. After all, when he was killed he was working at a blue-collar job in a winery. Why he was doing that, I don't know. He had been at this winery for several months, and I think he may have held other jobs after leaving the church and before coming to Crooked Lake. It sounds to me as if you and he had maintained contact after he left St. Anthony's. Is that right?"

"Yes," Sean said. "We hadn't been that close. I couldn't understand why he wanted to cut himself off from the world, go into the priesthood. But it was his choice, and he seemed to be happy. We used to see each other once in awhile, mostly at the Christmas and Easter seasons. Anyhow, a little over a year ago, Mother called me to say that she'd gotten word that Brendan had vanished. I remember that that was the word she used. He apparently just up and left his church. Didn't say anything to the diocese. Not even to his housekeeper in the rectory. Mother almost went crazy. There hadn't been a note, a phone call, nothing. He just dropped out of sight. Someone in the diocesan office got in touch with Mother to see if she knew anything, but of course she didn't."

Carol listened, fascinated, as Sean supplied a few of the missing pieces in her jigsaw puzzle. But there was still the question of what had caused him to walk away from St. Anthony's so abruptly. She hoped he would tell her. Better not to interrupt.

"I don't recall just when it was that I heard from Brendan. It was back in the winter. He called one day, right out of the blue. How was I? How was Mother? I really lit into him, told him it was a terrible thing he'd done to us. Especially to her. And him a priest. He apologized, but he never explained himself. 'It was a personal thing,' he said. And he refused to tell me where he was or what he was doing, just that he was okay. I'm pretty sure he made that call from a pay phone. I was mad. It was obvious that he was worried that I'd say something to someone, which suggested that he'd be in trouble if I did. Anyway, when he hung up all I knew was that he was alive and maybe in some kind of trouble."

At this point Carol did interrupt.

"Are you sure that he didn't say anything that even hinted at where he was living?"

"I'm sure. He was very cautious. If I didn't know better, I'd have thought he figured his phone was bugged."

"I doubt it," Carol said. "He was probably calling from a pay phone, like you said."

"He called me again later. Two more times, the last one about two months ago, give or take a few days. I didn't keep a record of the dates. Anyhow, it was always the same. He never told me anything except that he was okay and not to worry. But I got the distinct impression that he was afraid of something. Or someone. Don't ask me why."

"I agree that he was afraid, and I think it was someone. Maybe even more than one someone. He left a diary which was just about as nonspecific as he was when he phoned you. And in the diary he sometimes sounded afraid. I guess he had good reason to be afraid. Did he call your mother, too?"

"Eventually. He didn't want to. He wanted me to pass along the word that he was all right. I think he thought she'd do something like go to the diocese and tell them he'd been in touch. It was clear he didn't want that to happen. I really gave him what for. Imagine, never talking to your own mother, never telling her you're alive, never letting her hear your voice. I must have gotten through, because she told me he called. But I'm sure he never told her any more than he told me."

It was now clear to Carol that she wasn't going to discover any more pieces to the puzzle that was Brendan Rafferty. Not from this conversation with his brother. But she had to ask one more question.

"Let me ask you to think back to the time before your brother left St. Anthony's. Did he ever talk about people he knew in East Moncton? People in his church? I mean specific people. How about somebody whose initials are gf?"

"Like I said, we weren't close. I don't ever remember him talking about people. Oh, I guess he said something about his housekeeper being a pretty good cook."

"Do you remember her name?"

"No. I'm sorry I can't be—" Sean paused in the middle of his apology for not being more helpful. "I just thought of something. Probably unimportant."

"Tell me anyway, Mr. Rafferty."

"There was a time, maybe a month before Brendan disappeared, when we had a brief conversation. He seemed dispirited, like he was discouraged by the human condition. In fact, I think that's exactly the way he put it. I even remember thinking that he might be regretting that he had entered the priesthood."

"Did he offer any reason why he was discouraged?" Carol asked.

"Yes, in fact he did. It seems that there had been a ruckus involving an abortion clinic, one of those demonstrations that turned violent. Some of his parishioners had been involved. I remember that he sounded disappointed—terribly sad, really. Not with the clinic, although he hated the idea of abortion, but with the demonstrators. People he knew, people who sat in his church. He felt very strongly that violence wasn't the answer."

"Did he mention any names?" Carol was not optimistic, and he didn't surprise her.

"No. I wouldn't have known them anyway. But I hadn't thought about that conversation in a long time. Do you suppose he was already contemplating leaving the church? Maybe he had lost confidence in his ability to make a difference in the lives of his flock."

No, Carol thought, Father Rafferty's abrupt departure from St. Anthony's was precipitated by some immediate crisis in his life, not by his discouragement with the human condition. That may have helped explain his purchase of *The God Delusion*, but it could not explain the tone of fear and anxiety that ran through his diary.

She promised Sean Rafferty that she would speak to his mother and share the sad news regarding her other son. It was possible but unlikely that she would learn more from the mother than she had from the brother. But it was a call she had to make, even if she knew that Sean would also be calling her.

It was suddenly important that she do something else, and that was to put Officer Byrnes to work tracking down a news story about violence at an abortion clinic somewhere in or near East Moncton, Massachusetts, and sometime in late summer of the previous year. Byrnes was good at this kind of assignment. She'd ask him to pay special attention to any names which cropped up in news accounts of the trouble. She was interested in all such names, but she hoped that one of them might have the initials gf. As soon as she had Byrnes' report, she'd be in touch with Kevin. It would be one more lead to follow up on when he took his trip to Massachusetts.

CHAPTER 28

When she went to bed the night before, Carol had had no idea what she would be doing at 8:30 the next morning. What she was doing was driving east on the New York State thruway, her destination the town of Verona. The decision to drive to Verona was the result of her inability to sleep well. She had awakened on three different occasions, and each time she had had trouble getting back to sleep. The third time she had gotten out of bed and gone to the kitchen to make herself a cup of warm milk. Whether warm milk would help she didn't know, but it had been a family remedy since she was a little girl and it was worth a try. She had sat in her bedside chair, milk in hand, waiting for it to take effect.

It was while she was waiting for drowsiness to overtake her that she remembered something. Something she should have thought of several days earlier. One of the gaming sites which had been mentioned to her by John Rucker and Bernie Stolnitz was a place called Turning Stone. In fact, another of Rafferty's fellow cellar rats had said something about it even earlier. Rafferty had apparently inquired about where he might pick up some money. Slots and poker had been mentioned. And his colleague had suggested Turning Stone, only to have Rafferty dismiss the idea. Too far away, he was reported to have said.

There in her chair, between sips of the warm milk, Carol suddenly put together the name Turning Stone and the references in the notebook to a place with the initials ts. She couldn't imagine why it hadn't occurred to her before. The diary had mentioned ts when Rafferty was discussing a place, a place which he had reservations about visiting but a place which he seemed drawn to. And ts was always referred to in the context of his worries about money. Why? The answer was obvious. If he gambled and won, he would make the money necessary to stay afloat at a time and in a place when the church's security blanket was no longer available to him.

But the Turning Stone, if indeed it was Rafferty's ts, didn't always treat him well. He may have won sometimes, but he also incurred losses. The diary strongly suggested that he ultimately lost more than he won. Much more. As Carol pieced it together, it sounded very much as if someone called s had helped him over the bad times by lending him money, money with which he continued to gamble. His losses had continued to mount until a time came when s declined to lend more. A time when s demanded to be repaid. Unable to make the payment, Rafferty had taken flight once again, hoping to escape from his creditor. And she was willing to bet that his creditor was a man who typically wore a red vest.

Much of this was mere speculation. But it made sense. Moreover, if she was right, Rafferty still needed money, even after moving to Crooked Lake. Money to pay his rent to Jenny Stafford, among other things. He wouldn't have the credit or the references to obtain a conventional loan. He may even have acquired a gambling addiction, in which case his debts would have grown, his predicament becoming worse. Small wonder that he had been inquiring about gaming sites, had even visited one of them with Stolnitz. But it hadn't been Turning Stone for obvious reasons.

Not surprisingly, Carol had never gone back to sleep. Suddenly there was too much to think about. There was the fact, according to Stolnitz, that he had seen a man in a red vest at the Finger Lakes Race Track. Rafferty may have seen him, too, which could account for the fact that he had left the track precipitously that evening. There was the fact that Parker Jameson, Random Harvest's treasurer/bookkeeper, had recently lost some $30,000 dollars. Who needed money, perhaps a lot of money? And who was familiar with the winery and might have known how to get into Jameson's office and fiddle the books? Rafferty?

In any event, she would be at the thruway exit to Verona in another twenty minutes. She had considered calling Bridges and asking him to make the trip to the Turning Stone Casino. It would have made his day. But Carol was once again not in the mood to delegate. This was a trip she wanted to make herself. She wasn't sure how long she'd be gone. It all depended on what she learned, and at the moment she didn't even know whom she'd be talking to. If it took a second day, so be it. She'd brought an overnight bag, prepared to put up in a motel somewhere in the vicinity if necessary. Sam might regret missing out on Turning Stone, but he had seemed pleased to be put in charge back in Cumberland for the second time in a week.

Carol had never visited Turning Stone. She had no interest in gambling. In fact the only time she had ever been inside a casino occurred back when she was seven. Her parents had driven all the way across the country to visit her mother's brother's family in LA. She couldn't remember why they had chosen to drive rather than fly, only that she had been very unhappy, cooped up in the car day after day. But the road west had gone through Las Vegas, and they had stopped to see what all the fuss was about. She had not been allowed in the rooms where people actually gambled, so her parents had taken turns inside while she cooled her heels in a lobby. It had not been an experience conducive to developing an interest in casinos.

Finding the place was no problem. Carol was surprised at its sheer size. Not just a casino, but several lodges, a variety of restaurants, golf courses—the works. It looked like a huge, self-contained village. And in view of the number of cars she could see as she drove onto the grounds, it was every bit as popular as she had heard it was. The nation's economy may have been in the doldrums, but there was little evidence of it at Turning Stone. Perhaps people were trying to compensate for losses in their 401Ks.

Not sure where to park, Carol drove around for awhile, getting her bearings. She finally found a lot that looked appropriate for people like her, people who weren't staying at one of the lodges. She had given a lot of thought during the drive to how she would go about gathering relevant information about Brendan Rafferty. It had looked like a formidable task. Now that she was actually on the grounds of the casino, it looked even more daunting. Where to start?

Inasmuch as Rafferty had almost certainly never had enough money to stay at one of the lodges, there was no point inquiring at their front desks whether anyone with that name had registered there in the past year. The logical place to make inquiries, therefore, was the casino itself. The playground, as she had heard it called, was vast. Gaming tables everywhere, most of them already occupied in spite of the early hour. It was an eye-arresting sight, something out of a James Bond movie. Except for the fact that the men were not wearing tuxes, nor the women elegant evening dresses. Turning Stone personnel were busy doing their thing at the tables. She thought she recognized other casino employees, scattered throughout the room, some simply standing still and watching the action, others moving quietly from one table to another. Probably house security.

She would, of course, keep an eye open for a man in a red vest, although she found it hard to believe that he always wore that vest and she had no idea what he looked like. Other than that man—was he s?—she had no way of knowing who else would be likely to know anything about Rafferty. She didn't know where he had spent his time. At a poker table? Or was it bingo? Or even baccarat? She could imagine stopping at every table in every room in the playground, showing a doctored picture of Rafferty, asking if he had once tarried there. Somewhere there would be people who took your money and paid out winnings to those who were lucky. They might be in a better position to remember Rafferty than those in charge of the various games. Still, the odds of winning a pot looked to be much better than chancing upon an employee of the casino who remembered him.

If he owed the casino a lot of money, somebody in management would know it. But she doubted that a place as orderly and well run as Turning Stone would let one of its guests run up a big tab. No, far more likely that he had paid the casino in full. Paid with money borrowed from the man in the red vest, the man he had referred to as s.

Carol was thinking about this man who must have loaned money to Brendan Rafferty. While Turning Stone would be happy for customers to keep coming back to try their luck, even if they had to borrow to do it, the casino would not want loan sharks operating on their property. Was the man in the red vest a loan shark? Perhaps she should seek out someone in the casino's upper management, someone responsible for setting policy, someone who would be likely to know who "red vest" is and what arrangement the house had with him, if any.

She had made a conscious decision not to wear her uniform. It would have made Turning Stone's guests nervous, even if they had no reason to be. If she were to ask the casino's higher management to discuss "red vest," they would presumably be nervous, too, whether she was in or out of uniform. They would immediately be anxious, wondering if the authorities had reason to believe that organized crime was suspected of having penetrated one of New York's most popular tourist sites. She would have to be at her diplomatic best. After all, she was not a stalking horse for the FBI, nor was she an agent of some anti-gambling crusade. She was just the sheriff of a small upstate county, trying to solve the murder of a man who happened to have done some gambling at their casino sometime during the past year.

It took Carol the better part of an hour to work her way through the Turning Stone hierarchy, beginning with one of the people she had identified as a security guard in the playground. But eventually she found herself sitting in the office of one of the casino's senior officials, Gene Ramis, displaying her sheriff's badge and credentials for the fourth time that morning.

"I suppose I could begin this conversation," he said, "by telling you that Turning Stone has nothing to hide, that we are a well-run organization that is proud of its reputation. But I'm sure you know that, and I do not wish to waste your time. So please, why don't you tell me just why you are here and what you think I may be able to do for you."

"Thank you. I promise to be brief," Carol said. "I'm not sure what you've been told about my problem, but it concerns the murder of a man in my jurisdiction. It occurred at a winery near Crooked Lake, southwest of here. We have had some difficulty in discovering exactly who he was, but we now have evidence that he spent some time within the past year in this area and that he gambled fairly regularly at Turning Stone. We also know that he was hard pressed financially, and that he met a man here at the casino who loaned him money. We have reason to believe that he did not pay that man what he owed him. He eventually moved to Crooked Lake, and one of the reasons for moving was that he was fearful of what the man he owed money to would do to him."

"And you are here to ask me about the man who loaned money to the murdered man."

"Yes, although I'm also interested in whether you recognize the name of the man who was killed. His name was Brendan Rafferty. Have you ever heard of him?"

"No, I'm afraid not. We have thousands of guests every week."

"I understand. How about the man who loaned him money? We don't know his name, only that he usually was seen wearing a red vest. The man whose murder I'm investigating mentioned him in a diary he was keeping. He didn't use a name, only said he wore a red vest."

"That would be Sadowsky. Carl Sadowsky. But I don't think you need to consider him a suspect in your man's murder."

"Why is that?" Carol asked.

"I know Carl. He's a decent sort. He worked in a casino on a cruise ship for many years. But he had a series of strokes, couldn't do it anymore. He missed it, and took to hanging around here. Not so much to gamble as to soak up the atmosphere, reminisce about old times, whatever you want to call it. He's been a regular for several years. I think he makes the circuit of the casinos, the tracks, places like that. But we're his home away from home."

"You say you know Mr. Sadowsky. How well?"

"Pretty well. I see him around here two, three times a week."

"But do you know him socially? Does he enjoy a drink with you once in awhile? Talk about his family, things like that?"

"Well, no, we aren't friends in that way. But I know he's a good guy. If you think he could have killed your man, I'm sorry, but you're wrong."

"Do you know if he has a lot of money?" Carol asked.

"I couldn't say. I'd heard that once in awhile he loaned some to people in the casino, but no one ever mentioned a figure."

"Doesn't it seem odd that a man would loan money to complete strangers just so they could gamble? In the case I'm working on, he loaned a lot of money to a man he couldn't have known well. Nobody knew Mr. Rafferty well, not even his family or people he worked with."

The man who was speaking for Turning Stone was beginning to feel uncomfortable. Even annoyed. He obviously didn't like the way this conversation was going.

"Look, Sheriff, I know you've got a crime to solve. But I want you to know that our casino has nothing to do with it. Mr. Sadowsky is welcome to help somebody who's down on his luck if he wants to. He's been there, knows how it feels. Like I said, he's a good man. You make it sound like he's mixed up with some kind of organized crime operation. Turning Stone would never allow even a whiff of something like that, from Sadowsky or anyone else."

Carol was sure that he meant what he said, but she was equally sure that he didn't really know Sadowsky well. She had known several people who were personable, even charming, but who were also nasty when crossed. The way she had read Rafferty's notebook, he had clearly crossed Sadowsky by not repaying his debt, and Sadowsky, the man who had been simply s, had turned nasty. Whether he would have killed Rafferty she didn't know, but the ex-priest had believed that he might.

There was no point in further discussion of the man in the red vest, so Carol took her leave. She was determined to meet Sadowsky herself, even if it meant staying overnight. In the meanwhile, she decided to spend her afternoon trying to find where Rafferty had lived while he was staying in or near Verona. This meant, for starters, developing a list of cheap motels in the area. Identifying rooms for rent in private homes would be a much harder task. She hoped it wouldn't be necessary.

CHAPTER 29

Carol toyed with the stale Danish in front of her, then pushed it aside and took one final sip of coffee. She disliked motels, and she decided that she disliked this one more than most. The room needed a facelift, and the fact that a bad breakfast was included did nothing to compensate for the add-ons which made the cost of the room more than the price she had been quoted. It was still early, too early to go back to Turning Stone in the hope of catching Carl Sadowsky. She had no intention of returning to her room with its bad lighting and unmade bed. Instead she took a seat in the small lobby and made an effort to find something worth reading in a local newspaper.

In all probability she had learned all that she was destined to learn about Sadowsky's relationship with Rafferty, but she had chosen to stay overnight on the chance that "red vest" would show up at the casino today. Following her visit with the manager at Turning Stone, she had spent several hours in search of the place Rafferty had stayed in the time he had lived in Verona. She had been lucky. After she had come up blank at a fifth motel, all of them cheap, the woman on the desk asked if she had tried Simmons Boarding House. She hadn't, but, with directions in hand, she pulled up in front of what was obviously an old motel which had been turned into rock-bottom efficiency "apartments" for people who were one step above homeless status.

Simmons, if that was the owner's name, did not have an office on the premises, but a posted notice provided a phone number and she soon learned that Brendan Rafferty had indeed lived there for the better part of a year. To her surprise, she also learned that when he left he had paid his rent for all but the last week. This suggested that, whatever his luck at the Turning Stone, he had had a job and that when he packed up and headed for Crooked Lake he did it in a hurry. The person with whom she had spoken did not sound particularly angry that Rafferty still owed her money. It seemed to be a fairly common occurrence where residents of the "boarding house" were concerned. The ex-priest was apparently better than most.

Having killed thirty minutes or so, Carol paid her bill, collected her overnight bag, and set off for the casino once again. This morning she was one of the early birds. For awhile she stayed outside, people watching. She decided that if there were such a thing as a gambling type, she couldn't detect it from appearances alone. None of those who passed her on their way into the casino wore red vests. She doubted that Sadowsky always wore his red vest. Or perhaps he had a closet full of them, allowing him always to be in his casino uniform.

If he were a night owl, he might not show up until afternoon. If he was hanging out at some other casino, like the one where Stolnitz thought he had spotted the red vest, he might not show up at all. Carol was regretting her decision to stay an extra day in Verona. But her desire to meet the man who had threatened Rafferty won out over her reluctance to stick it out for a few more hours. She looked at her watch. 9:28. She would wait until the lunch hour.

It was just ahead of noon when a short, stocky middle-aged man approached the entrance. He was bald, and he had a rather large cigar stuck in the corner of his mouth. It didn't appear to be lit. But what was distinctive about the man was the bright red vest he was wearing under a brown plaid sport coat. He was chatting with a taller, thinner man who was more conservatively dressed. They passed Carol, disappearing into the casino.

She waited a moment, then followed them. They stopped to speak with two other men just inside the door. It was another five minutes before the group broke up and went several ways. Anxious to take advantage of the fact that Sadowsky—for she was certain that it was Sadowsky—was temporarily alone, she hustled after him. She tapped him on the shoulder just as he was about to sit down at one of the first tables in the large room.

"Excuse me, but I believe you are Carl Sadowsky," she said as he turned to face her. She had put on her best smile, hoping it would help break the ice.

"Yes?" He looked as if he was trying to place her among his many acquaintances.

"I was hoping I would find you here," Carol continued. "I believe we have a mutual friend, and I wanted to talk with you about him."

"Who's this mutual friend?" he asked, his tone of voice neutral.

"Brendan Rafferty. How do you happen to know him?" Carol watched his reaction to her question. He had tried to mask his surprise, but wasn't successful.

"Who are you?" he asked.

"A friend. We attend the same church." She was not a friend, and the only time she had attended his church in Clarksburg was after his death. "You were going tell me how you know Mr. Rafferty."

Sadowsky was being evasive.

"I'm sorry, but I'm not following this conversation. Who told you that Rafferty is a friend of mine?"

"He did." Another lie, but a necessary one, at least until Sadowsky showed his hand.

"I can't imagine why. I don't have a friend named Rafferty."

Very good, Mr. Sadowsky, very good. The man is clever. And technically honest. He and Rafferty had most definitely not been friends.

"Okay, maybe friend is too strong a word. But surely you know him. What is the nature of your relationship?"

"Would you mind telling me your name, ma'am?" Carl Sadowsky was no longer puzzled. He was annoyed, and he wanted her to know it.

"First, I'd like to tell you what I know about your relationship with Mr. Rafferty. At one time, not that long ago, he lived near here. He spent a fair amount of time in this casino. He needed money to gamble, and you were kind enough to lend it to him. But circumstances were such that he had to move. He didn't have a chance to say good-bye to you. So I thought I could say a belated good-bye on his behalf."

The expression on Sadowsky's face told her that he wasn't buying it.

"I wasn't born yesterday. You aren't here to say good-bye for anybody, are you? Why don't you just cut out the nonsense and tell me who you are."

"Of course, and you will tell me about your relationship with Mr. Rafferty. My name is Carol Kelleher. I'm the sheriff of Cumberland County—if you're not familiar with it, it's in the state's Finger Lakes region, about a hundred miles west of here. That's where I met Mr. Rafferty. And where I learned from him about you and the fact that you had loaned him money. I also learned that he was unable to pay back the loan, and that you were not happy about it. In fact, it is my impression that he left Verona because he was afraid of you."

"And why should he be afraid of me?" The man in the red vest had finally shown his hand. He did know who Rafferty was.

"I just told you. In any event, you know why. You wanted him to be afraid of what you would do to him if he didn't repay you. You threatened him, and inasmuch as he didn't have the money to pay you, he decided to disappear without saying good-bye. Or leaving a forwarding address."

"How is my friend Rafferty?" Sadowsky's face was wearing what looked for all the world like a smirk.

He knows, doesn't he, Carol thought. But how does he know? Had word of the ex-priest's murder spread throughout the upstate area? He would know, of course, if he had killed him, but why would he tell the sheriff, whom he must know was investigating Rafferty's death? Did he think he had an alibi, proof that he couldn't have committed the crime because he had been someplace else when it occurred? But if he had an alibi, then he hadn't murdered Rafferty and she was back at square one.

"Mr. Rafferty is dead, as I believe you know," she said. "He was killed recently over near Crooked Lake. A beautiful lake, a nice part of the country. Not a place where murder is welcome. I have the responsibility of identifying the person who killed him. And I expect to do so. In view of the fact that you are among the people Mr. Rafferty feared might want to kill him, I thought I should pay you a visit."

She reached into her purse and handed Sadowsky her card and a notepad.

"I hope that you will let me know if you think of anything that could help me track down Mr. Rafferty's killer. And if I need to talk with you again, I think it would be helpful if I didn't have to come up to Turning Stone. Why don't you write down an address and phone number where I could reach you if something comes up?"

Sadowsky gave her a self-satisfied smile as he pocketed the card and bent over the table to write his address on her notepad.

"I'll be looking forward to hearing from you. Especially if you have information about what happened to our friend Rafferty."

"I promise to keep you informed," Carol said as she tucked the pad into her pocket. "But I think you could clear yourself of any suspicion if you would simply tell me where you were the night of October 20th. There would then be no point in my bothering you further. Does that sound reasonable?"

"Very reasonable, Sheriff," Sadowsky said with a grin. "I'll be very glad to be of assistance. It's been nice meeting you. I'm only sorry I never got to say good-bye to Mr. Rafferty, and that you won't be able to pass along my best wishes to him. Now if that's all, I do have some business to attend to here."

He got to his feet, tugged at the red vest, which had ridden up a bit as he sat slumped in his chair, and set off in the direction of the poker tables.

Carol was left to wonder whether she had handled her tête-à-tête with Sadowsky as well as she should have. She was confident that he had already known about Rafferty's death. He hadn't accepted her invitation to tell her anything about his alibi, and she hadn't expected him to. But to her surprise, he had given her a sample of his handwriting. She would compare it with the note she had found in Rafferty's Bible when she got back to Cumberland. In any event, it was way too soon to be focusing on him as the priest's most likely killer. She thought she had made some progress, but she had not liked the way the meeting had ended. It would not be an exaggeration to say that the unpleasant little man in the red vest had been gloating as he walked away from her, presumably on his way to put the hook into somebody else who needed cash.

CHAPTER 30

The elegantly carved wooden sign at the side of the road told Kevin that he was entering the village of East Moncton. Established in 1756. Population 2,100. Night was falling rapidly, but it was light enough to see the very old headstones in the cemetery off to his right, some of them listing at a precarious angle. The village was a pleasant mixture of residential streets, open fields, and the occasional wooded acre. A swift flowing stream coursed through the village near its commercial center. It was a reminder that East Moncton had once been a thriving mill town. The mill itself had been converted into a 21st century multipurpose building, but in the gathering gloom it still evoked an earlier era when it had been the beating heart of the village's prosperity.

Kevin had made no motel reservation. He had been confident that finding a place to sleep would pose no problem, but by the time he reached the far end of East Moncton he had not seen a motel, much less a lighted bed and breakfast sign. Did this mean that the village had fallen on hard times, that it no longer attracted visitors? Fortunately, about a mile east of town, he at last spotted a motel. The vacancy sign was lit, but that was hardly necessary because the parking area contained only three cars.

By nine o'clock, Kevin had checked in, returned to the village for dinner at a chain restaurant that was surprisingly busy, and once back at the motel settled into an uncomfortable chair in front of the television set. He had opted for *House*, then changed his mind and pulled out his cell phone and punched in Carol's number.

There was nothing he needed to report. He had paid no attention to the Rafferty case since he had last talked to her, concentrating instead on a class which he felt was not shaping up as well as it should and a report he was preparing for his dean. But talking with Carol over the phone had never been primarily about law enforcement issues. It had typically been about their personal relationship, and Kevin remembered how difficult some of those conversations had once been. For some reason they had felt more like strangers on the phone than they did in person. Now, however, after three summers of sharing both the excitement of solving a crime and the pleasures of the big bed at the cottage, they were comfortable on the phone. Neither of them cared much for the sterility of e-mail or text messaging. They needed the sound of each other's voice, the easy laughter, the little silences that said as much as the words they exchanged.

"Hello, Sheriff Kelleher speaking." Carol had talked about getting caller ID for a long time, but she had never gotten around to doing it.

"Hi, it's me, and I want to speak with Carol, not the sheriff."

"Just a second. I'll put her on," she said. "So, where are you?"

"East Moncton, Massachusetts. They've just taken up the sidewalks. I haven't talked to anybody yet. Didn't get in until it was almost dark. I'd originally planned to make the drive tomorrow morning, but then I decided it might make more sense to give myself the whole day up here. So I left right after my last class. How are you doing?"

"Personally or in my official capacity?"

"Yes, in that order."

"Personally I'm lonely. A week ago we were having dinner at The Cedar Post. Tonight I'm cleaning up the kitchen and missing you. Does that make you feel better?"

"I hate to feel good about you feeling bad, but, yes, I'm glad you miss me. Next week, remember? I'll be there a week from tonight if you're kind enough to pick me up at the airport."

"I'll be there. What's your impression of Rafferty's old hometown?" Carol asked.

"Like I said, I didn't get to see much of it. Too dark. But I think it's what you might call New England quaint. Certainly not bustling. And it's smaller than I expected. I'm going to start at St. Anthony's first thing in the morning."

"Well, I made a little progress today. I met and talked with the guy that wears a red vest. Do you remember Rafferty's diary, the stuff about a man he called s? It turns out that s is Carl Sadowsky. I met him at a casino just north of the New York thruway. Turning Stone—that's where the ts comes from. What's more, this man Sadowsky gave me his address. Wrote it out for me. I've compared it with the note in Rafferty's Bible, and damned if I can tell whether he wrote the note or not. In some ways the note looks as if Sadowsky could have written it, but I'm no handwriting expert and I can't be sure."

"That still sounds like progress. How did you manage it?"

"It's called putting two and two together. You pretty much had it right when you told me what you thought about Rafferty's diary. Sadowsky hangs out at gambling joints like Turning Stone. I'd call him a loan shark. Anyway, he got his hooks into the priest. I think it's very possible that he's our killer. Possible. That's as far as I'm willing to go. I think he already knew Rafferty was dead. Knew it before I told him."

"Nice work. How did he know about Rafferty? Of course if he'd done it he'd know. But I doubt he'd tell you."

"He didn't say," Carol said. "I had the feeling that by that time he thought he was getting the best of me. Cocky son of a gun. I think Rafferty was right to be afraid of him.

"Oh, and by the way, I talked with his brother. Rafferty's I mean, not Sadowsky's. Interesting conversation. He tells me that not long before Brendan left St. Anthony's, there was some sort of violence at an abortion clinic near there and that some of his parishioners were involved. Apparently the priest found it terribly depressing, the resort to violence in a religious cause. I think the brother feels that maybe that had something to do with his decision to leave the church. I don't have any names of the people involved in the violence, but I've got one of my men on it. Keep your ears open. It may be important."

"I'll do what I can. If I'm lucky, I'll find out who gf is. That'll complicate your life, giving you another prime suspect to worry about. Even if I don't meet him, I expect to get to the bottom of this church cover-up or whatever it is. I'm sure they know more than they were willing to tell you. I find it awfully hard to believe that their priest just disappeared without them having some pretty good idea why."

"I'm inclined to agree with you, but take it easy. You don't have any official standing to be demanding information about Rafferty and how the diocese is handling his disappearance. They won't be very happy to discover it's some agnostic professor of music who's badgering them about one of their priests."

"Wait a minute. In the first place, I don't badger. Have you ever known me to badger anyone? In the second place, when did you decide I was an agnostic? You never heard it from me."

"It's a woman's intuition. And a Catholic woman's at that. As far as I know, you never go to church. Come on, when was the last time? You know I don't care, but why not admit it?"

"Excuse me for asking, but didn't you attend mass last Sunday because you needed to talk with some acquaintances of Rafferty's? I don't remember you saying anything about a need to commune with God. And didn't I see you reading *The God Delusion?*"

Carol laughed.

"You love to change the subject, don't you? You know perfectly well why I was reading *The God Delusion*. Anyhow, let's make a pact not to talk about religion. Or politics. Everybody says that more relationships hit the rocks over those two issues than any others. You can be a Zoroastrian for all I care. Or a card carrying monarchist. I'd still love you."

"And me you," Kevin agreed. "By the way, I promise not to do any badgering at St. Anthony's. And I'll let you know the minute I beat the truth out of gf."

"You make me nervous, Kevin."

"I know. It's part of my long-range plan."

CHAPTER 31

St. Anthony's Roman Catholic Church sat on the corner of Princeton and Lexington, an old red brick building of no architectural distinction. A rectangular, glass-enclosed board beside the front steps announced the name of the church, that of the presiding priest, and the days and hours at which mass would take place. The building next to the church on Princeton Street was connected to it by a covered walkway, but was dissimilar in appearance from the church. It had been built of stone in a style long out of favor. It was low and squat, while the church, with its spire topped by a cross, was tall and rather slender. While there was no mention of the low building's function, Kevin assumed that it was the rectory. The board in front of the church said that Father Julius Merton was the priest in this parish.

Father Merton, who had apparently succeeded Father Rafferty, was one of the people with whom Kevin wished to speak. He preferred to talk with the rectory housekeeper first if he could. Of course the housekeeper might not be the one who had served Father Rafferty's needs, and if that were the case it wouldn't much matter whom he spoke with first. One way or another, he'd soon know. He rang the front doorbell at the rectory.

The woman who came to the door was gray haired and slightly stooped, but her face was unlined and her eyes positively sparkled. Although she obviously wasn't much interested in preserving the illusion of youth, Kevin thought that she looked as if she were comfortable in her own skin.

"Yes, sir, what may I do for you?" she asked.

Kevin had given quite a bit of thought to how he would approach his quest for information about the priest who had disappeared from St. Anthony's. It would necessitate a bit of misrepresentation, but he had acquired a knack for it while working with Carol on a couple of her cases.

"Hello. My name's Kevin Whitman. I'm an old friend of Father Rafferty. It is my understanding that this is his church. At least that's what he told me. I was passing through and thought I'd stop by and say hello. But it says outside that the pastor is Father Merton."

The look on the woman's face said that this wasn't the first time she had been confronted with this problem.

"I'm afraid that Father Rafferty isn't with us anymore. Would you like to see Father Merton?"

"I don't know him. It was Father Rafferty I wanted to see. Maybe you can tell me where he is. Does he now have a different parish?"

Was it his imagination or did the woman suddenly look less friendly, more guarded, than she had when she opened the door?

"I'm sorry, but I don't really know. You'd have to speak to somebody in the diocese."

This was the same kind of response Carol had gotten when she had phoned the church, seeking information about what had happened to Father Rafferty. Kevin wasn't prepared to be so easily put off.

"Am I right that you're the housekeeper here at the rectory? Father Rafferty always spoke highly of his housekeeper, but I don't know if you're the person he talked about."

"I'm Emma Burley, and yes, I was here when Father Rafferty was our priest. But I'm afraid I can't help you. He's been gone for awhile, and they don't tell us where they send their priests."

"He hasn't been in touch with you?" It was a simple question, and it was clear that Ms. Burley was having a hard time coping with the obvious implication: that it was strange that a priest she had served, a priest who had complimented her to this stranger, had never informed her of where he had gone when he left St. Anthony's.

"No, he hasn't. I guess he must be terribly busy. Like I said, you'd probably learn more if you spoke with the people in the diocesan office."

"I shall do that," Kevin said, then decided to open a new line of questions. "Maybe you can tell me if Father Rafferty had any parishioners who might be in a position to help me find him. I'm thinking of people who may have spent more time with him, people who came by the rectory from time to time. I know priests seek good relationships with all members of their flock, but I wonder if you can recall any special relationships."

It was something of a shot in the dark, but Kevin hoped that Ms. Burley could be induced to mention a name or two. He needed a place to start, and she seemed to be the person most likely to know where and with whom that place would be.

For some reason, it was apparently easier for Ms. Burley to respond to this question than it was to tell him anything about when and why Rafferty had left St. Anthony's and where he had gone.

"He was good to people," she said. "I used to think he was somewhat like a doctor who had a good bedside manner. I'm not sure I can tell you about any particular situation, but his office was always open. There were a couple of people I think I remember him seeing quite a bit of. A man named Clemens for one. I think his name is Michael. Yes, I'm sure it is, Michael Clemens. And Jody Winters. I can remember him and the Father laughing at something. Maybe they were telling jokes. There was another man, but I think their relationship was a bit different. His name is Flanagan. He didn't laugh like Mr. Winters. Much more serious. I may be wrong, but I thought I heard him arguing with the Father once."

So, Kevin said to himself, the housekeeper is free to talk to me about Father Rafferty as long as she doesn't violate an order from the diocese not to discuss the circumstances surrounding his departure. Is it possible that the church has known that it has a pedophile on its hands and has tried to keep a lid on it? Fortunately, Ms. Burley is willing to talk—to gossip?—as long as she has not been specifically instructed not to. And now she has mentioned a man whom she heard arguing with the priest, a man whose last name is Flanagan. Could this be gf?

"I really want to get in touch with Father Rafferty," he said. "Perhaps one of these people you have mentioned can help me. Michael Clemens. Jody Winters. What was the other one? Flanagan, you said. I didn't get his first name."

"It's Gerald. His sons have been altar boys here at St. Anthony's."

It was all Kevin could do to suppress a satisfied smile.

"Have you ever heard any of these men, or anyone else, for that matter, say anything about where Father Flanagan might be?" Kevin knew he was pressing his luck.

The housekeeper hesitated, apparently trying to decide whether whatever she might say violated her instructions.

"Just once," she said, "but I never put any stock in it."

"As you can see, I'm anxious to find Father Rafferty, so I'm willing to consider rumors, even if they sound far-fetched."

"Well, there's a man here in the parish who claims he saw the Father. It was quite recent, as a matter of fact. He had been off somewhere to see a daughter who's in college, and he thinks he saw Father Rafferty."

"Did he say where he thinks he saw him?"

"That's one of the reasons why I'm sure he's mistaken. This college was somewhere in New York. South of Rochester, he said. But he says he saw the Father at a winery. He thought he was working there. That's pretty unlikely, don't you think? I mean, you know him. Can you imagine him working at a winery?"

"No, I can't." Kevin shook his head, hoping the look on his face conveyed the impression that he found the very idea ridiculous. "You said you didn't put any stock in this man's story. Is that just because the Father wouldn't be working at a winery?"

"I don't like to tell tales on people," Ms. Burley said as she prepared to tell just such a tale. "But Mr. Prentiss is—well, I shouldn't say he's a drunk—but he doesn't know his limit. I heard Father Rafferty say once that he'd consider his pastorate a success if he could persuade Mr. Prentiss to go on the wagon. Anyway, if you take the winery story plus his drinking habits, I'd say he just saw someone who looked like the Father and figured it would make a good story."

"Yes, I'm sure that's what happened. I'm always spotting someone I think I know, only to have it turn out that they just looked somewhat alike. I saw a guy recently that I'd have sworn was Harrison Ford. You know, the actor, the one who played Indiana Jones. But when I turned to get a better look, he didn't really look like him at all."

Kevin was about to ask what Prentiss's first name was, then decided against it. No need to sound too interested in the man's story. He'd have no trouble tracking him down in this small town. There couldn't be that many Prentisses.

"By the way," he put one more question to the housekeeper, "as far as you know, did Mr. Prentiss tell other people in the parish that he thought he'd seen Father Rafferty?"

"I wouldn't know. It wouldn't surprise me if he did. But I'm pretty sure other people would have reacted same as I did. Mr. Prentiss, he's got a reputation, if you know what I mean."

It was time to move on. He wanted to locate Gerald Flanagan, and the man named Prentiss. They suddenly looked more important to his mission than Father Merton.

"I appreciate your sharing this information with me," he said as he got ready to leave. "I hope someone can help put me in touch with Father Rafferty. We used to call him Brendan, by the way. I still think of him as Brendan. I'm sure you'd like to hear about him, too."

"Indeed I would," Ms. Burley said. "I would appreciate it very much if you would let me know if you find him. You could just call the church. We're listed. It's been hard, all these months, worrying about him, the church not saying anything. He was a good man."

Little did she know that her use of the past tense was correct. He had been a good man. At least that was her opinion. Whether he had in fact been a good man, Kevin did not know. Neither did the sheriff. It was doubtful if they would know until she solved the case. Maybe not even then.

CHAPTER 32

"Pull up a stool and I'll tell you about it."

The man who invited Kevin to take a seat at the bar in East Moncton's Ye Olde Shamrock was Paul Prentiss, whom he had finally located, thanks to the man's wife. By the time he had found the pub and identified the man he wished to speak to, he had learned that Prentiss was a former policeman, retired on disability pay, who seemed to divide his time between occasional security jobs and the Shamrock. Mrs. Prentiss, an elementary school teacher who appeared to be of the quietly long-suffering type, had told him that her husband had gone into town for an extended happy hour.

Assuming his new role as an old friend of Father Rafferty's, Kevin had approached the ex-policeman with the question that had been prompted by what the rectory housekeeper had told him.

"Excuse me, but someone said that you ran into Father Rafferty recently. I'm an old friend of his, and I've been looking for him. Would you mind if I joined you?"

Prentiss apparently enjoyed talking with people, and the subject was one on which he was the local authority. Without further prompting, he launched into his version of the story.

"It was funny, you know, his disappearing from St. Anthony's like he did. You do know about that, don't you?"

"I didn't until today," Kevin replied. "I hadn't seen him in quite awhile, but I knew he had the parish here in East Moncton. Or thought he did. But they told me over at the rectory that he'd been gone for over a year. The housekeeper didn't seem to know where he had gone, or why, but she mentioned that you thought you'd seen him."

"I didn't think I saw him," Prentiss said, almost vehemently. "I did see him."

"That's good news. This business of his leaving the church so suddenly really surprised me. But if you can tell me where he is, I'll be able to get in touch with him again."

"It was just by chance. People around here had pretty much forgotten about him going away. You know how it is, out of sight, out of mind. Of course it was a big deal when it happened, no one knowing where he was, what he was doing. But we were getting used to Father Merton, me just like everyone else. Then back in September, Penny—that's my daughter—she went off to college. She had a girl friend from the class ahead of her who'd gone there, so she had to go, too. What I mean is she had to go to this place called Brae Loch College. It's away off in New York. It was a dumb idea. She should have gone to BU or some place nearby, but she had her mind set on linking up with Katie. Then she ups and gets homesick just two weeks after I'd taken her to that little God-forsaken school."

Kevin wished that Prentiss would get to the point, but he recognized an inveterate storyteller when he heard one, and he was willing to indulge him—as long as he eventually got around to Rafferty.

"Anyway, there I was back at that college on the lake, arguing with my daughter about whether she should stick it out for a semester or come back home. Frankly, I think she should transfer, but I guess it's hard to do that after just two weeks. She sort of calmed down a bit, and I figured it was safe to leave her. One of the things she mentioned while we were talking about what she should do was that Katie had worked over the summer in the gift shop at some winery. I didn't know anything about wineries, but Penny said that there were a lot of them around the lake. So when it came time to come home, I thought I'd see what this winery stuff was all about. I'm a beer man, myself. I knew that they made wine out in California, but never heard about it here in the east. Anyway, I took a short drive around this lake, and made a stop at a place up on a hill. There was a sign out front, said it was Random Harvest Vineyards."

Prentiss, suddenly aware that his glass was empty, called out to the bartender for a refill from one of the draft taps.

"You having one?" he asked.

"Later," Kevin said. He had no idea how many beers Prentiss had had before he joined him, but this was his second in not much more than ten minutes, and he knew he couldn't and shouldn't try to keep up.

"Where was I?" Prentiss asked himself.

"You were about to go into the Random Harvest winery," Kevin said.

"Right. It wasn't a very big place, but I have to admit, it had a great view. The lake looked nice from up on that hill. I was surprised how many cars there were in the parking lot. Well, I just followed some people who'd gotten out of one of those SUVs. We all went into what was a place where you get to sample different kinds of wine. Quite a crowd, all sounding like they were having a good time. I wasn't interested in the wine, so I started looking around. They had all kinds of stuff for sale, not just bottles of wine. You know, corkscrews, coasters, glasses, T-shirts with the name of the place on them, things I didn't know what they were for. I was thinking about taking something back for Nancy—that's the missus—when I saw this guy who looked kind of familiar. It dawned on me, all of a sudden, that he looked like Father Rafferty!"

Prentiss paused to take a long drink of his beer.

"Well, I really should have called out to him. But he wasn't dressed like a priest, and I thought maybe I was mistaken. Anyhow, by the time I was sure it was him, he'd gone out that door. It had a sign on it, said employees only. I asked a woman at the end of the counter where all these people were sampling the wine if that guy was named Rafferty. She didn't seem to know who I was talking about."

There followed a moment when Prentiss pushed his glass around on the bar, leaving a trail of small circles. Kevin had the sudden realization that after this lengthy buildup, Prentiss had said just about all he had to say. He hadn't followed the man, hadn't pursued the matter with other Random Harvest personnel, and therefore hadn't talked with the man he thought was Rafferty.

"I should have gone after him," Prentiss said. "But it didn't look like they wanted people back there. Everyone was real busy. Anyway I know it was the Father. After all, I'd seen him on a lot of Sundays. And there he was, walking through a winery, acting like he worked there. It was strange."

Kevin could picture exactly where this encounter, or near encounter, had taken place. Would Prentiss have had a good enough look at the man to positively identify him? Too bad he had not acted on what must have been his natural impulse to satisfy his curiosity. There was no point in asking him whether he was absolutely certain it was Rafferty. He'd already said he was sure, and further questions about the identity of the man would only annoy him.

It was time to ask a different question.

"It certainly must have been a shock to see your old priest, and at a winery so far away. By the way, did you say anything about seeing Father Rafferty to anyone when you got home?"

"Oh, sure, my wife, the kids. I stopped at the rectory and told Ms. Burley. Fat lot of good that did. She looked as if I was on a bender or something. She was always holier than thou. I'd bet she was always keeping watch to make sure Father Rafferty wasn't sneaking a nip now and then. Probably the same with Father Merton."

"That's all? You didn't tell anybody else?"

"I probably said something to a lot of people. After all, it was quite a story. But most everyone thought he'd just decided the church wasn't for him. Maybe it wasn't. It can't be easy preaching about sin all the time, praying day and night. No matter how good a Catholic you are, you have to get tired of all those 'hail Marys.'"

"It must have been disappointing when people weren't much interested that you'd seen Father Rafferty."

"Yeah, I guess so. There was one exception, though. Gerry Flanagan. He paid attention. But then he never much cared for Father Rafferty, thought he was soft on abortion, homosexuals, that kind of thing. He probably figured he was better off working in a winery than lecturing us on our sins."

The conversation drifted off into other areas, such as the inadequacy of disability compensation, the state of the nation (miserable according to Prentiss), and the relative merits of the beers the Shamrock had on draft. When Kevin left, he expressed the hope that Penny would ultimately find herself in the right college. Prentiss looked as if he might need a ride home.

———

Gerry Flanagan. One of the names on Officer Byrnes' list that Carol had e-mailed him had been Gerald Flanagan. They had finally found gf! Or so he hoped. He had set off immediately for the Flanagan residence, only to be told that Gerald would not be back from his office until late afternoon. Returning at 5:50, he discovered the man he needed to talk with pulling into the driveway just as he was climbing out of his own car at the curb.

"Mr. Flanagan, I was hoping I would catch you this time." Kevin extended his hand. Flanagan obviously had no idea who he was. "I spoke briefly with your wife earlier today, and she urged me to come back around now. I'm Kevin Whitman, and I wonder if I can talk with you for a few minutes about Father Brendan Rafferty. I'm an old friend of Father Rafferty, going back many years."

Flanagan's face gave no indication of how he felt about this invitation to discuss the ex-priest.

"Of course. Please call me Gerry." He led the way into a living room, where they were greeted by a large and aggressively friendly retriever.

"Excuse me while I duck in here to wash my hands," he said, motioning Kevin to have a seat.

"Now," he began, "what's this about Father Rafferty? I'm afraid I didn't know him all that well. I belonged to his church when he was our pastor, but that was more than a year ago."

"That's my problem," Kevin said. "I haven't seen Father Rafferty in several years. It occurred to me when I was in the Boston area that it would be nice to stop and say hello. I thought he was still at St. Anthony's. But the housekeeper at the rectory informed me this morning that he's no longer there. She didn't seem to know where he is, but when I asked if there was anybody around who might know, she mentioned you."

This was not exactly a fair accounting of what he had heard from Ms. Burley. He had asked her about people the Father might have known better than most, and Flanagan's name had been mentioned, not in a complimentary way. She had never said that Mr. Flanagan might know where the Father was.

"I can't imagine why Ms. Burley would have said that. Like I said, I didn't talk much with the Father, no more than his other parishioners—you know, hello, good-bye, before and after mass."

"She probably doesn't know members of the church very well. Maybe she was just mentioning some names that came to mind, trying to be helpful in getting me in touch with Father Rafferty."

"That has to be it, because I'm afraid I can't help you."

"That's disappointing. I really was hopeful that before I left town I'd find someone who might know where he is."

It was then that Kevin chose to drop the other shoe.

"One of the other people Ms. Burley mentioned was a man named Prentiss. She said that he thought he had seen Father Rafferty earlier this fall when he went to visit his daughter at college. I got the impression that after he got back to East Moncton Mr. Prentiss went around talking with other St. Anthony's parishioners about seeing the Father. Did he ever talk to you about it?"

"I don't remember any such conversation. Prentiss is a bit of a talker, especially when he's been drinking, which is most of the time. I suppose I shouldn't be saying such things about another member of my church, but I think you should take anything he says with a grain of salt. I do. In any event, if he ever said anything about Rafferty in my hearing I would have dismissed it."

"I remember Ms. Burley reporting that Prentiss had seen the Father—or thought he did—at a winery in the Finger Lakes. It's called Random Harvest Vineyards. Does that ring a bell?"

"No, it doesn't." Flanagan had maintained a civil tongue, but it was increasingly clear that he did not wish to pursue this conversation. Kevin, in turn, realized that it might be better to leave it at that. He didn't want Flanagan to become suspicious of his motive for seeking him out and persisting in his questions.

"Sorry to have wasted your time, Mr. Flanagan. It looks like I may be on a wild goose chase, although I don't like to think that an old friend has just fallen off the edge of the earth.

"By the way," Kevin said as he got up, "were you surprised that the Red Sox didn't make it to the series this fall? I'm a New Yorker, and I'm getting fed up with my Yankees."

"I'm afraid I'm not much of a baseball fan," Flanagan said, sounding more upbeat. "Don't much like these high profile professional sports. I'm a hunter. I'd rather be off in the woods by myself. Bow hunting is the best. Have you ever tried it?"

"No, never. I'm a city guy. Probably couldn't shoot straight if I got one in my sights."

"Try it sometime. I put in several days just a little while ago. Got myself a ten point buck. It's good for the soul."

Kevin shook hands and took his leave. It was not until he had gone down the front steps that he realized that someone was standing quietly at the window of the room adjacent to the one where he and Gerald Flanagan had been conversing. Standing and watching him, the curtain held aside to provide a better look at the visitor. He appeared to be a young man. More accurately, a teenage boy.

CHAPTER 33

October had ended, November had arrived. It was the last day of daylight savings time. That night everyone would gain an hour's sleep, but the sun would set an hour earlier the next day. It was a time of transition in the calendar. It was also a time of transition in the pursuit of a breakthrough in the Rafferty case, although neither Kevin Whitman nor Sheriff Carol Kelleher was yet fully aware of it.

Kevin had spent a busy Saturday talking with the current pastor of St. Anthony's and several members of his flock who had been identified by the housekeeper as more than casual acquaintances of Father Rafferty. But he had learned nothing of interest, unless one were to regard as interesting the fact that there were people who missed their former priest. Whether Father Merton's paucity of information about his predecessor was due to instructions from the diocese or the simple fact that he distrusted rumors and the people who spread them, Kevin did not know. By mid-afternoon he had come to the conclusion that he had accomplished all that he was likely to accomplish on his visit to East Moncton, so he said good-bye to the sleepy town and headed back to the city.

Carol had been pleased to hear from Kevin that he had almost certainly identified gf as Gerald Flanagan. Moreover, he had talked with a man who claimed to have seen Rafferty at the Random Harvest winery. What is more, he had later mentioned it to Flanagan. The people Kevin had talked with, Flanagan included, had treated the story about the priest having been seen at a winery with a great deal of skepticism. But Rafferty *had* been at the winery. If Flanagan disliked him as much as the priest seemed to think he did, might he have decided to see for himself if the story were true? There was much more to be learned about Flanagan, about his grievance with Rafferty, about his whereabouts when the priest had been killed. Nonetheless, Carol would have to think of Flanagan, like Sadowsky, as a possible suspect in Rafferty's murder.

Sadowsky was still very much on Carol's mind. She knew from Rafferty's diary and from her own experience that he frequented the Turning Stone Casino. She knew from what Bernie Stolnitz had told her that he may also have hung out at the Finger Lakes Race Track in Farmington. If the man in the red vest Stolnitz had seen there was indeed Sadowsky, he might have seen Rafferty and thus have learned that he was still in upstate New York. It was even possible that he had made it his business to follow when Rafferty and Stolnitz left the racetrack that night. If so, he would have known where Rafferty lived or where he worked. Perhaps both. Carol had given Bridges the task of going up to Farmington to see what he could add to their knowledge of Sadowsky's habits. Sam would love the assignment.

One thing Carol didn't have to worry about was Random Harvest's loss of thirty thousand dollars. At least that was what Earl Drake, the owner of the winery, had told her. It was his view that the matter could be handled internally, indeed that it had to be handled internally. Publicity would be humiliating and very possibly harmful to the future of the winery. Drake seemed to believe that if he allowed the sheriff's department to become involved, it would no longer be possible to prevent the problem from becoming general knowledge. Carol had no choice but to honor the owner's wishes. But she was not convinced that such a large sum of money had disappeared simply because Parker Jameson was careless. Nor did she believe that it would miraculously turn up one day when an auditor discovered a bookkeeping error or a misplaced file. She could not shake the nagging suspicion that the loss of the money and the murder of Brendan Rafferty were somehow related.

Then there was the matter of those other initials in Rafferty's notebook. They now knew, or were quite sure they knew, who gf and s were, as well as what ts stood for. But there were still two sets of initials the meaning of which was still a mystery. One was mc, who had apparently recommended that Rafferty pay a visit to Turning Stone. Carol hadn't given much thought to mc. He—or she—had been a minor figure in the diary, not one of the people who seemed to be a cause of the priest's anxiety. But on reflection, mc might be more important than she had first thought. Whoever it was, it had to be somebody who knew Rafferty and was familiar with the casino. Did mc also know Sadowsky? Carol would ask Byrnes to work some of his Internet magic and try to identify mc for her.

The other initials that had not yet been linked to a name were jc. Carol remembered briefly thinking that they might stand for Jesus Christ. It was a connection she had made only because the writer of the diary was apparently a priest and because the diary made a number of allusions to God and the Bible. But she was sure that those initials stood for someone whom Rafferty had known personally. He—and this time it was definitely he—had been mentioned in the very last entry in the diary, which made it highly likely that he was someone whom Rafferty had met after he had settled in the Crooked Lake area. From everything she had heard, the priest was uncomfortable in the company of his fellow men. She had heard the word "loner" used to describe him by numerous people, both at the winery and in Clarksburg. Whether he was a loner by nature or because he was keeping a low profile out of fear for his life was not clear. But in the case of jc, he seemed to have actually become involved in someone else's life. The only people she had talked to who admitted to spending time with him, other than in brief conversation, were Esther Rhodes and Bernie Stolnitz. Neither one could be jc. It was time to try to identify the man to whom Father Rafferty had been referring. Another job for Byrnes. And he would start with the employees at the winery and the citizens of Clarksburg. If that search didn't turn up a jc or two, Carol wasn't sure what her next move would be.

All in all, however, it had been a good two days, both in Verona and East Moncton. Several more pieces of the puzzle of Brendan Rafferty's murder were now on the table. Fitting them together would not be easy, and completing the puzzle would probably be impossible unless they were able to locate the many pieces that were still missing. But both Carol and Kevin felt more optimistic about the case when they set their clocks back an hour on Saturday night. Better yet, they could look forward to spending the next weekend together at the cottage on Crooked Lake.

CHAPTER 34

It was Sunday morning, and Carol, still in her bathrobe, had just finished the sports section of the paper. She hadn't made it to church. If she had been asked, she would probably have said that she had overslept. But the truth of the matter was that she hadn't set the alarm, which she would have done had she had any intention of attending mass. She poured herself a second cup of coffee and puttered around aimlessly for awhile. She considered reading *The God Delusion*, but decided it would be too depressing. Chesterton might be more in keeping with her commitment to a lazy day, so she picked up Rafferty's copy of the Father Brown mysteries, leafed through it in search of an interesting title, and finally settled down to read "The Invisible Man."

It took her a little less than fifteen minutes to finish the story. She hadn't much cared for Chesterton's style, and realized that she still couldn't understand Rafferty's interest in the little priest. But the central point of the story she found intriguing. The invisible man in the story was not, of course, really invisible. He was invisible only because people, when asked if they had seen someone, thought about family members or guests or visitors or someone distinctive. We forget about the trash collector or the meter reader or, in the Chesterton story, the postman. Such people come and go and remain invisible.

Rafferty himself had tried to remain invisible. Or at least anonymous. Everyone she had spoken with had emphasized his reluctance to talk about himself, his past, his interests. He had gone out of his way to avoid cultivating friendships. His diary was deliberately opaque. She herself had thought of him as Mr. Cellophane in the musical *Chicago*. People did seem to walk right by him and see right through him as if he weren't there.

But the invisible man in the Chesterton story hadn't been a victim. He had been the perpetrator of a crime, a crime which he was able to commit without being detected because no one noticed him even if he walked about in plain sight. The parallel with Rafferty ended there. Carol, however, couldn't stop thinking about that which was invisible. What, she found herself asking, was invisible even if anyone could see it? It was an interesting mental exercise, and it occupied her mind as she waited for her breakfast muffins to toast.

By the time she had showered and dressed, Carol had decided that there were more important things to do with her day than ponder the relevance of the fictional Father Brown to the investigation of Father Rafferty's untimely and violent death. The reference to Father Brown in the diary had nothing to do with invisible men. Instead, Rafferty had seemed to be preoccupied with helping save someone's soul, something Father Brown apparently did in the Chesterton stories, including the one she had just read. She recalled its final line, the line in which Father Brown "walked those snow-covered hills under the stars for many hours with a murderer, and what they said to each other will never be known."

In spite of her best efforts, however, Carol was unable to banish invisible men entirely from her mind. It was while she was midway through the process of making up her bed that something occurred to her that changed her plans for the day. What about the scarecrow? Might it have been the invisible man?

She went to her study and retrieved the camera with which Officer Barrett had photographed Brendan Rafferty on the scarecrow's cross in the Random Harvest vineyard. She scrolled through Barrett's shots until she found one taken from the road. It had been a bright, sunny day, and the photo provided a clear picture of the vineyard stretching out below the road toward the lake. There, in the far distance, was the scarecrow, with Carol and Bridges and the winery people standing around it. But it was impossible to tell who any of these tiny figures were. Too far away. The scarecrow looked like a scarecrow.

Carol collected her windbreaker from the closet and within a few minutes was in her car and on her way over the hill to Crooked Lake and, more specifically, to Random Harvest Vineyards. The weather was similar to what it had been when Rafferty's body had been discovered. It was a bit chillier, but the sky was blue, the visibility excellent.

She pulled off the road in very much the same spot where she and Barrett had parked nearly two weeks earlier. There was no one in the vineyard below her this time. The wooden post which had held Rafferty's body was now just a wooden post, its cross arm almost but not quite at a right angle. She squinted, trying to imagine that a scarecrow was lashed to the post. If it had been, she was sure she would have had a hard time describing it in any detail. The straw hat? Yes, she would have been able to see that. The color of the clothes in which it was dressed? Possible, but barely. Rafferty had been dressed in blue jeans and a dark blue shirt, but in Barrett's photo it had been impossible to discern the color of the shirt and the pants had been hidden from view by the grapevines.

Carol considered this. She was unfamiliar with the original scarecrow, which was now missing in any event. From what she could remember of Mason's description of it as reported to her by Barrett, the jeans had had a hole in the knee and the shirt had simply been described as dark. She would have to ask Mason to be more specific regarding the color of the scarecrow's shirt. But from what she knew, or thought she knew, Rafferty-as-scarecrow would not have looked appreciably different from the real scarecrow to anyone seeing it from the road. And she could think of no one who would have been likely to see it from a closer vantage point.

The man who discovered the body, Brad Robinson, had not gone down into the vineyard because he thought he saw a dead man there. He had seen what he thought was a scarecrow and simply wished to take its picture. She herself had made the same point the day they discovered the body: people see what they expect to see. What they would have expected to see was a scarecrow, and from the road that is just what it would have looked like.

The invisible man. When the body was discovered, she had asked herself two questions: Why had Rafferty's killer put the body up on the "cross" to resemble a scarecrow? And why had no one discovered the body sooner? Now she found herself asking whether there might be a connection between the answers to those two questions. What if the killer knew that there would be no pickers in that vineyard until after the first frost? And what if he did not want the body to be discovered right away? Now, for the first time, it occurred to her that Rafferty's body may have been substituted for the scarecrow precisely because the killer wanted it to remain invisible. And what better way to keep it invisible than to hide it in plain sight. The one thing the killer had not counted on was Brad Robinson.

CHAPTER 35

Tommy Byrnes was privately amused by the fact that his fellow officers regarded him as some kind of a computer whiz. While it was true that he knew how to navigate his iMac and was quite capable of troubleshooting most problems without an SOS to the local computer techie, he was well aware that his son was probably more proficient than he was. And his son was 16 and a junior in high school. Nonetheless, he was the member of the Cumberland County Sheriff's Department who was regularly called on to find a shortcut to information that the sheriff needed urgently. Like yesterday.

He had spent a good part of the last days of October assembling data on everybody that the sheriff thought could possibly be a factor in the Rafferty case. They included everybody who worked for the winery, from the owner down to the most recently hired part-time picker. They also included the citizenry of Clarksburg and property owners and renters living within a mile of the Kempers' home on Crooked Lake. Some of it had been easy, thanks to the cooperation of Earl Drake at Random Harvest. Some of it had been harder. But by the first Monday in November, Carol knew a few things which looked to be important.

One of those things was that nobody associated with Random Harvest lived anywhere close to Donnie Kemper's house on Crooked Lake. Only three of the winery's employees lived right on the lake, and they had residences way down near Southport. Carol had needed to know if the person Donnie Kemper thought he saw dumping a body into the lake lived nearby. She had doubted he had seen what he claimed to have seen, but she was prepared to believe him when he said that the boat he had observed had headed back to a point not far below the Kempers' cottage. This meant that whomever young Kemper had seen did not work at Random Harvest. Unfortunately, that did not mean that all winery personnel could be ruled out as suspects in

Rafferty's murder. But it did make it even more unlikely that what Kemper had witnessed was the early morning disposal of the winery's scarecrow.

Of considerably more interest to Carol was the revelation that four of the people at Random Harvest had the initials jc. That in itself was an unusual coincidence. But one of the four was a woman, Jessica Coyle, and there was no reason to worry about her. The priest had been quite clear that jc was a man. The other three were Jared Church, Joseph Clifford (known as Joe), and Jerome Copeland (known as Jerry).

Church was a veteran, having worked at the winery for more than twenty years as a jack-of-all-trades who was reputed to be something of a wine connoisseur. In other words, he was someone who both played a role in making the wine that went into the bottles and prided himself on judging the wine he drank from those bottles. Carol had never met him.

Clifford was the young assistant to Earl Drake, an up-and-coming vintner whom the owner seemed to believe had a promising future in the industry, perhaps even as his successor as president of Random Harvest when he retired from that position. Carol had not met him either.

She had met Copeland, who was one of the first of the winery's employees she had encountered the day Rafferty's body was discovered. He had been down in the vineyard, talking with Bridges, when she had arrived on the scene. A middle manager at the winery, she had talked with him twice and was inclined to the view that he was sensible and didn't seem to be concealing anything. But what did she know. After all, his initials were jc.

In a second coincidence, Copeland lived in Clarksburg, which made him both a neighbor of Rafferty's and a fellow employee at Random Harvest. In fact, according to Byrnes, Copeland was the only male resident of Clarksburg whose initials were jc. Carol knew that she would have to forget any positive vibes she may have had where he was concerned. Which left her with three candidates for the role of the man whose soul Father Rafferty had tried to save.

Or did it? Why was she assuming that the last person mentioned in his diary was someone connected with the winery or with the village where he lived after moving to the Crooked Lake area? It was a logical conclusion, but that didn't guarantee that it was correct. Maybe jc was someone he had met at the Finger

Lakes Race Track. Maybe he was someone from East Moncton who had somehow encountered Rafferty in upstate New York. Or if not East Moncton, how about Verona? For that matter, why must jc be someone the priest had known in any of these places? Maybe he lived somewhere in the vicinity of Crooked Lake and had met up with Rafferty somewhere in some way which she could only guess at. The more Carol thought about the possibilities, the more discouraged she became. I have to stop this, she thought. Right now I'll concentrate on Church, Clifford, and Copeland.

The search for mc was necessarily more complicated. Because the Turning Stone Casino was located in Verona, it had made sense to begin the search by looking for people living there. But Verona was surrounded by much larger cities with an aggregate population of over 100,000, and mc could have come from any of those nearby places. In any event, Byrnes had focused on Verona. His message contained all of the names and addresses of people living there whose initials were mc. But he circled one name, Mark Cahill, and suggested that Carol start there.

Carol reached Byrnes on his car phone.

"Thanks, Tommy," she said. "It's a nice piece of work. I'm not sure where it will take us, but it's a helluva lot better than looking for needles in haystacks. Why single out Cahill up in Verona?"

"Well, I tried to get as much information on those addresses as I could. A few phone calls ruled most of them out—neighborhoods too fancy for a friend of Rafferty's. At least that's what I thought. But this guy Cahill lives in a place that calls itself a boarding house. Owner's name is Simmons. It's really an old converted motel, not one of the nicer sections of town. I asked myself what kind of digs Rafferty, with all his money issues, might be living in, and it just seemed to be a place like that. You've said Rafferty didn't mix much, so I thought maybe the guy who cued him in to Turning Stone might have lived there, too. You know, they couldn't help but see each other, both of them living in this boarding house. Look, Sheriff, I know this is just a wild guess. But you've got to start somewhere, so why not Cahill?"

Carol was impressed with Byrnes' thinking. What is more, she knew he was right. She herself had found the place where Rafferty had lived in Verona. And now it looked as if Cahill lived there as well. She could have saved Byrnes some trouble by telling him that Rafferty had stayed at the so-called boarding house. He had saved her some time by suggesting that Cahill was the mc she should talk to first.

It was probably more important to pursue the men who might be jc, but she decided to begin with Cahill. No need, Carol thought, to frighten him with word that a sheriff wants to speak with him. She'd have one of the men do it. One of the men turned out to be Barrett, whom she briefed on what this was all about and what he should say and not say.

Not surprisingly, Cahill was not in. Barrett left the message the sheriff had spelled out for him to use: an old acquaintance, Brendan Rafferty, had called to see how he was doing, and could he please give him a call back. He left his own cell phone number. If all went according to plan, either she or Bridges would be meeting with Mark Cahill in the very near future.

There was no need to place calls to Church, Clifford, and Copeland. She would drive on over to the winery and talk with each of them today. What she had to decide before doing it was just how she should approach the issue. For a moment she debated whether to defer those conversations until the following morning, giving herself time to discuss strategy with Kevin that evening. But much as she would welcome Kevin's input, she knew that this was her job. She had handled her conversation with Sadowsky without Kevin's advice, and she had instructed him on how to proceed with Flanagan.

So instead of arguing strategy with Kevin, she got herself a cup of coffee, sat at her desk, and for the better part of half an hour argued with herself about just what she should say and what she should ask of these men, one of whom might be Rafferty's jc.

She would need to keep firmly in mind that it was entirely possible that none of the three was jc. She could not, or rather should not, be aggressive. She should, of course, ask them whether they knew Rafferty and, if so, how. She had already asked Copeland that question and learned nothing. She would ask them what they had heard about him since his death, leaving the impression, she hoped, that she valued their opinions on his mysterious death. It was no longer a secret that Rafferty had been a priest, although she did not know whether these men would have heard it. There was not only no reason not to bring it up, but also doing so might possibly elicit a reaction which would be telling. Carol went over in her mind the two entries in the diary which referred to jc, entries which she had by now committed to memory. Were there ideas in those diary entries, either written or hinted at, which she could toss out in a casual conversation? She couldn't think of any, inasmuch as what Rafferty had put down in the notebook reflected his own thought processes, not anything which he had said to jc.

Father Brown. Should she drop his name into the discussion? She tried to imagine what Rafferty might have said to jc. "Do you know the Father Brown detective stories? No? Well, perhaps you should read them, because they may tell you something about me and why I am interested in you." No, she said to herself, the priest, in his own mind, believed he was walking in the Chesterton priest's shoes. There would have been no point in his mentioning Father Brown to jc.

In the final analysis, what she would be doing was looking for any small hint that the dialogue with the sheriff was unwelcome or unsettling. A fleeting facial expression. A poorly chosen word. What looked to be an overly rehearsed manner.

Finally, Carol realized that she was stalling. She got to her feet, told Ms. Franks where she was going, and walked out into the chilly air of this first Monday in November.

CHAPTER 36

Carol was on her way to the Random Harvest winery to have a talk with three of its employees whose initials happened to be jc. Kevin, several hundred miles away, was on his way to a faculty meeting at Madison College. Both were doing what was required of them in their respective jobs, but Carol was looking forward to the day while Kevin was not. If she played her cards right and if one of the three men she proposed to interview was indeed Brendan Rafferty's jc, she might have in her possession at least one more important piece of the puzzle surrounding the murder of the ex-priest. If Kevin were lucky, he would be able to stay awake while his colleagues debated what he thought of as trivial points in an agenda which didn't much interest him.

It was not that Kevin hated faculty meetings. Only some of them, and this was going to be one of the ones he hated. For some reason, the smaller the issue, the more heated the debate. He had read the agenda for the meeting, thought of it as an invitation to reinvent the wheel, and decided to go because he was expected to. He took a back-row seat in the conference room and pulled out a yellow pad on which he could take notes or doodle, depending on how the meeting went. Some of his colleagues around the room opened their laptops, presumably to do something they regarded as more important than listening to the provost hold forth on the need to update the college's mission statement. While he may have agreed with their priorities, Kevin couldn't quite bring himself to be so conspicuously indifferent to the speaker.

The room began to fill up, and one of the latecomers was Lester Martin, the professor whom Kevin had consulted as to whether a Father Brendan Rafferty's name had come up in his research project on pedophilia. Martin saw Kevin, waved, and pulled out a chair next to him in the back row.

"Morning, Whitman," he said, his tone jocular. "Did you, by any chance, go up to Massachusetts this weekend?"

"Hello, Lester," Kevin said, shifting his seat to make more room for his colleague. "The answer is yes. I made the trip for science. I thought I might dig up something to add to your database."

"Sure you did," Martin laughed. "I'm guessing you did it for your sheriff. Learn anything interesting?"

At that moment the chairman called the meeting to order, and the two men settled back into their seats, resigned to two hours of boredom. Their expectations were not disappointed. Martin didn't fall asleep, although he nodded from time to time. Kevin filled half a page with the intricate doodles that his music department colleagues had come to regard as his trademark. It was five of twelve when the meeting finally adjourned.

"Do you have lunch plans?" Martin asked as they gathered up their papers.

"No. Want to make it the faculty club?"

"Sure. If we hurry, we might get a table."

They did get a table, and having placed their orders, turned to what was obviously Martin's reason for suggesting lunch.

"So, back to my question. I figured you'd probably be going up to that place outside of Boston. East Moncton, right? Anyway, I've been wondering whether you learned anything about that missing priest."

"I did, but nothing that says he either is or isn't a pedophile. The interesting stuff had to do with whether any of the locals knew where he was, and if they did, what they did about it. Anyway, nobody mentioned pedophiles. But there's a good chance that one man I met is someone the missing priest referred to in his diary. If I'm right, he had a run-in with the priest back before he abandoned his church and left East Moncton."

"Interesting," Martin said. "Any idea what the run-in was about?"

"From the priest's diary it seems like it concerned this man's son. But it's hard to tell. His entries in the diary are all pretty vague, as if he was afraid to be specific."

"How old is this man's son?"

"The priest didn't say. But I think I saw someone who could be his son when I talked with the man. He looked like a teenager. Of course Flanagan may have more than one son."

Professor Martin looked thoughtful.

"What if this man thought his son was being abused by the priest?"

"We've thought about that," Kevin said, "but we don't know. I didn't think it was my place to ask a direct question like that. Flanagan was described to me as anti-abortion and hostile to homosexuals, and that's not really surprising. But we didn't talk about the possibility of any relationship between his son and the priest."

"Flanagan. That's the man's name?"

"Yes. Gerald Flanagan. In his diary the priest referred to a man whose initials are gf. I think he was referring to Flanagan."

"What's your impression of Flanagan? I mean, did he seem like somebody who could have threatened the priest?"

"He didn't really talk about the priest. I had the impression that he didn't want to talk about him."

"I know this isn't any of my business," Martin said, "but you've piqued my curiosity. What you tell me makes me curious about this man Flanagan. Is there anything else you and your sheriff know about him?"

"Let's see. He dismissed a report by one of his fellow parishioners at the church that he'd seen the priest recently at a winery upstate—the winery where we know the priest was working and where he was killed. Flanagan said the man who reported seeing the priest there was just an unreliable drunk. He also described himself as an avid bow hunter who'd just got himself a nice buck. That's just about it."

Martin looked disappointed. Kevin remembered something else.

"It doesn't mention Flanagan," he said, "but one of the things the priest kept in his Bible was a clipping about a demonstration at an abortion clinic. I bring it up only because one of the people I talked to told me Flanagan thought the priest wasn't tough enough on abortion. There's probably no connection."

"Do you know what paper the clipping came from?"

"No, I'm afraid not, but considering that the priest was from East Moncton, it's a good guess it was from one of the Boston area papers."

Lunch arrived, and the conversation turned briefly to other subjects, including a post mortem on the morning's faculty meeting. But an idea had been taking shape in Professor Martin's mind, and he finally gave voice to it.

"Would you mind if I had my assistant try to see what he can find out about this man Flanagan?"

Kevin gave his table mate a knowing smile.

"You're a lot like me, Lester. Or do you prefer Les?"

"Les to my friends."

"Good. Like I say, we're really alike. Detectives under our academic robes. Your interest in Flanagan doesn't have much to do with your research project, does it? You're intrigued by the mystery of Father Rafferty, just like I am. So, by all means, let your man see what dirt he can dig up on Flanagan. If it helps, I'll be in your debt. So will the sheriff."

"He may come up empty, but Hungerford's pretty good. I'll bet he can find out where that abortion clinic demonstration took place and whether Flanagan was part of it. If he was, he may be able to put together a profile on him."

When they left the club and headed back to their offices, Kevin found himself weighing the odds that Martin's assistant might actually help to trap Father Brendan Rafferty's killer. The odds weren't good. But Kevin was as anxious as the sociologist to know what Hungerford would turn up.

———

It quickly became apparent that Professor Martin had put his assistant, Warren Hungerford, right to work digging up dirt on Gerald Flanagan. And Hungerford, like Officer Byrnes up in Cumberland, knew his way around the Internet. It was just a little after four p.m. when the phone rang in Kevin's office.

"Martin here," the sociologist said in a voice that made those two words sound almost triumphant.

"Don't tell me you've got some information already?" Kevin was surprised.

"I do, and I think you'll be interested. Told you Hungerford's a godsend."

"Good. Let's hear it."

"Well, it seems that in spite of the decline in readership among the big city papers, small towns still churn out local news. Sometimes it's just weeklies, but up Boston way a number of towns manage to keep the citizenry up to date on high school sports, piddling little debates about trash pickup, that kind of stuff. Warren managed to wade through it and, lo and behold, there was your man Flanagan. He was the featured speaker at the abortion clinic demonstration you mentioned. Actually, the story, written by a witty stringer, compared him to a soapbox orator on Hyde Park Corner. It took place in a town called Cranwell, close to East Moncton on the outer Boston beltway. But Flanagan was just getting started. He now has a web site called SHOUT, which stands for Stamp Homosexuals Out. I didn't know acronyms could be made up of initials and real words like that."

Kevin was enjoying the fact that his colleague at Madison was having fun with the Rafferty case.

"Anything about pedophiles?" he asked.

"Interestingly, no. But in view of what we now know about Flanagan, I'm sure he'd be upset about pedophile priests. Probably a lot more than upset. I suspect he'd go off on a rampage."

"I take it he has a record of going on a rampage."

"It looks that way, although Warren didn't spend a lot of time on it," Martin said. "He's certainly been outspoken about homosexuals and abortion, mostly on his web site, but there's also a record of him turning up at meetings and raising a bit of hell. Let's just say that his strong suit isn't reasoning together with those he disagrees with."

"He sounds like the man Father Rafferty said he was having a problem with. According to the diary, Flanagan was critical of both the priest and his own son. About what isn't clear, and that's what we need to know. Our guess has been that the priest was abusing the son—or that Flanagan thought that he was."

The line went quiet for a moment.

"Did you say that Flanagan was angry at both the priest and his son?" Martin asked, his tone of voice suggesting that something had occurred to him.

"I don't know about angry, but in his diary the priest said something about gf being wrong to judge him and wrong to judge his son."

"I'm trying to put two and two together. If the priest were a pedophile, the victim would almost certainly have been a little boy, at least a prepubescent boy. I can't see a father being angry with a son who's just a little boy; he'd be understandably furious with the priest, of course, but why judge the boy? Even if the father's a martinet, he should understand that the kid would be confused by the attention being paid to him by the priest, not complicit in what was going on. Which makes me think that maybe the son is older—like the teenager you saw. In that case, what you'd have would be a homosexual relationship, not pedophilia. And we know that Flanagan has a thing about homosexuals."

"What you're saying is that the priest wasn't abusing Flanagan's son, but having a sexual relationship with him?"

"It could be. Depends on how old the son is. I think you need to know more about Flanagan's family."

The conversation came to an abrupt end when Martin suddenly realized that he was going to be late for a seminar. Kevin remained at his desk, thinking about Rafferty, Flanagan, and Flanagan's son.

Was the young man he had seen beside the parted curtain when he left the Flanagan residence the son the priest had referred to? If so, what had been his relationship with the priest? What was his relationship with his father? The only thing Kevin knew for sure was that Father Rafferty had said that gf had been wrong to judge both him and his son. Of course the priest could have been lying to the reader of the diary. But why? The only reader the diary had been intended for was the priest himself. Had he been lying to himself? Again the question was why? The picture forming in Kevin's mind was that of a father who was convinced, wrongly, that his son and the priest were involved in a sexual relationship. A homosexual relationship. A relationship which would have been anathema for a man who had a web site named SHOUT: Stamp Homosexuals Out.

What would such a man do if he thought that his son was homosexual? It seemed likely that he would judge him, and judge him harshly. And what would he do about the person he believed had encouraged his son's homosexuality? Kevin hated to think about it.

CHAPTER 37

She knew that she should go directly to the winery, but Carol chose to get there by a roundabout route, a route that took her to Blue Water Point on Crooked Lake. She and Kevin had agreed that she would pick up a few things to have on hand for meals at the cottage when he returned to the lake on Thursday. There was no need to do it today; Thursday was still three days away. But Carol was scheduled to testify before the county council on her departmental budget on Tuesday, and on Wednesday she would be attending a memorial service for the recently deceased police chief of Southport. So she rationalized that it would be better to stock Kevin's fridge today, even if neither the budget hearing nor the memorial service would occupy more than a couple of hours of her time.

For the two-plus years they had known each other, Carol had accepted the fact that they would share summers but necessarily lead separate lives between September and May. But since Kevin had announced that he had arranged his teaching schedule so that he could return to the lake more frequently in the off season, she had become even more impatient to have him there. It was now early November, only two months since he had packed up and gone back to the city, and he had already come back to the cottage for two long weekends and would be back for a third in just three days. She knew that she should be satisfied, but she wasn't. Her desire to stop at the cottage, to spend a few minutes in his space, was almost irresistible.

Carol shut off the ignition, gathered up the sacks full of groceries, and let herself into the cottage. It was cool, almost cold inside, but she resisted the urge to turn up the heat. She didn't plan to stay long before going on to the winery. She wandered from room to room, the mental newsreel of their last weekend together running pleasantly through her mind. In less than three weeks she would celebrate her 37th birthday, but she felt almost like a schoolgirl in the throes of a crush. Kevin had left the cottage neat and tidy. Too tidy. The bed had been made up so perfectly that it could have passed a Marine Corps inspection. Carol impulsively threw herself on it, then got up and surveyed the result. She smiled and headed out onto the deck and from there down onto the beach.

There wouldn't be that many more nice days before the first signs of the approach of winter manifested themselves. Carol bent down and ran her hand through the water along the shore. It was cold. If the lake were to freeze over this winter, it wouldn't happen for at least another two or three months, but the temperature had already dropped sharply since the last day that she and Kevin had gone swimming. The hillside across the lake, so recently aflame with the reds and golds of an unusually brilliant autumn, was now almost bare except for those patches dominated by pines. How quickly it had changed. Two weeks earlier, on the day she had been standing in the Random Harvest vineyard examining the faux scarecrow, the colors of fall were still sufficiently bright to attract tourists to the Crooked Lake wine trail.

Carol indulged herself for a few more minutes. She selected a few flat stones from along the beach and skipped them out into the lake, delighting as she always did at the way they skimmed over the surface, bouncing along until they lost momentum and sank. She knew nothing about the hydrodynamics of what she had heard the English call "ducks and drakes." It was simply a childhood game which still gave her pleasure. Kevin was a stone skipper. She was in the mood for doing things they both loved to do.

Reluctantly, Carol made her way back to the cottage, locked the doors, and headed for Random Harvest. She had managed to kill a couple of hours, pushing her conversations with Church, Clifford, and Copeland into the early hours of the afternoon. There was a good chance that they would be at lunch. If so, she would drop by Drake's office and see if they had figured out what had happened to the winery's bank account.

The parking lot at the winery was much less crowded than it had been the day Brendan Rafferty's body had been found. By this time the fall's harvest would be finished, all, that is, except for the ice wine grapes. Some of the company's wines would be fermenting. Others would be in the process of being bottled. Cases of wine would be moving to market, and there would still be a few visitors in the tasting room and gift shop. There was always something going on at Random Harvest Vineyards.

Carol was walking into the main building just as Earl Drake, the owner, was on his way out.

"Sheriff Kelleher," Drake said, his voice surprisingly pleasant, "I was just on my way down to Southport, but I'd like to talk with you if you have a few minutes."

"Of course," she replied. "I'm here to see a couple of your people, but that can wait."

What, she wondered, could be on his mind? Since the discovery of Rafferty's body he had been impatient to have the minions of the law out of the winery. Perhaps he wanted to revisit the problem of the missing money, a problem he had previously told her he could handle himself.

Drake went back into the winery, Carol right behind him. They climbed the stairs and went into the owner's office. He shut the door, invited her to have a seat, and suggested coffee, which she declined.

"I think I owe you an apology, Sheriff," he began. "I may have been rude back when we first spoke about that man Rafferty's murder. It was a real shock, and I imagined that the wine-tasting business would drop way off. Well, it didn't, and your people have been very civil."

Had he expected them to go running around the place like gangbusters, making demands, interfering with the day-to-day operations of the winery?

"No apology necessary," Carol said. "It's a puzzling case, and we've had to talk with a number of your employees. In fact, I'm here today to speak with several of them. We still don't know who killed Mr. Rafferty, and a couple of those who might have done it aren't related to the winery in any way."

"I'm glad to hear that," Drake said, obviously relieved.

"You should know, however, that I haven't ruled out the possibility that the guilty party could be an employee of yours," Carol said, anxious to make it clear that her investigation hadn't exonerated everyone in the winery's small staff. "But I don't think you changed your plan for the noon hour to bring me up to your office to apologize. Is there some new problem I should know about?"

"Not really a new problem. We talked about it briefly last week, and I said it was my worry, not yours. I'm talking about what looks like bookkeeping fraud."

"Have you decided that it may have something to do with the murder?" Carol asked. She had considered raising the issue with him, but was surprised that the winery's owner was willing to bring her into his confidence regarding what was surely a humiliating subject.

"No, nothing like that," Drake said. He paused, cleared his throat, and went on to say something which appeared to cause him pain.

"The problem is, I'm worried about Parker Jameson. Like I told you, he's an old friend. We've known each other since back before I got the bug to go into the wine business. We played golf together, belonged to the same poker group. Our wives are real thick. He didn't need a job, and the winery wasn't big enough to justify a full-time accountant. We were sort of like a mom-and-pop store, if you know what I mean. Anyway, I suggested he might come on board, give us a few hours of his time each week. He had the background, and it never occurred to me he couldn't be trusted with every dime we made. It's worked out just fine. We've grown a bit; his hours have expanded. But then this thing happened—the loss of that money."

Drake spun his swivel chair so he could look out the window. Carol had no intention of interrupting. He'd get to his point in his own way, in his own time.

"Parker isn't the neatest person I know. I assumed that somehow something had gotten lost or misplaced in that office of his. Figured he'd find it, we'd all breathe a sigh of relief and get on with it. But the money is still missing. It won't kill us, so I guess I've calmed down some. But I can't shake a growing suspicion that Parker's the problem. Hell, I don't pay attention to that stuff. Never had to, knowing that he knew what he was doing. It left me to worry about which way to take the company. Concentrate on the varietals? Chardonnay versus Riesling? How far to push the ice wine, which is pretty dear but kinda fun."

Once again Drake swiveled about, and now, facing Carol, he got to his point.

"I hate to say it, but I'm worried that Jameson's responsible for our problem. Not just that he's sloppy, but that maybe he's stealing from me. From Random Harvest."

"I can imagine that that would be terribly upsetting," Carol said. "A man you've known and liked, a man you've trusted. But I don't quite understand. Wasn't it Mr. Jameson who came to you and reported that the books didn't balance, that a lot of money was gone? Why would he defraud you and then come and alert you to the fact that something was awry? If he knew that you gave him a free hand, that you didn't bother yourself with the books, wouldn't it be sensible just to keep his mouth shut if he was fiddling the books?"

Carol realized that she was defending Parker Jameson. Or at least suggesting that it was difficult to believe he was both a crook and a whistleblower. There had to be something else that caused Drake to suspect Jameson.

"I know," he said, "but something's wrong. It's false invoices. That's what Parker says. A bunch of them over the last few months, all paid. His signature's on the checks. I don't pretend to know who we get all our supplies from, but Parker says some of the invoices come from a couple of companies he doesn't know anything about. The Vintner's Friend, I think he said, and some place called Hatton's Supplies. He says he didn't realize it when he paid them, but now that he knows there's a problem, he's checked with receiving. And what he hears is that they never heard of these two companies and never received anything from them. I don't know beans about accounting, but I can't understand why Parker paid somebody if the goods hadn't been received and signed for."

Carol didn't know any more about good accounting practices than Drake, but she could see why the owner might be worried about Jameson. He seemed to have come to the conclusion that his friend might have set up dummy companies, created phony invoices, and paid them, pocketing the money himself. He would claim that someone else was the thief, someone who would, of course, never be caught because he was simply a figment of Jameson's imagination. And Jameson could hide behind his reputation as a disorganized bookkeeper. It was a stigma he could live with.

"Have you hired an auditor?" Carol asked.

"I guess I'll have to. I suppose I don't have any other choice. But I don't want to learn that Parker's dishonest. I'd forgive him if he was careless, if he cost us a chunk of our profits, but I don't know what I'd do if it turned out that he was ripping me off."

"Why are you telling me this, Mr. Drake?"

"I'm not really sure. Like I said before, I didn't want the police to be involved. But things don't look so good, and I thought you might have an idea. Not open up a formal investigation or anything like that. Maybe you could just give me your opinion on how I could go about dealing with this mess."

Carol was flattered that the owner of Random Harvest Vineyards thought she could help him find a way out of his dilemma. But she couldn't.

"I still think you need a thorough, chips fall where they may, audit. What a good auditor will find, I think, is that these bogus companies Mr. Jameson paid are nothing but post office boxes, that the paperwork is worthless. And, if it makes you feel better, I think that whoever's ripping you off isn't your friend but someone else here at Random Harvest. Remember all those keys you told me about?"

"I suppose that would be better than learning it was Parker," Drake said. "But not much. We're family here."

Carol had heard almost the exact same words from Drake the previous week. But she was pretty certain that Random Harvest was anything but family. Somebody in the winery's modest complement of managers and laborers was very probably a thief. Were his initials also jc?

CHAPTER 38

By the time that Carol was again able to focus on the men who might be Father Rafferty's jc, two of them had come back from lunch and were in their offices. The third, Joe Clifford, was out sick. She stopped by the gift shop and purchased a candy bar which she would make do for her lunch. It was almost 1:30 when she knocked on Jerome Copeland's door.

He looked up from his desk and motioned for her to come on in.

"Good to see you, Sheriff," he said, then added, as a broad smile lit up his face, "that is unless you've come to arrest me."

"Why would I be doing that?" Carol asked.

The smile disappeared from his face, as if he realized that he might have miscalculated the sheriff's mood.

"Sorry, I didn't mean to make light of your investigation."

"It has been my experience, Mr. Copeland, that the more people I talk with, and the more times I talk with them, the more I learn. It is then, and only then, that I contemplate arresting anyone."

Carol was amused by the sound of her own voice. And by the rather pompous tone she had adopted. She would have to be careful not to take herself too seriously.

"I'm here because I'm interested in how things look to you," she continued. "About the Rafferty murder, that is. But I realize that I don't know much about your association with Random Harvest. I know you're a manager here. What do you manage?"

"Oh, that." Copeland's smile returned. "We're a small company, as you've probably observed. Manager's sort of an inflated title. Ask around, you'll probably discover half a dozen managers. What's that, close to one in six of our employees? Fact is, I have responsibility for keeping us stocked to do our thing.

Supplies, everything from bottles to boxes. I deal with companies that we order stuff from."

Well, well, Carol thought. Back to Earl Drake's money problems. And so soon.

"So," Carol summarized, "you negotiate with the company's suppliers, maintain inventory, put in orders, unload things when they arrive, pay the bills. Is that it?"

"Not quite. I don't pay bills. That's Jameson's job. But otherwise, that's about it."

There seemed to be no reason why Carol should act as if she were ignorant of the troubles she'd just been discussing with Drake. The owner had said that Jameson had learned from receiving that they'd never heard of two companies, much less received shipments from them. The "they" in receiving would presumably be Copeland.

"Have you ever ordered anything from Hatton's Supplies?" she asked.

The question was not one Copeland had expected.

"You know about Hatton's?" he asked.

"I've heard of it. And of a place called The Vintner's Friend. Why don't you tell me about them?"

"I don't understand. What do you know about those firms?"

"That's what I'm asking you."

Copeland leaned forward in his chair as if to share some secret with the sheriff.

"I never placed an order at either place," he said in a low, conspiratorial voice. "And that's the honest truth. I'd never heard of them until a few days ago."

"Is there such a place as Hatton's? Or The Vintner's Friend?"

"Not around here there isn't," he answered. "Maybe Albany or Buffalo."

"I take it then that you know the supply houses in the upstate area."

"Of course. That's my business. We're always on the lookout for good suppliers that are reliable."

"So you never had to sign off on any delivery from those places?"

Jerome Copeland wasn't just uncomfortable. He was nervous.

"Never. I already told Mr. Drake, I don't know anything about it." And then, as if to erase any doubt: "It's not my fault."

Carol had no reason to think it was Copeland's fault, but she could understand why he might be worried.

"Tell me, how long have you been with Random Harvest?"

"Just under four years." The look on Copeland's face said that he was puzzled by this change of subject.

He stroked his bushy mustache, something he seemed to do when he was thinking. Or uneasy.

"Did you know Mr. Drake before that?"

"No. I'd been working for the state extension service, but thought it might be interesting to get into the wine business. I dropped off a résumé at several of the wineries in the Finger Lakes area, and one day Mr. Francis got in touch with me, asked me to stop by and talk with him."

So he had been hired by Doug Francis, the man who didn't bother to check for references. Much as she had been interested in what Copeland had to say—or not say—about the winery's current financial scandal, it was time to get back to her reason for being in his office.

"Let's talk about Brendan Rafferty. How well did you know him?"

"I thought I told you last time we talked. I didn't know him at all."

"That's right, you did. Let me put it this way. What did you know about him? Were you aware somebody of that name worked here?"

Once again, Copeland looked a bit apprehensive, as if trying to figure out where the sheriff was going with her questions.

"I probably saw him around. I mean, this isn't a big operation. But I don't recall ever speaking to him or him to me. Nobody mentioned him to me, at least not as far as I can remember."

"Okay, he was a stranger. What have you heard since his death? I'm sure it must have been the talk of the winery these last two weeks."

This seemed like an easier question. Copeland became more animated.

"You're right. He's been topic number one. No one can understand why he was killed. Word is he was a nobody. Why kill a nobody? It couldn't be anybody here at Random Harvest who did it. I know it doesn't sound very nice, but no one here knew him well enough to kill him. Know what I mean? People don't go around killing someone they don't know."

Carol, of course, was quite prepared to buy that. What Copeland had told her was very much what she expected to hear from all of the winery's employees. And it made good intuitive sense. The problem was that Brendan Rafferty was not unknown. The question was who, if anyone, among the winery personnel *did* know Rafferty well enough to have a reason to kill him.

"I understand you live in Clarksburg."

"Right," Copeland answered, immediately aware of what was on the sheriff's mind. "And you're going to tell me that Rafferty lived there, too. I know. A couple of the guys have asked me if I knew that's where he lived. I guess it's general knowledge now. But I didn't know it until this last week. He probably didn't mix any better over there than he did here."

"He seems to have had some friends in his church," Carol said. "You don't belong to St. Leo's by any chance, do you?"

"No, that's the Catholic church. I'm kinda one of those irregular Protestants. You know, Christmas, Easter."

"Ever do any gambling?"

Once again, Copeland was caught off-guard by the unexpected question. But nothing Carol saw in his reaction suggested that he viewed the question as a trap.

"Gambling? Not on my salary," he said, smiling at what seemed to strike him as the absurdity of it. "There's a pool here at the winery for the World Series, the Super Bowl, March Madness, that kind of thing. But that's just peanuts. Why do you ask?"

"Just thinking out loud, I guess," she said, not explaining what she was thinking about.

"Oh, I almost forgot. One more question. Do you happen to know a guy named Carl Sadowsky?"

"Sadowsky? No. Should I?"

"Short, heavyset, middle-aged. Almost always wears a red vest."

Copeland shook his head.

"Sorry, I can't help you there."

And Carol was prepared to believe that he couldn't.

Several minutes later she was seated in the office of another of the men with jc as initials. His name was Jared Church.

"Mr. Church, I'm sure you know that we're trying to find out what caused one of the winery's employees to be shot and then strung up like a scarecrow down in one of your vineyards. My colleagues and I have been talking to all of you, learning what we can about the victim. I'm sorry not to have gotten around to you earlier, but it takes time. All I want to do is listen to what you have to say about Mr. Rafferty and what you think may have happened here. Okay?"

"Of course, Sheriff."

Church's office, if it could be called that, was smaller than Copeland's, more of a small cul-de-sac at the back of a room which looked more like Carol's remembrance of her high school chemistry lab than it did like a place where wines were made. They sat in a crowded space, no more than two feet apart.

"I understand that you've been here longer than almost everyone."

"I suppose so," he said. "This was just a little experiment for Mr. Drake back then. I was just out of high school. The Vietnam War was over; things were getting back to normal. It was a pretty good time to be growing up in Southport. But I had no idea what I wanted to do. Anyway, I knew Mr. Drake's daughter. We'd been in school together. Never dated, just enjoyed each other's company. One day Pam suggested that I ought to talk to her dad about working at the winery, which I did. I remember he gave me a hard time, wanted to know if I'd been screwing his daughter. Said if he found I'd messed around with her he'd have my hide. I must have looked innocent or something, because he took me on. I've been here ever since."

"What is it you do here?"

"It'd be easier to tell you what I don't do. But to answer your question, I'm sort of the go-to guy. I guess I spend most of my time in fermentation, but Mr. Drake encourages me to do almost everything. And lets me do it. I don't mean to show off, but I'd bet I know more about the business than almost anybody here. They're a good bunch, but they all have their own jobs. Mine is wine. I love it. If Mr. Drake wants an honest opinion about our 2007 Chardonnay compared, say, to Silver Leaf's or one of the others, he'd ask me."

"It sounds like this is your life," Carol said, impressed with Church's verbal bio.

"I suppose it is," he said. "There was a time I thought maybe it'd be nice to marry Pam, but it wouldn't have worked. She went off to college, got herself into another life. I found myself a nice girl over in Elmira. We've got three kids, a pretty good spread outside of Cumberland. I'm a lucky guy."

This couldn't possibly be Brendan Rafferty's jc, Carol thought. But she knew she shouldn't be jumping to that conclusion. Church seemed honest, down to earth, comfortable in his own skin, but she really knew nothing about him other than what he had told her and how he had told her. There were other questions she needed to ask, questions about the man Copeland had referred to as a nobody.

"What can you tell me about Brendan Rafferty?" she asked. It was an open-ended question. She'd let him decide how to address it.

"A good man, I think. Quiet. Not unfriendly, but someone you'd probably never get close to. We hardly ever talked—it just wasn't his way—but I got the impression he was smart. About wine, I mean. He probably knew more about wines than most of the people here, and not just because he drank wine."

"You knew him as a drinker?"

"That's not what I meant. Maybe he drank wine, maybe he didn't. I mean he was probably knowledgeable about wines. We didn't talk about it, like I said, but I'd bet he knew a few things about both viticulture and enology."

Church obviously had seen Rafferty as something of a kindred spirit. He was the first person she had spoken with other than Bernie Stolnitz who seemed genuinely interested in the ex-priest. The Rhodes woman over in Clarksburg, she decided, didn't really count.

"Do you have any thoughts about what happened to him? Why he was killed like he was?"

"I've wondered about it. I suppose everyone has. It just doesn't make sense. If he had enemies, well, I can't imagine any of them belonging to Random Harvest. No one knew him well enough to be an enemy. What could he have done to make someone angry enough to kill him?"

"Did he ever say anything to you about any problems he had? Not just here but before he came to Random Harvest?"

"No," Church said softly. "It's like I said, we never really talked. I tried once or twice, but he didn't go along. I mean, he wasn't unpleasant, but you sort of knew he didn't want to."

Carol made a spur of the moment decision to do something she had planned not to do.

"Mr. Church, I'd like to share something with you. Brendan Rafferty kept a diary. He didn't write in it often, and he didn't say much. But near the end of the diary he made mention of someone. He never spelled out a name, but he did use this person's initials. They're JC."

Carol emphasized the initials, turning the ex-priest's lower case into capitals in her own mind. She watched Jared Church closely as she did so.

"He doesn't say the person he is referring to is someone at Random Harvest," she continued. "I mention it only because they come at the very end of the diary. Your initials are JC. Can you think of any reason why Mr. Rafferty would have mentioned you in his diary?"

Carol had encountered good dissemblers in her life, but it would have been hard to feign the look of puzzlement on Church's face.

"Me? That makes no sense at all. He didn't know me. What was it he said about JC?"

This was something Carol was not prepared to divulge.

"Frankly, it isn't clear," she said. And she was being frank. "We don't think we'll know until we find out who JC is. If it isn't you, we'll just keep looking. But there's one thing I am sure of. We will find him."

When Carol brought the conversation to a close, she had left Jared Church with something to think about: Why had that silent and distant man, Brendan Rafferty, mentioned him in his diary? And if not him, who?

CHAPTER 39

Tuesday morning brought two pieces of news to the Cumberland County Sheriff's Department. One was not wholly unexpected, the other came as a surprise. The bearer of the first news was Officer Byrnes, who caught the sheriff right after the staff meeting. He had been on the trail of Hatton's Supplies and The Vintner's Friend.

"They're both just P.O. boxes," Byrnes said, "one in Binghamton, the other in some place called Lyons. There's no evidence that there's any company linked to either of the boxes. I checked with the local Chambers of Commerce. Nothing. It looks like they're dummies."

"That's what I thought," Carol said. "Do you know when the boxes were opened?"

"They're both recent. One was rented two months ago, the other one a little less than six weeks ago."

"Any names? I mean personal names."

"The signature card for Hatton's shows the name of Barnaby Rudge. For the Vintner's place it's Franklin Pierce."

"Wonderful." Carol sounded sarcastic. "Somebody's got a lousy sense of humor. A Charles Dickens' character and one of America's forgotten presidents. Excuse me while I laugh."

"Anything you want me to do about it?"

"I'll be seeing the owner of the winery today. We'll see what he'd like to do. But yes, chances are, we'll be trying to identify Rudge and Pierce."

The second piece of news came when Carol called Random Harvest to see if Joseph Clifford had recovered from whatever ailed him and had reported for work. The answer was yes, but of equal, perhaps greater, interest was word that there had been a phone call asking for Brendan Rafferty. Needless to say, this got Carol's attention.

"Who took the call?" she asked the woman who answered the phone at the winery.

"I did," said the woman on the other end of the line. "Blanche Sweet."

"Then I'd like you to tell me everything you can about the call. First, what was the caller's name?"

"Philip Flanagan."

This was news that made Barnaby Rudge and Franklin Pierce fade into insignificance.

"What did you tell him?" Carol asked, barely able to control her excitement.

"Well, I wasn't sure quite what to say. I mean, I knew you people were looking into Mr. Rafferty's death and all that. And Mr. Drake had told us not to discuss Mr. Rafferty with anyone. It was early, and Mr. Drake wasn't in yet, so I couldn't ask him what I should say."

"So what did you say?" Carol's impatience showed.

"I told him he wasn't here."

"That's all?"

"Yes, but he wanted more information. He asked when he'd be back. I felt stuck. I'd just have looked silly if I tried to make things up. So I said he wasn't coming back. And that's the truth, isn't it? I didn't lie to him."

"So you didn't say he was dead?"

"No. Should I have?"

Carol wasn't sure herself what would have been the best thing to say. She skipped past Ms. Sweet's question to ask one of her own.

"Did Mr. Flanagan ask you where Mr. Rafferty had gone? Where he could get in touch with him?"

"Yes, but I just said I didn't know. I guess that was a lie, wasn't it?"

"Did you ask him for his phone number?"

"I didn't see much point in it. I mean Mr. Rafferty wasn't going to be calling him back, was he?"

Carol knew that getting the number would not be a problem, provided that Philip Flanagan was a member of Gerald Flanagan's family and was living in his home. Was this the son that Father Rafferty had alluded to in his diary? That thought prompted another question.

"How old would you say Philip Flanagan is? Based on his voice, how he sounded over the phone? An adult? A teenager? A kid whose voice was changing? A little boy?"

Mrs. Sweet sounded uncertain.

"I don't have any boys. Just girls. So I'm not really sure. But I don't think he's an adult. Definitely not a kid either. It's just a guess, but I'd say in his teens."

"Did Mr. Flanagan ever say why he wanted to speak with Mr. Rafferty?"

"No. Like I said, he didn't really say much at all. When I told him that Mr. Rafferty had gone away, he sounded like he didn't know what to do next."

"So he didn't ask to talk to anyone else at the winery?"

"It seemed like he was thinking about what he would do. But in the end all he did was thank me and hang up."

Carol wished that she had been the one, not Mrs. Sweet, to handle the phone call from Philip Flanagan. But that wasn't fair. The woman had done as well as could be expected. It was doubtful that anyone else at Random Harvest would have done better. Maybe Drake. Or Bernie Stolnitz. She dismissed that thought. It didn't matter.

Carol instructed Byrnes to find the Flanagan phone number in East Moncton and took off for her meeting with Clifford at the winery. It was a trip that was getting tiresome.

———

She realized that Clifford was one member of the relatively small staff at Random Harvest whom she had not seen around the winery on any of her previous visits. Young—early thirties, she guessed—and handsome, he was one of those people who make a strong first impression based on appearance. A rich deep voice helped. He also exuded self-confidence.

"So, our sheriff finally gets around to me," Clifford said, a smile on his face. "I was beginning to worry that I wouldn't be given the honor of an interview. Presumably you want my opinion of the late Brendan Rafferty."

Carol's first impression of Clifford faded quickly. She didn't find his welcoming remarks amusing. This man is rather too full of himself, she thought.

"Yes, I am interested in your opinion of Mr. Rafferty, but I'd prefer to start by asking you to tell me how well you knew him. What was the nature of your relationship with him?"

"I hate to disappoint you, but I didn't know him at all. So you see, I can't really have an opinion."

"Had you ever met him? Ever talked with him?" Carol tried to pretend that she didn't find young Mr. Clifford annoying.

"I'm afraid not. Of course this is a small place, as I'm sure you've noticed, so I'd seen him around. But he was just one of the guys from the cellar."

It had not been Carol's intention to bring up Rafferty's diary when she began her interviews with the men whose initials were jc. But she had done so on the spur of the moment with Church, and perhaps she should do it again. It just might induce Clifford to take their conversation more seriously.

"Okay, you and Rafferty had no relationship. Didn't even talk to each other. How then do you account for the fact that he referred to you in a diary he kept?"

The smile—or was it a smirk—on Clifford's face disappeared. It was only for a split second, but Carol was sure of it. As quickly as it had vanished, it reappeared, this time with a chuckle.

"He mentioned me?" he asked, his voice making clear that he thought the very idea was absurd. "He must have been hallucinating or something. He wouldn't have known any more about me than I did about him. What did he say?"

If Joe Clifford was in fact jc, his brain would be working overtime behind the smile, trying to imagine what it was that Rafferty had said about him. Should she level with him? She already knew how he would react to word that Rafferty had mentioned him. How would he react if he knew that Rafferty had not used his name but only his initials? Carol decided to tell the truth.

"He didn't use names in his diary," she said, "just initials. He called you jc."

"JC?" The smile gave way to a look that Carol chose to read as relieved. "That's not me. I'm sure he was referring to Jerry Copeland. You'll have met him. I've heard him called JC."

Carol had not heard Earl Drake or anyone else refer to Copeland as JC. Perhaps Clifford was right, though. She'd ask around. It shouldn't be hard to find out whether there was a

Random Harvest employee who commonly went by those initials. One way or another, she was interested in the fact that Clifford had immediately pointed to Copeland as the person Rafferty meant. Was it because he was known to his colleagues as JC or because Clifford wanted to point the finger of blame elsewhere? And if blame, blame for what? He certainly couldn't know what Rafferty had written about jc—small case—in his diary.

"I shall be talking to Mr. Copeland," she said. "But let's you and I talk about Mr. Rafferty's death. What do you hear? It must be on everyone's mind. What are people saying? Any ideas as to why he was killed? Why he was down there in the vineyard, looking like a scarecrow?"

"Lots of speculation. Uninformed, of course. The favorite explanation is that someone out of his past did it. He hadn't been here long, and no one seems to know where he came from. So why not some enemy he'd made somewhere else?"

"Is that what you think?"

"I like to think I form opinions based on evidence, Sheriff. Inasmuch as I don't know anything about Mr. Rafferty, it has seemed best not to have a theory. I'll be as interested as the next guy when you find out what happened, but for the time being I'm just Mr. Drake's assistant, doing my job."

"What about the scarecrow business? Doesn't that strike you as a bit odd?"

"Sure. It is odd. Maybe it was meant to make an example of him. You know, sort of a warning—a 'don't mess with me' message."

"Whom do you think the killer would be warning?" Carol asked, interested in the fact that Clifford, having said he didn't wish to speculate, was now speculating.

"No idea. It's just a thought. You'll have to ask him when you catch him."

"You're close to Mr. Drake, aren't you?"

"I am. I guess you'd say I'm his right hand. He hasn't made any announcement, probably won't for another year or so, but I know he's thinking about asking me to take over the operation of the winery when he retires. We talked about it."

"I take it you like the business. Was it your field in college?"

"Not quite. I grew up in California, went to Fresno State. Shifted majors a few times, took a course in enology, but got my degree in business administration. My being here in New York is nothing I planned. It's my wife—she's from this area."

"I think you made a good choice. I'm sure your wife's very nice, but I mean settling in upstate New York."

"I like to think so."

When they had finished what Clifford had called his interview, Carol was feeling somewhat less annoyed with him. Young and a bit brash, but not a bad sort. Of course he had fingered Jerome Copeland as Rafferty's jc. And he couldn't pretend that his own initials weren't jc. Otherwise—

But that was the case with Church and Copeland, too. She had trouble seeing any one of them as Father Rafferty's killer. The diary references didn't say that jc was associated with Random Harvest. In fact, Random Harvest was never mentioned. However, the priest had been worried about jc. Whoever jc was, Rafferty had believed he needed to be saved. Saved from what?

As she left the winery that afternoon, Carol could feel her frustration level rising. She was still aware that too many pieces of the puzzle were still missing.

CHAPTER 40

Sam Bridges, Deputy Sheriff of Cumberland County, rarely got to travel outside of the county in his official capacity. Today was different, and Sam was enjoying the drive. He was not a gambling man, nor was he particularly interested in the ponies, but he had never visited the Finger Lakes Race Track and he welcomed the change of scene. Moreover, it was not a trip on which he was expected to solve a specific problem or provide an answer to a specific question. The sheriff's instructions were simply to find out what he could about Carl Sadowsky. She knew, and so did Sam, that it might prove to be a wasted day. On the other hand, with luck and perseverance, it might help them to further clarify the role of Sadowsky in the Rafferty case.

Carol had briefed him on what she had learned about Sadowsky from her visit to the Turning Stone Casino, including a detailed physical description and something about his taste in clothes, including the red vest. He knew that Sadowsky was in all probability a person who had loaned money to Rafferty, money which the ex-priest had been unable to pay back. And that he had threatened Rafferty over nonpayment of the debt. In spite of what Turning Stone's management had to say about him, Carol suspected that Sadowsky was in some way involved in borderline criminal activity and that he might well be a dangerous man to cross.

Sam did not know whether Sadowsky was a regular at the Finger Lakes Race Track. He was going there because one of the winery's employees, Bernie Stolnitz, had seen Sadowsky there and had reported the sighting to the sheriff. He did not expect to see him today; if he did, it would simply be an unexpected bonus. In any event, Sam was in no hurry to talk with anyone. He had decided to take a look around first, get a feel for the place.

After half an hour of doing so, Sam decided that it might deserve a return visit. Maybe he and the wife could spend a day there one day soon, even bet a few bucks. But that wasn't his mission on this Tuesday in early November, so he started to look around for someone who might know something about Carl Sadowsky.

Sam was out of uniform, and had no intention of stressing his law enforcement status if he didn't have to. The tracks and the casinos had their own security people, and were presumably tightly monitored by the state. He was not there to accuse anyone of wrongdoing or of turning a blind eye to shady dealings. But raising questions about Sadowsky would inevitably send the message that he was under suspicion of some sort, and, rightly or wrongly, that would quickly be translated to mean that the track itself was under suspicion. Sam would have to be at his diplomatic best. He knew it wasn't his strong suit.

Over the course of an hour of casual conversations with various employees, Sam learned a little about Finger Lakes Race Track but nothing about Carl Sadowsky. But he was patient, and it paid off when he asked someone who looked like a veteran of the establishment if he knew Sadowsky.

"Sure. Hard not to if you've been here as long as I have."

"We're talking about the guy who likes to wear a red vest, aren't we?" Sam asked, making sure they were thinking of the same man.

"Well, yes, but Sadowsky's sort of a team. Know what I mean? There's Carl—he does wear a red vest—but there's also Heckman and Travis, once in awhile a guy named Castellano."

"What do you mean by a team?"

"Just that you almost never see Sadowsky alone. You see him, you see the tall guy, Travis. And the guy with the cauliflower ear, Heckman. Sadowsky's number one, I guess, but they're sort of like the Three Musketeers. I think they're his muscle."

"His muscle? He needs protection?"

"Not here, he doesn't. It's just that they remind me of stuff I've seen in the movies. You know, those gangster films."

"Are you telling me that you think Sadowsky and his buddies are gangsters?"

"No, no. The boss wouldn't let 'em in if they were. But that's what they look like. They're always polite, pay their bills, don't cause trouble. But I wouldn't want to be around if they did. Cause trouble, that is."

Sam found this interesting, and he knew that the sheriff would, too. It is also interesting, he thought, that I haven't had to identify myself as an officer of the law. If the track veteran he'd been talking with knew he was a sheriff—okay, a deputy sheriff—maybe he'd share more of his impressions of Carl Sadowsky and his friends.

"I'm interested that you see this team of Sadowsky's as possible trouble. Want to tell me why?"

"That isn't really what I meant. Like I said, they mind their own business. And they're big spenders."

"Let me introduce myself. My name's Sam Bridges. I'm the deputy sheriff down in Cumberland County. Somebody was killed recently down our way, and one of the things we're investigating is that he apparently owed somebody money which he lost gambling. We think that somebody might have been Carl Sadowsky. I'm not accusing Sadowsky of anything, but the guy who got himself killed was obviously afraid of him. So I wonder if there's anything you can tell me that might help us figure out what happened. And why."

For Sam it was a long speech. It didn't elicit the response he had hoped for.

"I don't want to cause any trouble for the racetrack," the man said. It was obvious that he thought he might already have said too much. "We don't have any trouble with Sadowsky."

Who is the man afraid of, Sam wondered. His boss or Sadowsky?

"I understand. There's never been any allegation that Finger Lakes has problems. This man whose death we're investigating borrowed money and lost it at another casino, not here. And I'm not accusing Mr. Sadowsky of anything. He's entitled to lend money. As far as you know, does he do that here at the track?"

"I think so, but you'd have to ask someone else."

"It's my impression that Sadowsky makes the rounds of the gaming places. Is he here much?"

This was obviously a less sensitive question.

"I can't be sure because my schedule varies. But I think he's here a couple of times a week. Sometimes more, sometimes less. I think he hangs out mostly at Turning Stone. That's that big casino over near Utica."

"I didn't know that he was part of what you call a team. I'm not very good at names. I think you said Travis—can you give me their names again?"

"Travis, Heckman, Castellano." The names were recited reluctantly.

"Thanks. I'll want to talk with them. No need for me to say where I got the information. By the way, I don't think you ever gave me your name."

"Lenny Davis. I'd rather that you not mention that we've had this conversation."

"Of course. I could have heard it from any number of people. I just happened to talk with you first. Remember, we aren't accusing Mr. Sadowsky of anything. I'm just doing my job. Like you are."

Sam left Lenny Davis to worry about whether he'd said things he shouldn't have. He was also angry with himself. Instead of persuading Davis to talk more frankly about "the Sadowsky team," his announcement that he was investigating a murder had caused the man to clam up.

He struck up conversations with several other Finger Lakes' employees before he decided to call it a day. They either were unfamiliar with Sadowsky or spoke of him much as Davis had, if less colorfully. It was clear that he was not your ordinary racetrack bettor, but it was equally clear that no one knew just what he was. One thing was clear, however. He made people uneasy. No one was quite certain why, but if there was consensus, it had to do with a sense that he and his small entourage were in some indefinable way threatening.

Before returning to Cumberland, Sam sat in his car for awhile and made notes of what he had learned. He had come to the realization some time ago that it paid to write things down while they were still fresh in his mind. In this case the most important thing to write down was the information he had obtained about Sadowsky's team, especially their names and physical descriptions. He wasn't sure whether there would be a need for this information, but he had a hunch that he or the sheriff or one of their colleagues would be running into Heckman or Travis or Castellano and that it would be useful to be able to recognize them.

The drive was pleasant. Sam was listening to Shania Twain, enjoying a cloudless day and the procession of attractive barns and silos which were a testament to the endurance of the farming culture in the area. The only negative thought he entertained during the trip was the prospect that Carol's appearance at the budget hearing might not be going well. She would be arguing for a couple of new officers, cars to put them in, and better health benefits for the force. Given the state of the economy, she had told her colleagues not to be optimistic.

By the time he came within sight of Crooked Lake, however, he was thinking positive thoughts again. One of them was his opinion that Brendan Rafferty's murderer was going to turn out to be Carl Sadowsky. Of course it was only a hunch, a hunch bolstered by the way the Finger Lakes Race Track staff had portrayed Sadowsky as a menacing figure. In any event, he'd share his hunch with the sheriff when he made his report.

CHAPTER 41

The budget session had ended inconclusively, but Carol could not shed the feeling that her department's needs would not be met. She would be lucky if there were no cuts. It was almost with a sense of relief that she sat down to hear Bridges' report.

It confirmed the impression she had formed after talking with Sadowsky at the Turning Stone Casino. The news about his "muscle" only strengthened her belief that he was a dangerous man. It also told her that the tall man she had seen with him at the casino was probably the one Sam referred to as Travis. As they talked, it occurred to her that they still needed to talk with Mark Cahill in Verona, another possible source of information about Sadowsky. She had planned to do it herself, but her calendar was full and Sam seemed to have developed an interest in the man in the red vest and his team. She'd send her deputy up to Verona.

Later in the day, she turned her attention to Philip Flanagan and his phone call to Random Harvest asking for Rafferty. If this was the son that Rafferty believed Gerald Flanagan had misjudged, she very much needed to talk with him. Byrnes had produced the phone number at the Flanagan household in East Moncton. She had Ms. Franks place the call for her. It was only a matter of seconds before a woman was on the line.

"Hello, my name is Carol Kelleher. I was told that I could reach Philip Flanagan at this number. Am I right, and is he there?"

Carol did not wish to say she was a sheriff if she didn't have to. It would be hard to explain. Happily, the woman didn't ask her why she was calling.

"Yes, he lives here. But he's not here right now. In fact, I'm not sure where he is. Can I take a message?"

Was it Carol's imagination or did the woman sound worried? Her voice was that of a mature woman, not a sister of Philip. Probably his mother. She decided that the less she said the better.

"That's okay. I'll try again later. When do you expect him to be back?"

"I don't know. He's been gone since early yesterday."

"Thanks very much. Have a nice day."

She hung up, feeling quite certain that the woman she had been talking to was not having a nice day. If, as she suspected, the woman was Philip's mother and Philip was as young as she thought he was, she would be anxious. Where was her son? He had obviously not been at home the night before, and had apparently not told anyone where he was going. Teenagers were quite capable of being irresponsible, Carol knew full well. She had been there, done that. There was no reason why she had to jump to the conclusion that Philip's absence from the Flanagan house was in any way related to his recent phone call to Random Harvest. Nevertheless, Carol felt that she should take steps to forestall possible problems.

So she placed a call to Random Harvest. It was Blanche Sweet who answered the phone.

"Mrs. Sweet, this is Sheriff Kelleher again. I'm sure you remember taking that phone call from Mr. Flanagan, asking for Mr. Rafferty. If Mr. Flanagan calls back, would you be the one to answer the phone?"

"Usually, yes. This is what passes for our front office. Of course I'm not always at my desk."

"There's something I want you to do. If Mr. Flanagan calls—and I really have no idea whether he will—I want you *not* to say anything about Mr. Rafferty being dead. And I want you to give him my number in Cumberland and tell him please to call that number. Don't say it's the sheriff's department. Just tell him that someone at that number can help him. One more thing. Be sure that if you aren't at the desk, whoever takes calls will do what I have asked you to do. Do you understand?"

"Yes, ma'am. Do you think Mr. Flanagan's calling might be about what happened to Mr. Rafferty?"

"It's possible, but the truth is I don't know. That's why I don't want you talking to other people at the winery about Mr. Flanagan. It would just start a rumor circulating, and that wouldn't be very helpful right now."

Carol hoped that Mrs. Sweet would do as she'd been asked, although it was probably unnecessary to tell her not to mention Flanagan's phone call. As far as she knew, no one at the winery knew that somebody named Flanagan had in any way been involved in Brendan Rafferty's life. Or might have been involved in his death.

That little matter taken care of, Carol busied herself with other things. It came as a surprise when, less than an hour later, Ms. Franks buzzed to announce that Mrs. Sweet was on the phone.

"Hello again. This is the sheriff. Has Mr. Flanagan called back?"

"No, Sheriff, he hasn't called. He's standing right here in front of me at the winery."

If the call from Mrs. Sweet was a surprise, the news that Flanagan was at the winery, less than half an hour's drive away, was a stunner. Suddenly, nothing on her desk was important. She needed to get to Random Harvest post haste.

"Make him comfortable but don't tell him anything about Mr. Rafferty. Get him coffee or a soft drink, whatever he wants. Say that I'm on my way and that I'll be there in about thirty minutes."

The traffic was light and the trip took even less time than she had said it would.

"Good afternoon, Mr. Flanagan," Carol said as she walked into the reception area, extending her hand to a boy-man who looked to be in his middle to late teens. "I'm the sheriff of this county, which I'll explain in a minute. I trust that Mrs. Sweet has been taking care of you."

"Yes, she's very nice, but I don't know what's going on here. She doesn't want to tell me about Father Rafferty. That's why I came."

"I know. And I'm the one you need to talk to, although I'm sure you didn't know that when you left home. Tell you what. This isn't the place to have that talk. Mrs. Sweet has things she needs to do. Why don't we go out to my car, maybe take a short drive."

"If you say so," Philip said, "but you haven't told me what's happened to Father Rafferty."

"Come with me and I'll explain," Carol said. And they headed for the parking lot.

Carol chose not to set out for Cumberland right away. Instead of starting the car, she half turned in her seat behind the wheel, the better to face the young man beside her. He was informally but neatly dressed in the typical uniform of a high school student. Average height and weight for a boy who looked to be in his middle teens. Not much facial hair. Mercifully free of acne. A head of curly dark hair. No smile.

"May I call you Philip?" she asked.

"Whatever you like," he said.

"You may already have guessed, but you should know that Father Rafferty is dead. I'm sorry to have to tell you this, but it's the sad truth. I assume that you have come all this way because you hoped to see him. Do you want to tell me why you thought he might be here at this winery?"

Philip Flanagan sank back against the passenger side door of the car. He looked exhausted. It had been a long trip, and for nothing.

"I thought maybe something bad had happened," he said, his voice low. "It seemed funny when I called. The woman I spoke to didn't seem to want to tell me anything. Same thing today. I'm old enough to hear bad news. Why is everyone treating the Father's death as such a secret?"

"It's because he didn't die of natural causes. But I'm sure you know that. If he had, why would I be the one sitting here telling you about it? We are trying to find out who killed Father Rafferty. And why. Now that you're here, perhaps you can help us. I asked you why you thought Father Rafferty was here at the Random Harvest winery. How did you learn that this was where he was working?"

There was a long moment of silence before Philip said anything.

"Is there some place where we can sit down and maybe have something to eat?"

"Of course," Carol said. "Why don't we take a drive up the lake to a place I know. It opens early. I take it you haven't eaten today."

"Not much. I had breakfast when the bus stopped. That was before I hitched a ride down here. This place is awfully isolated."

It hadn't occurred to Carol that Philip might not have a driver's license yet. Or if he did, he might not have a car. Getting from East Moncton to Crooked Lake would not have been easy.

The trip to The Cedar Post was a quiet one. Philip seemed to prefer it that way, so she drove without trying to make conversation.

"Do you think you can tell me about it?" she asked after the Cokes had been set on their table and they had placed their order for chicken wings.

"I suppose so." It wasn't an enthusiastic response, but young Flanagan seemed to have decided that he could talk to the sheriff.

"Good. Take your time. I'll try not to ask too many questions."

"Father Rafferty was a wonderful man," he said. For a moment it looked as if he was going to choke up, but he took another sip of his Coke and went ahead.

"He was the priest in our church, and I used to be one of the altar boys. He was a good listener. I shared my problems with him, and I knew he'd never lecture me. I don't like to say it, but it wasn't like that at home. Anyway, just when I needed the Father most, he disappeared. One day he was there at the church, and the next day he was gone. Nobody knew what had happened. I tried to find out why he'd left and where he'd gone. A lot of people must have asked the same questions. But nobody knew. Or at least they didn't tell us. There's a new priest, and he's okay, but it's not the same."

The wings arrived, and Philip tackled them eagerly. Carol wasn't hungry, but it made her feel good to see him temporarily distracted from what was clearly the painful loss of Father Rafferty. First in East Moncton, and now hundreds of miles away on Crooked Lake. Eventually Philip resumed his story.

"I thought about the Father every day, even after all those months went by. And then just last week a man came to our house, a man I'd never seen before. He talked with my father for quite a bit. I happened to overhear some of their conversation, so I know they were talking about Father Rafferty. This man said he was a friend of his and was looking for him. But one of the things the man said was that one of the members of the church had seen the Father at some place around here. My dad told this man he shouldn't pay any attention to him. His name is Prentiss, by the way. Maybe Mr. Prentiss didn't know what he was talking about, but I knew I had to see him, ask him about the Father."

Carol was fascinated by this retelling of the meeting between Kevin and Gerald Flanagan from a different perspective. So far it tracked perfectly with what Kevin had told her of his meeting with gf.

Philip asked for a time-out so he could finish his wings. Carol ordered two more Cokes.

"I know Mr. Prentiss. Everybody does. They say he's a lush. But he wasn't drunk when I saw him, and he said he'd seen Father Rafferty. Not that long ago and at a place called Random Harvest on Crooked Lake. So I got the number and called them. That's when they said the Father wasn't there. It didn't sound right to me, so I decided to cut school for a couple of days and come and see for myself."

He seemed not to know what to do with his hands. They found the salt and pepper shakers and started moving them around in small circles.

"You must have been very fond of Father Rafferty," Carol said. "From what you tell me, he was a very special person. I'm afraid I never knew him while he was alive. Have you ever wondered why he left your church and your community? It couldn't have been easy for him to do. Priests aren't in the habit of just walking away from the church, not after taking vows and making it their life. I'm a Catholic, so I know a little bit about it."

"No, I don't really know. But I think it might have had something to do with some of the members of the church who didn't think he was strict enough. Do you know what I mean? I think some people felt he didn't always take a hard line on some of the church's teachings."

They were now on sensitive ground.

"What teachings are you referring to, Philip?"

"Oh, different things. I mean he wasn't going against the church. It's more like he didn't want to put down somebody who was having trouble living like the church said he should."

"Have you had trouble living like you think the church says you should?"

Silence again. And then—

"I think so. The Father and I talked about it."

"I'm sure that Father Rafferty was right," Carol said, hoping that her support of the late priest would induce Philip to be more candid. Whether it did or not, the young man gave her a wan smile and came to the point he had been avoiding.

"This is hard to talk about, Sheriff. But I think I'm attracted to guys. The Father was understanding. He didn't get angry. He listened to me."

Philip was close to tears.

"My problem is worse than you can imagine," he said. "It's my own father. He means well. I mean he's a good man, probably a more devout Catholic than I'll ever be. But he can't understand that I might be homosexual. He thinks I can just put some steel in my spine—that's what he's always telling me. I don't know how many times he says I've got to straighten up and fly right. I think he heard that dumb expression from his father, and it's been his motto ever since."

"I take it you've argued with him about it many times."

"No. There's no argument. He won't listen. And I know he blames Father Rafferty. He thinks the Father made me this way. One time he even accused me of having sex with the Father. I mean, that's completely ridiculous. But he won't listen to what I have to say. If it weren't for Mother, I think he'd actually throw me out of the house."

This was catharsis. For all Carol knew, it was the first time since Father Rafferty fled East Moncton that Philip had ever spoken so openly about the issue.

"I'm sure this has been very difficult for you. Why are you telling me about it?"

"It's just gotten so bad at home, and there's no one I can talk to. I was hoping I'd find Father Rafferty again, but now—"

Philip began to breathe heavily. Suddenly he brought his fist down hard on the table. The silverware rattled against the plates.

"It'll be all right," Carol said.

Her voice was quiet but firm. She didn't believe it, but it was one of those things that had to be said.

"How did the Father get killed? It wasn't by an arrow, was it?" Philip asked. He had regained control of himself.

"An arrow?" The unexpected change of subject surprised Carol. "No. Why do you say that?"

"I'm not sure. For a minute I guess I thought my father might have done it. He went deer hunting last month. He's big into bow hunting. Usually he goes up to New Hampshire, but this time he said he was going over into New York."

Carol had considered the possibility that Gerald Flanagan had killed Rafferty. It was the reason she had gone along with Kevin's plan to visit East Moncton and talk with the parishioners of St. Anthony's Church. But the idea that Flanagan's son might think his father was Rafferty's killer came as a shock. She wasn't quite sure what to say. She was sure, however, that if Flanagan had been bow hunting in New York State around the time the priest was killed, his status as a suspect in the priest's murder increased exponentially.

"In the first place, Philip, it was a gunshot that killed Father Rafferty. In the second place, I think you shouldn't be imagining your father as someone who could have done this. He may have disliked Father Rafferty, but murder is a very different matter. It's bad enough that you've lost a thoughtful man who understood you. Try not to be too hard on your father."

What Carol wanted to ask Philip was just when it was that his father had gone bow hunting, and precisely where in New York he had gone. It was important, perhaps critically important, that she know these things. But if she pursued the matter, it would only stimulate Philip's fear that his father was in fact the priest's killer. She tried to finesse her problem.

"You don't know whether your father was anywhere near Crooked Lake when Father Rafferty died. He may have taken his deer-hunting trip earlier. Or later. Maybe he spent it in the Adirondacks, which is a long way from here. So let's not be too quick to judge."

"I guess you're right. It's awful to think of your own father as a murderer, isn't it? If I didn't know how much he hated Father Rafferty, I wouldn't have—"

His voice trailed off, but he didn't need to finish his thought. Their conversation had made it all too clear that tensions in the Flanagan household had been running dangerously high. Unfortunately, Philip had not chosen to clarify exactly when or where his father had gone bow hunting. She would have to look elsewhere for that information. It wouldn't be easy.

Carol was faced with a more immediate dilemma: what to do with this young man who was a long way from home and without the solace he had been seeking from his former priest. In the end she did what she knew she had to do. And wanted to do. She gave him some money and dropped him off at a motel in Yates Center after calling Officer Barrett and arranging for him to drive Philip up to the thruway in the morning to where he could get on a bus for the trip back to East Moncton.

Gerald Flanagan, then known as gf, had been a suspect or at least a person of interest in Rafferty's death ever since she had read the diary. The priest had certainly been afraid of what

Flanagan might do. But for all she knew, Flanagan had been watching TV with his family the night of Rafferty's murder. Or bowling with friends, a great many miles from the rented flat in Clarksburg. Not to mention the likelihood that Flanagan's anger had cooled in the months since Rafferty had left East Moncton or that it had never been so great that it could lead to premeditated murder.

Nonetheless, when Carol retired for the night, she knew that she was going to have to take steps to learn more about Gerald Flanagan's deer-hunting expedition. The fact that she fell asleep thinking about it probably accounted for a strange dream, one in which the huntress Diana brought down a scarecrow with her bow and arrow.

CHAPTER 42

"That's one sad young man," Officer Barrett said the next morning when he stopped by to report that he had driven Philip Flanagan to a thruway stop where he could get a bus for the trip home.

"I'm sure he is," Carol said. "He's lost the one person he believed he could confide in, and he's on his way back to a home where he has to contend with his fiercest critic, his own father. That can't be easy. Anyway, thanks for helping."

"What's the problem? His dad sets impossible standards for the kid?"

"That's one way to put it. But it's really more a matter of fundamental beliefs. I don't know anything about your views on religious issues, and it's none of my business. Young Philip Flanagan thinks he may be gay, and I gather his father would rather throw him out on the street because of it than live in the same house with him."

Barrett did not offer his own thoughts on the subject of homosexuality.

"I was lucky," he said. "My dad was great. He used to take me fishing, and we bowled together right up to the time he had his stroke and couldn't do it anymore. I don't ever remember us getting into an argument."

"That's the way it was for me, too. Anyway, I hope that we don't find out that his father killed Rafferty. However much they're estranged, I wouldn't want Philip to have to live with the knowledge that his father is a murderer."

After Barrett left for what would be a routine day on the county roads, Carol turned her attention to a stack of reports in her in-basket. Her attention to those reports was almost immediately interrupted by Ms. Franks.

"It's a Mrs. Stafford on the line," she said.

Carol hadn't thought about Brendan Rafferty's landlady for several days, and could not imagine what she would be calling about.

"Mrs. Stafford, it's good to hear from you. What can I do for you?"

"I don't suppose you can do anything for me. Unless, that is, you can cover the rent that Mr. Rafferty didn't pay me."

The way she said it made it clear that Jenny Stafford had no expectation that she would ever be collecting the money the ex-priest owed her.

"I'm calling because there's something you ought to know," she continued. "At least I thought you'd be interested. I'm sure you remember that Mr. Rafferty never had anybody come calling on him. I told you that. Well, someone actually did come to the door, wanted to see him. It was actually two men. But it happened after you came to see me. After Mr. Rafferty was dead, that is. So I didn't think much of it at the time, figured it didn't have anything to do with what had happened to him. But yesterday I got to thinking about it, and it occurred to me that maybe I should have said something to you about those men. I mean it was sort of strange, him having no visitors while he was alive and then two of them show up right after he's dead."

"I appreciate you calling me, Mrs. Stafford. I agree, it may not be important at all, but I'd still like you to tell me the names of those men."

"Well, I can't do that. I didn't ask them their names and they didn't say who they were. They just asked if Mr. Rafferty was there and could they see him. Of course he wasn't. He was dead, and I told them so."

"You said Mr. Rafferty was dead?" Carol asked. Mrs. Stafford had just answered that question, but Carol wanted to be absolutely certain.

"That's right. You didn't tell me not to, did you?"

"Did you say he had been killed or just that he was dead?"

"I think I said he'd been murdered."

"No names, you say, but maybe you can describe these men."

"I was cooking dinner, and was eager to send them along. So I didn't pay much attention. But one of them was tall, really tall. I'm not a good judge of such things, but I'd guess he was as much as six foot six. Thin, with dark hair, a kind of sallow complexion. The other man was shorter, nothing unusual except he had a funny ear. Something wrong with it. I mean it didn't look like what you see on people. Sort of all bunched up, like it would be hard to hear out of."

They sounded very much like Sadowsky's muscle, as reported by Bridges.

"Do you remember the day they came to your house?"

"It was a week ago Saturday. I remember, because I was annoyed that all I could seem to get on TV was those damn football games. They must think nobody watches anything but those big lugs mauling each other. One channel after another."

Carol smiled to herself. She liked football. She liked most sports. But she had to concede that the networks could be guilty of overkill.

"I want to thank you for sharing this information with me. We're still working on the case, and I hope to catch whoever killed Mr. Rafferty soon. If you think of anything else that might help, please call me."

"I'll do that," Mrs. Stafford said, and doubtless felt pleased with herself when she hung up the phone.

It was no more than three minutes later that the sheriff was again interrupted, this time by Officer Byrnes.

"Mind if I bother you?" he said, standing half in and half out of the doorway to her office.

"No. Come on in."

"I think I got something wrong the other day," he said. But he didn't look as if he felt too badly about it.

"About what?"

"Addresses. No, not exactly addresses. You wanted to know about winery people who lived near where that Kemper boy thought he saw somebody dumping something into the lake."

Carol, her thoughts still on what Mrs. Stafford had told her, had not been paying full attention. Byrnes had now changed that.

"Somebody at the winery does live there?" she asked hopefully.

"No. He doesn't live there. But he keeps his boat there. I'm talking about Joseph Clifford."

"Really?"

"Right. I was going over those addresses again and spotted it. Clifford has a small right of way on the west arm of the lake, not more than a quarter of a mile from the Kemper house. He maintains a powerboat there. It's only about nine feet wide, just enough for a path down from the road to a dock and a boat hoist."

"I'll be damned," Carol said, her mind already in the business of rethinking her decision to dismiss Donnie Kemper's story. "You don't happen also to have discovered what kind of boat Mr. Clifford parks over on his right of way, do you?"

"I do," Byrnes replied, his face now wearing a big smile. "It's a nine-year-old Four Winns."

There was no guarantee that either Jenny Stafford's or Tommy Byrnes' news would turn out to be important. But they opened up interesting avenues of speculation. It was while she was speculating about the visit of Sadowsky's friends to the house on 125 Maple Lane that she thought again about the note in Rafferty's Bible.

The note was in a locked cabinet along with other items relevant to her investigation. She could easily have retrieved it, but that would not be necessary. She remembered the message, word for word.

> Surprised to hear from me, aren't you? It has taken me awhile, but I always knew I would find you. Expect a visit from me soon.

She wasn't sure, but she was of the opinion that the note had been written by Sadowsky, and that his henchmen were carrying out the note's implied threat when they showed up at the Clarksburg address. The problem, of course, was that Rafferty was already dead when Travis and Heckman showed up. Does that mean that Sadowsky could not have been responsible for his death? It could certainly explain how he knew he was dead. Carol was trying to make sense of what she had heard from Mrs. Stafford. Perhaps one of Sadowsky's men had killed Rafferty earlier and then came back in broad daylight, asking for him, in order to confuse those investigating the crime. Well, I'm investigating the crime, Carol said to herself, and I'm surely confused.

Perhaps none of it is relevant, she thought. Flanagan could have written the note, having heard from Prentiss where to find Rafferty. And then he had come to Crooked Lake to kill the priest he believed had turned his son into a homosexual. Or had he? Carol made up her mind to stop speculating. Too many puzzle pieces were still missing.

CHAPTER 43

Tomorrow, Carol thought. Tomorrow Kevin will be here, and she was already looking forward to the change of scene. She much preferred the cottage to her house in Cumberland. After her father's death, she had moved into the family home when she assumed his job as county sheriff. It was both familiar and convenient, and she had been too busy to spend time looking for a place of her own. But it was an old house, in need of work. What is more, Carol had never much cared for her father's taste in furnishing. Since her mother's death a decade earlier, he had gradually filled the walls with what she thought of as second-rate art, most of it with a nautical theme. And then there was the stale smell of cigar smoke. She doubted that it would ever go away.

Carol knew that she should give it a fresh coat of paint, change the drapes, try to find pictures to hang which were more to her liking. Either that or sell it and move to an apartment. But since she had met Kevin, her interest in sprucing it up or moving had waned. She gave herself the excuse that she could always spend time at his cottage, which to her delight was both brighter and cozier. It also had the advantage of being right on the lake. If they were to get married—the perennial big if—they would surely move into the cottage. Depending, of course, on whether he settled permanently at the lake. But how could he do that when his job was in the city? How many times had she revisited this dilemma?

Enough of this, she said to herself. There were more important things to do than indulge in daydreaming. She couldn't do any of these things by sitting in her office. One of the things she most wanted to do was to talk with Parker Jameson. She was not investigating the imbalance in the winery's books. Not officially. But she continued to believe that there could be a connection between the missing money and the death of Brendan Rafferty. The person most involved in Random Harvest's financial affairs was Jameson. And she had never spoken to him. She had no idea what she might learn, but it was becoming clear to her that if no thief were found, Jameson was the one who would take the fall for the disappearance of thirty thousand dollars. First Rafferty, then Jameson. Two victims in what would be remembered as a very bad year for Random Harvest Vineyards.

Carol strapped on her sidearm, the gun she had never fired and hoped never to fire, and set off for the winery. It had become a near daily trip.

As it happened, Carol never did get to speak with Parker Jameson that day. It was due to the fact that the first person she encountered at the winery was Mary Rizzo. Mr. Francis's assistant was just returning from lunch when Carol pulled into the parking lot. They got out of their cars, exchanged hellos, and walked into the winery together.

"Do you think you know who killed Mr. Rafferty?" Ms. Rizzo asked.

Carol remembered how sad the young woman had been when she told her that Rafferty had been killed. And how eager she had been to befriend him when he had first joined the company. Her friendliness seemed to have come naturally to her. Carol doubted that she had treated others at the winery differently than she had treated Rafferty. She was willing to bet that Mary Rizzo was one of those people who almost reflexively likes people. She decided to spend a few minutes with her before going upstairs for her meeting with Jameson.

"I'm afraid we aren't there yet," she answered Mary's question. "Do you have a few minutes?"

The woman's eyes lit up. The prospect of chatting with the sheriff was obviously pleasing.

They sat down in Mary's small anteroom. Mr. Francis was not in his office, which was fine with Carol.

"There's not much to say about how things are going," Carol said. "We're making progress. Slowly, I should add. But I'm more interested in asking you a couple of questions. We haven't spoken in quite awhile. It's now more than two weeks. I remember that you tried to make friends with Mr. Rafferty and that it wasn't easy. You seem to be interested in people. And observant. Perhaps you can help me to get a better picture of the people here at the winery. I'm afraid I still have trouble sorting you all out."

The last bit was somewhat disingenuous. Carol had a good memory, and she was quite sure she could recognize every

Random Harvest employee she had met and even a few others who'd been pointed out to her.

"Sure," Mary said, anxious to please. "Are you suspicious of someone?"

"No, no," Carol said, laughing. "I'm not making book on anyone. I guess I just get people mixed up. It's not a good thing for a police officer to do."

"I know. It could be embarrassing. Mr. Rafferty did that once. It was kinda funny. But I was able to set him straight."

Mary Rizzo, by her own admission, had found Brendan Rafferty difficult to draw out in conversation. But she had just remembered a time when the two of them had apparently had a discussion about someone.

"That's interesting," Carol said. An understatement. "Why don't you tell me about it?"

"It wasn't all that long ago. I mean not long before his death. We hadn't talked much, but one day he stopped by and started talking about Mr. Jameson. Or a man he thought was Mr. Jameson. But when he described him, I realized he was talking about someone else. He had them mixed up, just like you were saying you do sometimes."

It was probably an unimportant matter. But it must have been important enough that the normally taciturn Rafferty had chosen to talk about it with Ms. Rizzo.

"Do you remember who he thought was Mr. Jameson?"

"It was Joe Clifford. He's Mr. Drake's assistant. They don't look at all alike, which was why I was so surprised that Mr. Rafferty had confused them."

"You're right about the two men not looking like each other." Carol was being very careful not to leave an impression that she suspected either Jameson or Clifford of a role in Brendan Rafferty's murder. But she suddenly had the feeling that what she was hearing might indeed be important. "Why do you suppose Mr. Rafferty didn't know one from the other?"

"I don't really know. He probably hadn't met either one of them before. What he said that made me realize he had made a mistake was that the man he'd been talking to was wearing gloves."

"I don't understand," Carol said. "Why would gloves tell you that he was mistaken?"

"Well, Mr. Rafferty said the man he thought was Mr. Jameson had a rash. That was why he had to wear gloves. It didn't make sense. I'd never seen Mr. Jameson with gloves on, and that's what I told Mr. Rafferty. It was then that he asked me to describe Mr. Jameson and we got it figured out that it was really Mr. Clifford he was talking about."

Carol was suddenly very proud of Mary Rizzo. Particularly proud of her memory of the details of a conversation which must have seemed inconsequential at the time.

"Tell me, did you ever see Mr. Clifford wearing gloves?"

"No, now that you mention it I never did. Oh, maybe back last winter when it was cold. Of course, Mr. Jameson might have worn them, too. But we were talking about a pleasant autumn day, not winter."

"Did Mr. Rafferty mention what kind of gloves Mr. Clifford was wearing?"

Ms. Rizzo looked puzzled. Carol knew that she had possibly asked one question too many.

"Never mind," she said. "It sounds like one of those mix-ups I have to be careful to avoid. Anyway, I'm here today to talk to more of the winery people. It would help, I suppose, if everyone had on one of those little nametags, but I guess that wouldn't make much sense in a small place like this."

Carol chuckled as if she had just made a silly remark. But Mary Rizzo's little vignette led her to revise her plan for the afternoon.

They talked for another five minutes, the sheriff trying to create the impression that she needed help in forming mental pictures of some of the winery personnel. She wanted to tap into Ms. Rizzo's observational skills for information regarding one or two other Random Harvest employees, but figured that doing so would only convince her that those people were under suspicion. Perhaps they should be, but it wouldn't be wise to leave Mary with that impression.

Instead of going in search of Parker Jameson, Carol followed up her impromptu meeting with Mary Rizzo with a visit to the wine-tasting room. She had no business to conduct there, but she was anxious not to have it known that she went directly from Rizzo's office to Clifford's. So she chatted with her friend Pat for several minutes, then browsed through the memorabilia in the gift shop for several more. Feeling slightly guilty about leaving without buying anything, she selected a bottle of Kevin's favorite Chardonnay to take with her. It was only then that she took the stairs to the second floor.

Joe Clifford was in his office, his fingers moving rapidly around on his computer keyboard. The office was neat, not at all like the picture Mr. Drake had painted of Parker Jameson's office. Carol rapped on the glass window.

"Ah, our sheriff is paying me the honor of another visit," he said as he opened the door. "Do come in."

As on her earlier visit, Carol's impression of the young assistant to Earl Drake was negative. She had left their earlier meeting feeling somewhat less annoyed with him than she had been at first, but his welcome on this Wednesday afternoon set him back once again in her estimation.

"I don't propose to keep you long, Mr. Clifford, but I would like another word with you."

"By all means. Here, have a seat."

He pulled out a chair, made a thing about brushing it off, and waited for her to sit down before resuming his own seat.

"Is there something else I can do for you? Something that I forgot the other day?"

"Yes, there is," Carol said, anxious to put an end to Clifford's little charade. "When we had our talk, I mentioned that Brendan Rafferty had kept a diary and that he had commented on a conversation he had had with a man he called jc. Just the initials, no name. You told me it could not be you he was referring to inasmuch as the two of you had never met. You did say, however, that he must have meant Mr. Copeland. Like you, his initials are jc. Why did you tell me that Rafferty must have been referring to Mr. Copeland?"

"Who else could it have been? As you say, Jerry Copeland's initials are JC."

"True enough. But you said that Mr. Copeland is called JC. I've talked with almost everyone here at the winery, and I'm sure I've never heard anyone call him JC."

"Maybe he tries to discourage it. You know, too much like Jesus Christ. Jerry's a very religious man."

Hadn't Copeland told her he was an irregular Protestant, that he rarely attended church?

"But Mr. Copeland isn't the only jc working for Random Harvest," she said. "What about Jessica Coyle?"

"Coyle? That's ridiculous, isn't it? Rafferty and a woman? I'm sure you've heard that our Mr. Rafferty used to be a priest."

"Yes, I've heard. Actually, I'm the one who told Mr. Drake about Mr. Rafferty's background. But I don't understand why that rules out Ms. Coyle as his jc. Maybe he left the church because he didn't like the celibate life."

"You haven't met Jessica, have you?" Clifford wore a big smile. He was enjoying the conversation.

"No, as a matter of fact I haven't. And I'm not suggesting that Mr. Rafferty was talking about Ms. Coyle. Or for that matter that he was seeking a woman's companionship. I was only saying that people other than Mr. Copeland have the initials jc."

"Point taken. But you really should meet Jessica."

"I'll do that. What about Jared Church?"

"Makes about as much sense as Coyle. I mean he's all wine, all the time."

"Why not? This is a winery."

"Of course, but if you knew Jared you'd know what I mean. He doesn't have a life outside of wine. He could be one of those guys who does blind tasting and never guesses wrong."

Carol could see no reason why this should disqualify Church as the jc in Rafferty's diary, but decided to let it go. It was increasingly apparent to her that Clifford, for some reason, wanted her to believe that Jerry Copeland was Brendan Rafferty's jc.

"I'm sorry to be taking up your time like this, but I'm still chasing loose ends. That's what investigations like this are all about. Loose ends. There's one other thing. Have you ever had an occasion recently to wear gloves?"

"I'm afraid so," he said, his face expressionless, his voice calm. "I had an annoying rash awhile ago. But it cleared up about as fast as it came on, thank God. Simple over-the-counter stuff did it."

Carol was impressed. Clifford had responded to her question without any hint of uncertainty, much less anxiety. She was tempted to lie and say that Rafferty had made some comment in his diary about jc wearing gloves. Instead she resorted to a half truth.

"I have a problem with stories that conflict with each other. Unfortunately, I am faced with just such a conflict. You have told me that you didn't know Brendan Rafferty. Another person here at Random Harvest has told me that Mr. Rafferty spoke of talking with you. Do you see my problem?"

"Who told you that? He's either got me mixed up with someone else or he's lying. I never met Mr. Rafferty, much less had a conversation with him."

It hadn't been a he, but a she. Her name was Mary Rizzo. And she hadn't said that Rafferty told her he had spoken with Clifford, only that he had apparently mistaken Clifford for Parker Jameson.

"Well, I suppose people can remember things differently," Carol said. "A variation, you might say, on he said, she said."

She could pursue the matter further, but not much further without actually accusing Clifford of something. She wasn't quite ready to do that. She chose to pose one more question.

"I understand you live down in Southport, but that you keep a powerboat on the lake up near West Branch. Is that right?"

"It is, but I'm afraid I don't understand. Why do you ask?"

"It's just that somebody reported seeing your boat out on the lake at a very early hour a couple of weeks ago. Six o'clock, I think he said. He thought that was odd."

"What is odd, Sheriff, is that some busybody should take the trouble to bother you with reports of other people's morning habits. Some of my acquaintances fish at six a.m. I know people who simply enjoy the peace and quiet on the lake at that hour. For what it's worth, I haven't used my boat since the Labor Day weekend. Not in the morning, not at midday, not in the evening. Not at all. To be perfectly frank, I find all of these questions irritating. And offensive. If you suspect me of something, then say so. Otherwise, I wish you would concentrate on finding that man Rafferty's killer."

"All I am doing, Mr. Clifford, is gathering information," Carol said, her voice calm. "I have been talking with many people since Mr. Rafferty's death, some of them affiliated with the winery, some of them not. I'm sure no one welcomes my questions. But it's my job."

When Carol finally left Joseph Clifford's office, she once again was doubtful that he had been dumping the remains of a scarecrow into Crooked Lake on the morning after Brendan Rafferty's death. She did, however, feel reasonably certain that the young, red-haired heir apparent to Earl Drake's job as president of Random Harvest Vineyards had been less than straightforward with her. What, she wondered, had been his real relationship with the late Father Rafferty?

CHAPTER 44

Confident that he had plenty of time in which to make his appointment with a man named Cahill in Verona, Sam Bridges pulled off the New York State thruway at the Port Byron plaza to get a cup of coffee. He was tempted to have a burger and fries as well, but his conscience told him that that wouldn't be wise, considering his doctor's recent admonition regarding his cholesterol.

It was close to four o'clock, well past the lunch hour, and there were plenty of empty seats. Sam could have taken the coffee back to the car, but he wanted to kill some time. Better to do it here at the plaza than in Verona while waiting for Cahill to get home from work. He took a seat near a window which gave him a view of a lot of asphalt. The occasional car passed by on its way to the gas pumps.

Sam could have killed ten or fifteen minutes with a crossword puzzle, but he left the puzzle in his pocket and thought about the Rafferty case while he drank his coffee. What bothered him most about the case was that the prime suspects, according to the sheriff, were not from the Crooked Lake area. It was almost with a sense of pleasure that he recalled the Britingham case. All of the suspects had lived right on Crooked Lake, many of them neighbors of the victim. But now they were faced with a crime in which one suspect lived way off in Massachusetts while another seemed to spend his life in an endless circuit of gambling spots all over the state, none of them close to the lake. The problem, of course, was that Brendan Rafferty, the former priest, had come to Crooked Lake from Massachusetts by way of one of those gambling places, leaving in his wake people he had made angry. It made for a complicated case that involved people and places with which no one in the Cumberland County Sheriff's Department was familiar.

If there was an upside to the case, it was that it had given him an opportunity to travel a bit. He hadn't been asked to go to that town near Boston where Rafferty had come from. Something the sheriff had said suggested that her friend Whitman had been there. But he had experienced a change of scene as a result of the trip to the Finger Lakes Race Track and now this one to Turning Stone Casino. Today's mission didn't officially include the casino, but he intended to spend an extra hour checking it out after he had spoken with Cahill.

Cahill, the man whom the sheriff was fairly certain had steered Rafferty to the casino and to Carl Sadowsky, benefactor of gamblers and scourge of those who don't honor their debts. Cahill, the person identified in Rafferty's diary as mc. He had returned Barrett's call and had agreed to a meeting, which had been scheduled for today after he got back from work. He still did not know that Rafferty was dead. Not knowing how well he had known the former priest, Sam had no idea how he would react to the news. But that wasn't the purpose of the meeting. What they needed was his impression of Sadowsky, plus any knowledge he may have had about Rafferty's problems with the man in the red vest.

In spite of his stop for coffee, Sam still got to the Simmons Boarding House well ahead of the time when Cahill expected him. The converted motel badly needed a coat of paint, not to mention some plantings to dress up the façade which faced the street. Sam felt certain that it would also be in need of structural improvements on the inside. The few cars that were parked in front of the building looked to be as old as the "boarding house" itself, but by no stretch of the imagination were any of them vintage vehicles with any claim to historic interest. It was a sad sight. Sam felt sorry for Mark Cahill.

So this is where the late Father Rafferty had lived when he settled briefly in Verona. Even a priest, accustomed to a life with few amenities, would have been unhappy here, Sam thought. Mrs. Stafford's house in Clarksburg was no show place, but it was a major step up from this eyesore. Sam wondered what Father Rafferty's rectory in East Moncton had been like.

He sat in his car and watched the comings and goings of "boarding house" residents for nearly twenty minutes before the man who proved to be Mark Cahill drove up in front of number 21.

Sam initially doubted that it was Cahill. The man who got out of the dusty old Ford was wearing well-pressed slacks, polished loafers, and a well-tailored blazer over a turtleneck sweater. Not what Sam had expected. But the man came over to the car announcing itself as belonging to the Cumberland County Sheriff's Department and waved at Sam.

"Sheriff Kelleher? I'm Mark Cahill. Sorry if I've kept you waiting."

"I'm Sheriff Kelleher's deputy," Sam said as he stepped out of his car. "Name's Bridges. Pleased to meet you. And you're not late; I'm early."

Cahill led the way into number 21, where Sam was greeted with another surprise. He had expected a tiny, dingy efficiency apartment. It was indeed tiny, but not in the least dingy. The furniture looked new and comfortable, and, most surprising of all, the walls were decorated with several pictures that looked more like something he thought he had seen in an upscale museum than they did like motel knockoffs.

"Please have a seat. I'll be right with you." Cahill disappeared into what was presumably the bathroom, leaving Sam to study the art. It wasn't to his taste, and it very probably wasn't original, but he knew that the man he'd be talking with wasn't the man he had pictured on his drive over to Verona.

"So," Cahill said. He had shed his jacket. "The word I got is that you're here because I know Brendan Rafferty. The man I spoke with didn't say much, just that a sheriff down in the Finger Lakes needed to talk to me. How can I help you?"

"In the first place, I'm interested in how you knew Rafferty. What your relationship with him was. But I think you should know, first of all, that he's dead. He was killed just a few weeks ago, and we're investigating his death."

"He was killed? I take it that it wasn't a car accident, or the police wouldn't be asking me questions."

Mark Cahill hadn't reacted as a close friend would have. Surprised, but not obviously shaken by the news.

"That's right. He was murdered. At first, we didn't even know who he was. We still don't know much about him. But we did discover that he had been living, at least briefly, around here. That he was a neighbor of yours."

"That's interesting. Just out of curiosity, how did you find my name?"

Sam smiled.

"Mr. Rafferty left a small diary in which he mentioned several people. He only referred to them by their initials, but he did mention somebody with the initials mc. That gave us a start, and the next thing you know we had your name."

"I'm sorry to hear that Rafferty is dead. He seemed like a nice man, although I hardly knew him at all. We weren't friends. I don't mean he wasn't friendly, it's just that we didn't spend any time together socially."

"Did he ever confide in you? Tell you about himself?"

Cahill thought about it.

"Not really. If you mean did he ever tell me where he came from, had he been married, did he have kids—things like that—the answer is no."

"But I gather you and he did have the occasional conversation. What did you talk about?"

"I remember that he seemed to be hard pressed for cash. One day he stopped by my humble little abode and before he left he said something about money problems. I think he was intrigued by my place, probably figured I was doing okay. That's probably what got him to ask for my advice about getting out of his financial hole. Anyway, we were having coffee one day when he brought up the money problem again. I said something about maybe he'd be interested in going up to Turning Stone, that there might be some money in it for him."

"Did he ever tell you why he was in a financial hole?" Sam asked.

"No. I assumed he'd had some hard luck. Lost big in the market, something like that."

"It's no secret any longer, Mr. Cahill. Brendan Rafferty had been a priest. He'd never had much money, and when he left the church, he didn't have the security blanket the church provides."

"A priest. No kidding?"

"When you were talking with him about money and Turning Stone, did you ever happen to mention a man named Carl Sadowsky?"

"I may have," Cahill said. "Yes, come to think of it, I did. Sadowsky has a reputation as a go-to guy if you need cash to pay up at the casino."

"Do you know Sadowsky personally?"

"No. Why? Is he somehow involved in Rafferty's death?"

"Not that I know of," Sam said, following Carol's orders not to raise the possibility that Sadowsky might be Rafferty's killer. "It's just that his is another name that cropped up in that diary."

"Funny, you mentioning Sadowsky. I hadn't gone to Turning Stone for quite awhile. Probably three months. Then my birthday rolled around back in October, and a couple of friends and I decided to try the tables over there. Just a little celebration. It seemed like old times, even Sadowsky in his little red vest was making the rounds."

Sam would later congratulate himself on thinking to ask the next question.

"What is your birth date?"

"October 19th. It was three weeks ago Monday. I've been all of forty years old for three whole weeks now."

"Did Rafferty ever tell you why he was leaving Verona?"

"No. He didn't even tell me was leaving, much less why. In fact I didn't know he'd left the boarding house until somebody else asked me if I'd seen him recently. Turns out he'd been gone nearly a week."

There isn't much more to be learned here, Sam thought. He was curious, however, about the presence in this shabby ex-motel of a man who, by the look of things, had both money and style.

"None of my business, really," he said, "but I can't help but be curious about how come you're living here. This is a nice little apartment. It looks like it belongs in another part of town."

Cahill smiled. This wasn't the first time someone had expressed a similar thought.

"I'm in a witness protection program. The seedy exterior is a great cover." The smile turned into a laugh. "Sorry, that's just a joke. Truth is, I'm satisfied. It's cheap, lets me spend on things that matter. I was never a green lawn, white picket fence kind of guy."

Sam was already on his way out the door when it occurred to him that there was another question he should ask. Carol would rightly be annoyed with him if he didn't.

"By the way, I've heard that Sadowsky hangs out with a few close friends. Always seen together. Does that sound right to you?"

"Sure. Usually two buddies, one a real tall fellow, the other looks like an ex-boxer."

"Do you happen to remember whether they were with him the night you had your birthday party at Turning Stone?"

"I'm sure they weren't there that night. Dutch—that's one of my friends—he commented on it at the time."

CHAPTER 45

Following her meeting with Joe Clifford on Wednesday, Carol had decided not to go straight to Parker Jameson's office. It had been her intention to meet Jameson and form her own impression of the man whose carelessness may have contributed to the loss of thirty thousand dollars of Random Harvest's money. But her conversation with Mary Rizzo had changed her plans, and she had gone instead to speak with Clifford. That conversation, in turn, had persuaded her that she needed time to think more carefully about what she needed to ask Jameson. As a result, Carol spent much of that afternoon back in her office, the door closed, with Ms. Franks instructed not to interrupt her unless it was an emergency.

She wasn't exactly sure what would constitute an emergency. Certainly a call from Gerald Flanagan or Carl Sadowsky. Possibly the discovery of the original Random Harvest scarecrow. None of these things was likely to happen. She would have to trust Ms. Franks' good judgment.

When a situation called for reflection, Carol liked to have a yellow pad handy. So, she had noticed, did Kevin. They both liked to capture fugitive thoughts, thoughts which at the moment seemed insubstantial, even frivolous, but which might later merit another look. If she jotted them down, they wouldn't be lost in the ebb and flow of the day's business. Otherwise, there was a good chance that they would simply vanish, leaving her with a nagging sense that something was bothering her, something that she could not recall, no matter how hard she tried.

The yellow pad in front of her, a pen in her hand, she went over in her mind the conversations she had had with Mary Rizzo and Joe Clifford. And what she knew about Random Harvest's missing money. And about Jerome Copeland. And Jared Church. And, while she was at it, Doug Francis. The yellow pad filled up with notes about invoices and post office boxes and checks and receipts. And gloves. Carol found herself writing Brendan Rafferty's name. Could he have been the thief who stole the thirty thousand? After all, he needed money. But then she crossed out his name. It made no sense. She couldn't imagine that in his very short time at Random Harvest the ex-priest had become familiar enough with its finances to come up with a scheme that had fooled Jameson and defrauded the winery of thirty thousand dollars.

Moreover, the thought of Rafferty as a thief didn't square with his last diary entries. He had been trying to save another man's soul. What had the other man done that caused him to think like a priest? To think like he imagined Father Brown would? As Carol stared at the pad and her jottings about the missing money and the people with the initials jc, it occurred to her that the man Rafferty was referring to might be the thief. If true, how would Rafferty have known that he was stealing from Random Harvest? Had he actually seen him in the act? That seemed unlikely. Whoever was fiddling the books at the winery would not have been so careless as to do it where he could be observed. Unless, of course, that person was Jameson. Anybody observing him would have assumed that he was simply doing his job. But Jameson's initials were not jc.

The idea that Rafferty's jc might have been engaged in the theft of thirty thousand dollars wouldn't go away. What if he had been caught in the act by the ex-priest, leaving aside for the moment the question of how and where and when? What if Rafferty had confronted him, urged him to restore his ill-gotten gains? The more she thought about it, the more such a scenario came to resemble what Rafferty had written in his diary. She could imagine that a priest, even someone who was no longer a priest, might prefer to forgive the sinner than report him to the authorities. Or to Earl Drake.

And how did the gloves enter into the picture? The obvious answer, following her own line of reasoning, was to avoid leaving fingerprints. She wore them herself when collecting potential evidence. The person Rafferty had seen wearing gloves had been Joe Clifford, according to Mary Rizzo. Clifford, when asked about it, had claimed that he had a rash on his hands. Which was quite possible. Why should she doubt him? Only because Brendan Rafferty had referred to a jc in his diary.

Carol had the feeling that she was going around in circles. The gloves might be irrelevant. Rafferty's diary entries might have nothing whatsoever to do with the missing thirty thousand dollars. And what did any of it have to do with the scarecrow in the vineyard? It was time to go back to the winery and see Parker Jameson. The only thing her little private brainstorming session had added to her list of questions for the Random Harvest accountant concerned his relationship with Joe Clifford.

Jameson's office was not as untidy as she had been led to believe. She preferred a cleaner desk than the one between her and Earl Drake's old golfing partner, but the papers on it were in orderly piles. In all probability, the problem of the missing money had inspired a modest housecleaning.

"I should have been around sooner," Carol said. "It's been more than two weeks since the death of one of your employees brought me out here to the winery. I can imagine that things have been a little hectic."

She knew that things had been hectic, and where Parker Jameson was concerned it was not Brendan Rafferty's murder that had made them hectic.

"That's an understatement, Sheriff," he said. "Are you any closer to solving the murder?"

"Let's say I know a lot more now than I did when we found Mr. Rafferty's body. I think I know of several reasons why he may have been killed. But I'm afraid I'm not that close to making an arrest."

"It still seems impossible to me—that one of our people could be killed in that way. Wine making isn't what you think of as a violent business."

Carol found this an interesting observation.

"I'm sure it isn't wine making that had anything to do with Mr. Rafferty's death. Anyway, I'm interested in how things look from where you sit. Did you know Mr. Rafferty?"

"No. I'd seen him, but I doubt that we ever spoke. Those of us up on the second floor here don't get to mix much with the people who really do the work."

Carol smiled and changed the subject.

"I'd welcome any thoughts you may have about Mr. Rafferty, but I'm also interested in something which must be even more worrisome to you. That's the matter of what happened to the money that seems to be missing. That's not what I'm investigating, of course. It isn't our responsibility. But I have to keep in mind the possibility that the missing money may be related to Mr. Rafferty's death."

Was it her imagination or did Parker Jameson suddenly look paler?

"Do you think that the two things are related?" His tone of voice suggested that he couldn't believe that they were.

"Like I said, we can't rule it out. That's why I need for you to tell me what you think happened and why."

Jameson was less comfortable talking about the state of Random Harvest's finances than he was about the murder of a man he'd never spoken to.

"Well, if I knew what happened, I'd be a much happier man. And you'd probably know whether it was in any way related to that man's murder. What I do know is that I signed some checks paying for winery supplies that were never delivered to us. What's more, the companies I paid aren't people we do business with. In fact, we think they're bogus companies. Which means somebody's set up a racket and is getting rich at our expense."

"That's pretty much what I've heard. On the face of it, it seems as if ripping Random Harvest off wouldn't be that easy to do. It would mean that somebody would have to have access to the books, would have to know quite a bit about the details of how the company works. Who beside yourself has been in a position to pull something like this off?"

Jameson had to be aware of his lackadaisical reputation. It could not be pleasant to have to answer the sheriff's questions.

"I hope you don't think that I have been defrauding the winery. I am an old and dear friend of Earl Drake. I'd never do anything like that to him. Or to anybody else. I wish I could say that no one else could be doing it, but the evidence says otherwise. This is a small company. It's been run very informally, almost like a family enterprise. You know, open doors, everybody trusts everybody. Someone has taken advantage of our open door policy. Funny, but while I want to know who, in a way I don't. It hurts to think that someone you know has betrayed your trust."

"I can appreciate that," Carol said. "But let's talk about specific people. Forget for a moment whether anyone is guilty. What I want to know is whether there's someone—maybe even several someones—who hypothetically could have stolen from Random Harvest. Let me rephrase that. Is there anyone besides yourself who pretty much knows the ins and outs of the winery's financial system?"

"Sure, if you put it that way. Drake does. Of course he doesn't pay it much attention. He relies on me. But if he had to, he could take over. Copeland knows a lot because he handles supplies. And Grabner. He does marketing. I can't think of anyone else except Clifford, and that's just because he's trying to learn all he can about the business. Earl plans to let Joe take over when he retires, so it makes sense for him to get up to speed on everything."

"And how does Mr. Clifford go about getting up to speed in your area?"

"He comes down the hall to my office from time to time, sits there where you're sitting, asks questions. He's a bright guy. I think Earl's made a good choice."

"Do you think it's possible that Mr. Clifford would be able to make thirty thousand dollars disappear?"

"That's a terrible question," Jameson said. "Good God, Sheriff, he's Mr. Drake's right arm. He's the heir apparent here. Why would he steal from the company that's his future?"

"Okay, why would Mr. Grabner? Or Mr. Copeland? I'm not suggesting that Mr. Clifford is guilty. Or anybody else. I'm just seeking information, and I'm doing it because I'm trying to figure out who killed Mr. Rafferty."

"I realize that, and I'm not questioning your judgment, Sheriff. But frankly I just can't imagine any of my colleagues stealing from us. Or, for that matter, killing Mr. Rafferty. All I know is that my ass is in a sling, because it seems I've been too hands off when it comes to bookkeeping. It's a hell of a way to end a solid, decent career."

Carol actually felt sorry for the man. He's taking the blame for the financial scandal, while at the same time he's sticking up for the people most likely to have been taking advantage of his sloppiness.

"Mr. Jameson, do you think it would have been possible for Mr. Rafferty to be your thief?"

"Rafferty?" For a brief second, something flickered in his eyes, suggesting that Rafferty-as-thief would lift a terrible burden from his shoulders. But just as quickly he rejected the idea. "No way. Like I said, I didn't know him, hardly ever saw him. I mean, how could a guy who was laboring down in the cellar have the smarts to game the system like that?"

This was not the time to explain that Brendan Rafferty was almost certainly a very smart man, quite capable of stealing from the winery if he put his mind to it. But unless her image of him was totally out of focus, it was not the kind of thing the ex-priest would ever have put his mind to. In any event, she agreed with Jameson. The late Father Rafferty was not responsible for the accountant's problem.

There was one other question she needed to ask. She didn't expect an answer that would help her.

"Have you seen any of your colleagues here wearing gloves?"

"Gloves? I don't think so. Why?"

"I ask only because I overheard someone say that you were seen wearing gloves one night. It appears that that person must have been mistaken. It was someone else who was wearing them. Either way, the question remains: why would it be necessary for anyone to be wearing gloves in the winery on a warm October night?"

"I guess I don't understand. In any event, it wasn't me. Why is it important?"

"It probably isn't," Carol said. "But it does raise the possibility that someone was wearing gloves to avoid leaving fingerprints somewhere in the winery. It's worth thinking about."

When Carol left his office, Parker Jameson was deep in thought, thinking about gloves and fingerprints and whether he might be wrong about the trust he had placed in his colleagues.

CHAPTER 46

Carol was due to pick Kevin up at the airport at 5:45, but before embarking on that pleasant mission, there were many things to attend to and she was having trouble prioritizing. She needed to see the signature cards for the boxes at the banks where Parker Jameson was sending the checks to the bogus supply companies. That should not pose a problem. She would also like to take a look at the bank accounts of the Random Harvest employees with the initials jc to see if any of them showed substantial deposits which might tell her where the thirty thousand dollars had gone. That would be a dicier matter. Sooner or later she would need to persuade Judge Olcott to issue a warrant to search the home of one or more of the winery's jcs. Unfortunately, she knew that she didn't yet have sufficient evidence to meet the probable cause standard for such a warrant. And then there was the matter of authorship of the note she had found in Brendan Rafferty's Bible. It bore a vague resemblance to the address Sadowsky had written out for her, but vague wouldn't cut it. She was worrying about how she could obtain a sample of Gerald Flanagan's handwriting when Ms. Franks signaled that someone wanted to speak with her.

"It's that Flanagan boy. Long distance," she said.

Carol had no idea what to expect, but it was with nervous trepidation that she picked up the phone.

"Mr. Flanagan, this is a surprise. Are you all right?"

"I think so," he said. "You know my situation up here."

"I know what you've told me, and I worry about you. There hasn't been more trouble with your father, has there?"

"Not yet," Philip said. "But I've learned something which will interest you. You remember I told you that he'd gone bow hunting in New York, back around the time that Father Rafferty was killed. Well, I couldn't get it off my mind that he might have gone down to that lake where you are and done something to the Father."

Philip hadn't wanted to say the word, but it was obvious that what he meant was that his father might have killed the priest.

Carol tried to imagine the mental and emotional torment the young man was going through. He was probably horrified by the idea that his own father might have done such a terrible thing. But he was also alienated from his father, a man who refused to try to understand him. And he clearly had regarded the priest with a great deal of respect and affection.

"I'm sorry, Philip. Sorry that you're having to cope with what must seem like a nightmare. But try to leave the worrying to us."

It was too late for such advice.

"What I'm calling about," he said, "is that I know when my father went bow hunting and where. Well, most of it anyway."

Carol wanted to slow him down, but Philip had a story to tell and he rushed ahead with his explanation of what he knew and how he knew it.

"Father is neat." The way he said it made it clear that it was no compliment. "He never throws a receipt away. He stores them in a box in his room. And he's always criticizing Mother when she forgets to let him have her receipts when she's been shopping. So I figured he'd have the receipts from his hunting trip—you know, for motels, restaurants, gas stations, places like that. I waited until him and Mom and my brothers were out of the house and I went through his receipt box. You never told me what day Father Rafferty was killed, but I can tell you that he spent October 16th and 17th in a motel in some place called Chestertown and the next night, the 18th, at one in Eagle Bay. I looked at a map and those towns are a long way from Crooked Lake."

Carol knew what his next question would be.

"Was the Father killed on any of those days?" It was impossible to tell from his tone of voice whether he hoped that her answer would be yes or no.

She could have said, no, he was killed on the 20th. She didn't.

"Let me first ask you a question, Philip. Make that two questions. First, when did your father leave on his trip? And second, when did he get home?"

"Does that mean that the Father was killed before the 16th or after the 18th?"

"Let's take it one step at a time. Why don't you give me those dates."

"Okay. He left early on the 16th. And he got back on the 21st. Does that mean that he could have done it—after he left Eagle Bay, that is?"

There was no way she could put his mind at rest unless she lied, and that didn't seem like a good idea.

"Father Rafferty died the night of October 20th. That does not mean that your father had anything to do with his death. We have discovered no evidence that he was in this area, or that he has ever been in this area. Are you sure you didn't miss a motel receipt for the 19th and 20th? Or one for a gas station?"

"There weren't any more motel receipts, and the only ones for gas were on the 17th and the 21st."

"Where was the gas station he stopped at on the 21st?"

"Right near here. Shrewsbury. It's a place between Worcester and Boston."

That would have been a long drive from the vineyard at Random Harvest. Long, but not impossible if Gerald Flanagan had hit the road shortly after hoisting Rafferty up on the scarecrow's cross in the wee small hours of October 21st.

"Do you happen to know at what time your father got back to East Moncton on the 21st?"

"No, I'm afraid not. He was home, taking a nap, when I got back from school, and I never asked him. I don't think I should ask him now."

"Absolutely not, Philip. There is no reason for you to strain your relationship with your father any further. Like I said, I have no evidence suggesting that he was anywhere near here when Father Rafferty was killed. It's more likely that you overlooked a receipt or maybe your father lost one along the way. Try to put it out of your mind."

Carol knew that that would be impossible. At least until the murder had been solved. And perhaps not even then.

There was something else she needed to know. Which meant that there was another decision to make while Philip Flanagan was on the line. She took a deep breath and asked the young man to do something for her, something which she felt quite certain would guarantee him more sleepless nights.

"Is there a way in which you could send me one of those receipts? One with his signature on it. No, wait a minute. Can you

get a picture of it so we could bring it up on the computer screen
here in the office? Like today?"

"Sure, no problem. Just tell me where to send it. But why
do you need his signature?"

"What I want to do is eliminate your father as a suspect in
Father Rafferty's death if I can. I believe a clear signature would
do it. It's complicated, but sometimes matching—or in this case
not matching—handwriting can be very helpful. I hate to ask you
to do this, Philip, but it really might clear things up."

It might also make it more likely that Gerald Flanagan had
written the note to Rafferty, and thus that he had tracked him to
the Random Harvest winery and killed him. She knew that young
Flanagan was too smart not to see this. But she had done what she
could to suggest that his cooperation would lead to his father's
exoneration. Is that what he wanted to happen? She hoped so. It
would be a terrible thing if Philip, consciously or unconsciously,
wanted his father to be convicted of murdering the priest. Carol
shuddered involuntarily.

She gave him the information he needed to send the
signature which might or might not make it likely that Gerald
Flanagan had written the note. The note that said that Brendan
Rafferty's effort to escape his past had been a failure.

Carol was not pleased with herself. She was involving a
troubled young man in her investigation of a murder, a murder
which his father may have committed. She tried to move on to
other things, but found it hard to do. It was not until Sam Bridges
walked into her office with news about the phony post office
boxes that she managed to put Philip Rafferty out of her mind.

"Franklin Pierce and Barnaby Rudge," Bridges said.
"Where did he come up with that one? Never heard of anyone
named either Rudge or Barnaby."

"It's Dickens, Sam. He liked to give his characters crazy
names. Like Martin Chuzzlewit or Uriah Heep."

Carol bit her tongue. She was showing off, and she knew
it. Bridges would not be impressed, nor should he be.

"Sorry. It's the handwriting that matters. What do you
have?"

"Both signature cards are in the same hand," he said.
"Nice and clear, easy to read. Now this is what you'll want to hear.
I went back to the winery, spoke with Mr. Drake, and got his okay
to compare the signature with those of his employees. I focused on

the people you said were most likely to be involved in the winery's financial transactions. Guess what? First one I checked was a match. At least it looked like one to my untrained eye."

Carol, unable to restrain herself, interrupted Sam.

"Who is it?"

"Mr. Jameson. You know, he's—"

"I know who he is. But I don't believe it. Did you compare the signature card with anyone else's John Hancock?"

"I did. Copeland, Grabner, Clifford, Church, even the guy who does their hiring, Francis. While I was at it I checked a few others, but it didn't seem necessary to go through the whole roster. After I saw Jameson's, it looked like a waste of time."

She would probably have reacted just as Sam had. But the idea of Jameson setting up bogus mail drops made no sense to her. On the one hand he was the most logical candidate, given his position at the winery. On the other hand, however, it was hard to imagine that he would be the thief. After all, he had reported the fact that the books were inexplicably out of balance. And his initials were PJ, not JC.

After Bridges had left, looking quite satisfied with himself for having taken care of the Rudge/Pierce problem, Carol sat back in her chair and considered the implications of what he had told her. If Jameson was guilty of stealing Random Harvest money, the theft had nothing to do with Rafferty's attempt to save the soul of jc, whoever jc was. And if that were so, neither did the theft have anything to do with Rafferty's murder.

She decided that she was unwilling to accept Sam's judgment. Hers, she knew, would be no better. What they needed was the opinion of an expert. She remembered that Gretchen Ziegler, a fellow lawyer she had known when she worked in the capital, had a reputation as a handwriting expert. She hadn't spoken to Gretchen since she had left Albany to become sheriff of Cumberland County. But they had been good acquaintances back then, and Carol was confident that Gretchen would be willing to take a look at the signatures.

She was lucky. Mrs. Ziegler was still with her old firm, and she was in her office when Carol called. This was too important a matter to be left to the vagaries of the mail, so it was quickly agreed that Officer Barrett would drive to Albany with the documents the following morning, wait while Gretchen evaluated them, and drive back that afternoon. It occurred to her that she could kill two birds with one stone. She'd retrieve from the files the note that Rafferty had kept in his Bible, clip it to Gerald Flanagan's receipt and the paper with Sadowsky's address, and add a brief note to Gretchen Ziegler, asking her to offer her opinion on these handwriting samples as well.

It was while Carol was explaining his mission to Barrett that Ms. Franks announced that something had come in from Philip Flanagan. It was, as expected, the photocopy of one of his father's receipts from the bow-hunting trip, a receipt containing his signature. Had there ever been a day when handwriting had occupied more of her time than it had today? If so, she could not recall it.

It was immediately apparent that Gerald Flanagan had not penned the note she had found in Father Rafferty's Bible. There would have been no reason for him to have disguised his handwriting on either the note or the receipt. The two handwriting samples were about as different as they could be. Philip Rafferty would be pleased to hear this. At least she hoped that he would be pleased. The differences in the two documents made it more likely that the note had been written by Carl Sadowsky. It did not, however, prove that Sadowsky had murdered Rafferty. Nor did it prove that Flanagan hadn't murdered him.

CHAPTER 47

Carol had been careful not to give Earl Drake the impression that she wanted to take over the investigation of the missing thirty thousand dollars. But it was becoming increasingly difficult to leave Random Harvest's "other issue" alone. She found herself thinking about it almost as much as she did Brendan Rafferty's murder.

She was putting her desk in order, preparatory to picking up Kevin, when she decided there was something she would have to do, something which would require Drake's support. So she set off on the upper lake road with the intention of paying the owner of the winery a visit on her way to the airport.

Fortunately there was no one with him, so she was promptly waved on into his office. He looks unusually tired, Carol thought. And worried. She came right to the point.

"Mr. Drake, I have a request to make. As you know, it has occurred to me that there may be some relationship between Mr. Rafferty's death and the fact that someone has been stealing money from your winery. I don't know whether it is true or not, but I can't get it out of my mind. Mr. Rafferty said something in his diary about a conversation he had had with someone whose initials are jc. He doesn't say what the conversation was about, but the more I've read his words and thought about it, the more I believe that the jc he refers to is one of your employees and that the subject of that conversation was the winery's finances."

"Why would Rafferty have been interested in our financial matters?" Drake said, obviously not prepared to accept the sheriff's thesis.

"We may never know," Carol said, her voice calm. "But what if I'm right? I believe that there are several people here at the winery who go by the initials jc—Mr. Copeland, Mr. Clifford, Mr. Church, Ms. Coyle. I would like to have your authorization to search the offices of those people. Not now, not while they are around. After hours, on the weekend. There is no need to say anything to them. After all, in all probability none of them is in any way involved in your money problem. I'm just as interested in clearing their names as you are."

"But search their offices?" Earl Drake made it sound as if she had proposed subjecting them to a strip search. "That implies that you think one of them is guilty of stealing from me. That's impossible."

"It may be unlikely, Mr. Drake, but it isn't impossible. Surely you want to know what happened to the money. All I'd be doing is looking for any papers that don't belong in their offices, papers or anything else which suggests that they might be privy to information which isn't their responsibility. Odds are, I'd find nothing. But as of this moment you still don't know what happened to the money, and I don't know who killed Rafferty. It can't hurt to pursue the possibility that there's a connection, a possibility that I believe is implied by Rafferty's reference to a winery employee with the initials jc."

Earl Drake gazed out of the window at the grey waters of the lake far below the winery. For a long minute he said nothing.

Finally he spoke, his voice barely audible.

"Could this be done quietly—and carefully—so they'd never know I'd questioned their honesty? Their loyalty?"

"Of course. And if word somehow got out, you could say that I required you to allow me into their offices. But word will not get out. If you can tell me when the building will be deserted, when these men—oh, and Ms. Coyle—will absolutely not be around, I'll arrange to do it then. It won't take long. We aren't on an open-ended fishing expedition. I'm just looking for something that would connect someone to Rafferty and to Parker Jameson's records."

"Does this mean that you're sure Parker had nothing to do with the loss of the thirty thousand?"

"I can't say with absolute certainty, but I think it is highly unlikely. I'd stake my reputation on it."

Carol wasn't sure why she had said that. It was a foolish assertion, and quite out of character. But she was desperately anxious to get into those offices.

Drake said he would think about it. She hoped he meant he would think about what would be the best time to do it. They agreed to meet the next morning at nine.

When she left for the airport, it had started to rain, a light drizzle which made it necessary to turn on the windshield wipers from time to time. She tried to shut out thoughts of the Rafferty murder, the better to focus on the prospect of several days with Kevin. Normally, that prospect would have made it easy to forget everything else. But for some reason it wasn't as easy today. Maybe it was the gloomy weather. More likely it was the fact that another day had passed without a glimpse of the solution to a crime which had been committed more than three weeks earlier.

Kevin would be eager to help. He might even have a good idea or two. But he had been little involved in the investigation. She would need to spend quite a bit of time filling him in on what had transpired in his absence, reminding him of who was who, what they had done, or what they were suspected of doing. And while she didn't mind sharing all of this with him, she would much prefer to unwind and enjoy a romantic weekend.

The small handful of people in the regional airport waiting room were treated to the sight of a uniformed officer of the law warmly embracing an arriving passenger who was carrying a briefcase and a small handsomely wrapped package. Moments later they released each other and stepped out into the evening drizzle.

When they pulled up behind the cottage, Carol urged Kevin to freshen up while she readied supper.

"Take your time," she said. "It's not going to be anything special, but I thought I could prove that I know my way around a kitchen. There's a bottle of your Chardonnay waiting."

When Kevin emerged from the bathroom, soft music was coming from the Bose in the living room.

"What's that?" he asked.

"It's Fauré," Carol answered. "Something from *Pelléas and—*"

"Yes, I know," Kevin interrupted. "But what is it?"

"Oh. It's a little something I bought for you. A CD with the charming title *Bedroom Adagios*. I thought you might like it."

"And I do. You're full of surprises, aren't you?"

"Actually it was the title that intrigued me. I don't pretend to know most of the numbers. Let's open the wine."

Kevin poured the wine, and while Carol curled up on the couch, he went back to the bedroom.

"I don't know what prompted you to honor me with a gift," he said as he returned, hands behind his back. "Not my birthday, you know. But it looks like great minds run on the same track. I decided to surprise you, too."

When he brought his hands out, they were holding the package, neatly wrapped in silver paper with a bright blue ribbon.

"I've been wondering what you've been carrying. For me?"

"No, it's for Deputy Sheriff Bridges. Of course it's for you. Just a way to say how much I've been missing you."

"Am I allowed to open it now?"

"I suppose we could wait until after dinner, but now that *Bedroom Adagios* is playing, why don't you go ahead and open it."

Carol tore off the paper, opened the box, and pulled out an attractive rust-colored nightie.

"You are a devil, aren't you?" she said, getting up from the couch to give him another hug.

"I considered red and I considered black, but decided they were too obvious. When in doubt, be subtle, I thought. Will you promise to model it for me tonight?"

"Now or after supper?" she asked.

"I think we can sustain the mood, don't you? I wouldn't want to ruin that nice dinner you've created. Let's eat and then model."

There was a lot that needed to be said about the Rafferty case, but there was no urgent reason why it couldn't wait until the next day. So they drank their wine and enjoyed the first ever dinner that Carol had prepared at the cottage. And then the bedroom beckoned.

CHAPTER 48

Kevin rolled over, pushed himself up onto his elbow, and looked at the clock. 8:50. Carol was long gone. She had nudged him awake some time ago, told him that she was on her way to the office, and announced that tonight it was his turn to do dinner.

He lay in bed, reveling in the fact that this was the first day of another long weekend at the lake cottage. And recalling the night before. Carol had looked great in her new nightie. Of course she had looked great with it off as well, but he was congratulating himself on the impulse which had led him to buy it for her. He was on his own for the day, but she had promised to be back before six and after that there would be nothing to interfere with their enjoyment of each other's company until the following Monday. Or so he believed. As it happened, he was wrong.

As they had agreed, Carol met Earl Drake in his office at nine. The winery's owner spent the better part of ten minutes insisting that he had full confidence in his employees, especially those whose offices the sheriff wished to search. He recited their many contributions to Random Harvest's success, ticking them off on his fingers as he spoke. But it soon became apparent that he would not stand in the way of Carol's plan. He only wanted to establish the fact that if things went wrong, the blame would rest on the sheriff's shoulders, not his.

They decided that the best time to conduct the search would be Sunday morning. Carol invited Drake to accompany her when she went through the offices, but he demurred, worried that his presence would suggest that he shared Carol's belief that something incriminating would be found.

On her way out of the winery, she ran into Mary Rizzo.

"Good morning, Sheriff." The young woman was her typically good-natured self. "Any good news?"

"Hi, Mary. If by good news you mean am I ready to arrest somebody, the answer is no. But I think we're getting there."

Carol hoped she was getting there. She was more optimistic some days than others. Maybe Sunday would give a boost to her optimism.

It was early afternoon when Ms. Franks buzzed to say that a Ms. Ziegler was on the phone. Carol had assumed that she would be getting the report on the handwriting when Barrett got back late in the day. But apparently Ziegler preferred to speak to her personally rather than rely on a note that Barrett would be bringing back from Albany.

"Hi, Gretchen. I take it my man made it and that you've seen the handwriting specimens."

"He did and I have," she said. "You didn't tell me what this was all about, but you've aroused my curiosity. It looks as if your course work in criminal law is more important to you these days than the stuff you did in your practice here."

Carol laughed.

"Right you are. I really appreciate it that you called. I've been getting antsy, waiting for Officer Barrett to get back. What can you tell me?"

"Well, first, let me remind you that I'm an amateur. I know you'll protest, but it isn't really my field. Not officially. But I said I'd help if I could, and I think I can. You gave me two cases. Let's start with the one involving the man called Sadowsky. I'm pretty sure that the note—the note about finding somebody at last—was written by the same man who wrote out his address for you. I'm not one hundred percent sure, but if I were called to testify, heaven forbid, I'd say they were by the same person."

"That confirms my hunch. Good. What about the other case, the Jameson signature?"

"That's another story. There's the man's signature that you say is authentic, and there are the signatures on the post office box forms. Same name, and they sure look alike. Superficially. But I'd lay money that they're not by the same hand. When you examine the signatures closely, it looks like they were written slowly, as if somebody was trying very hard to get them just right. Most people just write their signature quickly. After all, they've done it thousands of times. But in this case the line isn't quite steady, as it wouldn't be if the writer was being very conscious of how it should look. I have no idea whether this is what you want to hear, but I'd say whoever wrote the name Parker Jameson on the post office forms isn't Parker Jameson."

"That's fantastic," Carol said, and she meant it. "I've been hoping it was someone else, but in my business you need the truth, not what you might like to be the truth. I owe you a full account of this case I'm working on. It's complicated, and there's no way I can do it now over the phone. But I promise to fill you in when we wrap the case up, assuming we do. In fact, I'd love to take a trip over to Albany and do lunch."

"That would be great, Carol. You might even be able to convince me that I'm in the wrong profession."

"I doubt that, but I mean it. Lunch. After I've closed my case. You know, of course, that there's a possibility you may have to be called as a witness."

"I figured as much. I'd rather not, but I'm available if the prosecution needs me."

"Many thanks. You've been a big help."

Yes, Carol thought as she considered what she'd learned, but I still don't know who faked Jameson's signature. Nor do I know whether Carl Sadowsky followed up his note to Brendan Rafferty by paying him a visit in Clarksburg and killing him. Cahill up in Verona gives him an alibi, and why would he be lying? Maybe it was his muscle, doing the dirty deed for the boss. Yet they had made an appearance at Mrs. Stafford's after Rafferty's murder. Did that exonerate them, and by extension Sadowsky? Or were they cleverly trying to cover their tracks?

———

Kevin had once again borrowed the Morgans' car to run a few errands, but had returned it and was taking a stab at his article on Verdi and *King Lear* when Carol drove up. It was 5:50.

He set aside his notes, of which there were very few, and rushed to the kitchen door and a welcome-home kiss.

"Quick," Carol said as she tossed aside her jacket. "I'm ready for whatever's cold. Beer or wine."

"Let's finish the bottle we opened last night," Kevin said, taking down two wine glasses from the cupboard. "Good day?"

"I think so. Nothing dramatic, but I've got that feeling. It's probably because you're here."

"Glad to be of assistance, but I'm way out of the loop. Except for a few scraps, I don't know much of anything that's happened since I got back from East Moncton last weekend."

Carol took her wine to the living room. Kevin peeked into the oven, and satisfied with what he saw, joined her.

"Tonight I'll tell you everything. Everything except who killed the priest. If you promise to keep your mind on the case and your hands off me for an hour or two, I think I can tell you pretty much everything that I know. Then you can weigh in with your opinion. Maybe I should make that opinions."

"Good. Right now I'm ready to argue that Flanagan is your man. But that's because he's the only one of your cast of suspects I've met. So you have to make the case that it's someone else."

"I really don't have a prime suspect. There have been days when I wonder if our killer is somebody we haven't even considered. But I'm still inclined to believe that it's going to be Flanagan, Sadowsky, or jc. Remember him? There are four jcs working at Random Harvest, one of them a woman. If we go by Rafferty's diary, we can disregard her. I'm going to search all of their offices this weekend. With the permission of the owner, of course. But I've got a hunch that Rafferty's jc is going to be Joe Clifford, the winery's golden boy."

"Golden boy?"

"Yes. He appears to be the man the owner wants to succeed him when he retires, which looks to be about two years away. He's smart. And a smart-ass. Very self-impressed. I don't have any particular reason to think he's our jc. It's just that the other jcs seem like nicer specimens of humanity. But then, what do I know?"

"Clifford. Want to tell me about him?"

"Sure, but let's wait until after dinner. It's a long story."

"I've got an idea."

Carol felt a familiar feeling rising in her chest.

"An idea? What now? You haven't heard anything yet. How can you have a new idea?"

"I know. But I trust your instincts. If you're suspicious of this guy Clifford, I'll bet it's not just because he's a smart-ass. Tomorrow's Saturday. Presumably he'll be at home, and home can't be all that far from here. What if I were to pay him a visit? I could pull that 'friend of Father Rafferty' routine, just like I did up in East Moncton. He doesn't know me. The only time I was at the winery was when we were doing the wine-tasting circuit, and that was a Saturday. I've become a pretty good liar, and I could size him up, see how he reacts to what I have to say about Rafferty."

"You're bored with teaching, aren't you?"

"No, not at all. I just think I could do you some good. Provided you give me a good briefing on him tonight."

"Kevin, I've talked with Joe Clifford. I've talked with him twice. And at some length. I've talked about him with Mr. Drake, the owner. I can't imagine what you'd learn that I haven't or that I couldn't."

"We'd be playing different roles. You're the cop. If he's guilty, he'd be on his guard. I'm an old friend of Father Rafferty. Just an innocent friend of the deceased."

"Why would an innocent friend of the deceased choose to seek out Mr. Clifford? Wouldn't that make him suspicious?"

"I'm a couple of steps ahead of you, Carol. This old friend had a letter from Rafferty, a recent letter. One in which he mentioned someone named Clifford at the winery. I hear my friend is dead; I want to hear what happened. I don't know anybody at the winery, but I have this guy Clifford's name. It would be the most logical thing in the world to look him up, talk to him."

Carol realized that the other side of Kevin's persona, the gung-ho amateur sleuth, was now in charge. She could—and probably should—simply tell him that she wouldn't allow it. But in spite of her understandable misgivings, she could see that it might work. He couldn't do it without a thorough briefing on the Random Harvest financial mess. She'd be telling him all about that in any event.

"I think it's time for dinner," she said. "Let me fill you in on where things stand after we eat. Then we'll decide whether your idea is a good one or not. No, let me revise that. Then *I'll* decide whether your idea is a good one or not. Okay?"

"What can I say? You're the boss. And tonight I'm the chef. How does southern fried chicken sound?"

"Fine. You praised my goulash last night. I'm ready to give your dinner a thumbs-up even before I pick up my fork."

After dinner, the discussion of the missing $30,000 and ancillary issues occupied the better part of two hours. By the time that Carol and Kevin decided to call it a night, it had been agreed, with a few important caveats, that Kevin would pay a visit to Random Harvest's heir apparent the following day. In light of the fact that Clifford might have heard rumors that there was someone named Kevin Whitman in the sheriff's life, they had settled on a new alias. The late Father Rafferty's friend would introduce himself as Wilson Vollmer. Carol thought the name was a bit pompous, but Kevin prevailed, arguing that it was an improvement on Barnaby Rudge.

CHAPTER 49

After a week of uncertain weather, the skies cleared and the sun made a welcome appearance on Saturday morning. Kevin punched Carol on the shoulder and announced that he'd like to take the canoe out before starting breakfast. She responded by burrowing deeper under the covers.

He couldn't blame her. Why not sleep in when the opportunity presented itself? But the sight of the sun on the quiet waters of the lake after too many days in the city was simply too inviting. Kevin crawled out of bed and started rummaging in the closet for a sweatsuit he knew was there.

He turned on the coffee pot, wrote a short note for Carol, and went out to what passed for his boathouse to haul out the canoe. Two minutes later he was paddling south along Blue Water Point. It was a chilly morning, and little curls of steam were rising from the surface of the lake. This is pure heaven, he thought. A lovely night with Carol, a lovely morning on the lake. Why don't I do this more often? There were, of course, reasons why he didn't. Why he couldn't. But he was pleased with himself that he had at least struck this bargain with the college and his conscience to spend every other weekend at the cottage.

As he paddled, he tried to focus on what he had learned from Carol about the missing $30,000, as well as her impressions of Joe Clifford. It would have been easier to focus on these things had it not been for the distracting call and then the sight of a kingfisher. Or if a flight of Canadian geese had not approached, veered toward the bluff, and then settled down not far off to his left. Or if a fish, probably a large bass, had not broken the surface in search of some flying insect not twenty feet ahead of the canoe. Kevin found himself wishing that the water temperature were just a bit warmer. Warm enough for swimming. He stopped paddling and trailed his hand in the lake for a moment, testing the temperature. Unfortunately, it really was much too cold.

He remembered a time, some years ago, when his lake neighbor Mike Snyder had told him about belonging to something called the Crooked Lake Polar Bear Club when he was a kid. It had apparently been less of a club than simply an annual January ritual, one in which a bunch of foolhardy guys trekked down to the town dock in Southport and jumped into the lake while their girlfriends and assembled townspeople stood on the bank and cheered them on. Kevin had never tried it, giving himself the convenient excuse that he was always down in the city in January. But if it was too cold in November, it would certainly be way too cold in January.

Kevin paddled on past Mallard Cove for another half mile, then turned and headed back for the cottage, a cup of hot coffee, and breakfast with Carol. He knew that she would again admonish him to be careful with Clifford, not to overplay his hand. He smiled at the thought. When had he ever overplayed his hand? By the time he pulled the canoe up onto his beach, he had counted at least a dozen times when that is exactly what he had done. Carol would be only too quick to cite several of them.

The smell of coffee and something baking in the oven greeted him when he came in.

"What have you got cooking?" Kevin asked as Carol came out of the kitchen, wrapped up in the bathrobe she had borrowed from him.

"Sorry to disappoint you, but it came from the bakery. I don't do breakfast muffins from scratch. Lake quiet this morning?"

"It sure is. Great day for communing with nature. I'd have stayed out longer if I didn't have to hassle one of your suspects."

"It was your idea, not mine," Carol said. "This'll be an odd day, won't it? You doing police work, me staying home. Anything you'd like me to do around the cottage?"

Kevin was ready to make a frivolous suggestion, but thought better of it.

"You're going to have to take me over to Cumberland to get your Buick. Then why don't you just take it easy. My little chat with Clifford shouldn't take long."

He had no idea how long it would take, or even whether it would take place at all. Clifford might not be home. Or he might find an excuse to send Brendan Rafferty's faux friend quickly on his way.

"Let's eat and get dressed," Carol said as she took the muffins out of the oven. "By the way, you're going to have to stop and fill the tank. It's almost empty. I'm not sure you'd make it to Southport and back without more gas."

It was a quarter to ten when they set out for Cumberland and Carol's other car. It was 10:40 when Kevin pulled out of the gas station and headed for Joe Clifford's home in Southport. It was close to 11:15 when he parked in front of the white colonial with green shutters at 35 Spruce Street.

Kevin had never met Clifford, but Carol had provided him with a good description of the man, both as to his physical appearance and his personality, insofar as she could gauge it after only two meetings with him. For some reason, he was looking forward to this meeting less than he had to the one with Flanagan the previous weekend. Perhaps it was because Rafferty's notebook, however sketchy, had provided more of a hint as to what Flanagan's problem with the priest might be. In Clifford's case, there was almost nothing to go on except the reference to Father Brown and saving souls.

The man who opened the door looked to be in his thirties. He was well over six feet tall, and appeared to be in excellent physical condition. But his hair was a fiery copper red, and that was enough to tell Kevin that the man who greeted him was Joe Clifford.

"Good morning. Would you be Mr. Clifford?" he asked, slipping into the role of a friend of the late Brendan Rafferty.

"Yes, that's me. What can I do for you?"

"First, my name's Wilson Vollmer. I was hoping you might help me to understand what has happened to an old friend of mine. Mind if I come in?"

Clifford looked puzzled, as well he might be. But he stepped aside and motioned the stranger into the house.

"Who is this friend you think I might know something about?" he asked as they took seats in the living room. A woman, presumably Clifford's wife, stuck her head around a corner, managed a half smile, and retreated to wherever she had come from.

"His name's Brendan Rafferty," Kevin said. Clifford tried to mask his surprise when he heard the name. He failed.

"Rafferty? He's the man who—"

Clifford caught himself in mid-sentence.

"Excuse me," he asked, "but what do you know about Mr. Rafferty?"

"All I know is what I was told at the winery where he was working. They said Brendan was dead, that he'd been killed recently. I was shocked."

"Yes, I can imagine you would be. It has been quite a story around here. Nobody seems to know what happened to him."

"That's why I'm here. I had come to Rochester on business and thought I could drive on down here and see how he was doing. I still find it hard to believe that he was killed."

"I don't see how I can help you, Mr. Wilson. I'm just like everyone else at the winery. No one has a clue why he was killed."

"It's Vollmer. Wilson Vollmer."

"Sorry. I don't understand, though, why you came to see me. I know we worked for the same company, but I didn't know Mr. Rafferty. We had very different jobs."

"The reason I'm here, Mr. Clifford, is that Brendan mentioned you in a letter he wrote to me several weeks ago. He wasn't in the habit of talking about his friends or his fellow workers, so your name stuck in my mind."

"That's strange," Clifford said. "Why would he mention me? Like I said, I didn't know him. I doubt we ever spoke. He must have had me confused with someone else."

Kevin was no expert at reading body language. But if he were asked to describe the man who sat across from him in the living room of 35 Spruce Street in Southport, he would have said tense.

"Perhaps he was confused. But his letter didn't read that way."

"What was it he said about the person he thought was me?" The question did not surprise Kevin. If Clifford were indeed Rafferty's jc, he would want to know what had been said about him. If Clifford had killed Rafferty, the content of that letter would be of utmost importance to him. There was, of course, no letter. Only a couple of opaque notes in a diary.

Clifford's question posed a challenge for Kevin. He had created a false relationship for himself with Rafferty. Now he had to fabricate a relationship between Rafferty and Clifford, a relationship based on speculation as to what had transpired between the two men that led to those frustratingly vague diary notes. Kevin had thought a lot about what he would say. He had even spent a restless hour in the middle of the night worrying about it.

"What he said makes sense only if you know that Brendan Rafferty was a priest. Did you know that?"

"There's been word back at the winery that maybe he used to be. I didn't know whether it was true or just an unfounded rumor."

"It's true. I knew him when he was a priest. He had an existential crisis somewhere along the way. He never liked to talk about it, but it bothered him a lot. I mean it bothered him that he'd chosen to leave the priesthood. I know he agonized over it. I think he thought he may have abandoned people who needed him. That's what comes through in his letter about you."

There was no longer any question about it. Joe Clifford was indeed tense. But he said nothing.

"The way he told it," Kevin continued, "you were troubled by something. You admitted—I think that's the word Brendan used—you admitted that you had done something you should not have done. Being a former priest, he saw it in terms of sin. He spoke of you as having sinned. What was interesting to me about the letter was that Brendan said that he wished he were still a priest because he wanted so badly to hear your confession. He thought he could help you make things right again, right with God and right with whomever you had harmed."

Kevin let it go at that. He waited for some reaction.

"It's an interesting story," Clifford finally said. "But it has nothing to do with me. I never said anything like that to him. I wonder whom he was talking about."

He had never said anything like that to Rafferty. Did that mean that he *had* talked with him, just not said what Kevin had said he said?

"Anyhow," Kevin went on, "I think you can see why I came to see you. I had the impression that you and Brendan were quite close. In a strange way, perhaps, but close enough that you could tell me what had really happened to him. As I said, he never mentioned anybody else at the winery."

Throughout this brief conversation, Joe Clifford may have been tense, but he had been patient, willing to hear this stranger out. Suddenly, as if his patience had finally run out, he stood up.

"Mr. Vollmer, I believe I've said it now several times. I did not know Mr. Rafferty. We never had a conversation, much less a conversation like the one you've described. So you're talking to the wrong person if you want information about Mr. Rafferty's death. I have no idea how it happens that he confused me with someone else."

Then he seemed to have another thought on the subject.

"I know that he was a friend of yours, but from what you tell me about him—his leaving the church and all that—maybe he was experiencing mental problems. That could account for his confusion."

"I'm quite sure he was mentally fine," Kevin said.

"Okay, so maybe he was in his right mind. Whatever the reason, he was confused. I can't spend the rest of the morning wondering what Mr. Rafferty's problem was. All I know is that he's dead."

Clifford headed for the front door, obviously expecting his visitor to follow him. The conversation was over.

When Kevin had arrived half an hour earlier, Clifford had been puzzled but willing to listen. Now he was clearly impatient to get rid of the man who had been telling him things which were not true. Or were they true enough to be deeply unsettling, even threatening?

As Kevin drove away, his mind was on Joe Clifford's reaction to the imagined content of the nonexistent letter. And to the fact that on one of the shelves of a bookcase near where he had been sitting in the Clifford living room was what looked like a complete set of the novels of Charles Dickens.

CHAPTER 50

Carol had joked about the fact that it was Kevin who would be working on this Saturday in November while she enjoyed a lazy day at the cottage. But she hadn't been entirely idle. There were still too many loose ends to be tied up, and she found it impossible simply to sit and read or watch TV or otherwise put the Rafferty case on hold.

What she had done with most of the morning was to place calls to every motel and B & B in the immediate area. The purpose of those calls was to find out whether Gerald Flanagan had stayed on or near Crooked Lake the night when Father Rafferty had been killed and strung up like a scarecrow in the Random Harvest vineyard. The answer everywhere—at least everywhere she could think to call—was that no one by that name was on their guest list for the night in question. In view of the possibility that Flanagan had used a phony name and paid in cash, she had asked whether any of their guests had been driving a car with Massachusetts plates. Once again she came up empty, although several of the places she called admitted that they didn't know.

For Philip Flanagan's sake, she would like to believe that the negative replies to her question meant that his father could not be Father Rafferty's killer. But she knew better than to make that assumption. Maybe he had slept in his car, thereby avoiding the possibility that someone would remember him. Maybe he had prudently stayed in someplace further away—down in Elmira, up in Auburn, some place other than Crooked Lake but within a relatively short drive of it. She could think of several reasons why he still belonged on her small list of suspects.

Carol's thoughts shifted from Flanagan to Clifford. It was now after one o'clock, and Kevin should be back soon. She doubted that he would have learned anything. She hoped that her preferred candidate for the role of Rafferty's jc had accepted Kevin's claim to be an old friend of the priest. But he struck her as much too smart to lose his cool and change his tune regarding either Rafferty or the missing $30,000. She was more optimistic about finding something in his office that would point to him as the thief. Whether that something would also make it likely that he had killed Rafferty was another matter.

Where was Kevin? How long could he have sustained the story he had concocted for his meeting with Clifford? How many times could he have found another way of persuading the winery's golden boy to make a damaging admission? What if she was wrong and Clifford had had nothing to do with the theft? And what if, in spite of what Mary Rizzo had told her, Rafferty and Clifford didn't know each other and Clifford was not the priest's jc?

"Hi, I'm home," Kevin called out as he opened the back door.

"Thank God. I'd started to worry about you."

"You shouldn't have. Everything went according to plan. I did make a stop at Random Harvest to pick up some wine, but it's only a minute or two after one."

"No, it's 1:24 according to the clock over the stove. And the watch on my wrist."

Kevin gave Carol a big kiss.

"That was nice," he said as he set the sack of wine bottles on the kitchen table. "A good prelude to lunch, don't you think?"

"Agreed, but I think I'm more interested in what you have to report than I am in lunch."

"No reason we can't have it both ways. Why don't you pull a couple of things out of the fridge while I go and wash my hands. I wouldn't want to eat without first scrubbing away that man's handshake."

"It was that bad?"

"No, not really. But I think you've got him pegged. He's a slippery cuss."

"Like I said. Go ahead and wash up. We've got two nights' worth of leftovers to snack on."

It was a long lunch. Carol had to concede that Kevin had done everything he could to lure Clifford into a discussion of his relationship with Rafferty. But it hadn't worked. Either the two men had been virtual strangers or Clifford was a master of the art of deceit. Carol suspected the latter. Kevin was sure of it. When she pressed him, however, he was unable to offer convincing evidence. Clifford's body had been tense. He had clenched his jaw. There had been something shifty about the movement of his eyes. In essence, Kevin had not liked the cut of his jib. Neither had Carol, but she had hoped that a different approach, by someone who was obviously not an officer of the law, would yield a different result.

Having disposed of the Q & A part of his meeting with Clifford, Kevin mentioned the man's collection of Charles Dickens' works.

"You said that the post office box for one of the phony companies somebody was using to rip off Random Harvest was in the name of Barnaby Rudge. Rudge? Come on. Who would pick a name like that? Only someone who knew his Dickens. And most people have never heard of Barnaby Rudge. He's not exactly top drawer Dickens. But your friend Joe Clifford had a whole shelf full of Dickens, everything from *Oliver Twist* to *Edwin Drood*. So it's a reasonable guess that Rudge came to mind when he was trying to come up with a phony name for his PO box. Maybe he considered Pickwick and Marley, too, but he settled for Rudge. There's my evidence."

"It's an interesting theory, but it won't stand up in court, Kevin."

"Maybe so, but don't you think it makes it likely that Clifford's the guy who's cheating the winery?"

"He was my candidate anyway, so, yes, it makes sense. It's just that a good defense lawyer would demolish it as admissible evidence. Besides, it doesn't say anything about Clifford being Rafferty's killer."

"Okay. It's your case. Want to tell me who the killer is? Who shot the priest and turned him into a scarecrow?"

Carol's answer was "no," but she soon found herself in a discussion of what she knew and didn't know about the men she had come to view as her prime suspects.

"Here we are," she said, "weeks after his death, and the best witness for the prosecution is still Rafferty himself. We don't know much other than what he tells us in his notebook. And there's not a word in there about a threat to his life."

"But it's there," Kevin objected. "It's obvious he felt threatened."

"I know, but we're talking about hard evidence, not the jottings of a paranoid ex-priest."

"It seems to me he was paranoid with good reason."

"Let's look at what we have," Carol said. "Take Flanagan. He's supposed to have hated Rafferty, hated him for what he thought he had done to his son. We have the son's word for that. It's quite possible that he's responsible for Rafferty's decision to leave East Moncton and the priesthood. We know that Flanagan didn't mellow once the priest had gone away. Philip tells us that his relationship with his father is still pretty tense. We also know that Flanagan had heard that Rafferty was working at Random Harvest, that he went bow hunting in New York State just before the priest was killed, and that there's no record of where he was the night it happened."

"See? You're making my case. Flanagan had motive and he had opportunity."

"I like to think so, but I can hear a defense attorney cross-examining Flanagan. Did you hate Father Rafferty? Of course not; he was my priest, my confessor. Did you know that he was working on Crooked Lake? I had no idea where he was. A chronic drunk who's always making things up said he thought he saw him there, but why would I believe a crazy story about a Catholic priest working at a winery? Did you go to Crooked Lake on your bow-hunting trip? Absolutely not. Do you have a motel receipt for the night of Mr. Rafferty's death? No I don't. It's obvious that I lost it. Haven't you ever misplaced a receipt?"

"Which side are you on, Carol?"

"I'm just trying to think like a lawyer. Do I think Flanagan had motive? Yes. Opportunity? Very possibly. Do I think he killed Rafferty? I don't know."

"Does he strike you as someone who'd turn his victim into a scarecrow?"

"All I know is what I've heard. You met him. What do you think?"

Kevin thought about the question for a moment, then shrugged.

"Depends on why the killer went to the trouble of trussing the priest up like that. It didn't make sense when you first told me about it, and it still doesn't."

"I remember thinking it looked like a crucifixion," Carol said. "And if that's what the killer intended, it makes Flanagan the most likely suspect. Here's a man who believes his priest doesn't honor the teachings of the church. He thinks of him as an apostate. Why not mock him? Treat him like a hollow man, a fake Jesus?"

Kevin shook his head.

"It's a possible explanation, but I don't buy it. Scarecrows always look like that—upright, arms stretched out at right angles to the body. If the killer wants to turn his victim into a scarecrow, he can't help but make him look like he's being crucified. No, I don't think the scarecrow business was intended to demonstrate the killer's anger over the priest's apostasy."

"That sounds reasonable," Carol said, agreeing with Kevin's logic. "What about Sadowsky?"

"I've met Flanagan and Clifford. I wouldn't know Sadowsky if I ran into him at the supermarket. He's just a guy who makes money off gamblers, another of the men Rafferty felt threatened by."

"Okay. Like Flanagan, we know him mostly because Rafferty seemed to be afraid of him. The diary again. We know Sadowsky loaned him money, that he couldn't pay it back, that he eventually left Verona to escape this particularly nasty creditor. We're pretty sure that Sadowsky found out where he was and wrote him a note saying that the game was up. But we also know that Sadowsky was elsewhere the night Rafferty was murdered. Unless, that is, Cahill got his dates mixed up, and that isn't likely because it was his birthday. Which brings us to Sadowsky's muscle. Why kill the priest himself? Chances are, he'd let his henchmen do it for him."

"Right," Kevin said, "except you told me that those guys showed up at Rafferty's place days after he'd been killed."

"That doesn't prove anything, one way or another. Maybe they came for him too late; somebody had beaten them to him. But maybe they'd already done the deed and then came back later to create an alibi."

"And you're going to tell me again that a good defense lawyer would make mincemeat of all of this. What's your theory as to why Sadowsky or those bodyguards of his would make a scarecrow out of Rafferty?"

"I suppose it would be to make an example of him. You know, this is what happens to people who don't pay their debts. It would send a 'don't trifle with me' message."

"Do you believe that?"

"I can't think of another reason," Carol said.

"Well, I can't imagine Sadowsky doing anything so stupid. If he kills Rafferty, he won't be collecting. If he strings him up in that vineyard, who's going to see him? Who'll get the message?"

"Maybe his bodyguards, or whatever they are, screwed up. Maybe they misunderstood Sadowsky's orders. Just a couple of guys with muscles in their brains as well as their arms."

But Kevin could see that Carol didn't believe what she was saying.

"And then there's Clifford," he said. "The diary isn't much help where he's concerned."

"I think there's a good chance that he can be nailed for the theft of winery money. Trying to link that to Rafferty's murder will be a lot harder."

"But unless he's indicted for embezzlement, or whatever the technical term for it is, I don't see how he can be tied to the murder."

"That's true," Carol said. "Our only reason for thinking Clifford may have killed Rafferty is that the priest's diary refers to his effort to save the soul of someone whose initials are jc. And that takes us into the land of 'if.' If jc is Clifford. If the reason that his soul needed saving was that he had stolen from Random Harvest. If the priest promised not to expose the act of theft if Clifford returned the money. If Clifford didn't believe Rafferty and killed him to prevent him from informing the owner. If, if, if."

"You're going to tell me that the defense attorney will have a field day, aren't you?"

"I think what I have to do is concentrate on the missing money and hope that we can get an indictment on that score. Maybe, just maybe, that will produce information that opens a link to Rafferty's murder. That's why I'm searching the jc offices at the winery tomorrow. All of them, even the one belonging to Jessica Coyle. I don't want Clifford to know that I've singled him out. Not yet."

"If I understand what you're saying—or is it what you're not saying—you believe that Joe Clifford killed Rafferty. Am I right?"

"I might be saying that if I could think of a single reason why Clifford would put Father Rafferty's body in that vineyard, masquerading as a scarecrow. I've racked my brain. I just don't get it."

"I know," Kevin said. "You'd think that the last place a winery employee would want his victim to be found would be on winery property. Why not dump the body in the woods? Or weight it down and toss it in the lake? Anywhere but in the winery's own vineyard."

"So Clifford doesn't seem to make sense. But when you think about it, at least he knew that there was a scarecrow in the winery's vineyard. How would Sadowsky or Flanagan have known that? I have a hard time imagining either of them thinking 'okay, he'd dead, now what—how about turning him into a scarecrow and sticking him down there with the ice grapes.' The scarecrow business just doesn't seem to fit any of my suspects."

Carol sighed and looked at her watch.

"Are you as tired as I am? We've been at this for nearly two hours. Let's take a break. In fact, why don't we call The Cedar Post and make a dinner reservation. I'll make the call if you'll promise me that we won't discuss the Rafferty case over dinner. Or for that matter after we get back to the cottage. I'm sure we can find better things to talk about if we try."

"I know we can. I can even think of better things for the two of us to do. Want to join me?"

"I thought you'd never ask."

CHAPTER 51

Kevin had wanted to accompany Carol to the winery on Sunday morning when she searched the offices of the small handful of employees whose initials were jc. But she vetoed the idea. She didn't expect to see or be seen by anyone, but if her expectations proved to be wrong, she didn't want to have to explain Kevin's presence. So shortly after 7:30 she set off alone in the Buick, leaving Kevin to do whatever he felt like doing. What he felt like doing was taking a hike up the nearest ravine.

When Carol got back to the cottage, he had shed his shoes, socks, and pants, all soaking wet from a fall into the stream, and was sitting in his bathrobe, engrossed in Father Rafferty's copy of *The God Delusion.*

"What are you doing?" Carol sounded surprised.

"Reading," he said, stating the obvious. "But I have been up and out. Had a little accident is all."

"What happened?" Carol now sounded alarmed.

"I took a short hike up the ravine and managed to fall in. This is my post-ravine outfit."

"And I see you're boning up on the 'God is dead' catechism."

"I'm trying to figure out why a Catholic priest would have been reading an atheist tract. It's an interesting book, but not, I suspect, one that the Vatican recommends."

"Or any other practicing Christian. Anyway, we'll never know what Rafferty was thinking. Want to know what I found up at the winery?"

"Of course," Kevin said, putting the book aside and making room for Carol on the couch.

"It was even better than I had expected. I think I'm close to nailing Clifford."

"He's going to be Rafferty's killer?"

"That remains to be seen. But I'm sure he's the one who's gotten away with the money. The rubber gloves were there, tucked conveniently away in a desk drawer. Better yet, there were several papers with Jameson's signature on them. Nothing special about the papers, but it looked to me as if he'd been practicing tracing the signature. I think we've now got enough for a search warrant for both his house and his bank. In fact I'm going to call Drake, tell him what I'm doing, then get in touch with Judge Olcott. Sorry, but I'm going to have to go over to Cumberland and do the paperwork just as soon as I have a bite of lunch."

"I take it you didn't find anything in the other offices."

"No, and I didn't just give them a once-over lightly. Found some interesting stuff, but nothing that smacked of involvement in the theft. Coyle, that's the lone woman in the bunch, which rules her out as Rafferty's jc in any event—she had a whole collection of ducks in her office. Wood carvings, glass and china ducks, you name it. Must have been thirty or forty. A couple of them could be really valuable. But no, Clifford's was the only one where I found anything suspicious, anything that didn't belong there. Oh, by the way, Clifford has a gun in his desk. A Smith & Wesson 642. Looks like he's exercising his Second Amendment rights."

"Do you suppose it's the gun used to kill Rafferty?"

"No idea. When he's arrested, we'll check it out. What matters at the moment is that we've got what could be hard evidence that the golden boy is the one who was cheating on his boss."

"If you have to get started on the warrant, let's first see what there is to eat."

Half an hour later, lunch finished, Carol set off for her office in Cumberland, and Kevin began to think about the fact that he would be heading back to the city the next day. A day when the sheriff's case might well be winding down to its conclusion. How could he be teaching a bunch of twenty-year-old undergraduates about music appreciation when something as momentous as arresting Father Rafferty's murderer could be taking place? Maybe he should call his assistant and ask him to take his Tuesday class. The chairman of his department would understand. At least he hoped that she would.

Carol made quick work of her quest for a search warrant. Earl Drake was no longer in a position to insist that it was his problem, not the sheriff's. The drafting of the request for a warrant was easy, easy because she framed her argument narrowly, making it clear that she was not on a fishing expedition. She refrained from mentioning Rafferty's murder, arguing only that $30,000 was missing from the winery, that there was probable cause to believe that Joseph Clifford was responsible, and specifying the documents she sought. It was to her advantage that Judge Olcott had a high opinion of her judgment, and by the end of the day she was in possession of his authorization to search the Clifford house and take a look at his bank accounts.

It was close to six in the evening when Carol pulled up in back of the cottage. It was obvious to Kevin that she was experiencing an adrenaline high.

"We're going to do it," she said. "How about getting your favorite sheriff a beer?"

"Coming up."

"God, I can't believe we're in the home stretch."

Carol walked on into the living room, kicking off her shoes and shoving them into a corner. Her uniform jacket came off next, followed by her gun and holster.

"That's a relief." She took a deep breath and turned on a big smile. "I'm off duty!"

Kevin produced two beers and joined her on the couch.

"You sound pretty confident that Clifford's your man."

"I am. Unless he's been a lot more careful with his own house and his bank accounts than he was with his office at the winery, I think we've got him."

"For murder, too?"

"I know it's not like me," Carol said, "but I've got a feeling that this is going to be one of those cases where one thing really does lead to another. So, yes, I think he killed Father Rafferty, and I think the Father had it right when he had second thoughts about trying to save jc's soul."

"When do you plan on doing the search?"

"It's known as executing a search warrant, Kevin, and we're going to do it tomorrow. Tomorrow morning. I've already lined up my men. I'm going to leave the house and the bank to them. I want to be at the winery when Clifford hears what we're doing. And I'm sure he'll hear, right away. If I were Mrs. Clifford, the first thing I'd do when Parsons and Barrett walk in with the warrant in hand is call Joe. If for some reason she doesn't, I'll have the pleasure of telling him what's happening."

"What about me?"

"Tell you what," Carol said, reaching over to take his hand. "I'll let you come with me to the winery. On one condition."

"Which is what?"

"You stay down in the foyer, or in the gift shop. Or in the car if you'd rather. It's tight quarters up there on the second floor. Narrow corridor, small offices. Just room for me and Clifford. Okay?"

"You're the sheriff."

CHAPTER 52

Monday had turned into a glorious day. A stiff breeze kept the waters of Crooked Lake in motion, but a bright early morning sun in a cloudless sky promised to take the chill out of the air. Carol and Kevin were up early and on the road to Random Harvest Vineyards by 7:40.

When they pulled into the winery's parking lot, it was empty except for three cars. Carol took note of the fact that none of those cars was Joe Clifford's. She drove to the far end of the lot and backed into a space in front of a loading dock. A sign announced that the space was reserved for Random Harvest vehicles, but it provided a good view of the rest of the parking lot and Carol chose to ignore the sign. She and Kevin settled back in their seats to enjoy their coffee and watch as winery employees, one by one, arrived.

Just ahead of eight, a second county patrol car drove into the lot. Bridges. He chose a parking spot some distance away from the sheriff's car, shut off the engine, and busied himself reading a paper. Finally, at 8:25, Clifford's car turned into the lot and found a vacant space close to the main entrance. Earl Drake's tall heir apparent got out of the car, ran a hand through his wind-blown red hair, and walked into the winery.

"Parsons and Barrett are due to arrive at his house at nine. I'll wait until five of. You can stay here if you like."

It all seemed a bit overly dramatic to Kevin.

"Why don't you just arrest him?"

"We will. But I want to see how he reacts to the news that we're searching his house. He doesn't know we suspect him. Or if he does, he's too cocky to take it seriously. There's a chance that he'll say something that gives him away when he's confronted with the news that we've got a search warrant."

They lapsed into a companionable silence. It wasn't long before most of the spaces other than those set aside for visitors were filled. It was nearly 8:55 when Bridges left his car and headed for the main entrance.

"Okay," Carol said. "Here I go. You staying here?"

"Hell, no. I want to be as close to the action as I can. I'm going to poke around the gift shop."

"There won't be any action. At most you'll see Bridges or me marching Clifford out of the winery and into Sam's car. Then we'll go have lunch and I'll take you to the airport."

"I was hoping I might get to stay an extra day," Kevin said.

"Why? Rumor has it that you have a few students waiting for you down in the city."

"Rumors, rumors. Covering my class won't be a problem. I'd like to see what happens after you make an arrest."

"It'll be boring. There's paperwork, the question of bail, legal stuff."

"I know, but this won't be routine. We're talking about murder, Carol, not DUI."

"We'll see. Got to go."

Kevin watched as she walked across the parking lot, on her way to confront a thief and in all likelihood a murderer. He realized that he was fiercely proud of her.

Random Harvest was alive with activity as people exchanged Monday morning stories about their weekends and got themselves organized for the day. Carol spotted Mary Rizzo as she headed for the stairs to the second floor and waved good morning. No one thought it strange that the sheriff was at the winery. Her presence there over the preceding weeks had been so common that it no longer caused comment.

By the time she reached the corridor leading to Joe Clifford's office, Carol had said hello to several people she now knew by name, plus several others she knew by sight. She paused in front of the open door, watching Clifford stirring sugar into his coffee. He looked up, flashed her a broad smile, and with a theatrical bow asked her to come in.

"Care to join me for a cup of coffee, Sheriff? It's an inferior brew, but it beats what comes out of that vending machine downstairs."

"No, thanks. I've had my daily quota."

"Of course. I suppose you've been up since the crack of dawn chasing down Cumberland County's miscreants."

"Not quite. But I thought I'd stop by, see how Random Harvest is weathering its troubles."

"We're doing just fine," he said. "Things have settled down considerably since poor Mr. Rafferty's death. Can you believe, the last couple of days last week I never heard his name mentioned. Not once. It looks like the winery's moving on."

"I'm afraid I don't have that luxury, Mr. Clifford. It's not a cold case yet."

"No, I suppose not. Is there something I can do for you?"

Carol had expected Mrs. Clifford to call her husband the minute Parsons and Barrett showed her their search warrant. Had they been delayed? Had she opted to defy them, to make a scene? She doubted it. Parsons was the veteran on the force, a man whom she never remembered being late. And he would not have let himself become embroiled in an argument with the woman. Why had she not done the natural thing and called to report this outrage, to ask her husband what she should do?

No matter. Carol would explain the situation to Clifford herself.

"Yes, there is something. I'm here this morning to—"

The sound of a cell phone ringing interrupted her. It was his, not hers.

"Sorry, Sheriff. I'll just be a second."

It was immediately clear that this was not a routine call regarding winery business. The smile he had put on for the sheriff disappeared, to be replaced first by an expression of surprise and then by one of anger.

"Stop it, Annie!" he said into his phone. His voice was not pleasant. "Stop it. Calm down, do you hear me? Now tell me what has happened."

He listened as the woman he had called Annie told him what had happened. He looked at Carol while he listened.

"Now here's what I want you to do," he said, his voice tense. "Stay where you are. I'll be right home, and I'll take care of it. Those people have no right to be in our house, none at all. I'll call our lawyer. They're not going to do this to us."

Clifford's voice rose as he spoke until he was virtually shouting at Annie when he put his cell phone down on the desk.

"That was my wife." He practically spit out the words. "She says that two of your goons are in our house right now, rummaging through our things as if they owned the place. What the hell do you think you're doing?"

"What I'm doing, Mr. Clifford, is collecting evidence that will be used to prosecute you for stealing funds from the winery. And I'm here to place you under arrest."

Carol said it without raising her voice. The man across the desk from her continued to raise his.

"I think not." He yanked open the desk drawer and pulled out the gun Carol had found there on Sunday morning. He got to his feet as he said so, and came around the desk, waving the gun at her.

"Back up, Sheriff. Just back up, slowly. We're going downstairs and out to my car. If you don't want this place turned into a charnel house, you'll do as I say."

Carol was shocked. She had assumed that Clifford would be angry. That he would be full of bluster. But she had never imagined that he would do what he was now doing. How could he possibly believe that he could get away with it? He was already in trouble. Now he was putting himself in an impossible situation. She hoped she had not put herself in an impossible situation, too. The man she had thought of as cocky, rather too full of himself, was making it very clear that he was also very dangerous. As she backed through the door, she forced herself to think, not of why Clifford had apparently lost it but of how she could avoid a disastrous ending to what she had assumed would be an unpleasant but uneventful arrest.

"Turn around," he said, pushing the business end of the revolver into her back as she did so. "Now walk straight down this corridor. If we run into someone, don't say a word, just keep walking. We're taking the stairs ahead, then out through the foyer. If you think I won't shoot if I have to, you're even dumber than I thought you were."

That last remark stung. She didn't doubt that he'd shoot her. Where is Bridges? When she'd seen him last, he was in the foyer. It wasn't his fault; that's where she had told him to wait. They encountered no one before they reached the stairs. Clifford ordered her to stop. He quickly slipped out of his jacket, which he then draped over his arm, hiding the gun.

"Okay, now move."

They were near the bottom of the stairs when Mary Rizzo, who was just coming out of her office, spotted them.

"Oh, Sheriff Kelleher, can I have a word—"

It all happened in an instant. Distracted by the sound of her voice, Clifford turned in that direction. The pressure of the gun against Carol's back momentarily eased. She brought her elbow back sharply and caught him in the stomach. He staggered for a step or two, nearly falling off the bottom step, as she twisted to her left, reaching for her gun.

It would have worked except for the fact that, in stumbling down that last step, Joe Clifford bumped into Mary Rizzo. He reacted quickly. Recovering his balance, he grabbed Mary around the throat and pulled her to him as a shield.

They stood for a moment, a frozen tableau of three frightened people. Two guns were visible. One in Clifford's hand, its muzzle flush against Mary's head. The other in Carol's, useful only if she were willing to risk Mary's life.

Clifford realized that he had the upper hand.

"Stand back. Everyone!" he shouted to the small knot of people who had been attracted by the confusion in the winery foyer.

Taking crablike steps backward, he dragged his hostage across the tiled floor toward the door to the parking lot. When he got there, he reached around behind him to push the door open. In that instant when the gun was briefly not at Mary Rizzo's temple, a shot rang out and Clifford released his grip on the young woman. He sank to his knees, his hand on his shoulder, probing for the spot where he felt the pain and where the blood had begun to flow.

Mary hesitated, barely aware that he was no longer holding her. Carol took three quick strides toward the door, her gun pointed at Clifford. The small crowd in the foyer stood motionless, stunned by what they had witnessed. Two members of that crowd seemed to be shaking. One of them was Kevin Whitman, who had experienced the transition from horror to almost unbearable relief in the space of no more than five seconds. The other was Deputy Sheriff Sam Bridges, who had fired his revolver for the first time since he had left the Marine Corps six years previously.

Clifford was now on the floor, his gun in a spreading pool of blood under his right arm.

"You're under arrest, Mr. Clifford," Carol said. It was only with some effort that she said it in a calm, controlled voice. "I suspect that you will be facing shoulder surgery, but it's not life threatening. That shoulder is going to be the least of your worries."

She turned to the winery employees behind her and asked that someone go and get some towels. Bridges had appeared at her side and set about the task of shepherding Mary Rizzo back to her office.

"I'll take that gun, thank you," Carol said as she reached down to move Clifford's arm.

But he beat her to it. His face reflected the excruciating pain he must have experienced in the effort to move his injured shoulder.

"It was that meddling fool Rafferty's fault." They were the first words Clifford had spoken since Bridges had winged him. He struggled to say something else, but failed. It would not have surprised Carol had he fainted.

The gun was now in his left hand, but he made no effort to point it at the sheriff.

"That gun's of no use to you now. Let me have it."

As Carol held out her hand, Clifford brought the gun up as if to comply with her order. But that wasn't his intention. When he pulled the trigger, the bullet caught him just above his left ear. The force of it pushed him over onto his broken and bleeding shoulder. The second shot fired that morning in the Random Harvest winery was instantly fatal.

CHAPTER 53

Three weeks earlier, news of the human scarecrow in the vineyard had spread through the winery like a slow fire through wet grass, stirring curiosity and gossip as it passed from room to room. On this second Monday in November, the drama in the winery's foyer had generated a wave of disbelief that reverberated instantly throughout the building. Those employees who had not witnessed it materialized from the cellars and offices and other corners of the complex that constituted Random Harvest Vineyards, quickly filling the room where Joe Clifford lay dead in a pool of his own blood.

Carol Kelleher and Sam Bridges, representatives of law and order in Cumberland County, struggled to gain control of the confusion that swirled around them.

"Everybody stay back," Carol ordered in a voice that she hoped would be heard above the clamor. "Way back. Better yet, go back to your jobs."

She turned to Sam, who was trying to block the sight of Clifford's body from dozens of prying eyes.

"Just keep them away from him. I'm going to get Drake to send everybody home."

As she started for the stairs which she had so recently descended, a gun at her back, the owner himself arrived by way of those same stairs. She wasted no words.

"Mr. Drake, Joe Clifford has been shot. He's dead. We need to close the winery. I want you to send your people home."

The owner of the winery looked ashen. Obviously in shock, he displayed none of the irritability with which he had greeted the sheriff after Rafferty's death.

"What happened?" he asked. Carol was sure he had already heard. In any event, this was not the time for explanations.

"We'll talk about that, but first I must ask you to clear the winery. Have a notice posted telling tourists that the winery is closed today. Are you hearing me?"

Carol reached out a hand and steadied Drake as he came toward her.

"Yes, I hear you. They said it was Clifford."

"That's right. Mr. Clifford is dead. He committed suicide, right there by the front door. We have a crisis here, Mr. Drake. The coroner will be along shortly. An ambulance will follow. There will be a number of my fellow officers in the building within the hour. We are going to need room to do our job. So I must ask you to send your people home. Otherwise I shall have to do it myself."

Drake made a visible effort to pull himself together, nodded to the sheriff, and went off to do as she had asked.

It was while she was placing a call to the coroner's office that Carol remembered Kevin. The fact that she had momentarily forgotten him surprised her. It said volumes about the traumatic events of the morning. Where was he? She walked back in the direction of the gift shop, through a thinning crowd of Random Harvest employees, looking for him. He was in a corner of the shop, unsuccessfully pretending to study the labels on a rack of red table wines.

"So sorry to have ignored you," she said, putting her hand on his shoulder.

"Are you okay?" Kevin asked. "You are okay, aren't you?"

He made it sound as if his saying so would make it so.

"I'm fine, but I really didn't mean to forget about you."

"You have a job to do. A pretty unpleasant job. I'm just trying to stay out of the way."

They would have loved to hug each other. They knew they shouldn't, and they didn't.

"Look, you've got to get out of here, get back to the cottage," Carol said. "I'm going to be awhile. Like all day. I'd give you the car, but we have rules about letting unauthorized people drive county cars. Let me see if I can get you a ride with someone."

"Don't worry. I'll stay out of sight."

At that moment Carol spotted Bernie Stolnitz.

"Mr. Stolnitz," she called out to him.

The man who had accompanied Father Rafferty to the Finger Lakes Race Track, surprised to hear his name, turned toward them.

"Yes?"

"We're closing the winery, and my friend here needs a ride down to his cottage. It's not far, and I'd very much appreciate it if you would give him a lift."

Kevin raised a hand in protest.

"That's not necessary. I'll be okay."

"No, Kevin, I want you to go home." Carol doubted that she had ever spoken so sternly to him. "Mr. Stolnitz will be glad to take you."

Stolnitz smiled. It was probably the first smile to be seen at the winery since the brief hostage scene and Clifford's suicide.

"Of course. Whatever our sheriff wants him to do, Bernie does." The smile disappeared. He cast a glance toward the foyer door where Bridges was in the process of spreading a towel over the late Joe Clifford's face. "Never thought I'd see something like this."

In a matter of minutes, Kevin and Stolnitz had departed, as had most of the winery's employees. Carol had contacted Parsons at the Clifford residence and Byrnes at the Upstate Bank and Trust, instructing them to finish what they were doing and meet her at the winery. She also gave Parsons the unpleasant task of telling Annie Clifford that her husband was dead.

———

It was not until seven o'clock that Kevin and Carol sat down on the couch in the cottage living room to talk about the dramatic ending to the latest murder to roil the normally calm waters of Crooked Lake. It had been an insanely busy day for Carol. As for Kevin, he had been uncommonly restless. He had tried to read and had given it up. He had tried to listen to one of his favorite operas, only to discover that he was unable to concentrate on the music. He had set out on a walk down the road behind the cottages on Blue Water Point, only to abandon it after less than a quarter mile, worried that Carol might call while he was out of the cottage. And he had called his assistant at the college, asking him to take his Tuesday class.

By the time Carol arrived and they had uncapped two beers, Kevin was something of a nervous wreck. He was anxious about her, curious about what had happened since he had left the winery, and aware that the morning's crisis marked the end of yet another chapter in the relationship he had developed with the sheriff over the short span of a little more than two years.

"Were you scared?" Kevin asked.

"Only a fool wouldn't have been. I may have done some foolish things in my life, but I'm not a fool. The worst moment was when I took a chance and elbowed him in the gut at the bottom of the stairs. I didn't know whether his gun was loaded or if it would go off when I hit him. Yes, I was scared."

"Me, too. Scared for you. Right up to the moment when he shot himself. Why'd he do it?"

"We'll never know exactly what was going on in his mind, but what we learned today pretty much tells us why. Ready for my debriefing?"

"I've been waiting for it ever since you sent me home from the winery."

"I won't keep you in suspense. If his suicide didn't tell us we were right, what my men found did. If he wasn't stealing from the winery, I'm in the wrong business. And it's a near certainty that he killed Rafferty."

"Want to tell me about the priest first? After all, that's the crime you've been working on now for three weeks. You and me, that is."

Carol reached across the couch and patted Kevin on the arm.

"Right. My crime-fighting partner." Her smile turned into a little laugh. "Can you believe that we might still not know whether he'd killed Rafferty if Clifford had survived that rumble in the foyer. The search warrant was narrowly drawn. It mentioned only things that might prove he was taking money from the winery, things like checkbooks, account records, that sort of thing. There was nothing in it about looking for stuff that could tie him to the Father's murder. But once Clifford was dead, once his wife knew he'd committed suicide, the door was open. I think Parsons helped give it a push. Anyway, he says the wife seemed devastated, but that she gave him her okay to go looking for anything that would help explain his suicide. Want to guess what they found?"

"No. I think you're enjoying this, so why don't you just tell me."

"The scarecrow. Or what was left of it. There's a big shed out back of their house, place where Clifford kept his hobbies as well as the garden tools—golf clubs, a hunting rifle, all kinds of boy's toys. His wife said it was his territory, that she never went in it. Barrett shot the lock off and voilà—there was the original scarecrow. It looked like Clifford had tried to take the clothes off it. Maybe he originally thought he'd put them on Rafferty. But it wasn't working. You know, the result of years of rain, sun, all kinds of weather. Anyway, there was plenty of straw, still in the pants and shirt, but also all over the floor of the shed."

"Are you sure it's the same scarecrow that used to be on Rafferty's cross?"

"Ninety-nine per cent certain. I'm going to have Mason, their expert on scarecrows, take a look, but I'm sure. Moreover, the bullet that killed Rafferty was almost certainly fired from the same gun that Clifford committed suicide with. The gun that he stuck in my back as he marched me down the stairs at Random Harvest. We'll run ballistic tests, but I'm sure it's the same gun. Which pretty much proves that Clifford was our murderer."

"And that what that boy saw being dumped into the lake could not have been the original scarecrow. Sounds like this makes the money matter superfluous."

"Not really. Clifford's records tell us he deposited fairly large checks in his account, then shifted them later to an account we didn't know he had. They add up to almost exactly the amount that's missing. And by the way, this was another part of their life that his wife was kept out of. I think she was afraid of him.

"Now here's the really interesting part, and another black eye for Doug Francis, who does the hiring for Random Harvest. Clifford had a history of stealing. His wife told us a lot. Just a guess, but I have a hunch she was afraid we'd think she and Joe were in it together. So she made it a point to let us know that she knew he'd been in trouble before, but that he'd promised her that that was all in the past. She made it sound as if she'd insisted on him straightening out his life before she'd marry him."

"Did she sound credible?" Kevin asked.

"Yes, she did. Parsons thought so, and when I talked with her this afternoon, she told me just what she'd told him. But Clifford's luck finally ran out. The wife said he'd gotten off with a fine and community service on one occasion. His biggest stroke of luck, back when he was working for a computer-servicing outfit, came when the owner fell for a sob story about a sick father or something like that. He paid the money back and the charges were dropped. It looks to me as if Clifford moved from one place to another just often enough to avoid acquiring a local reputation. I'd also be willing to bet that there have been cases where he simply never got caught. Anyway, he gets this job at Random Harvest, smooth talks Earl Drake, and sets himself up for a chance to steal big-time. Until Brendan Rafferty comes into his life."

"Drake must be sick at heart," Kevin said.

"He is, and he doesn't even try to hide it. Blames himself for being taken in by a smart guy, a quick study who'd boned up on the wine business and had an air of assured competence. Random Harvest is going to be a different place. Jameson retired, Francis fired, and Clifford, of course, gone to boot hill or wherever his wife chooses to inter him."

Kevin got up to get two more beers.

"One thing I still don't understand, though," he said when he got back from the kitchen. "Why the scarecrow gambit?"

Carol looked at her watch.

"I'd rather discuss scarecrows than eat, but don't you suppose we ought to give some thought to dinner?"

"I figured we'd make do with leftovers."

"What if I could still get a table at The Cedar Post?"

"Even better."

She went into the study, called to say that Sheriff Kelleher hoped they had a table for two available, and returned, thumbs-up.

"Nine o'clock. Can you wait that long?"

"Yes, if you can explain the scarecrow in the vineyard."

"I'll give you my best guess, but I suspect we'll never know just what Clifford was thinking. Ready?"

"I've been waiting for this since the day you first told me about Father Rafferty."

"I may have mentioned it, but I got the idea awhile back when I was reading one of the Father Brown stories. What if the killer decided to hide the body in plain sight? Nobody would think a scarecrow way down in the vineyard was a real person. It could be days before anyone noticed that anything was wrong. And let's say Clifford needed time to wrap up the theft plot he had launched. Aha, he thinks, I'll hide Rafferty's body in the vineyard. But why not hide it someplace where it would *never* be found? Because he would want it to be found, just not right away."

"That's crazy, Carol." Kevin's face made it clear that he had problems with her reasoning. "A tourist who'd been at a wine tasting found it the very next day. Besides, what's the point of hiding it if he wanted it to be found?"

"I know. Clifford knew there were ice wine grapes down there, that there wouldn't be any pickers around. What he didn't anticipate was a tourist who was determined to go running down into the vineyard to take a picture. But who would have expected that to happen? Anyway, why might he want to first hide the body and still want it to be found later? Now this is a guess, pure and simple. But it has a certain logic to it. Clifford's smart. He'd know that if the body was found on winery property people would immediately think somebody at the winery did it. But then he'd think again, and it would occur to him that the police are smart, too, and that they would reach the conclusion that no winery employee would be dumb enough to leave his victim right there in the winery's own vineyard. So they'd start looking for other suspects who'd have their own reasons for creating the false scarecrow."

"Clever," Kevin weighed in. "Very clever. Except that as far as we know, Clifford never knew that Flanagan and Sadowsky existed, not to mention whether either one of them had a grudge against Rafferty. Hell, they probably didn't even know there was a Random Harvest winery, and if they did, they wouldn't have had any idea that there was a scarecrow in one of its vineyards. So whom did Clifford think he might be framing?"

"Probably no one in particular," Carol said. "But it was a good idea. After all, we kept thinking about Sadowsky and Flanagan as possible murderers. We gave them what at first seemed like good reasons for wanting to string Rafferty up like a scarecrow. Clifford could have been thinking along the same lines, except he wouldn't have had those guys in mind. One way or another, it would have kept the cops guessing. And we were guessing, weren't we?"

"Yes, and we still are. This is going to be one mystery we'll never solve. Let's go eat."

"I'm ready," Carol agreed. "Let me dump the rest of my beer. I can't afford to have one of my men pull me over en route to The Cedar Post."

It was after 8:30 when they got away from the cottage.

"You'll be interested to know that I got a call from Philip Flanagan this afternoon," Carol said as they headed north along the west lake road. "I didn't get to speak with him. But he left a message with Franks. The kid has obviously been fixated on the possibility that his father killed Father Rafferty. I've tried to persuade him to let it go, but he can't. His message says he was still looking for hotel and other receipts from the bow-hunting trip, and finally found one when he went through his father's wallet one night. That must have been a risky bit of business. Anyway, the receipt he found was for two nights, including the night Rafferty was killed. The motel was nowhere near Crooked Lake. It was in Warrensburg. That's the southeastern part of the Adirondacks."

"Do you suppose he's relieved or disappointed?"

"Relieved, I think. Franks said he sounded pleased with what he had to report. I'm going to try and get in touch with him tomorrow. This doesn't solve his problem with his father, but maybe it will help. I hope so."

"Want to know about a small coincidence?" Kevin asked, well aware that Carol was skeptical of coincidences. "It concerns your friend Stolnitz, the guy who drove me home this morning."

"Stolnitz?"

"Right. We got to talking, and I asked him what had brought him to Random Harvest Vineyards. He obviously thought I found it odd that he'd be working at a low-paying job in a winery. Which I did. You'd told me he was really smart, well informed. And that's how he sounded to me. So he sort of threw the question right back at me, something about my thinking his job was beneath him and saying he'd heard I was a professor. I was embarrassed about where the conversation was going, but I said that, yes, I was a teacher.

"And that's where it got interesting. He told me he'd been a teacher, too. At an upscale private boarding school downstate. But it seems some kid told his parents Stolnitz had been molesting him, and that a lot of parents began acting like vigilantes. It wasn't long before the kid said he'd been lying, that it was just a hoax, but the damage had been done. He didn't like the way the school had responded, didn't like how nasty some of the parents had been, so he told them all to go screw themselves—that's exactly the way he put it. He pulled up stakes and came up this way, ending up at Random Harvest. How's that for a coincidence?"

"Amazing. He never told me any of this."

"I know. He said he thought that, like me, you wondered about him working at the winery, but he didn't think you'd believe his story. By the way, he asked me not to tell you any of this."

"Then why are you telling me?"

"Because I know you and he doesn't. I know you always believed Father Rafferty was innocent of any wrongdoing, and I'm sure you'd give Stolnitz the benefit of the doubt, too."

"Strange, isn't it? And, for a change, a real coincidence."

They drove into The Cedar Post's chaotic parking lot, found a space, and were soon seated in a favorite corner.

"You must have clout, getting us this table on such short notice."

"Oh, yes," Carol said. "It's not because I'm the sheriff, but because I have such a winning personality."

Neither of them was particularly hungry, but they went through the motions of a light dinner, Carol settling for coffee in her role as the evening's driver.

It proved difficult to move the conversation away from the sudden and dramatic ending of the Rafferty murder case.

"Is there much left to do?" Kevin asked.

"I'm afraid so. This is when the paperwork really becomes burdensome. And then there is Mrs. Clifford."

"Is she going to be okay?"

"I'm not sure. She seemed to really believe that he had reformed. The fact that he hadn't was almost as much of a blow as his suicide. Thank goodness there aren't any kids. How would you explain to little ones that their father was a thief and a murderer? I don't like to think about it."

"I've been thinking," Kevin said, "Clifford has paid for what he did. Well, not from a legal point of view, I suppose. You could say his suicide cheated the state out of seeing that justice was done. But what about Flanagan and Sadowsky? They share responsibility for what happened to Rafferty, and they haven't paid. If it hadn't been for Flanagan, the Father would still be tending to the needs of his flock back at St. Anthony's. And Sadowsky. If it hadn't been for him, Rafferty would probably have gotten the gambling monkey off his back and never run away to Random Harvest. They'll both get off scot-free."

"And they'll probably continue to cause trouble for other people," Carol added. "But, unfortunately, Rafferty had a hand in his own death. If he'd stuck to his low-profile posture, the man nobody knew, he'd still be with us. For some reason, he decided to be a priest and confessor again, a real-life Father Brown. What if he had just ignored what Clifford was doing, and not tried to get him to return the money? There wouldn't have been any reason for Clifford to think he had to shut him up."

"I know," Kevin said. "But ironically, the priest died because he was trying to do something right. I guess you could say that in a sense Father Rafferty never really abandoned his priestly calling. And paid for his life because of it."

"People are always calling every misfortune a tragedy. But I think this was really a true tragedy. Wouldn't you agree?"

"I would."

Carol changed the subject.

"Will you still be coming back to the cottage every other weekend? Even if there's no crime to solve?"

"I will. That's a promise. I even got away with an extra day this weekend, and no one down at Madison College is going to suffer from it. I'm getting used to this commuting existence. I love it."

Carol drained the coffee from her cup and folded her napkin on the table.

"You ready to go?"

"I'm more than ready," Kevin said. "Funny thing, though. I never realized what an aphrodisiac murder could be. Just talking about it puts my libido in high gear."

"That's ridiculous, Kevin. Since when have you needed the excitement of a murder to give a boost to your libido?"

"Okay, so I exaggerate. Anyway, why don't we hurry back to the cottage and see what develops?"

"My thoughts exactly."